The Snake Report

By u/wercwercwerc

Special thanks to all who have supported me.

Online
At home

Ren, thank you for everything.

Cover art by the talented
U/Inpfh

Additional art by the wonderful
Magda Zwierzchowska

The Snake Report

Chapter 1

Death.

There are a lot of great things in life, but Death isn't one of them.

I'd go so far as to say, that if I were to line every experience in life from best to worst, I'd put that fun-sucking bastard right at the very bottom.

Because Death? Well, it's simply not something I recommend.

Really, I find it difficult to believe we're all so okay with the process. I mean, it's just down-right terrible, you know?

… Well no, I guess you don't.

Relax- that's not your fault, I just forget myself when I ramble.

Of course you don't know: no living person I've ever met has ever really gotten through that mess and come back to tell me about it, and if they said they had? I wouldn't believe them.

That's exactly why it's such an unpleasant experience, why it's so god-damn awful.

Because of that Fear...

Horror...

Dread...

Fading off into the black...

Oh, it's no fun.

From birth to the grave, death is all of those above coming at you at once.

Each one rolled into the last as seamless as can be until it's just a giant sphere of black. One great pill to swallow down, right at the end without even a hint of choice in the matter. Down come the curtains, and all you really get is the assurance: the guarantees of that bolded ink patiently waiting on the last page, of the last chapter, of the last book.

The End.

Or… maybe not.

Chapter 2

For context, we should probably talk about out-of-body experiences.

Random subject? Sure, but I'm pretty confident that everyone gets them now and again. I myself can say I've definitely had at least a couple over the years, generally under the pressures of stress and lack of sleep.

I think the last one was back at university... or maybe when I pulled that double shift?

Exhaustion can do funny things to the mind, it's true, but I'm not really confident that's what's happening now.

No... unfortunately, I'm starting to think this is something else.

See there?

Yeah, right below, ten feet down. Squint a bit, I know, it's dark out.

See it now?

There's something on the ground. Laid out like a sack of smashed tomatoes on the concrete.

That's me, I think.

No, actually- I don't *think*: I know.

That's me.

I'd recognize that shoddy-looking frame anywhere. I'm more than just sure, that's my body on the blacktop.

Slowly dying.

Even from all the way up here, it's not pretty. So much left to live for, and yet... there I go.

One wheeze at a time.

It's a bummer.

From the spectator's seats here, I think speaking objectively is still an option. So that base, I really wish there was a way I could tell you that this came about for a good reason.

The dying, I mean.

It's what I'd like to do. Tell you that my body down there meant something, that there was a purpose in the final moments here.

I'd be lying though.

There's no good reason.

None.

No matter how hard I think on it, there's not even a single decent explanation for the whole unpleasant mess. This is what you can safely call a pointless death.

Safe for you, at least. Not for me.

Hey, that's the way it goes though, right? It's not like no one ever warned me that this was going to be at the end of the road. Maybe I should be a good sport about it, accept things as they are.

That would be the highroad to take, I think.

It's a nice evening, after all. The atmosphere is... actually, it's really quite pleasant. This is the kind of weather that only comes a few times a year: a nice night of "not-too-warm" and "not-too-cold."

Comfortable, and not buggy.

No storms, no sirens. Decent cloud coverage.

This isn't the type of night you leave your house thinking "I might die" but it might be one of those "I could die happy right now" sort of nights.

Still, I'm not happy.

No… no matter how hard I try to make peace here: I'm not happy at all.

I can't live this this… die with this? Whichever this happens to be, I can't. My acceptance of this isn't in the cards.

It could have been- maybe if it were an accident, I would take it with a bit more grace. But that's the problem.

This wasn't an accident.

Ah, so what does that leave? Something health related? Heart attack, or some freak brain aneurysm?

No, I mean- obviously. On account of all the blood, it's not either of those.

Besides, pleasantly plump looking or not: I'm way too young for either of those. I'd probably need another decade of life-style creep before those threats should have the opportunity to set in.

So... what?

What happened?

Ah, glad I asked, because that's really the question of the night, now isn't it? Multiple-choice has narrowed somewhat, and that there's only a few options left.

See, benefit of the doubt or no: a guy like me doesn't have any heroic-acts to play through. Dying here isn't the result of some sort of noble deed, saving some child from an inbound vehicle. What preceded this was not a moment of valor.

I didn't save anyone.

And before you ask: it's not even like I've even lived a humble life, dedicating my service to others. I absolutely did no such thing.

No such luck.

So... ruling out natural causes or accidents, really we're only left behind one obvious source.

Oh yes.

I've clearly been murdered.

Well... almost murdered.

I guess it's a give-or-take ten minutes sort of scenario, but I'm really on my way towards getting there. Dead-center in the heartland of suburbia, laid out in an unseemly sort of face-plant sprawl.

A soon-to-be victim of a homicide.

What a joke.

What ridiculous joke.

Why me?

Seriously, why? It's a valid question.

I'm not exactly the prime target for violent crime. The body down there doesn't look much like a real catch. There's no gang affiliation related clothing, clearly I don't look rich, my sweatpants have chicken wings stains and a hole in them.

So why?

Is dog-walking really that deadly a profession? If it is, no one warned me escorting a chihuahua could be such a dangerous gig.

Damn it all.

Who would shoot a guy who's only got a doggy-bag on him? What could they possibly hope to gain from that?

Just dropped on the blacktop with a surprised look, like a pile of wet rags. Nothing but surprise and pain.

Ah... shit... I guess this is it.

Hoo... I'm coming back down.

Back towards the ground, towards the pavement...

Hoo... Hooo...

Closer and closer, it seems like the out of body experience is slipping.

I can taste the blood again.

God that's awful.

Ah... that's really unfortunate.

It hurts.

Shit.

Everything… everything hurts.

Painful.

This is really painful.

Locked in, no escaping from it now.

Fire and burning in my ribs- and for what? What kind of death is this anyways? Didn't even see any of it clearly, and all I can see now is... pavement.

I don't even know who did it.

What kind of death is this, where I don't even know who killed me?

Even that... stupid dog... ran away.

Shit…

I'm... slowing down...

Everything's slowing... down...

down...

down...

down...

down...

down...

down...

down...

down...

down...

How long... have I been laying here?

I... don't know...

Seconds... minutes... hours? I can't tell, but I think... someone's here... To help?

No...

Ah... someone's going through my pockets.

Of course.

Those seven dollars and a coupon for almond milk...

Does this mean I'm worth seven dollars... or is it better not to ask this sort of question...

Ah... can't say anything... voice isn't working. Breathing... is enough work. I just wish... it didn't hurt so much.

Lungs are moving... but they're not doing their job. Slipping...

It's dark... Darker than the night... I remember walking into. Dark tunnel of nothing... That's what... they always say it's like... right?

Guess this... is it...

Damn... shame...

I could...

Have done...

More.

I could have done more.

Chapter 3

Nothing.

Nothing.

Nothing.

Something.

Cold.

It's... really cold.

More oppressive than anything... Cold, chilly and damp. Surrounding me, wrapping my body up in it.

I can't even scream.

Where am I?

Something is holding me.

Pressure.

I feel pressure. I need to get out.

I need to get out.

Push?

I can push.

It's moving... I think.

There… if I work at it, I can feel a difference…

A little more…

Little more…

"Crack"

There: it's moving.

Something's moving.

"Crack-crack"

It's working!

"Crack-thump"

AH!

COLD!

COLDER!

FREEZING!

"Hisssssssss"

What was that? Where am I? Why can't I...

"Hisssssssss"

Wait a second, is that me?

"Hisssssssssssss"

Are these... scales? Is that a tail- do I have a tail? Why the hell do I have a tail-

"Hisssssssssssss-"

Oh.

"Hiss"

It's because I'm a snake.

Chapter 4

Hisss...

Hisssss...

Hisssssssss...

That's what horrified screaming sounds like in snake language.

It's my screaming, which really just makes things all that much worse.

Hissssssssssssssssssssssssss.

Yes, those are the hisses of a man turned serpent.

Dignity is forgotten in this place.

In the empty void that it had once taken up, there is nothing but fear and confusion, and... skin.

Mountains of it.

Long piles of skin.

They're huge.

Even the smallest of them is easily twice my size. I get the feeling like that's not a very good thing.

Was I the runt of the litter?

… do snakes have litters?

Hissssssssssss...

That's me again.

For some reason, it's making me feel a bit better.

Stress management, or something close to it.

This... this is going to take time.

This is definitely going to take some time. Why the hell am I a freakin' snake-

HISSSSSSSSS-

Okay... alright, tone it down. Roll it back.

I gotta calm down.

Deep breaths... don't think about how those feel weird too. Chill, relax, calm... calm...

Calm.

Okay.

It's okay.

Even if I'm a snake, I can probably decide to approach the matter with some semblance of stoicism. Rational thought can defeat almost anything, given enough time... probably.

Let's first consider the positives, give optimism some well-deserved exercise.

It could have been worse.

Reincarnation is real, for one. Check that off the list of life's mysteries.

Benefits? Well, clearly not dead, even if I'm dead.

So that's nice.

I guess it's easy enough to take another step here and be thankful I wasn't reborn a fish or something.

All things random, I probably could have been born a bug, or a bacteria... or something. Maybe even a tree.

What if I had been born a tree? Would I have known I was a tree?

Is that a thing?

Come to think of it, snake brains aren't very big: how have I been I thinking like this?

I'm still thinking like a human, but clearly I'm lacking some required hardware.

Can a snake brain think like a human brain?

That makes no sense...

This makes no sense...

Nothing makes any freaking sense-

Hisssssssssssssssssssssssssssss

Serpent-migraine.

Okay, just cut the thoughts off there. Clearly I'm a snake with the mind of a dead guy.

Like a ghost, only scaly.

Move on, next question: where am I?

That's important. I should find out.

Was it just dying that happened? Was there some fine print I missed? Did I fall asleep in the spiritual DMV?

There's another couple questions.

I can't answer them.

Okay, back to the first. More pressing, where is this?

Right now, where do I happen to be?

Hisssss...

It's a cave.

Has to be a cave.

A dark, cold, moist and unpleasant cave filled with snake-sheddings.

Oh.

Something moved.

Hiss-No.

Might be best to stay quiet for a second… movement…

Yes, there is indeed movement.

My eyes are different... that's something.

This isn't like what I remember seeing being like.

Little bit difficult to interpret.

Like grayscale, but not? Human-side here is picking up on it.

But even if seeing is a bit weirder than I remember, that's most definitely movement.

Slowly but surely it seems to be shaking... almost. Slow but steady.

Listening... I find this even weirder, honestly. Not like a human ear, but more like a rattling inside my head. Like my ears are covered and muffled a bit.

Only I don't have ears.

Huh.

"Don't you dare move!" Instinct is shouting.
"But I want to see what it is!" Human side complaining.

"Crunch"
"Snap"

If I still had normal skin, I think would be feeling the prickled scalp sensation by now.

Prickled scale?

Something is... not good.

"Crunch"
"Snap"
"Crunch"

It almost sounds like... jaws?

Like something is munching down on food of some kind.

Well, it's not moving much.

Noises aside, I think I'm probably alright for now. There are other things to look at anyways, and they're not so far away. Like right here, beneath me there's some cold rock, a little bit moisture.

Above me looked like a... ceiling? It's a stone sort of rounded ceiling, so I'm in a cave? Maybe?

Do snakes like caves?

Hmm... I don't know, maybe some of them do. I guess that makes sense.

Now what's this here behind me...

Oh.

Scales.

Wow, that's a lot of scales.

Different scales: these aren't shed. These look like they're very much still on something's body.

I don't think they're scary though, is that weird? Instead, I actually feel a bit of kinship here...

I wonder...

Is this... Mama snake?

Oh my god, I think it is.

This is mama snake.

Do snakes normally know their mothers? Do they imprint like ducklings?

Maybe?

I wish I wasn't so clueless here. Should try to get her attention?

Hmm...

Weird.

Mama Snake doesn't seem to be moving much.

At all, actually.

But there's that noise still...

"Don't move!"

Ah, there it is. Instinct holding firm here: don't move. Gotcha-Gotcha... but y'know, I'm not really sure what that leaves me with.

To do, I mean...?

Am I just supposed to stay here forever?

Just sort of sit still and wait until... what exactly?

What am I even waiting for?

Heck with that, I want to slither a little. Couldn't do that as a human, I bet it's at least a little fun.

Instinct: *"DON'T-* **[Vetoed]**

Heck with that. Human side is in control here little snake mind. Human-side wants to take a look-see.

"Crunch"
"Snap"
"Crunch-"
"..."

Hmm... it seems the *"Crunching"* has stopped.

Instinct: *"DON'T MOVE!"*

"Crunch"
"Snap"

Hmm... it started back up. Weird, wonder what that's about.

Instinct: *"DON'T-* [**Vetoed**]

We're about to slither more. Waiting still is lame and that noise is still a little far away to see clearly. Seems a little big though...

Actually, isn't that a little too big? Whatever it is, this thing huge, and are those... are those legs?

Yeah, those are legs.

A lot of legs.

"Crunch-"
"..."

Hmm. It stopped again.

Instinct: *"DON'T MOVE! DON'T MOVE! DON'T-"*

Well I'll be darned, Instinct sure is screaming. Honestly though, how bad could this really be? Snakes are usually at the top of the food chain, if I remember right.

"Crunch"
"Snap"

See? It started back up, no worries. Slithering for a better look never killed anybody, relax.

So this thing... it's a bug of some kind? It must be a bug, looks like a bug.

A centipede?

"Crunch"
"Snap"

Lots of legs... body segments.

Yeah, that must be it. It's a huge bug- I hate bugs. Human-side hates bugs, and snake-side just seems to be half a second from pissing itself.

Instinct: *"DON'T MOVE! DON'T MOVE! DON'T-"*

Can snakes piss themselves?

There's a question.

I'm blocking instinct out, but man is that thing screaming. It's just a bug! What's the big deal?

I mean, as a human I used to swat these guys with my shoe. A giant centipede or no, I'm not that scared.

"Crunch"
"Snap"

What is it eating though? I wonder, I mean it's still going to town on whatever it is...

Pretty big meal...

Hmm... it's...

Oh.

It's eating Mama snake.

"Crunch-"
"..."

I think it's looking at me.

Chapter 5

Slithering:

Entertaining? Yes, yes it is.

Labor intensive, somewhat clumsy? As luck might have it, also a yes.

It's the kind of motion that makes a reincarnated human wish for more efficient methods of travel. This is especially true when contemplating slithering away from a giant predator.

Fleeing in some way..

Slithering is going to be my only option, but that suddenly doesn't seem so great.

In fact, moving at all seems impossible. I'm frozen stiff.

Like a statue, made of snake instead of stone.

It seems that human curiosity has lead me to a terrible place.

This is a stare down with death.

What if I had been born a cat instead of snake?

I'd already be dead- that's what.

See, there's a giant centipede in front of me.

It has as a bunch of eyes. They glow, each a little bit more evil than the last, and they're all peering over the half eaten corpse of Mama snake.

They're watching me, or around me.

I can tell that much. They're just waiting, patiently watching for the slightest hint of motion. Scanning the ground.

I can only pray it can't sense fear.

If it can, I'm doomed. That's all I am right now.

Staring back at clicking mandibles, twitching legs. It has way, way too many legs…

Oh, this is not okay. I mean, I just died, and that was pretty scary- but this is worse. Horrific and gruesome as any b-rated horror film I caught on the latenight sci-fi channel.

Only it's not fake.

Not fake, too real.

I am almost certain I'm about to be murdered.

Instinct: *"STAY STILL! DO NOT MOVE!"*

Human: "SURE THING BOSS."

The temptation to try and slither to safety is there, but slither to where?

I have no idea where I am.

A cave? What good does that do me? Which cave?! WHERE?

Calm.

Gotta keep it together here.

I could run, sure- but what if there are other creatures like this one? What if this one just follows me and eats me? It's eating a snake that has got to be thousands of times my own size.

Not a good plan.

Just need to stay still.

Wait.

Wait it out.

Wait it out.

How long is this thing going to stare at me?

Forever?

Oh my god, this is bullshit.

Barely five minutes alive, and it's already game over.

Worst spawn-point ever.

Instinct: *"Don't move."*

Instinct is still holding firm on this one, which is good, because human-side is trying to go about making peace with life for the second time today.

I guess I did live a decent life as a snake. I hissed a little, slithered a little, got devoured by a terrifying subterranean insect. All in all, I'd give it a six out of ten.

Instinct: *"Don't move."*

Part snake, part human, part statue, part at peace with the universe: *and though I slither through the valley of the shadow of death...*

Wait. Something else moved.

"CRAAAAAAAW"

"HISS-Eeeeeeeek!"

Oh god. Oh Jeez. Oh holy shit snakes- the centipede just struck something.

Oh god, it's like some sort of shelled lightning covered in blood.

"EEEEEeeeeeeeekkkk..."
"Crunch"
"Crunch"
"Snap"

I just witnessed a murder.

Perhaps a sibling, or maybe just an unsuspecting bystander.

"Crunch"

They're being eaten. Oh god, those mandibles are like razors. Giant evil razors of doom.

Instinct: *"Move... move slowly"*

Human: *"Yes boss."*

Slowly but surely, I am slithering.

Like I have never slithered before, I am slithering.

There are horrific glimpses of razor mandibles snapping down on some unfortunate and unknown soul to my far right.

Oh crap. Oh crap.

Just a bit farther. Down this path, away. Gotta get away.

"Crunch-"
"..."
"..."

Instinct: *"Move faster-*

"... Creeeee?"

Instinct: *FASTER! MOOOOOVE! MOVE MOVE MOVE-"*
Human*: "YES BOSS, ANYTHING YOU SAY BOSS!"*

"CRAAAAAAAW"

Oh fuck

Oh fuck

Oh fuck

I wish I had legs, oh god do I wish I had legs, gotta get away. Gotta-

Ah! Hole in the floor!

Dive! Dive! Dive!

"CRAAAAAAAW!"

Instinct: *"HIDE! HIDE HIDE HIDE-"*
Human*: "YES BOSS! SURE THING BOSS!"*

This is insane.

I haven't even been alive an hour, and I'm having an almost intimately close encounter with death. Barely half a foot away from me, there's a set of glowing compound eyes and smashing mouth-pincers trying to rip up my hiding place.

All I can do is wait.

The hole doesn't go down any farther.

"CRAAAAAAAW!"

I'm so dead. It's right above me.

"CRAAAAAAAW!"

It's like an inch away, slipping closer.

"CRAAAAAAAW!"

I'm so dead- This isn't fair! I was just born for god's sake!

"CRAAAAAAAW! Craaaaa..."

"..."

"..."

"..."

"..."

Is it…

Wait a second, is it gone?

I don't see it up there anymore.

Is it just waiting for me now?

Oh… oh my god, I bet it is. Probably just sitting there, patiently waiting for me to stick my head out.

No.

I'm staying in this hole, forever.

This is a safe place.

This is nice.

Nothing trying to kill me here.

Unless... unless…

No.

No, there's nothing here. Just me, some rocks. This is a nice little divot in the ground.

Safe space.

Hisss...

I'm so tired...

So tired.

I feel like I just ran a marathon, and I still don't have a single goddamn clue what's going on-

[Spawn survival: SUCCESS]

Wha-

[LEVEL UP:]

What is thisssss-

[Current: Level One]

Level? Spawn? What?

[CHOOSE STARTING ABILITY]

Hisssssss

Chapter 6

New Game.

I used to play video games when I was younger. I knew my fair share of goob-lore, but... I think I've been thrown in a bit too deep.

I've heard of a [*New Game Plus*] but this is something else.

[*New Game Minus*]

Advanced and skilled players only. Starting over again, but highly disadvantaged. A more difficult play through.

That kind of vibe.

But... y'know, that's really not such a great option for someone who didn't even make it to middle-aged in his last life. Not exactly setting the bar high there.

And as much as I liked games, I wasn't great at that them.

Hiss...

So... what? This is hard mode?

Make it more difficult, take away arms and legs. Take everything away and make them a snake, and put them in a cave filled with things that might eat them.

That sounds super fair to me.

Really, this is great.

Just great.

NO! This is freaking rigged! This game is rigged! This is bullshi-

Hissssss!

[CHOOSE STARTING ABILITY]

The words are still there.

They're not a projection exactly, but a hallucination maybe?

[CHOOSE STARTING ABILITY]

Oppressive and demanding.

So... this is a game?

No... it doesn't seem much like a game, I feel very much alive and serpent-like.

This is real, I think.

Real life: The toughest game of all.

Maybe I've cracked under the pressure and I'm having one of those DMT experiences I read about online.

It's not like I've ever claimed to be the toughest when it came to mental fortitude. I couldn't even put up with cold showers.

Death is probably a lot worse than a cold shower.

[CHOOSE STARTING ABILITY]

Geez. It's aggressive.

It's like a microwave that beeps until someone opens it.

[CHOOSE STARTING ABILITY]

Irritating and unrelenting.

I wonder what I'm supposed to do, exactly? Touch the image with my tail? Reach out with my mind? No... that's not working.

So my tail then? It's not like I have any hands-

[UNLOCKABLE BRANCHES:]
[Venom]
[Consumption]
[Massive]
[Magic essence]

Oh. It worked. Who would have thought it?

Hissssssss...

Not me.

This is all rather bizarre, but I suppose this is something to be grateful for. It's a chance. They sound like useful abilities: things that keep a tiny little snake like myself from getting eaten by giant centipedes or whatever else is hiding in the cave.

Still...

> **[Venom]**
> **[Consumption]**
> **[Massive]**
> **[Magic essence]**

Well, there are some interesting choices here. But I can't be exactly certain I'm doing, or exactly what they mean. A more detailed description would be nice.

Hissssss...ssss?

Hmm. Nope, Nothing.

It was worth a shot, at the very least. Doesn't hurt to ask. I guess the forces of deductive reasoning will have to compensate for ignorance at the moment. What have we got for options...

> **[Venom]**

Well... That's probably a reasonable branch. Poison-bite of some kind. Snakes have that on occasion, makes perfect sense. Human-side is helpful here.

> **[Consumption]**

Hmm... either some disease, or maybe something to do with eating things. Not entirely sure. Not going to bet on it.

> **[Massive]**

Makes me bigger? Maybe... Maybe... Would it kill to have some details be included? I mean, this could mean anything. Would that mean like mama-snake? Or just a little bigger?

> **[Magic essence]**

Well.

Hissssss...

Well, well, well...

Magic. No matter how long I stare at this, that word isn't changed. It clearly is reading Magic.

Giving off a very RPG style vibe all of a sudden.

Horribly difficult and unpleasant [Praise the sun] kind of vibe, but still a vibe.

Options, options, options... as if I even really have a choice here.

[Magic essence: Selected]
Mana unlocked.

[No Spells unlocked.]
No spells available

[10 Skill points to allocate]

Hissss... Point based? Really? Is that number a lot, or a little?

[Available Skills – Starters discounted!]

- **[Basic Heal: Level I]** Cost: 5 points

  Unlocks future Healing magics.

- **[Flame element: Level I]** Cost: 5 points

  Unlocks future Flame magics.

- **[Earth element: Level I]** Cost: 5 points

  Unlocks future Earth magics.

- **[Water element: Level I]** Cost: 5 points

  Unlocks future Water magics.

- **[Knowledge element: Level I]** Cost: 100 Points

  Unlocks future Knowledge magics.

Hisssss... So, one of these things is not like the others. For now, as I certain do not have enough to buy it, I'll pretend that last option isn't there.

If I remember anything about games, that option is either super useful, or it's a trap. Like something an evil developer might put in place to screw over first-time players.

That sort of thing.

If I only start with 10 points, that last option seems insanely expensive. I'm leaning towards a trap. First a giant centipede, and now a trap.

Not falling for it.

Even if I had the points to fall for it, I'm not falling for it. That's the kind of thing that gets a poor little snake killed before it can grow old and die peacefully of old age and over-eating.

[Healing] and [Flame] selected.

[Spells unlocked: Points deducted!]

[Fire breath]

[Fireball]

[Weak Heal]

Well, this is interesting.

Speaking of eating, I'm hungry.

Chapter 7

Exploring the cave.

I won't shake my tail at the notion of exploration.

It's scary.

Really scary.

From the divot in the cave floor, just poking my head above ground is enough to shake me a bit. The thought of waiting pincers that might lop my head are still all too real, and I've got a real bad feeling about the circumstances of my continued survival.

If I'm going to die, I think getting insta-killed seems more than plausible- but luck? She's on my side.

For now.

Thankfully, sticking my head above ground does not get me insta-killed. The God of Tiny-Snakes must be watching over me.

Must be it.

There are probably better gods, but it's not good to complain when divine favor is bestowed upon one's scaly head.

Hissss...

Having leveled up now, I can see a slight difference from before.

It seems I came into this world as a level zero, but now that I'm up to level one I must have received some sort of benefit. I can move a bit easier. Not much, but it's noticeable- and I can see a bit farther.

Again, that's not much of a change, but it's a good sign. I guess basic stats are at play here.

But level one isn't going to cut it.

What I see in the cave before me is anything but good.

I was right, originally: this is completely rigged. Not a newbie friendly environment.

Danger lurks.

There are your typical cave formations. Stalagmites rise up here and there. Light seemed to glow off weird looking mushrooms along these, a nice color. Blue I think. The sight is a bit weird though, so I can't be too confident. The ceiling is much the same, some stalactites and more glowing plant-like things.

But there are also monsters.

Yes: monsters. It's safe and reasonable to call what I'm seeing exactly that.

I was willing to hold off on my judgement, writing off the Giant Centipede as a freak occurrence before the terrified eyes of a tiny little snake, but the animals in this place are absolutely not normal.

Perched in regal form not ten full slithers ahead of me is a giant frog.

It has two heads.

One of them is covered in spikes, the other in warts.

Watching this frog fills me with the urge to vomit. Instinct is screaming just for poking out my head.

"HIDE! NOW!" Instinct is yelling.

But I can't.

I'm frozen again as I watch this frog with horrified curiosity.

Dozens upon dozens of my body couldn't hope to rival its size. No matter how I look at it, this frog is simply way too big.

There's wind.

Instinct is screaming again, something new.

Oh. I see.

The Frog is gone.

It's being carried away with a look of deep sadness and acceptance by a large creature with wings.

Ah... a bat.

Now I understand.

There are bats on the ceiling.

Giant bats.

Easily as big as the centipede, hanging and crawling around. That drip-dropping sound I'd be ignoring?

Guano.

Haven't worked up the courage to move, but this divot is suddenly much less appealing.

So… we have giant bats, huddled mostly towards the far side, If where I'm now looking now is the arbitrary "North" then I would say the bats are to the far, far West.

That's not to say there aren't other bats flying around in all directions, just to confirm that the majority seem to be happily sleeping on the ceiling to the West.

Hundreds of them.

Beyond than that, it seems that the cavern goes deeper.

So this is clearly a large cavern. Supporting this many living things, I imagine it's got to be much more than what I'm able to see from my hole in the ground.

Because of that, I don't have it in me to move just yet. The desperation just isn't there.

I'm not inclined to end up like the frog did. He sat in plain sight admiring the beauty of the cave, and that resulted in a gruesome demise. Nature is a cold-hearted bitch.

That's why my prayers go towards the Tiny Snake God.

Rest in peace two-headed Frog. You're not a tiny snake, but I feel it's only just to mourn for you anyways.

You didn't try to eat me, after all, and that counts for something.

So… giant bats to the West, and a gradual rising slope towards the East. North and south end with massive walls.

There, that summarizes my visual assessment.

Like exploration, but safer. You can lump this in as the snake equivalent of a submarine poking out its periscope for a bit.

I don't want to die.

But eventually, I know I'm going to have to leave the little hole in the ground.

I'm starting to get hungry- not just "*I could really go for a snack*" hunger, but "*I might end up starving*" hunger.

This makes a bit of sense.

I was born. I fled in terror. I never ate anything.

Living things need to eat.

This cave probably doesn't have a grocery store, so the question emerges.

What can I eat?

Everything in this cave looks more likely to eat me.

Frogs, centipedes, bats: zero chance of victory.

Less probably less, maybe even negative chance…

Oh, wait. Something is happening.

Bats.

Lots of bats are airborne. The West has come alive, hundreds of them are swarming in the air. Even shrinking down into the dirt doesn't seem to help me much, instinct might as well have a megaphone to my head.

I'm not moving.

But the bats... they're moving. Oh. They're flying overhead, going East.

AH!

They're leaving the cave.

A moment of clarity here. My human-side is still good for something it seems.

One minute... two minute... three minute. They're mostly gone now. Ceiling might as well be empty.

Hissss...

I guess that means it's time to get something to eat.

Chapter 8

Eating.

In a place where everything is much more likely to eat me, the concept is daunting. As a living creature, I'm going to have to eat something. This makes sense.

The question is what?

Frogs? No, that would result in [Certain Death]

Bats? No, that would result in [Certain Death]

Centipedes? No.

The idea is straightforward. I'm at the bottom of the food chain, I'm small, and all I have going for me is that I leveled up.

Once.

I leveled up once. That's not much.

Healing and fire though, at least I think I chose well. Fire is something that scares most animals. Healing? That's probably obvious. Taking injuries and not being able to do anything about them? I feel that the chances of survival might drop dramatically.

Snake's don't get healthcare.

But this, all of this is irrelevant if I starve to death.

And really I might starve to death.

With the giant bats gone I've taken the liberty slithering around a little. I've seen and learned quite a bit through this experience.

Mainly: there is nothing I can possibly eat.

Bats, frogs, centipedes- I already considered these impossible prey, but even the smaller things lurking around the cavern look dangerous.

Spiders for example.

There are many kinds of bugs and insects, as one might expect in a cave, but I also saw several spiders. Each of them happened to be larger than myself, and each of them happened to be munching on something with scales.

Instinct didn't like them much. Neither did human-side. "Kill it with fire." Both were in total agreement.

Unfortunately, though, I don't think I'll be able to kill anything with fire.

I practiced one of those attacks with high hopes after the bats left, thinking to myself rather optimistically: "If there's a magic that might make a tiny snake think better of themselves, it would be this."

Hiss... I was wrong.

[Fire Breath]

That was the spell I tried. The one that might not attract attention.

In theory, it sounds like it would turn me into a wingless, limbless dragon.

But no.

It's pitiful.

If I had to give it a power rating, I would say maybe on the scale of a match with some hair-spray behind it. One single puff of bright fire, and then it's used up. Maybe I could scorch something, but it probably wouldn't die.

At best case it might run, and at worst it might eat me.

So it's not looking good.

With that, I've confirmed the terrifying reality.

I am the bottom of this food chain.

But I also confirmed something else. Something potentially life-saving through careful study and observation.

The glowing mushrooms are unique.

Nothing else seems to eat them, nothing else seems to get eaten by them. They are silent, inanimate, and utterly defenseless.

Human-side looks at this with hope and hunger. Instinct remains silent.

Under normal circumstances, I don't believe that snakes eat mushrooms.

But these circumstances are not normal.

Not normal at all.

Hisss...

Next to my hole in the ground, there is a rising pillar. A pillar once belonging to the recently deceased frog. There are many mushrooms on this. Dozens of them, in fact. Enough to remind me of a spooky-looking totem pole.

Starving... That's an awful way to die.

I am going to eat this.

Chapter 9

Snake Report:

I ate the mushroom, and now I'm dying.

I only ate part of it.

A really tiny part. Without hands it took me a long time to do this. I had to creatively use a rock.

I even cooked it with [Fire Breath]

Then I ate it.

And again, I'm dying a pitiful death.

I've cast [Weak Heal] on myself in an effort to survive.

Once.

I glowed white, and it worked for a moment. Like something had come and wiped away my pain, everything was better.

But then the feeling came back.

Twice.

It worked... Temporarily.

Three times.

I feel like I'm pouring water into a bucket with holes in the bottom.

Four times.

Oh. That's my limit.

Instinct tells me politely that if I try to do that again, something bad might happen.

But I might die anyways.

Now I'm hallucinating too. Outside my tiny hole in the ground, shapes are swirling, pillars are bending, shadows are twisting.

It's terrible.

One more heal. I'd rather die that way.

I call up the magic. [Weak heal]

Five times now.

Oh. I can't move. I feel better, but I can't move.

Hmm. My vision is blurring. I can't move.

Am I dea-

[POISON RESISTANCE: UNLOCKED RANK I]
[WEAK HEALING: UNLOCKED RANK II]
[UNIQUE TRAIT: OMNIVORE UNLOCKED]

[LEVEL UP:]
[Current: Level Two]
[Five Skill points to allocate]

Hisssss...

I'm not dead.

Well then.

Learning experiences, pushing boundaries-- These are very important things in life. Things I did not often do when I was a human.

I ate poison. I used all my tiny-snake magic.

Yet I survived.

In fact, I seem to have been rewarded for it.

[POISON RESISTANCE: RANK I]
[WEAK HEALING: RANK II]
[UNIQUE TRAIT: OMNIVORE]

I'm willing to believe this is related to leveling up. The moment I saw those words, I felt as though all my strength had been replenished.

I also shed my skin.

It looks really strange, like a snake sleeping bag. Regardless, I'm a little bigger now. Not much, but some.

So in summary, eating things is beneficial. Surviving dangers is beneficial. There are distinct rewards for this.

Weird.

Horrifying.

But there is possibility here. I'm a little bigger now, I think. If that mushroom a'la poison were to repeat a few more times, there's a chance I might be able to defend myself from at least some of the creatures in this place.

…this really only leaves me one choice though.

I'm going to have to finish it.

Chapter 10

Snake Report:

I did it.

I ate the entire glowing mushroom. Piece by painful piece.

It took longer than expected, and was only slightly less horrible.

I'm now [**Level Four**] with [**POISON RESISTANCE: RANK III**] and [**WEAK HEALING: RANK III**]

It seems that early levels are coming in quickly for now, but I haven't learned anything new like before. No further "Unique skills" or such like that. [Omnivore] was the only thing I got out of this.

I guess that makes sense, but I still have a lot of questions.

It feels like I'm blindly stumbling my way along here. Some open-forum question and answer would be helpful.

For example, in theory I now have fifteen [Skill Points] to spend, but I can't figure out how to do it.

I can't seem to bring up any of the glowing signal words at all unless something important happens. Either [Leveling up] or unlocking some sort of [Unique] ability are the only ways to get the menu to appear.

It really only seems to appear then.

But fifteen points… that could mean more powerful magic, or maybe different kinds of magic. Considering I'm still a tiny snake, I'd hazard a guess that magic is the only plausible way for me to go. Even level four, I'm still smaller than every other monster in the cave.

My size has not really scaled up much at all, so human-side is taking the initiative.

Even someone like me knows that camping and grinding is a perfectly legitimate strategy.

Under that mentality, I have retrieved more mushrooms from *Frog's-Pillar*. Seven of these glowing fungi now rest beside me in my hole in the ground.

The feast begins.

Chapter 11

Snake Report:

[Current: Level Five]

By the observed movements of the Giant bats, it has been five days since I first awoke in this place. At this moment, I have finally finished the final stockpiled glowing mushroom.

The level up fills me with both strength, and satisfaction. A job well done. I am stronger. I am no longer starving. I know I have secured a food source.

[POISON RESISTANCE: RANK V]
[BASIC HEALING: RANK I]
[UNIQUE TRAIT: TOXIC]

These are the fruits of my labor.

They glow in my vision, confirming what I already know: my weak heal is much more effective, and apparently it renamed itself. I think this is the natural course of spells, as they seem to improve over time.

Same with resistances: far from dying, the mushrooms now barely seem to upset my stomach.

What doesn't kill you, makes you stronger.

As a note, I've also gained an interesting bluish tint to my scales, first appearing upon my fifth shed layer of tiny-snake skin.

[Toxic] is likely the trait behind this. I believe it's highly likely that any creature wishing to eat me might experience the symptoms of food-poisoning. I have eaten so many mushrooms, I have taken on their attributes.

I have no intentions of confirming this.

Hisssss...

But, there is something else to report! More important than any of that, I've got something really fantastic to share.

I've learned new magic.

[Earth Element] was unlocked for the (apparently discounted) cost of 5 points. Upon doing so, it immediately granted me a single spell called

[Earth Manipulation I] which seems to do basically what the name suggests.

It can let me mold the ground a bit. Like play-doh sort of mold, but slower.

Much slower.

Still, that's enough to get me going.

I've expanded me hole in cave floor slightly, although it was rather exhausting. Even after all of that, the spell didn't rank up like healing which I felt was a bit of a rip-off, but complaints are for other people-turned-snake.

Not for me.

Life is good.

I'm not being eaten, I'm no longer starving, and there are no giant centipedes in sight.

Besides, I started with the boring spell.

[Earth Manipulation]? That's boring compared to what I've spent the other points on.

Five points for each level up. It seems that the more points I accumulate, upon leveling I can go and look at the magics I already possess. If there is an available skill, it seems to show up.

It reminds me of a menu.

A menu that let me look back into [Fire Magic] and [Healing Magic] and browse. There were a lot of spells, I think.

It's difficult to describe because I could only see a few. Things like [Fire Breath II] for 20 points, or [Fireball II] for 50 points. [Basic Healing VI] was available for 400 points.

Weird, but it looks like I can level up the skills I own, or just buy them with points. That said, buying them isn't a good deal, and trying to purchase some of the higher-ranked ones seems insanely expensive.

Probably a waste.

A not-so-subtle: *"earn it yourself."*

Hisss...

In a weird way, I could almost see some further options. Those choices just on the edge of my vision, but not quite there. The longer I tried to pull those up, though, the greater my headache got, so I've given that up for now.

But it was good to learn how the menus work. Let them go long enough, and there's no way to get them back. It's back on leveling or skill ranking to trigger them again.

Patience seems to be important here, but I'm getting the hang of it.

Anyways, before the [Level up] temporary menu closed, I made one more purchase.

My purchase was from the healing category: [Passive Regeneration I] for a full 20 points.

Excessive?

Yes, maybe- because it's likely going to start out useless. Still, something like that? I think it might be worth it. Unlike the [Basic Healing] I think this should work on its own.

I will be a healthy snake.

Chapter 12
Snake Report: Day Seven

A spider tried to eat me today. It was terrifying.

The good news is: spiders hate fire.

As in, fire kills them.

It really, *really* kills them.

Spider.

Spider webs.

Spider egg sacks.

All of these things are extremely flammable.

Like they're missing some warning messages, and brightly colored signs: *"Keep away from heat, sparks, open flames, and hot surfaces. No smoking."*

It was my fault, in the end.

To clarify, by "my fault" I mean human-side.

This sort of thing can be attached to human error, and thought the situation could have easily been avoided, I got careless.

The greed… that was what got me. The hunger for just one more mushroom. So it was, my foraging expedition to *Frog's Pillar* put me out a bit too far out into the open.

Out into the many watching eyes of predators. Apparently, even to the smallest of them I look like a tasty morsel.

I barely even saw the thing before it cleared whatever distance had between us.

A hunting spider.

They're fast.

Really fast.

Compared to my current body: they're also unpleasantly large. Easily three times my size, not even counting the extra length their legs provide.

Nightmare fuel.
Human-side dropped the ball, so Instinct can take complete credit for this round of survival. While panic had turned towards in full shock, Instinct managed to barf up a decent example of [Fire-breath] along with half a toasted mushroom.

Pitiful, but effective.

Super effective.

Like it was doused in gasoline, the eight-legged BBQ was lit.

The spider ran off and died, curling up with a smolder of complete defeat somewhere in the distance.

[Fire Breath] ranked up, twice.

I didn't stick around longer than that.

Hisss…

Torched spider smells terrible.

Chapter 13

Snake Report: Day Eight

I shed another skin.

That's a trend, or it seems to be the case with each new level: I break free of my old skin and emerge anew as a slightly larger snake.

Well… sort of.

Very slightly larger. I think I've grown a solid centimeter now. Which is some serious progress considering what I'm starting with, but still tiny when viewed by human standards.

Tiny snake… the title still fits, but I'm large enough now that been forced to renovate my hole in the ground yet again.

If I were to describe what it looks like presently, I'd have to say it looks like a regular hole with a small tunnel that leads to a peaceful looking rectangular space. At best guess, it's probably about the size of a shoe box.

It also shares the decorations of a shoe box.

Plain sides, and a bunch of annoying wrapping paper.

Only the wrapping paper is composed entirely of snake-skins.

I've decided those can pile up against the western wall of this space, and somehow managed to shove them over there. Eventually I needed assistance from [Earth Manipulation] on account of having no arms.

Something to get used to, for sure.

Anyways, I've managed to stack them up. Serious effort expended, but I don't know what else to do with them really.

Eat them? No… that's a bit too close to cannibalism.

Leaving them there for now.

Still, there's another part of snake camp [Shoe box] that's unusual.

Like I said, the walls are made completely from stone, but there's a sole exception to this wedged in one of them.

I've discovered a weird looking crystal, that seems to be embedded in the layers of the rock. Manipulating the stone to move around, and I pretty much ran right into it.

It glows a pretty color blue. Similar, but much, much stronger than the mushrooms.

I think there's a high possibility that it's radioactive.

Maybe.

Earth Magic is really hard though, so I've left it as it is. Currently settled for using the glow as a light source.

A weird lamp, if you will.

Yes, things are going well.

Outside of watching spiders, foraging has been relatively successful. I've had enough of a surplus to justify a small shelf for extra mushrooms.

Really, more of a hole in the wall near the weird crystal, but still.

Not so bad.

I don't really get hungry like I did that first day, but it's difficult to predict the way things will turn out. There is always the chance something will trap me in here, and I'll have to wait them out.

[Paranoia]

Behold: it's a Unique skill I possess even without the glowing letters of approval.

There is a problem though.

Frog's-Pillar is slowly, but surely, running out of mushrooms. So it seems that human-side's ambition has met its first true challenge: these glowing blue delicacies I've come to know and love don't spread very quickly. In fact, I haven't seen a single motion of the ones I've already eaten returning any time soon.

Perhaps this makes sense.

Even after a full week of living in this cave, I've still not seen another creature try and eat the mushrooms. I only ate a tiny sliver of one- after cooking it with fire no less, and I almost died even after healing myself several times. For a normal monster, this would probably result in the development of a **[Don't eat this]** sort of mentality. The Mushrooms are not seen as food by anyone except me.

But that doesn't mean they won't run out eventually.

There are other Pillars with less sentimental value and significance, but if I continue to grow the only accessible food-stuffs will be in dangerous places.

Places where Spiders, or Frogs, or Giant bats might swoop down and devour me.

Truthfully, I need to escape this place. I'm out of my league. It's like I spawned in the deep-end of the pool, never getting a chance to learn how to swim.

If I stay here, I'll drown.

My main focus is decided.

[Get out of this cave.]

Chapter 14
Snake Report: Day Nine

The arbitrary West goes down.

The arbitrary East goes up.

North and South are walls.

So it is, East is the direction I must go.

Simple and decided, behold the power of human logic.

Of course, it's not nearly so simple as just "going."

If only, if only: there are many variables in play, most of which could easily get me killed.

For one: the bats.

They fly out from West to East, and Return from East to West. It's a thing, and a pretty consistent one so far as I can tell.

That's both encouraging and troublesome.

If I am to go East, it can't be when there are a thousand bats flying around looking for food.

I'm food.

A fact that takes some getting used to.

So, if I'm going to move it needs to be timed wisely, lest I end up like my friend the frog.

For two: there are still other creatures in this cave.

It's not just bats, there are other monstrosities lurking. Huge things that pass by on too many legs, or things that make the ground shake so bad I don't even feel tempted to try and find out what they are.

Plus, ever since I set that spider on fire, the arachnid side of things has been much more aggressive.

They never approach, but I see their glossy sets of eyes watching me. Their mandibles make strange noises, and they move in groups that follow where I go.

I think they know what I did to their buddy, and now they want revenge.

Hisss... Creepy.

Monsters with intellect.

It might be possible…

Well, it is possible: I'm here, after all.

These things to consider… life used to make a lot more sense, I think. Human-me never had to wonder about any of this.

Ug.

Still, moving about unfamiliar territory is just as terrifying as it ever was, even if I know fire works on some of my enemies.

Still, I've started my efforts with earnest attitude. My work ethic on this subject is of top-tier quality.

[Escape the Cave]

I will accomplish this goal. I've set my mind to it.

The Tiny Snake God will be proud.

Chapter 15

Snake Report: Day Ten

A large group of spiders tried to eat me today.

Yes. It was terrifying.

There were dozens of them. From all directions: on the ground, on the walls, even in the air.

Spiders are very good at jumping.

That's terrifying as it is, sure: but what's much more horrifying is that they can use webs.

Oh yes.

They use webs, and those webs are very hard to see.

It's a problem. One that let them hang suspended and quiet above my head.

Maybe you can see where this is going.

Yes, a bigger problem.

Lots of them, starting with eight legs pouncing on me, and then wrapping me up. Of course, in addition to numerous painful, venomous, bites.

If I didn't make my living by eating poison, I think I would have died.

100% dead, without a doubt.

Ignoring the bites, I was pretty tightly wrapped in a web before I could think to escape. My shiny blue scales are apparently not so great in the way of armor or defense.

Come to find out they're not fang proof.

Bit of a bummer.

My great mission to [Escape the Cave] seemed to have met a premature end. I was a tiny little snake, wrapped in a tiny little cocoon, waiting for a tragic and terrible demise.

But then the spiders left.

They just sort of… skittered off, somewhere.

I don't know.

Off to do spider things.

So… I guess I was worried for nothing.

All this time, it seems there was no species-specific grudge: I think they just wanted to eat me.

Much more basic.

Looking around in the web they stuck me, there were dozens of similar occupants. Nobody was making much headway to escape, so I was being saved for later.

Trapped in the spider-pantry.

Not a great place to be, I wasn't particularly thrilled.

Not dead, sure, but very much stuck in a web.

What is a tiny-snake to do in such a position? Struggling wasn't getting me anywhere. I couldn't rip the threads, or cut them, or do much of anything.

Totally trapped.

Hisss...

Well, human-side might have panicked about then. Instinct might have panicked too, and that all lead to a very large mistake.

An error of magnitude.

I used [Fire Breath]

Chapter 16

Snake Report:

Do you know what's more terrifying than a swarm of angry spiders?

[LEVEL UP]

A swarm of angry spiders that on *fire*.

[LEVEL UP]

Yes.

[LEVEL UP]

Much worse.

[LEVEL UP]

 Eight-legged predators skittering and screaming as their massive webs go up in flames.

[LEVEL UP]

I messed up.

[LEVEL UP]

The entire Eastern side of the cave is on fire.

[LEVEL UP]

There are even giant bats caught up in it, smacking into walls and falling to the ground as carbon monoxide inhalation takes them out. There's so much smoke rising it's blacking out the ceiling.

[LEVEL UP]

More of them are falling now. All the bats that took the night off and didn't fly out are trapped in here.

[LEVEL UP]

There's a giant spider running around now too. It's just spreading the flames as it goes, like an eight-legged, drunken elephant covered in gasoline.

[LEVEL UP]

It's running deeper, towards the West. Maybe there is water somewhere over there.

[LEVEL UP]

Oh. The West... where the bat's normally nest.

[LEVEL UP]

Under the bats, there is always a lot of...

[LEVEL UP]

Oh.

[LEVEL UP]

Guano is flammable.

[LEVEL UP]

Highly flammable.

[LEVEL UP]

Yeah. This was a mistake.

[LEVEL UP]

A tragic error.

[LEVEL UP]

I just wanted to escape the web.

[LEVEL UP]

[LEVEL UP]

[LEVEL UP]

[LEVEL UP]

[LEVEL UP]

[LEVEL UP]

[LEVEL UP]

Hissssssssss...

Chapter 17

Snake Report: Day Eleven

I used earth magic to the fullest extent of my ability.

Fear is an excellent motivator, and with its encouragement I managed to dig into the cave floor and seal myself in.

Now I'm just waiting for awhile, until the fire burns itself out.

Waiting patiently.

… very patiently.

See, although I'm fairly certain it's on its way to settling-

[LEVEL UP]

There- that's how I know it's still going.

[LEVEL UP]

I keep getting reminders.

Hissssss...

As of this moment, I'm now [Level Thirty]

I feel like that's a rather large number.

It's a reasonable understanding that the more levels I earned, the harder it was to get more. I noticed this just in the struggle to reach [Level Six] before I turned the cavern into Dante's inferno. Surviving to reach that wasn't a walk in the park, but I feel like reaching [Level Thirty] holds much more significance.

To have reached level thirty on mushrooms alone. I get the feeling that would have been almost impossible.

And endless grind that may have ended in fatal dysentery.

This thought hovers along, but there are others crowded in beside it.

Most of them are brought on and personified by the masses of glowing text in my vision.

[LEVEL UP]

[Level Thirty-One]

This is intimidating.

I feel the influence of this, seeping into me. There's a palpable effect from this big a jump. My vision, my sight, any of my senses seem to be crystal clear compared to before. I feel much, much stronger. It's a lot like… I don't know: like I had terrible eye-sight only to put on glasses.

Only, for everything.

Almost everything.

For some reason I'm still tiny. Size apparently isn't scaling up with the rest.

Reaching mama-snake's stature seems impossible, even now.

On the magic front, of course I've been getting messages as well.

For the most part it's pretty much just one spell influenced here.

[Flame Breath]

Probably should have expected that.

It ranked up.

A lot.

Extremely quickly, as in: moving so fast the mental images for words kind of blurred together.

That was before it hit some sort of invisible wall at the upper limits, exploded, and got replaced by something else. A line of text which now floats with the title of **[Leviathan Breath]**

So… yeah.

I think this makes me rather comically lopsided in my Magical growth. [Basic Healing], [Passive-Healing], [Earth Manipulation], [Fire-ball] and **[LEVIATHAN BREATH]**

One of these things is not like the others.

Not one bit.

But magic right now might be safely labeled as good news. It's good news that at least some of it has probably gotten stronger, and it's the other notifications that are turning out to be much more worrisome.

[UNIQUE TITLE: DIVINE BEAST]
[UNIQUE TITLE: LEVIATHAN]
[UNIQUE TRAIT: FIRE AFFINITY]
[UNIQUE TRAIT: LEGENDARY]

Ding, ding, ding: one after the other. These are all new.

As always, there is no explanation, they're just here now. No guide, no blurb about why, and trying to mentally poke or prod at them provides nothing of value.

They're just sort of "present" for some reason. Just like the **[125 Skill points to allocate]** is "present."

Hissssss...

A lot of points.

New spells? Of course, I'm just waiting here with no excuse not to check, not as though I haven't been looking. There's a really, really long list that seem to be available.

By a large number, I count more than before. It requires scrolling.

Problem is, most are insanely expensive.

I figured **[125 Skill points to allocate]** was a large number, but a lot of spells seem to indicate pretty damn blatantly that's not the case.

Four digits, sometimes five, and most of those hurt my brain to look at.

On the bright-side though, while all of the all of the advanced ones are still impossibly expensive, those original basic ones seem to have remained cheap.

Discounted? I'm not sure, it said that I think.

[Fire] has a whole bunch. [Flame Wall] and [Torch Skin] seem interesting, but they're both pushing close to a solid hundred a pop...

[Healing] has barely any options, which is weird. Apparently ranking in [Fire] doesn't help that much. [Earth] is pretty much the same boat.

But 125 points...

This is like winning a small lottery. Seems like a lot, but it's not nearly enough to quit the day-job.

Still... there's one other option.

I've got a number that's almost enough to be tempted.

Enough to charge headlong into the *Trap*.

- **[Water element: Level I]** Cost: 5 points

  Unlocks future Water magics.

- **[Knowledge element: Level I]** Cost: 100 Points

  Unlocks future Knowledge magics.

- *[Divine element: Level I]* Cost: 0 Points

  Unlocks future Divine Beast magics.

One reasonable option, one trap, one suspiciously free gift.

That's clearly one reasonable option, and two traps.

Yes.

All within budget.

Sign me up.

Chapter 18

Snake Report: Day Twelve

I bought them all.

Maybe that was foolish.

I'm trying not to have too many regrets.

Even if I mess up, I'm sure the God of Tiny Snakes will forgive me.

[Water element] Unlocked [Water manipulation I]

[Knowledge element] Unlocked [Voice of Gaia]

[Divine element] Unlocked...

Nothing. Maybe I should have figured as much, it was free.

First on the list, [Water Manipulation I] was the safe choice.

I already had [Earth Manipulation] so it wasn't like this process would be a mystery to me. It's exactly what it sounded like.

The powers that govern this messed up reality apparently accept that I can manipulate water.

I am the master of three elements now. Earth, water, and fire.

… and healing.

That last category doesn't fit, but whatever.

Anyways, it's neat I guess. Water stuff could be useful, I'm sure.

Here in the tiny-snake temporary lair this isn't a particularly useful magic. There's no water or anything, but I'm sure there's bound to be some puddles around somewhere. Maybe an underground water source? I'll put it to use somehow.

But then there's the real purchase.

[Voice of Gaia I]

That's a completely different story.

Oh yes, I'm snake enough to admit: I was wrong. I take everything back about the 100 points being a trap.

[Voice of Gaia] is no trap.

It's my long-awaited, desperately needed, wish upon a stalactite: mystical Q&A services.

Behold:

> "[Voice of Gaia]: Show me my abilities."

[TITLE: DIVINE BEAST, LEVIATHAN]
[BRANCH: **Magic essence**]

[UNIQUE TRAITS:]
[Toxic]
[Omnivore]

[Affinity of Flame]

[Legendary]

[RESISTANCES]
[Poison resistance: Rank IX]
[Fire resistance: Rank II] - Affinity*

[Skills]
[Healing:]
[Passive Healing II]

[Basic Heal II]

[Flame element] - Affinity*
[Leviathan breath I]

[Fireball II]

[Earth element]
[Earth Manipulation II]

[Water element]
[Water Manipulation I]

[Knowledge element]
[Voice of Gaia I]

[Divine element]
[None]

Hissssss...

Now how about that? I feel a bit of a drain. More than just a bit, actually-but it all shows up.

Just: Bam! There it is, I can look at it. I can see these things without leveling up, and what's more?

I can ask questions.

> "[Voice of Gaia] what is [Unique Trait: Toxic]?"
>
> *"Toxic: Toxic flesh. Deadly to consume."*

Hisssss.

Hear that?

Finally, I get some answers.

Short answers. Brief and not very detailed, but answers all the same.

The sensation of draining happened again though… rather substantially this time. Magical equivalent of getting pretty winded.

> "[Voice of Gaia] what is [Title: Leviathan]?"
>
> *"Leviathan: A beast of power. Known to lurk in the deepest depths of the Dungeons."*

Oh.

Dungeons.

The RPG vibe wasn't far off the mark after all. I'm starting to make sense of this, at least a bit.

> "[Voice of Gaia] what is [Title: Divine Beast]?"
>
> *"Divine Beast: A ____ ____ ____ __"*

Ah… huh.

Is this… hmm. Yeah, I think it is.

Messed up a bit.

I'm out of magic.

I can't move.

Shit.

Chapter 19

Snake Report: Day Thirteen?

I have awoken to the familiar look of shed skin. Quite a lot of it.

Gotta shed that skin. Snake-fact of life.

Still, strange as it sounds, I haven't gotten much bigger. I still fit in the hollowed lair I created. At best guess, I cant be much larger in mass than the average gardener snake. Maybe a bit smaller.

Weird, considering I have the title of [Leviathan]

Maybe I just need to eat more?

That's probably what granny-snake would be telling me, if mama-snake was still around to take me on family visits.

A real tragedy.

I might have killed half a cave of monsters, but all I've eaten are glowing blue mushrooms.

Not really "bulking-up" foodstuffs, but I've got more important things to try and gain than just a bit of weight.

Mana, for example.

Magic fire-power.

Stamina.

It was the hard way, but I'll consider it a lesson well-learned. Using too much magic is absolutely not an option for me.

Not to be repeated.

I have no idea how long I was out for, but unconscious in the Dungeon probably means certain death: easy meal and no escape.

So, getting answers using [Knowledge magic] is apparently dangerous. Caution for the future, strongly recommended.

Like, it knocked me out.

Had about five seconds of realizing I couldn't move, and then- Done.

D-u-n, done.

Clean out with a swift K.O.

From now on, I'm putting a limit on questions. One per day until I'm sure I can handle more.

All well and good when I'm sitting pretty inside the tiny-snake lair, but out in the open that sort of thing could be deadly.

Safety first.

Still, today is the day that I've chosen to emerge from my hiding place once more.

With [Earth manipulation] I will part the stone and sprout from the earth like a small sapling, surfacing among the ashes of a forest fire.

New life in the wreckage of the Tiny Snake God's sacrificial Pyre.

Yes… emerging… surfacing… Fresh air at last.

Perhaps I'm part snake, part periscope.

It is finally time to make my return to the world.

Hisssss...

Hmm.

Well, I don't really know what I expected.

It's very dark.

Pitch black, really.

Smells like… burning. Okay, that makes sense. Turning about, 360 degrees of motion here and…

Yeah, it's about what I figured.

Nothing moves but the faintest trails of smoke. Probably wouldn't see those if it weren't for being a higher level than before.

Ah... Right.

Well, this makes sense. It is a cave after all.

Or a Dungeon?

[Voice of Gaia] definitely called this place a Dungeon.

Doesn't really matter: there isn't going to be much natural light in a place like this. Light sources don't just grow on…

Oh, "duh."

I burned all the Mushrooms when the get Spider BBQ happened.

Aside from the weird crystals sprouting around here and there, it was the shrooms were what kept this place aglow.

I guess charcoal doesn't provide the same level of quality ambient lighting.

Hissss...

Well, somehow I can still see at least a little. It's dark, sure, but it's not completely pitch black. Everything is scorched though, which probably isn't helping much.

There... I can make out the familiar land marks. The Arbitrary West... The Arbitrary East.

It is time to go East.

Slight detours aside, mission **[Escape the cave]** continues.

Chapter 20

Snake Report: Day Fourteen

The arbitrary Eastern direction did not lead me to the promised land.

As such, I soon made camp, carving out a new temporary Snake Lair at the most elevated portion of the caves yet located.

Slithering along to the East lead me up, and up, and up: it's a long tunnel, just about as wide as it started, with more or less the same shape if just a little more polished. Strangely, not a single monster even made an effort to block my path.

In fact, I didn't see any monsters at all.

Maybe that's why.

Visibly, all I managed to see were scorch marks from the heat and smoke, so I'm guessing they all fled from the flames.

Kind of a marvel how far the fire managed to go, when I think about it.

Pretty decent amount of distance.

Still, this is perfectly alright. Leveled up or not. I don't know much about combat. I'm alive by either a fluke or a miracle. Important sounding titles brought up my floating words in my mind's eye make little difference.

I'm not going to take weird floating letters over a gut feeling of primal-dread.

Heck no.

As such, caution is still my first approach. When the slope began to dip back down, going much deeper into the unknown, I hit the brakes.

It troubled me, so I stopped to found temporary tiny-snake lair "Summit-Camp."

[Earth Manipulation] let me burrow into the North-side tunnel wall. A tiny hole leading to a rough cube of space, per-usual routine. I ended Day thirteen there and listened for the swarm of Giant Bats passing through the Tunnel.

None came.

I guess the fire really did scare them all off.

Hisssss...

Well, ecosystem destroyed or not, I didn't feel too much guilt over it.

Safe to reason the giant bats probably would have tried to eat me anyways, so good riddance.

Emerging from the temporary tiny-snake lair, though, was the moment I happened to be forced into confronting the unpleasant truth.

Continue going forward? That meant going down deeper into the Dungeon.

Steeply.

Down.

Down.

Down into the pitch black darkness. Further I go? That's probably where the more dangerous things will be.

The really horrifying stuff is always at the bottom.

Isn't that how these things work?

I think it was, in the games, I know that's exactly how this all went. The newbies usually start out with something easy, and then work their way towards a greater difficulty.

I'll trust that judgement.

But there's a Brightside to this.

Where there's an increased feeling of eminant danger, there's also an increased population of Glowing Mushroom.

Correlation or causation? I suppose it doesn't matter considering I don't have much of a choice besides turning around. On this steep incline, it seems I've found a bountiful supply of tiny snake rations.

Lucky.

Far as I can tell, the fire seems to only have spread with violence deeper towards the West, but here on the Eastern side it was quickly extinguished.

Guano free zone, from the looks of it., but it's not just that. From the floor, flowing up and along my scales, I can understand the more important factor.

There is a noticeable draft of cool air. Directional, moving relative East to West, I feel it slide along my scales. Wind... it's definitely a current of some kind, and I'm slithering into it.

This is good news.

Really good.

Even though the incline is heading down, it's why I'm confident that somewhere in this general direction, there is in fact a way out. Maybe this down will lead back up, and I'll be able to get out of this messed up place.

I mean, a draft needs to come from somewhere... right?

Maybe?

Here's hoping, but add that with the clear fact that those bats were always flying in this direction, I expect they were moving to leave the Dungeon. That's totally what bats do: every night they go out to eat, and then they return to rest after.

Clearly remember reading a National Geographic article that taught me this.

I feel confident about.

Yes, very confident.

But still... going deeper into the depths of a monster filled Dungeon.

I'm not so confident about that.

Hiss... there's compromise to be found in everything.

Win some, lose some.

I'm taking my time here. No rush, careful approach. Nibbling on a few glowing delectable here and there, exploring down one slither at a time. At this point, these fungi are the nicest things I've found in this place.

Almost killed me, but now I recognize that they're fun guys.

Ha... ah... oh, who am I kidding?

That wasn't funny.

Nothing is funny about glowing mushrooms, but that doesn't mean I'm not going to keep following them. I'll keep following the glowing edible things, so long as they don't try to kill me anymore.

Once a tiny snake passes their test, the shrooms will not betray trust.

Much like the Tiny Snake God, I have faith in the blue shrooms.

But... eating these...

It's strange. Such a sort period of time, but it's already so different from what I first remember. Much like when a person diligently trains themselves to eat spicier and spicier foods: there's a whole new level of flavor just waiting on the horizon.

The taste and sensation of being poisoned? Gone.

It has been replace by something new... something wonderful.

I won't say it's like chicken, but...

Well, it's not bad. Not bad at all. I don't even bother to cook them anymore, I'm past that, and besides- it ruins the taste. Instead I practice my Tiny-snake [Lunging Bite] and swallow them whole.

"Hisssssss-ah"

Another mushroom down the hatches. Another few hundred, and perhaps I'll finally put on some real weight.

"Hisssssss-ah"

Maybe grow a bit more. Get into the same weight class as some of the other monsters sitting around at the bottom of the food chain.

"Hissssssss…"

Honestly, if there is any residual damage from the blue mushroom poison, I don't even feel it after ten of them. You'd think I would, but it's as if-

[PASSIVE HEALING: RANK III]

Ah-ha! Rank up.

Well, that would be why.

It seems that a healing factor combined with resistance is a powerful thing, and I clearly chose to grind the correct attributes. Human-side wins again.

What's more is that, past level Thirty, I feel I probably have more health than before. I'm thinking that maybe some base stats have been boosted.

Invisible rank ups.

Maybe?

Hard to say, other than the basic senses it's a difficult thing to pin down- and even those are relative so now that I'm used to them, thinking back to before is tricky.

So it's a mystery of sorts. Working on it.

Clearly I've gained some benefits, but the only really obvious one is that I've probably got more magic firepower.

Still tiny, still just a snake.

Nothing else of noteworthy value to report, physically speaking.

Troublesome.

I really wish I could decipher how my base stats are tracked. I even took a risk and asked [Voice of Gaia] but all it gave me was one of those "_____" statements.

Gobbled up my mana regardless.

Kind of rigged, but [Voice of Gaia] has a rank attached, so it might just be a grinding thing. Maybe?

Given enough time, I'm sure I'll figure it out. For now though, I'm limited to describing some vague details as "more," or "less."

At best guess, I would say that I have twenty times more magical strength than when I started.

Like, I could cast one spell twenty times, instead of one time.

Guessing, as in: based on a gut feeling. Not dropping my mana low anymore if I don't have to. Not worth it, but I think I'm probably Super-snake if put side by side with when I hatched.

Super-snake.

I like the sound of that.

But it's very weird, this Eastern Tunnel. Down and down I go, yet I still don't see any other monsters. The fire was bad, but it wasn't like it even made it this far. On top of that, it burned out a whole day ago already. I'd expect spiders, or Frogs, or god-forbid- some Giant Centipedes.

Instead there's nothing but mushrooms growing on cave formations. That and a deep, deep silence.

It makes me nervous.

It makes instinct nervous, too.

"A little snake like me isn't meant to stumble into a place like this." That sort of nervous.

"Grrrrrrooooooooaaaaaaaan."

Instinct: *"Freeze"*

There was a noise, and there was a fitting reaction. Instinct took over the wheel, and there are no complaints from human-side.

None.

I'm frozen like ice: part snake, part statue. I am one with the world, both living and inanimate.

"Grrrrrrrrrooooooooaaaaaaaaaan."

Again.

There it is again, and it sounds terrifying.

Scary in a way that resonates with the unknown. I already know, it's not a living thing that is creating the noise I'm hearing.

"Grrrrrrrrrooooooooaaaaaaaaaan."

It's not approaching me… I can tell that now.

The source of this sound… it's still far off.

If I move closer though…

"Grrrrrrrrrooooooooooaaaaaa-**CRASH.**"

Like thunder. As if the clouds of the heavens smashed against the sea. Even without ears my head is ringing from the impact of such force. It's such a strange sound, out of place with this cavern.

Curiosity… my old nemesis has returned.

With great care, I will slither forward. Down deeper into the depths of shadow.

Chapter 21

Snake Report:

I was right. The source of this strange noise is not a living thing.

But...

Well, I feel in some way I was also wrong. Because it's not exactly "inanimate" either. Inanimate would suggest that it's not moving on its own, which would be wrong.

So to say it's not that it's not "living" is correct, but… misleading.

Yeah… this is a tough one., so I'll just say what I'm seeing.

Two words: giant skeleton.

Giant, as in: head to the ceiling.

Skeleton as in: made out of bones.

Fitting.

I'm surprised, in a really horrified sort of way.

There's something that should just absolutely not exist, and it's right over there. Standing in a massive open space, boney feet planted upon dark looking runic carvings that cover over a disturbingly flat and polished stone floor.

From a distance, I think on the massive skull, it might actually be wearing some ancient royal crown of stained and blackened gold.

Giant skeleton, wearing a crown.

It's a thing that's perfectly fitting for a Dungeon. The heavy rusted shackles on each of its wrists seem all too well, and if this were a video game, I'd expect it to suddenly stare at me.

To stare at me with dark and haunting flames in its eye sockets.

Yes…

It doesn't though- thank the Tiny Snake God, it does no such thing.

Instead, it simple smashes its massive arms against a large metal door.

No tiring, no wearing down. It just lays down one heavy-handed blow after another with a lumbering pace.

Spooky? Check. Evil? Oh, yes- check. Occupied with some immortal and never-ceasing task? Also… check.

It's cleared all the boxes, right down the list.

Crazy. Scary. A bit fascinating in the morbid sense, but there's something much more important. It's above all this, way- way up there.

Yessss…sssssss…ssss…sss- ahem.

Yes.

If I look up, I see what I've been waited for.

There, faintly visible, almost completely cut off along the twisting formations of jagged stone, but my eyes can make it out.

Freedom.

No mistaking that, no matter how weird this world is: I see sunlight.

Operation **[Escape the Dungeon]** is now entering phrase two.

Chapter 22

Snake Report: Day Fifteen

Noise pollution.

Anyone who's lived near a highway will tell you, that's a thing.

True, zoning boards can help, and if you pay your taxes sometimes they'll throw you a bone- but I'd rather not have a bone thrown, literally or otherwise at the moment. Instead I've taken matters into my own lack of hands.

I have moved my tiny-snake-base of operations to just outside the creepy giant skeleton's space. I call this base *Big-foot.*

It's probably my finest work. I plan on staying here awhile.

Now, I'll admit. The immortal giant skeleton makes a lot of noise. Far as neighbors go, it's not the best: the giant skeleton spends a large majority of its time banging on that giant and creepy looking door.

But like I said, I decided to solve this problem. I don't call camp *Big-foot* my finest work for nothing. Noisy or no, last night I slept perfectly.

Peaceful slumber.

Uninterrupted.

You see, if a tiny snake with some semblance of talent with earth magic covers up an equally tiny entrance way to their secret camp: no noise gets in.

Perfection? Maybe.

Genius? Most definitely.

But… well, there is one problem.

My goal is not to stay and live here beside the neighborly skeleton of doom forever. I'd like to not to that, if possible, and would much prefer to go up to the surface. To live out my days in the happy and peaceful utopia of the easy-levels, which I both hope and pray are a thing.

They better be a thing.

But that's the one problem, in a nutshell.

See, snakes are not good at climbing giant stone walls. Especially not domed ones that go almost entirely upside-down. That's not a good risk for a snake to take: the chance of falling it high, as is the height from the ceiling to the floor.

But if that wasn't enough?

Saying the fall doesn't end with pansnake, the results of touching that rather suspicious runic-carving floor might.

There's something weird about it.

I can observe that giant skeleton is touching that floor, so just by their presence I personally think they've made a rather compelling case against doing the same, but I'm actually rather concerned by the fact that it glows red and seems to whisper dark and mysterious words.

Sometimes.

When I'm staring at it for a bit too long, only to wake up from my trance and wonder what I was just doing.

Yeah… no, I'm not going to touch that floor.

Hell no.

At the same measure though: I'm not going to try and climb along the sloped walls of the ceiling and stupidly fall right into the middle of it either.

That would be an incredibly stupid way to die, fall-damage or otherwise. Instead, human-side of things has a plan.

A long, boring, cheating-the-game-mechanics sort of plan.

Operation [**Escape the Dungeon**] phrase two: [**Earth Manipulation that can pierce the heavens**]

It's a long name, I know.

Hissss...

But that's because it's probably going to take a long time.

Chapter 23

Snake Report: Day Sixteen

I think it's safe to call this "grinding."

The earth.

The stone.

My patience and magic reserves.

Onward and upward, progress continues until it doesn't.

It took me over four hours to run low enough on magic for instinct to start shouting at me to stop.

During those four hours, I managed to get about three whole full-length slithers worth of distance out of the stone.

Already, I'm having some slight doubts with my plan, but progress doesn't always start quickly. In this case, it's going to have to build up some momentum.

[Earth Manipulation: Rank III] Is going to have to be a reward in itself. If I can make the skill more efficient, this should get easier with time. I end my day early after taking a quick slither out of Camp *Big-foot* for a few glowing mushrooms.

The Giant Skeleton is still hitting the creepy door. Same as before.

Hissssss...

Consistency can be comforting in odd ways.

Chapter 24

Snake Report: Day Seventeen

Another four slithers upward in the manner of progress.

Not a lot, but I had to stop.

[Earth Manipulation: Rank IV]

Exhausting, I'm not going to complain anymore than that because this is much easier then yesterday.

Yeah, hard to believe, but it's true. This magic is tough- wicked tough to use for long periods, but I've been working a steady pace of a slow and winding spiral.

The base camp at the bottom, followed by a spiral upwards into another flat resting space, followed by another spiral into another resting place.

It's a very simple design.

I don't have arms or legs, so I feel like this is really the only way to do things even if straight up and down might be less distance to carve out. The stone down here is very tough, but if the surface is only a few hundred feet away, I think I can make this work out within a few months.

As I popped back out of the lowest level of my expanding camp, I collected another few mushrooms and watching the giant skeleton bang on the door.

It's a wonder he can just keep going like that. He must have recovery magic up the wazoo, otherwise I think his arms would have crumbled to dust ages ago.

Crazy.

Chapter 25
Snake Report: Day Eighteen

[Earth Manipulation: Rank V] was reached.

I'm getting better at this: maybe six whole slithers worth of height added to the total. Some real progress compared to yesterday.

Although… the trade-off is interesting.

Seems to me that now it's becoming more difficult to rank up the skill. Higher rank is starting to mean a much longer period of use before I advance with a notification.

Diminishing returns.

There's some tricks to this.

I can, on my side, control the magic in different ways.

From a pinprick of mana use, to cranking open the mystical faucet: I can focus and work very carefully with the output that's actually doing the work or I can be more efficient. I've noticed patterns, played around with methods depending on the type of stone… there's obviously a lot that can go into this, but in the end the fact is plain as day.

No matter how good I get with my techniques, I can't break the upper ceiling of this from skill alone.

Only a rank up can do that.

Moving from a four to a five.

So simple, yet so powerful. Mana, magical strength- they're intrinsically linked to the number attached to the spell. Nothing I do seems to hold even a candle to the difference these can make.

The mental flashing "ranks" have a very specific relationship with what I can or can't do. While working smarter has benefits, unlike my life before all this, practice does not make perfect: only advancing does.

It's different.

Not entirely bad, but different.

Certainly, this forces me to look at everything so far from another perspective.

Fundamentally, wherever I happen to be now is completely different from where I was before. Human to snake, the laws of reality here don't line up with what I used to take for granted.

In a weird way though, I think it's all evening out. Few more days of this, and at best guess I'm on track to be moving upwards in my tunnel at a reasonable rate. Holding to optimism, it's plausible that I can keep the pace of ranking it up at least a little each day as time goes on, continuing onwards with greater and greater distances per day.

Regardless of how much control I can gleam from using the magic itself, as long as I can managed to keep moving those numbers up, I know I'll be making some headway.

Still, there's trouble with planning that far ahead.

Especially in a place like the Dungeon.

What's the expression? "Look towards the horizon, and you'll be tripping over your feet."

Lack of feet.

Yet again, it was Instinct that saved the day.

I was so confident after the successful ascension, I almost slid out of camp *Big-foot* right stopping only at the last possible second- reverting into my trademark frozen posture at the edge of the entrance-way.

There, standing noble and regal as any monster might ever hope, a giant frog waited.

Dwarfing my size wasn't enough for this one. Much like my previous encounter with its type, that was already a given- but unlike the previous: this one had *three* heads. One spikey, one warty, one plain.

It also had an aura about itself.

Difficult to explain as this sort of attribute might be, I can say with confidence that the giant frog gave off a very sage-like and understanding sort of appearance. Dignified, professional, almost noble, as if holding some true understanding in its power.

Seated just along the edge of the cavern passage, inches from the polished floor of mysterious seals and runes, it waited as if in meditation.

It waited, and I waited.

Completely frozen, staring at this frog, Instinct screaming at highest volume- yes, I felt fear. Deep fear, primal fear: enough to make me question how I ever came to find myself in this terrifying place. My life flashed before my tiny snake eyes- yet the frog didn't so much as look in my direction.

Not with the spikey, warty, or even the plain head waiting on its mighty torso.

My mind's eye wandered, spurred on by the blended smoothie of fear and panic, and soon I found understanding.

I knew.

I knew why it had come here.

The absolute truth.

From the depths of the Dungeon, far, far to the West- it witnessed the horror of great fires that swept through the caverns. Its froggy brethren did flee, falling dead at his warty-green feet to pass a single message:

"Avenge us, Sage-Frog."

With tears streaming from all six of his eyes, so it was that the Three-Headed Frog carried on through the dark depths of the Western Dungeon. Travelling on, past the carnage, past the ashes of the damned, and towards the source. With greater and greater leaps, he bounded onward past over burnt husks of those who once lived in, not stopping until finally arrived here.

Here, where his journey had ended.

Yes… now, he stares at the giant skeleton. Behind those three froggy-faces lies deep and misplaced hatred: a desire for revenge on the Monster which wrought such terror upon his-

Oh.

He jumped in.

Chapter 26
Snake Report: Day Nineteen

I won't talk in detail what happened to the Three-headed Frog.

It's not right.

No... It's much too soon.

I will simply say that he was a hero among frogs. Never will I forget his noble sacrifice in the efforts of misguided justice.

Though I know little of the Frog-Gods, I believe he has performed in noble enough fashion to be seated at their great froggy table in the sky: to munch on insects and other gross amphibian-food for all eternity.

The memory of his efforts will not be lost so long as I live.

I truly believe that.

Hissss...

Once upon a time, I thought "Don't touch the floor with all the symbols on it." This was based on nothing more than fear.

Fear, and a hunch.

Now though... now I understand. It will be a rule from this point on: "Do not touch the floor."

Not now- not ever. This has been established. Touching the floor is a very dangerous thing to do. Something only to be done by madmen... or frogs.

Never snakes.

Life is short.

I realize this now.

So short, unpredictable. One wrong move... yeah, that's all it takes.

I've had a long time to think about this, reflecting on the subject while I take the day off. Instead of operation **[Earth Manipulation that can pierce the heavens]** I'm carving a shrine.

Yes.

A shrine to the Tiny Snake God and his trusted prophets: Two-headed frog, and Three-headed frog.

Though their shape is rough, I've made them look like quality. Here I have these two froggy figures standing beneath the small serpent in the sky. I've raised the ceiling to match a cathedral-style arch. Perhaps it's now three slithers high, four slithers wide.

The single most detailed, labor-intensive, and exhausting use of my powers I've ever committed to.

My mana reserves are all but completely expended on this effort.

I'm recovering slowly, but still: I can barely move.

Hissss...

This is alright.

I might be losing my mind, but this is fine.

Camp *Big-foot* is now a sacred place. This is holy ground.

[Earth Manipulation: Rank VI]

Ah.

A sign.

Proof I have pleased them.

Hissss...

I've most been under some level of stress since being born here. It's now more obvious than ever before. Laying here in the cathedral of the Tiny Snake God, I am feeling much like a person aware of approaching mental instability.

This is such a terrifying place.

Just out of paranoia, I chose not to touch the floor of the giant akeleton's lair.

Fear has kept me alive. If I'd been this fearful as a human, I never would have died: I'd have lived forever.

See, it's not the floor, exactly, that is dangerous. It's what the floor does.

For the unfortunate individual who steps on the rune-covered surface, fate is sealed.

Literally.

A barrier of glowing magics lift along the edges of the floor. The kind which will not let even the bravest of Frogs back out. A hidden trap: No escape from the space.

The Giant-Skeleton stops hitting the door immediately, and turns exactly like I imagined it might: With dark and haunting flames in its eye sockets.

Then…

Well, then it attacks.

Rest in peace Frog.

Chapter 27

Snake Report: Day Twenty

I have officially managed to reach the level of the giant-skeleton's height. About thirty slithers up from the ground level I started.

Today I made a tiny balcony to confirm this, and it's quite a sight. The giant skeleton and the terrifying ancient door make for an interesting view, all while I overlook the floor that shall not be touched.

Still, hard to believe it took me this long to get here.

Operation **[Earth Manipulation that can pierce the heavens]** is ridiculously difficult. I may have bitten off a little more than I can chew with this one.

I mean, sure, it's a good plan for someone who wants to avoid another early death, but time-consuming is an understatement.

Ug.

Well, on the bright side, I've gotten very good at recognizing my limits. This is like Mr. Miyagi's sort of training: repetition and endurance.

Wax on, wax off.

Only with heavy stone.

It's coming to me, the tricks of the trade. When I'm running out of steam, I now recognize it without Instinct screaming at me in panic, and I stop early. I'm getting more efficient, even without the rank ups.

Altogether, this has been nice.- if only for the sake of having energy left-over to explore a bit.

Explore?

Oh, yeah.

I know: not fitting to the mold for someone so fear driven, but having far too much free time is abrasive after days and days of magically molding rock and stone.

Boredom is a killer.

It also helps that I have some actual motivation to look around.

Back in the original tiny-snake-lair, back when I did little more than hide in the ground and wait for the Mushrooms to kill me, there was a glowing rock.

Yup.

A rock, that glowed.

Weird how quickly I'd forgotten about that, but I guess that can happen when you're trying not to die.

Anyways, I never did anything with it.

Used it as a lamp.

It just sort of glowed, looked pretty, acted as a light-source for my tail-version of shadow puppets. I could do one pretty good variation of a worm, and another convincing version of a…

Never mind.

Listen, as it turns out: there are more of them.

A lot more.

If a careless burrowing snake happens to break one, while digging upwards towards the heavens, this will result in a flash of light, and a sickly-sweet scent that might make a person panic and think they're about to die.

Yes, in fact that existential terror will hit like a freight-train: but it's important to note that they won't die.

Not even after hissing in terror and wriggling like they're going through death throes.

Nope.

Not dead.

As a bonus, this not dead individual will also recover a large amount of magical stamina.

Enough for almost a completely new full-day's work.

Mana rocks.

Pun intended.

Basically, I'm looking for crystallized magic. These seem to be a monster Dungeon's equivalent of mana-potions. Personally, I think this is a pretty ground-breaking discovery.

Again, pun very much intended.

… I'll stop.

I don't want to spoil the importance of this discovery.

It's a big deal.

Very big.

Because of this, tiny snake productivity has been off the charts.

I'm making a ton of progress. Magic isn't just for labor anymore, I'm practicing with it just for fun. Letting out some more creative steam, trying some new variations of how to channel it along.

Interesting stuff, actually pretty fun.

But these gemstones, or crystals, or whatever it is I decide to call them: I've managed to find a bunch now that I'm actually on the lookout for them.

Up along the cave walls, they seem to have a decent number.

Of course they're well within the giant skeleton's lair, so there's that, but I think the reason I didn't realize they were in there was because of all the glowing mushrooms that were acting as camouflage.

They look pretty close to one another.

Regardless, there are a lot of them, the trick is getting to them.

It's not a matter of motivation.

I can see clearly that these stones are worth the trouble. One broken crystal is a full day of magical energy. I can double my progress, carry on with operation **[Earth Manipulation that can pierce the heavens]**

But this is a more difficult respawn, a *New Life Minus*. More specifically: minus the hands, the fingers, the *thumbs.*

Without those, when slithering through a freshly made tunnel, there is only one method for a tiny snake to carry a crystal.

Can you say "open wide?"

Hisssssssss…

Well, in this manner, I will admit that I've made another mistake.

Upon discovery and collection of a rather large looking magic crystal, for once it seems that snake instinct has betrayed me.

I swallowed it.

Chapter 28

Snake Report: Day Twenty-one

I have made a terrible error, and despite my best efforts to remedy this, I am growing concerned.

Very concerned.

"[Voice of Gaia]: Show me my abilities."

[Level 31]
[TITLE: DIVINE BEAST, LEVIATHAN]
[BRANCH: Magic essence]

[UNIQUE TRAITS:]
[Toxic] - Toxic Flesh. Dangerous is consumed.
[Omnivore] - Capable of eating non-monster food-stuffs.
[Affinity of Flame] - Bonded to the Element.
[Legendary] - A rare being. Not often seen, known only to Legend.

[STATUS: **AFFLICTED**]
[MANA-BURN] - Magic exceeding capacity. Damage inflicted.

[RESISTANCES]
[Poison resistance: Rank X]
[Fire resistance: Rank II] - Affinity*
[Mana resistance: Rank V]

[Skills]
[Healing:]
[Passive Healing V] - Automatically being to recover from injuries. Mana drained as a result.
[Heal I] - Third rank of healing.
[Flame element] - Affinity*
[Leviathan breath I] - Rare ability. Advanced variation of [Flame Breath]
[Fireball II] - A launched ball of flame.
[Earth element]
[Earth Molding I] - Second rank of [Earth Manipulation]
[Water element]
[Water Manipulation I] - Ability to actively mold and shape water.
[Knowledge element]

[Voice of Gaia II] - Knowledge embodiment
[Divine element]
[None] - None

Maybe that will explain a little.

Well, in more ways than one, it should explain. More details at the very least.

In summary though: I messed up.

This is worse than the Mushrooms. It's a different kind of pain.

Imagine you ate something very spicy. It's a lot like that, only in every inch of my body. From the tip of my tail, to my snout, I am filled with a burning sensation.

"**[Voice of Gaia]**: What is that giant skeleton?"

"*[Veel'Osa, Lord of the Damned]*"

"**[Voice of Gaia]**: Who is Veel'Osa?"

"*[Veel'Osa, Lord of the Damned] is the cursed and Ancient Prince of the [First Men]*"

"**[Voice of Gaia]**: What are the First Men?"

"*[First Men] were ancient beings of intelligence. They are now extinct.*"

Questions- lots of questions.

"**[Voice of Gaia]**: What are beings of intelligence?"

"*[Beings of intelligence] are also known as the [noble races]*"

Okay, interesting.

You might have noticed and already begun wondering: what happened to the previous suggested caution for these things?

It's a reasonable question.

Wasn't using [Voice of Gaia] dangerous? Wasn't that a rule, not to use it too much?

Well... past tense? Yes.

But present tense?

No.

True, the **[Voice of Gaia]** uses a lot of mana. Too much. An unfair and unreasonable amount, and all I have to do in order to spend that is ask a question.

Ask a question, the magic will answer. Simple and easy.

Asking three or four questions, and I think normally that would just empty my reserves and I'd pass out.

Normally.

Emphasis here: it's still using a lot of mana, but that's exactly why I'm using it.

Because I'm *not* running out. Quite the opposite: I wish I could.

I think I'm dying.

It's like eating the spiciest pepper you've ever imagined, but instead of chewing it, you just gulped it right down.

And then waited.

Slow burn to start, getting worse... and worse... and worse.

Right now my reserve tank of magic is brimmed to overflow, past overflow. By the time I've asked one question, I already need to have another queued or-

Oh god, there it is.

I think my tail might actually be sparking.

Oh, it hurts.

"**[Voice of Gaia]**: Where are we?"

"*[Deep Dungeon]: A lower level in the Dungeon network which falls below the bed-rock of the surface world.*"

Hissss...

So, I ask a question. I get an answer. I've gotten past the point of really thinking too heavily on my queries. I haven't been able to sleep because the moment I stop using magic, I start to burn.

Like, dying at an accelerated pace kind of "Burn."

I tried to productively combat this with earth magic, with healing, with anything- but they don't have the capacity to pull out mana quick enough. They're like venting with a garden house, when I need to break open the whole damn pipe.

So I've come back down to this.

"[**Voice of Gaia**]: What species am I?"

"[Basilisk]: A monster-species often known for its capacity for poison."

Currently in my mentally exhausted state, after carving out another dozen feet of stone, turning the entire camp *Big-foot* into a human-sized bunker, and casting heal more times than I can count: this is the only thing keeping me alive.

I'm too tired to do anything else.

Like drinking an entire pot of coffee after an all-nighter, I'm tired but I can't sleep.

It sucks.

Miserable doesn't do it justice.

Everything hurts. I'm exhausted.

"[**Voice of Gaia**]: What is a Divine Element?"

"[Divine Element]: An element of divinity."

That's the most non-answer I think I've gotten yet. Even after it ranked up once, it still doesn't provide all that much in the way of details.

"[**Voice of Gaia**]: What is an element of divinity?"

"A [Divine Element]"

Well. that's useless.

Oh, I hate everything.

I really do. Everything but the Tiny Snake God and his two faithful Frog Prophets. The rest of this world can go to hell. This is too difficult. It hurts so bad, I feel like I'm about to experience spontaneously-combustion…

[Rank up]

[Mana resistance: Rank VI]

[Passive Healing VI]

[Voice of Gaia III]

Hisssssssssss... Hysterical.

I am being mocked, I think.

[LEVEL UP]

Yes. I am being mocked. This is hell.

Chapter 29

Snake Report: Day Twenty-two

[Mana resistance: Rank XI]
[Passive Healing: Rank X]
[Voice of Gaia: Rank V]

I will say no more. My brains, both human and snake, are close to madness.

I welcome death.

If I die in my sleep, so be it.

Chapter 30

Snake Report: Day Twenty-three

[Mana resistance: Rank XX]
[Passive Healing: Rank XIX]
[Voice of Gaia: Rank V]

I slept.

I really did, I slept and woke up, used magic and then went back to sleep.

Somehow... somehow I'm alive.

Like someone with alcohol poisoning, too stubborn to go to the hospital. I basically puked up magical spells and rolled back over into slumber.

I also shed my skin, several times from the looks of it.

Insert joke about onions [here] -no. Stop that.

Still.

Outside of asking the [Voice of Gaia] nonsensical and open-ended questions like "WHY?" over and over, I think I mostly used [Earth Molding]

Camp *Big-foot* is now a large human-sized bunker, complete with replica stone sofa, table, chairs, and book-shelf. At its center, the shrine to the little-snake-god still sits.
The absurdity is noted. Half-awake molding magic is just that. I made whatever would make the pain subside while I spammed questions.

Somehow though, I think I've now reached some sort of middle ground.

I feel sick. I still feel pain.

But I think it's less.

I'm going to attribute this to [Mana resistance: Rank XX]

Intense.

Slowly but surely, I am becoming immune. Like some ancient ninja that injects themselves with poison from a young age, the effects are lessening. First the mushrooms, now the magic crystal...

It seems I've taken the long and winding masochistic-route to survival. No pain, no gain.

As a plus, I've grown stronger.

It's not just the overflow from the crystal that has long since dissolved and poisoned the ever-hissing shit out of me. Though it's still overflowing a bit, my magical reserve is easily twice what it was before, maybe even more. The more I used magic, the more of it I seem to get.

Like a muscle… or something. Not only do I out-heal or out-resist pretty much any self-inflicted damage, in some strange way I'm almost 100% sure my mana reserves have also followed that trend… which is an odd feeling.

[Voice of Gaia] still won't reveal anything, not that I was really expecting much on that front, but I can feel I've got more magical firepower to throw around then I did before.

"[Voice of Gaia]: Show me my abilities."

[Level 34]
[TITLE: DIVINE BEAST, LEVIATHAN]
[BRANCH: Magic essence]

[UNIQUE TRAITS:]
[Toxic] - Toxic Flesh. Dangerous is consumed.
[Crystalline scales] - Increased Defense
[Omnivore] - Capable of eating non-monster food-stuffs.
[Affinity of Flame] - Bonded to the Element.
[Legendary] - A rare being. Not often seen, known only to Legend.

[STATUS: Lessening]
[MANA-BURN] - Magic exceeding capacity. Damage inflicted. Status is the result of consumption - Large [Mana Crystal]

[RESISTANCES]
[Poison resistance: Rank X]
[Fire resistance: Rank II] - Affinity*
[Mana resistance: Rank XX]

[Skills]
[Healing:]
[Passive Healing XIX] - Automatically being to recover from injuries. Mana drained as a result.
[Heal I] - Third rank of healing.
[Flame element] - Affinity*
[Leviathan breath I] - Rare ability. Advanced variation of [Flame Breath]

[Fireball II] - A ball of flame, capable of long-range.
[Earth element]
[Earth Molding III] - Second spell rank of [Earth Manipulation]
[Water element]
[Water Manipulation I] - Ability to actively mold and shape water.
[Knowledge element]
[Voice of Gaia V] - Knowledge embodiment. Spirit of the world.
[Divine element]
[None] - None

Hissssss... I can't believe I'm still alive.

Even the pretty looking rocks of the world want me dead.

Chapter 31

Snake Report: Day Twenty-three, Continued

I went about continuing my upward digging with a new resolve.

The magic crystal that I made the mistake of swallowing seems to have been dissolved a long time ago, but its effects are still hanging around. Before they completely pass, I want to make the best of things.

[Earth Molding III] makes this easier, and as of today we've reached a new record: over one hundred slithers in distance.

Vertically speaking.

On the small balcony I've made to confirm, the giant-skeleton and the creepy door are actually starting to look a bit small.

Or... normal sized.

I'd have to be twice as big as mama snake was to even come close to rivalling the skeleton, so I know this is all a trick of perspective. Still, they don't look nearly as scary from up here, which is nice.

What's more though, is that by being up here, seeing the sights: there's encouragement.

Positive reinforcement, I mean.

Breathe in deep, point your nose up: feel that?

That's the feeling of real moving air.

Wind: not stale, or tasting of cave guano, or burnt things, or dead things- no. This is a faint but pleasant flow, and it's reaching down from way above my head. If I look up, I can see the source, hundreds upon hundreds of slithers up along the massive crack between the two sides of the ceiling.

There is the faintest hint of light. At certain times, it can pass all the way down to the floor below.

The goal-line is finally in sight, I'm confident that my plan is working.

With this much mana, even if the overflowing effects of the crystal are lessening, operation, **[Earth Manipulation Molding that can pierce the heavens]** is in full swing. We're charging ahead, and even if the surface is as far as another thousand slithers away, I can still be there in a month at the worst case.

Fifty slithers a day, multiplied by twenty days- factoring in a steady improvement of efficiency. Best guess, I estimate twenty days or less until I reach the surface. Less than a month before I can escape this terrible Dungeon, and hopefully eat something other than blue mushrooms.

Soon.
Honestly, I would settle for just about any kind of human food. Eggs, chicken, rice, beans, bread, pasta: Anything. I'm not trying to complain, but blue mushrooms and shiny rocks haven't been the most appetizing menu items.

Both almost killed me.

If I can eat those things, I'm sure I could eat a sandwich or something.

Even if it tried to kill me, I think I could handle a sandwich.

Human food...

Human...

Hissss...

"[Voice of Gaia]: do humans exist?"

" ... "

Nothing... the magic was used... decent sized query there, but no answer.

" ... "

Hmm...

This has happened a few times before. When I asked "Why" a whole bunch of times because I felt like I was dying in a fire from the inside out. That sort of occurrence, mostly.

Because of that, I think this Magic seems to work better with direct context. In some way, I feel like that makes at least a little sense. It identifies things, it doesn't act as an all-seeing oracle. The questions need to have some basic reference to go off.

Hissss... Waste or not, the curiosity is killing me from the inside out.

"[Voice of Gaia]: What is that giant skeleton below?"

"[Veel'Osa, Lord of the Damned]"

"[Voice of Gaia]: Who is Veel'Osa?"

"[Veel'Osa, Lord of the Damned] is a cursed and Ancient Prince of the [First Men]"

First men... huh. There's something.

"[Voice of Gaia]: What are Men?"

"[Men]: Term and title for [Human] beings."

AH HA!

Wooooah! WOAH.

Woah. Hear that?

Humans.

Hiss.

Oh man, hold on a second.

That last question drained a lot.

Like, I'm getting a little woozy and lightheaded, so much more than normal...

Crystal burning is still in effect though, I feel that still. Ah, it's coming back, but that just wiped out 80% of my remaining magic in a flash.

Quite a cost for one question.

Maybe it has something to do with context? I feel like I bent some rules getting that answer. It's not like I've ever seen a human as a snake, just a giant skeleton banging on a giant door.

How would I normally know what a human is?

I wouldn't.

Hmm…

I think I'll wait for a few minutes. Take this time to collect myself to the musical tones of bone and iron smacking on a massive creepy door.

Soothing. From this height, I feel that these sounds have some nice acoustic qualities to them. Really impressive, probably the arching stone- presents some decent amphitheater-style effects.

Ah... Wow, this recharge time is really slowing down. I must be on the trailing ends of the magic crystal here. I'm not sure if that's a good thing, or a bad thing. Not dying to the horrible feeling of magical fire is well and good, but unlimited magic is also pretty over-powered.

Having at least something going for me was kinda nice.

Hisss...

Maybe I'll hold off on questions for now. Focus on heading to the surface instead.

If I have to decide between eating another crystal and going without a few answers, I think I'll be going without answers.

Chapter 32

Snake Report: Day Twenty-four

Today is not normal.

It started normal, but now it is most certainly shifted category to "not."

I've used most of my magic for the sake of operation **[Earth Molding that can pierce the heavens]** and I'm now watching from a previously made balcony overlooking the giant skeleton and the runic floor.

Only, there is not music to my lack of ears.

Holes in side of head?

At least I've got those.

But to reiterate: there is silence.

For the first time since Hero-Frog, the giant skeleton has stopped hitting the creepy door.

Instinct doesn't like this much more than I do. We're both waiting for the traditional horror twist: The evil turn and skull-grin with the smolder of an ancient hatred.

Maybe even some dark-gothic theme song in the background.

But that hasn't happened.

I almost wish it would. Just get it all over with so I can stop being so on edge over here. I've already slithered my way up and down the passage I carved out to check the mushroom tunnel that leads to the skeleton room, and though there are now a few signs of recent monster activity, nothing has approached the trap-floor.

No monster has been brave enough since the frog.

Yet, the skeleton is just standing there... doing nothing. It's perfectly still in the middle of the circular floor of runs.

Still... watching... waiting.

For what?

I have no answers to the question, and it's bothering me to no end.

The door?

That's the direction it's staring. Something about the door seems likely, but after trying to break the thing down for who-even-knows how long, I wouldn't expect the Skeleton to just give up on a whim.

Maybe sometimes even giant skeleton's need a break. That could be why. Every couple hundred years, he takes a breather from being evil and terrifying, to think about life and such.

Or undead and such. Whatever.

This could be a very important even, like Halley's comet, or a solar eclipse. The type of thing I'll one day tell my grand-snakes.

"Yes little snakelets, your grandfather was there when the evil giant skeleton of the Dungeon took a break. He stood around all day and did absolutely nothing at all, and by gods did he do it ominously."

Yes.

I can see it clearly even now.

... No, this is still bothering me.

The sudden stop like this, after being that skeleton has been consistent for days. Just pounding on the door endlessly, only to stop now?

Not okay.

Something is different, and I don't like it.

It makes me nervous.

Chapter 33

Elsewhere

"Keep running! Don't stop!" Grant shouted from the distance as Talia smashed the ghoul that blocked their path, clearing way just as the flash of wind magics sparking to light. "THUNDER!"

A gnarled scream met the crack of lightning that streaked through the air. A burst of heat and flame scorched her nostrils and throat as Talia kicked through the second fallen foe. Its bones crumbled under the steel and leather, shattering to fragments.

"We can make it Grant!" She hollered as the faith magics enveloped her weapon again, seals of protection threading along the surface as she rounded the Dungeon's narrow corridor. "We can make it!"

"GRAAAA-" Her mace struck down another foe, skull disintegrating under the heavy-handed swing.

"Keep running! Don't stop Talia!" The roar of fire lifted as the man behind her passed into the corridor at breakneck pace. Talia turned just in time to catch the final words of a deep chant, words rolling atop words with a message of power. *"Flames and gods, defend this sacred path."* The cloaked man lifted his staff, crystal atop its wooden frame blazing with heat as it slammed down towards the distant howls of pursuers: *"Wall of Fire."*

With a deafening wave, the floor erupted, smoke and heat spiraling down the tight passageways with a deadly hunger. The screams and screeches soon pitched and then feel silence, smoke and fumes all that remained of the creatures that once gave chase as the Wizard feel heavily to the floor.

"Grant!" Talia shouted, turning pace to drag the man back to his feet. With effort, she shouldered him on her left side, glowing mace illuminating their way as she pressed them forward. "Where in god's name are Rodrick and Joan? They should have met back up with us at the rally point!"

"Gone. " Heaving the word out, Grant let out a rough hiss as he steadied his feet to free himself from her shoulder to lean upon the wooden staff. "Our team's split up. Didn't see it clearly... the ghouls swarmed them... Joan might have made it. Rodrick was the one holding them back."

Reproachfully, he eyed the weapon in his white-knuckled grip, stare focused on the trails of misting cinder that lofted from the crystal piece affixed to its upper end. Exhaustion was evident.

"Oh Lord of light, Grant your blessing." Talia recited the words quickly as she raised he mace, left hand reaching out to touch the man's ashen forehead. *"Heal."*
The magic took effect immediately, bruises and weakness fading beneath the warm glow.

A sigh escaped his lips, breath escaping and replaced by a deeper breath.

"Can you walk, Grant?" Talia asked quietly. "We're not safe here." Her tone was hushed as eyes aglow with white-magics carried on in a scanning motion: alert and watchful of their surroundings. "I took us down a side-channel when we got cut off. It might take us some time to find our way."

"I can." A stern nod met her question, heavy breathes of the smoke-tainted air drawing in as the man straightened his back. Even healed, he looked as though he'd been thrown off a cliff; bags of tiredness settled heavy on his face. "Do you know the way?" The staff leaned towards the smoldering wreckage of the spell he'd cast. "We can't go back there." The smoke lifted and swirled, thick and oppressive.

There would be no way through that safely, Talia could tell from just a glance. She fumbled through the pouch at her hip with a spare hand, before reaching out to pass a small vial of glowing blue to her companion.

"I think so. Here, drink. This one's stamina." She gestured with the glass piece, mace settling to point in the opposite direction of the smoke. "Rodrick had the map, but I remember this level well enough. If we can find a major line, I think I can get us back without difficulty."

"Ah..." Tipping back the vial, Grant's eyes seemed to shimmer with the flood of magics that came with it. "So, we're not going to die in romantic fashion after-all then?" His grin seemed to glow in the dim light of Talia's magics and the strange Dungeon fauna that seemed to settle upon the walls. "That's a crying shame."

"Ha." Talia flashed a grin of her own. "As if- I'll have you know: I plan to die of old age."

"And I myself, being smothered to death by fair maiden's breas-" A light punch to Grant's arms silence him, as Talia pointed their way with a commanding expression.

"Lets get going. I don't think Rodrick's the type to die easy, and if Joan made it back to the rally point alone, you know she'll be a wreck." Her eyes narrowed, as a single hobbling figure emerged from the darkness before them. "Just follow my lead." She muttered, weapon readying.

"Yes Ma'am." Grant replied, humor forgotten.

Chapter 34

Snake Report: Day Twenty-five

A day or so has passed here in the Dungeon, and it did so without the giant skeleton moving an inch.

It's just standing there, terrifying as ever as it stares at the door.

This is starting to wear on my nerves.

Much as I want to continue on with operation [Earth Molding that can pierce the heavens] I'm scared to put myself at a disadvantage. I still think it might come down to the classic horror twist. This world has tried to kill me at almost every turn, I don't see why the evil Skeleton would be much different.

Everything is deadly. Trust nothing.

So there. No trust. The giant skeleton is plotting something.

Something terrible.

Something really terrible that's going to happen any minute now, any second.

Now.

No... Now.

Soon... Hissssss... I'm not sure.

It just keeps staring at the door. I don't understand.

The door... Maybe that's a hint. It's huge, its covered in runes and carvings that are all rusted over. No visible damage despite the beat-down that I had grown accustomed to, so probably magic.

Flat, no handles. Iron... or metal of some kind. Something that can visibly rust, so it's not gold or something fancy. Thirty something feet tall, at the very least. Covered in a bunch of symbols beneath all of that... it's spooky but not really any more than it was before. I can't see anything that would catch my attention, specifically: but the giant skeleton can.

It's waiting for something. It knows something- something that I don't. That's the only thing I can think of. It knows something about that door has changed, and it's waiting...

"THUMP."

"Grrrrrrrrrrrooooooooooooooan."

So that's it.

"GRRRRRRRRRRRRRrrrrrrrooooooooooooan."

It was waiting for someone to open the door.

Chapter 35

Elsewhere

In full, it had been at least a day, by Talia's best judgement. Possibly more, but it was difficult to know for certain. They had been moving without true rest, and any adventurer worth their salt knew that one's personal concept of time passing in the Dungeon was guesswork at best.

Surviving meant sleeping in short shifts, breaking portions of the few biscuits and dried meats left from Talia's pouch. While Grant stood watch, Talia might close her eyes for what felt as though it were the barest of moments before being awoken by a warning of enemies, and forced to continue again until they found another area of relative safety.

Talia was finding that even when using faith magic to reinforce and heal their exhaustion, the limit to such methods was quickly approaching. There were limits to healing no matter how efficient, it couldn't work without material to draw from. Low on rations, doing too much would be a potential danger in the long run. Besides that, even if they could feast like barons or lords at every meal, there was no denying these benefits wouldn't be enough to let her continue perpetually. Talia knew they would need to find safety soon, or face the consequences.

The problem was that they'd tried almost everything by now.

Grant was a talented mage with more experience than most, so he'd had a few ideas at the start. There were things one could do when they had talent for both soul and air magic, and he'd taken to trying them immediately: hashing out simple runes to mark their route along the tunnels and catch the attention of anyone else who might find their way down. Though he'd admit they weren't his strong suit, they glowed brightly enough that no who knew what to look for could miss them, and were effective in marking their path.

At first it had seemed promising. There was a fork in the road, that lead to another fork. One went down, but the other? That managed to actually lead into a slow incline that leveled out. It dipped, then rose, then dipped again, but it didn't go deeper, which both of Talia and Grant decided was a good sign.

Yet, after walking for hours, they'd found it lead back to the beginning: a loop.

So, Grant had tried some other things. He wasn't an [Adept] but he could try and use the earth and soul elements to try and get a sense of direction relative to previous sanctuaries. There was a resonance of some sort there, and though Talia had never quite understood the details, she knew that often in the upper levels of the Dungeon this could work.

Only they weren't in the upper levels, which meant it didn't.

Still, Grant was by no means was he limited to a trio of elements. He had a handle on almost all of them short of faith (though no mage could use faith for much of anything anyways so that wasn't really a surprise) so he'd tried several other things Talia wasn't quite sure about. Starting with some sort of earth and soul combination to try and "delve" the rock of the ceiling, which was remarkably clever of him in Talia's opinion, but only revealed only several more meters of rock. That attempt was followed by pouring an exact quantity of water into a small pot Grant kept in his pack for tea, and setting it to boil with a very precise source of fire magic.

Talia didn't understand the point of this, but Grant insisted there was a general sense of depth that could be obtained from the time it took for the water to begin bubbling. Regardless of what it was intended for, Talia didn't think he looked very pleased with the result.

So that left almost nothing, outside of faith or fire magic- which were of little value to escaping thousands of feet of rock. Talia joked that Grant might as well try using earth magic to dig their way out, but the frown on his face seemed to indicate that was a bust, so she'd let it slide and instead they returned to walking.

From bad, to worse. Every path they took lead only deeper into the network of caverns.

Turn after turn after turn, Talia hoped there would be something positive around the next bend: but none of them lead back to the main passages. Soon, she was starting to run low on strength, but she knew that Grant was even worse off. He'd cast more magics in succession recently than she had ever seen. Perhaps it was because they were as deep as they were in the Dungeon that he felt it was viable, as the mana density was higher, but Talia knew fatigue accumulated all the same.

To make matters worse, instead of upward, they'd been forced down further, significantly. Further and further down, no matter what Talia did, they were harried into the depths to the point where even the slightest misstep could be fatal even with a full team. This many layers down into the Dungeon, she knew just the two of them wouldn't stand a chance against some of the monsters that were known to lurk.

"We need to find a Sanctuary zone." Grant's voice was hoarse as he spoke. "There should be one on this floor nearby if Rodrick's map was right. If I remember it correctly, it was somewhere about this depth."

"Aye." Talia replied, eyes peering in the dark recesses of shadow ahead of her glowing mace. "Aye, there should be one soon."

It was both a lie, and a truth. They both knew it.

Grant was technically right: there had been one on the map. It had been one layer deeper in the Dungeon than they had reached before getting separated from the others, but it had been there.

He was also wrong: they had long since lost any clues to where they were, and Talia suspected they were hundreds of feet below it by now. Even if she kept a stoic face, it didn't change the facts.

They were completely and utterly lost.

"Craaaaaaaaaw!"

Talia froze, holding position at the next intersecting passage as a feeling of dread ran down her spine. Carefully peeking around the stone, she caught sight of what she'd feared: another monster swarm. It seem this time, it was spiders. There was a large group milling about with disturbingly quick movements brought about by skittering legs.

"Craaaaaaaw…" Beneath their onslaught, some unfortunate creature cried out as their fangs sunk in to pass the paralyzing poisons with a pitiful "Craaaaaa..."

"We're going left." Talia whispered, nodding quickly to Grant's waiting stare. She couldn't believe how tired he looked. Face sunken, exhaustion teetering on the edge of collapse. She held a forced grin as she continued. "To the right… I think there are some Tar-spiders, but the left looks like it widens out to a larger passage-way. It might be the Sanctuary."

The mage's mana reserves were probably holding, but everything else was at his wit's end.

"Let's go." Grant replied, weak nod passing agreement and feet trailing softly behind her own as they crept forward.

Talia steeled herself for the end with each quiet step. She awaited the cry of hunger from some unseen monstrosity, the sound of motion or ambush with every twisting corner.

But none came.

Instead the hall widened. It grew larger, and larger, and larger still. It passed into a massive tunnel-byway, carved stone molded with giant bricks; as if some ancient castle had once stood where they now tread.

Perhaps it had, for all Talia knew of the world's history. Behind her, she could see Grant staring in bewildered and exhausted wonder.

"Where in all the hells have we wandered, Talia?" He whispered quietly, hand tracing along the stone of the cavern. "Work like this... no I've never known the Dungeon could manifest something of this nature."

"The ancients then?" Talia replied weapon ready, "Some Guilds have found wreckages before."

No monsters seemed to show, but neither did Talia's guard settle. This place lacked the familiar hum of magics often associated to the precious zones of Sanctuary, and the floor had not a single rune, instead falling to bricks of heavy stone. It was as if they were in a castle. A structure of hands and design, deep beneath the earth.

"It might just be..." The haggard reply settled into huffing breaths as they continued on into the unknown hall. "Maybe a sunken portion of some long forgotten city... certainly from before the Empire if I'm to interpret the architecture. There have been some expeditions that have come across similar sights in the past, but not to this scale..."

"Did it turn out well for them?"

"I'd say it's an even-split between rich and dead."

"Ah."

They settled back to silence after that, neither willing to attract unwanted attention. After an hour of marching, without a single monster approaching or blocking their path, finally Talia forced them to stop. Turning to Grant, she grinned as she watched his head tilt back, eyes widening in awe at the strangeness before them.

A giant set of doors, arching up ten wide paces high and covered in the ancient scripts of long-forgotten runes. The familiar hum of magics settled atop the stone with a static filled buzz, almost music-like in quality.

"Do you think this is it?" Talia asked, staring at the tired man beside her. "Or is it something else?"

"Well, we can't be sure..."

"But?"

"But..." Grant let his hand fall to stroke the thin hairs of an approaching beard coming in atop his chin and jaw. Tired as he was, his eyes seemed to hold the glimmer Talia often saw in him when he was running at full-strength. The look of excitement, that turned to her with a wide smile as he pulled free one last potion from his belt. "There's only one way to find out, isn't there?"

Chapter 36

Snake Report:

The door opened.

Doors* actually.

I now stand… no: slither corrected.

Seems there were two doors the whole time, meeting in the center. I just couldn't tell because the surface was so covered in rust and magical weirdness. Staring at it for days, and I didn't have the slightest clue.

But the door, or the doors: those don't matter now.

They don't matter at all compared to what just wandered directly into the giant skeleton's floor trap.

People.

Two tired looking, exhausted, beaten-up and dirt-covered, people: an armored warrior-woman of some kind, and a Mage that looks like Gandalf in his late-twenties. They marched right in like a couple of bad-asses, staring down the unknown with grim determination.

Then the barrier activated, and they spent a good ten seconds just staring in slacked jawed horror as the evil-theme music started to play.

Watching from my lower-balcony roost, overlooking this affair at Giant head-level, I find it difficult not to pity them.

Snake-side instinct doesn't care about humans at all, but I've got a whole mental and spiritual frame-work in common with them. I was a human for about 25 years before the Tiny Snake God granted me a second chance at life.

Watching two humans get slaughtered into fine red paste isn't what I'd like to see. Not one bit.

Hero-Frog was more than enough for one lifetime.

Still, I can't look away.

It's like target fixation and morbid curiosity all rolled up into one. There are humans! Here! In this god-awful Dungeon! We're easily hundreds of feet from the surface, and yet somehow there are people?

Does this mean something? Does this hold significance? Is this a blessing sent by the Tiny Snake God?

If they die, will I have missed a chance for a better life?

I don't know, but as I watch from the balcony of cliff and stone:
The battle is starting.

Chapter 37

"A trap." Grant cursed beneath his breath as he raised his staff. "Of course it would be a trap."

"Oh, Holy guardian of Light."

Talia began her chant even as the growing sensation of horror began to over-take confidence.

"Grant me strength to protect. If others are your sword, I am your Shield"

The white magics flowed, a layer almost like glass forming with the essences of mana as they domed over; rising from the ground like a bubble. Focusing her mind, she began to channel mana further, steady drain pulling down.

"It's not just a trap Grant." She managed to reply, eyes focused ahead at the approaching monstrosity. Each step towards them seemed to shake her bones, strumming through her chest like the beats of a drum. Still, she kept on, letting the glow of white magics intensify. "Look at the floor: this is a Sanctuary."

"This is a pretty sorry excuse for a Sanctuary, Talia." Grant spoke as energy collected atop the crystal piece of his weapon, eyes focused on the rising shape of a giant monstrosity just now taking its first step. "Not exactly hospitable, compared to the ones I remember."

"We were on the run for a long time, I think must have gone down into an undiscovered layer." Talia poured her magics into the shield above their heads, imbuing it with faith. "All of the ancient sites of the Dungeon originally possessed guardians."

"Guardians huh? Never through we'd be the types that went racing ahead of the expedition teams." More mana collected into the staff, torchlight and smoke burning atop the piece with the craft of a master-magician. "How much gold do you think a Sanctuary is worth?"

"More than you can spend Grant. Do we have a plan?"

"Well, we have a choice to make." His hands lifted the wooden piece, muscles on his forearms stretching to their limits as the glow intensified. "I either try to break us out of the barrier by the doors, or I hit this thing really hard. Either way I'm going to be spent, this is everything."

"You're leaving this to me?" Talia almost lost her focus, mana slipping before the flow rightened itself again to continue their defense. Onward it went, with layer upon layer of faith blanketing the air above them.

"It's a skeleton of some variety, so it's clearly undead. That monster's roots are certainly not in the natural elements." Grant's voice trembled as the feeling of mana-burn seemed to radiate into the air above his head. "There's no telling what this is capable of. Even if we run back out, we both know there's slim chances we're going make it back up to the higher layers."

"What are you saying?"

"I'm saying that if you're willing to fight, I'll fight."

"Grant..." Talia closed her eyes as she poured out the last readying spell of defense, opening them once more to a dome of milky white crystal. Beyond the strange translucent fog of purified mana, she could barely even see the beast approaching. All she could feel was the drumming steps.

Boom.

Boom.

Boom.

This was her strongest skill. Of all the faith magics, the barrier was one Talia had always felt an affinity with. Truly, layered as it was now, the shield of white-mana was likely strong enough that could turn any normal undead to flame in cinder just by touching it. Perhaps in its current state, it might rival a lesser Saint-class miracle, but even so: she doubted it would be enough.

Boom.

Boom.

Boom.

The steps approached, each more terrifying than the last. This was no ordinary undead. Whatever creature coming for them was something far more sinister.

Grant was right.

They were veteran adventurers. They were members of one of the strongest freelance teams operating in the Northern continent and had more than enough experience to back such a claim- but this would be the last time they could fight at full strength. To run was to die slow and pitifully. To fight was a chance.

The floor guardian before them was at a disadvantage to their professions, not a giant spider or beast- but an undead. Her affinity might be enough to pull a victory, but at the same time, backing out and trying to flee would likely only earn them a slow and miserable death. It was now, or never.

"We fight." Talia whispered.

"That'a girl." Grant replied. "Let's give it hell."

"Blood and thunder."

Chapter 38

Snake Report:

Hissss...

Magic things are happening.

The suspense is terrible.

This is real deal, crazy impressive, magical stuff. The kind I remember seeing in movies. A battle for the history books: Two heroes versus the great ancient evil.

Compared to the Earth Molding and the Q&A talks I've been having, this is on a different level.

As the giant skeleton has made its approach, the two humans have readied themselves. I've never seen anything like it.

There's a barrier of some type.

The human duo made a shield by the door, like a glass dome made out of magic. More time that pass, the more difficult it is to see through, so my guess is that it's getting thicker. Glossier, pale and cloud-like.

Difficult to see through or not, though, it's hard to miss that there's also going on with young-Gandalf and his staff.

He's collecting energy or... I don't know. Condensing air? Pushing fire magic into it? It looks like he's bottling up a storm.

Seriously, my scales are tingling a bit. As if there's a current in the air: I think something crazy is about to happen.

Maybe an all-out wombo-combo style attack.

Either good, or bad. I can't tell yet.

That remains up to the giant skeleton to determine, with his equivalently giant-fists and wrist shackles.

"GRRRRRRRRRAAAAAAAAAAAAAAAW"

And the fist comes down-

CRASH

It's on fire. Holy smokes, the Giant's arm is on fire. The other arm is coming down now, but that shield magics holding up to it.

CRASH

Wow. That's some crazy barrier.

It's looking a bit less white and foggy than before though.

CRASH

Ah, the Skeleton is really on fire now. It's looks a bit like Burning Man, flames reaching up its arms and covering its shoulders and head.

Can they really kill it? A immortal monster like that doesn't exactly seem the type that will go down with a bit of heat.

There's a price to pay too, That shield is almost gone. If I called it a bubble before, it's about to pop. Almost invisible compared to the white orb that was in place at the start.

Ah... I see it.

That was the plan all along.

This was all to bide time.

To stall for young Gandalf.

"THUNDER!"

"THUNDER!"

The shout was overwhelmed as the magic erupted over Talia's head, passing force knocking her to her knees as the shield released from the inside out.

With impact that shook the white fires of faith free to the air of the giant room, the skeleton shuddered, its chest agape as the magic forced its way inside, pulsing and burning a path of fury. Yellow, blue, red and orange mixed in a single pillar of force that surged from the crystal piece atop Grant's staff. Even as he too fell towards the ground, his hands clutched the wood, barely capable of kneeling as the magic continued.

"NOW TALIA! DO IT NOW!" His shouted command was barely a whisper over the roar of magics, but Talia moved all the same, responding with all her remaining effort.

As the last whispers and sputters of the magic fell to their ends in threads and spitfire, She rose with her Mace held high to shout the crucial words. *"TURN UNDEAD!"*

"GRAAAAAAAAAAAAAAAAAAAAAAAAAAA-" The giant skeleton howled in agony, head thrown back and arms raised towards the distant ceiling as the magic struck it- but it was not enough.

Again Talia shouted:

"TURN UNDEAD!"

Her words lashed out with the glow of faith. Her power crucial ability as a paladin, a weapon against the scourge that haunts mankind. *"TURN UNDEAD!"* It stuck out again, and again. *"TURN UNDEAD!"*

Behind her, the clatter of a staff rolling upon polished stone confirmed what she already knew. Grant slumped to the floor unconscious, completely spent by his massive efforts. How he'd even had so much power left, Talia didn't know, but she knew that it was down to this last spell.

Mace raised high with all of her remaining strength, she shouted the last of her magics:

"TURN UNDEAD!"

As her energy left her, she stared as the great skeleton fell to the ground before her. It crumpled beneath its own weight, slouching downward as flaming fists of bone and shackles landing to either side of her.

The skull, too, approached in much the same way. Slowly bending, as its own weight dragged. In the dark caverns of its eyes she could see smoldering coals of hatred. Black and desperate things, raging against the pain that had lashed out upon its body.

Then, the flames which covered its bleached bones faded.

In horror, Talia watched on as those holy fires were snuffed out. Only receding at first, then faltering, then disappearing entirely. Those terrible eyes stared at her, as its jaw clacked in a mockery of laughter.

The giant skeleton began to rise, once again.

It was all she could do, but Talia held her ground, knees shaking along the effort just to stand as it towered upward before her. Higher and higher, back to its full stance, easily thirty paces of scorched and ashen bone. Egregiously wounded it might have been, but not quite defeated. That hated smolder looked down at her with such pressure it threatened to break her very spirit.

This was the end.

Unconscious behind her, Grant lay still, and Talia offered a silent prayer for him. They had done all they could. They had thrown everything they had, and come up short. Ever so short.

She knew, already it was recovering.

Eyes wide, she waited for the end, mace ready to strike out with one final swing as a massive fist raised high for the coming downward motion. Like a mountain, towering and waiting to collapse.

Then, it stopped, turning its head as if in reaction to something. The dark coals behind its eyes seemed to flare up in rage as its mighty jaw opened to bellow out a shout-

-and instead swallowed fire.

Terrible green flames, so hot that her skin was blistering even from a distance, forcing her to cover her face and eyes with a shout. Between gloved fingers, Talia watched in awe as the ungodly cone of fire erupted: absorbing the giant skeleton within as it did its work.

With horrible cracks, those massive bones began to shatter. Those hollow eyes raged as they were filled from within, tendrils of bright and ghostly green flames wicking through with relentless pressure.

Instead of a shout, Talia was sure it screamed.

Then, finally, the flames relented- and for a single moment, all was still.

She watched as the skeleton stood, immobile.

Still standing, even after all that. Like a statue, carved from black volcanic stone.

Crack.

She heard the noise, as much as she felt it.

Crack.

She heard it again, and then…

The massive skeleton began to turn towards her, bringing with it the fear she'd been holding at bay. It still wasn't defeated, it was still coming for her, even now-

An arm felt, then crumbled to the floor.

CRASH!

Then another-

CRASH!

Then the ribs, the spine: as they hit the floor, slag and dust spread out. Piece by piece, they tumbled down, until finally the skull too landed with a resounding explosion of crumbling dust.

Before Talia, started two gaping holes, in which there was nothing left but bone. Then, that too disintegrated.

Talia stared in wonder, turning slowly to look in the distant direction which the sudden blast had come from.

Someone had saved them, but how? Who?

Her legs wobbled, then gave out, forcing her to her knees. Staring off across the room, she could see the slightest glow of blue moving along the dark stone of the Dungeon wall. It paused, as if staring back, before disappearing completely.

"Thank you." Talia whispered.

Then, the strength she'd pressed far beyond her normal limits fell to gray, fading with the last light of her magics. Talia's legs gave out, then her knees, and then even her head slumped to the cold surface of the polish runic floor.

Without a further thought or question to how or why, she embraced by the sweet comfort of nothingness.

Chapter 39

Snake Report: Day Twenty-six

[LEVEL UP]

[Level 40]
[TITLE: DIVINE BEAST, LEVIATHAN]
[BRANCH: Magic essence]

[UNIQUE TRAITS:]
[Toxic] - Toxic Flesh. Dangerous is consumed.
[Omnivore] - Capable of eating non-monster food-stuffs.
[Affinity of Flame] - Bonded to the Element.
[Legendary] - A rare being. Not often seen, known only to Legend.

[STATUS: None]

[RESISTANCES]
[Poison resistance: Rank X]
[Fire resistance: Rank II] - Affinity*
[Mana resistance: Rank XX]

[Skills]
[Healing:]
[Passive Healing XX] - Automatically being to recover from injuries. Mana drained as a result.
[Heal I] - Third rank of healing.
[Flame element] - Affinity*
[Leviathan breath II] - Rare ability. Advanced variation of [Flame Breath]
[Fireball II] - A launched ball of flame.
[Earth element]
[Earth Molding V] - Second rank of [Earth Manipulation]
[Water element]
[Water Manipulation I] - Ability to actively mold and shape water.
[Knowledge element]
[Voice of Gaia VI] - Knowledge embodiment. Spirit of the world.
[Divine element]
[Royal Spirit of Man – Acquired]

So… I did something.

In memory of Hero-Frog, vengeance was swift and righteous. I was an instrument, a tool for the Tiny Snake God's wrath.

The giant skeleton has been defeated.

I am the victor.

Ssss…

The two humans almost did it on their own, I think they actually might have come pretty close. One more hit, maybe.

But then they ran out of steam.

Young Gandalf essentially used hyper-beam, then took an immediate dirt nap. The paladin woman let loose one heck of a "Turn undead!" on the skeleton, but I guess being an evil immortal giant has some perks.

Hard to kill something that's already dead.

On fire, rib-cage displaces and chain-smoking magic fumes, peppered with the white glow of some sort of holy-faith laying an all-mighty beat down on it: the skeleton just didn't die.

So, yeah… made my move.

I'm not sure if I should call myself a credit-stealing bastard, or a hero.

A bit of both, maybe?

Tiny Snake God forgives though.

It's alright.

Morality is in the eye of the beholder anyways, and really that's just me because neither of the humans have woken up since the fight. They're just sort of lying there, like rag-dolls.

All limp-limbed at what not.

I went about my daily upward expansion operation as normal, came back, and they're still there: out-cold by the creepy door.

Doors?

Doesn't matter, really. What does matter, is that it's open- by the way. There is a long and ominously dark hallway beyond it. Probably a whole section of the Dungeon that has been shut-away for centuries.

Now, I'm not totally heartless. I was a human once. I really don't think I have a tremendous amount in common with these people, considering when I was a human Magic was a fiction-only sort of thing, but I'd help them if I could.

But I'm not sure that's going to work out.

The problem is that they're still on the creepy floor, which now gives off a different vibe of paranoia-inducing sensations than it did before.

This sort of *"your kind is not welcome here"* type of feeling that bothers my monster-instincts a whole bunch.

It's weird, but not *"you'll get trapped and crushed beneath a giant's fist"* sort of weird. More like a *"Don't walk on this, you're not supposed to sort of weird."*

But in that, lies the problem.

Literally.

Those two humans are still unconscious, and I'm starting to wonder if they'll die. It's been a day or so, if my concept of time is even somewhat accurate.

They're in bad shape.

Hissss...

Chapter 40

Talia awoke to the sweet burning of mana, and the smoking trails of recent flame.

In her lungs, in her nose. It was as if all her strength had suddenly been returned, and then some. It actually hurt, like the air was just slightly too hot to breathe.

"We're... alive?"

Beside her, Grant stirred, head turning towards her as he slowly sat up. Next to them, his staff lay quietly beside patches of dust and ash. He reached for it, cautiously, as he looked about. "Talia... you killed it?" Sitting up further, he seemed incredulous, eyes locked to Talia's own with a look of true surprise. "You killed it!" He repeated.

Standing on wobbly knees, Grant leaned forward picked up the weapon, shoulders heaving with laughter.

"Ha! Oh: if Rodrick and Joan could see us now! By the Light Talia! You've cleared a new floor- probably the first one in over a hundred years! You're a bloody hero for the History books! You're a living legend! If we get to the surface alive, we're going to have Royalty knocking on your door!"

"Now wait a second." Sitting up carefully, Talia coughed at the rich air. It was fading now, but still harsh on her tongue and throat. "Wait just a minute, ack-" She heaved out another cough. "Grant, I don't think I did. I really don't."

"You don't think you killed it?" The Wizard turned to her, arms spread wide to gesture at the dust and metal fragments scattered across the floor. "What do you call this? It's certainly not alive and trying to murder us." He kicked at the partial fragment, iron and rust perhaps once belonging to a giant wrist-cuff. "If you didn't kill it, who did?"

Rolling over, Talia felt her hand run along shards of glass. Among the dust and bone fragments, blue tinted pieces of crystal seemed scattered about, settled among a tiny smoldering impact on the floor beside her. Curiously, she picked up one large portion, raising it to the ambient light of the fauna that glowed along the walls and ceiling.

"Hey now, is that a Mana Stone?" Grant leaned in, squinting as he plucked another one of the shards off the floor. "Wow. Talia, you know how much some of these pieces could go for?" Carefully, he picked up another shard, pecking the ground with his free hand like a hen. "Each one of these could make twenty... no- *Thirty* mana potions. Light and Gods, just these and we've got ourselves enough money for a year. Do you know lucky this is?"

Talia coughed out the last of the sickly-sweet air, breathing in deep as she wiped her cheek. Uncertainly, she stared out along the far wall, opposite to the door, catching the faintest flash of glowing blue before it disappeared.

"I can't say I do." Talia replied honestly.

Chapter 41

Snake Report: Day Twenty-Seven

The two humans have woken up and made camp in the middle of the rune-covered floor.

Coming clean here: I might have had something to do with it.

It took some ingenuity.

Camp *Big-Foot* ground level, I tried to see what would happen if I put the tip of my tail down on the room's floor. It was an experiment, just a curiosity to know if it was just all in my head.

Well, my tail started smoking almost immediately. Those pretty blue scales of mine were singed like I'd gone and rolled it around in hot coals.

It seems that the terrain is most certainly not-ok for me to enter. Strangely enough, it seems that the Humans are unaffected. When I asked [Voice of Gaia] "what gives?" The magic replied with "[Sanctuary space]" so I'm going out on a non-existing limb to consider as intended.

The Big-bad-boss was defeated, and now the heroic adventurers have a safe space to rest. That sounds about right.

So, how did I wake up the humans? There's a question with an interesting answer.

I threw a rock at them. When it landed, the rock broke and they huffed some of the fumes.

I'm a bit proud of this, mostly because I lack arms so throwing should have been impossible. I can pick things up with my tail, but it's still a bit tricky to lob anything with accuracy.

I had to get creative.

Against my better judgement, I put another one of those glowing crystals in my mouth. Then I spit the thing so hard it practically exploded on impact.

I call it: [Fire-ball II: Rock-launching]

First try, one shot. Not bad, if I do say so myself, but I'm a bit nervous now.

Hissss...

Some things only become obvious upon reflection, you know? The details I was casually overlooking for the sake of species preference.

I'm still a just a snake.

Probably best to keep a wide berth of them from here on out.

Chapter 42

Snake Report:

I carved out another twenty feet of rock and stopped early.

Something is different about the stone now. I think I might have broken through a layer, or possibly moved up into a different evil level of the caverns. For all I can tell, I'm about to tap into a new section- maybe even another tunnel.

Hard to say for certain, and I decided to cool it, because of that.

I'm hesitant to move upwards any further just yet. There's some notable concern I'm going to pop out in the middle of some dangerous place, only to get myself eaten.

Caution, it's not a bad thing.

Instead, I'm thinking about heading horizontal and breaking back out into the split ceiling pieces. I can probably mold out a ledge to travel along the way, and hopefully avoid any surprises.

Of course, I could also potentially fall hundreds of feet, land on a floor that will set me on fire… and then, maybe have two startled humans brutally murder me.

Trade-offs.

I'll decide tomorrow.

Now, onward to the human report.

Ahem.

Snake-Watching-Humans Report: Part 1

The humans have walked along the entire border of the giant skeleton's domain. They were very thorough, and I think they were looking specifically for traps.

They also walked to the Westward opening into the room that I came from originally. I have had to reseal Camp *Big-Foot* with [Earth molding] to avoid detection. From what I can tell, they've only gone a little ways up that tunnel before turning back. Since then, they've only gone in and out of the giant doors (which seem to have been permanently opened) and not back towards the arbitrary West. Instead, I guess they've been sticking to the Arbitrary South-East.

Weird all around.

Completely guessing, but I think they're trying to find a way out of the Dungeon. Probably scouting back the way they came.

I heard some shouting, so I think they might have run into monsters once or twice. I know near the sealed entrance to Camp *Big-Foot* there have been some predatory visitors. Things are finally moving back into the area since the fire, and I've even seen some Giant bats fly past my balconies at night.

So... yeah. There's that.

As for the humans right now, the day is winding down and the wizard has made a weird magic camp-fire in the center of the room. from my vantage spot overhead on my lower balcony.

I can say with confidence that they're looking pretty miserable.

I'm thinking it's the food situation. Pretty abysmal, really.

They're both staring at a tiny piece of... bread or something. Even from here it looks like a moldy rock, but the way they're eyeing it would make an onlooker wonder if it's a roasted turkey with a side of green-bean casserole.

The struggle is real.

Not like they can eat the poisonous mushrooms that I've been making do with, but if they starve to death down there I'm probably going to feel guilty about it.

No... Scratch that.

I know I'll feel guilty.

Hisss...

Chapter 43

Journal entry: 53

A monster fell into the Sanctuary this morning. Even after the floor magics were done with it, Grant's absolutely sure something hit it with a fire-ball. So, a magic spell- and a reasonably powerful one at that.

It looks like it's a giant bat, or once was a giant bat.

The thing landed only a few feet from where we've made camp, scared Grant so bad he actually sparked a bit of lightning into the air. His hair is all frizzed up, almost like one of the Noble Aristocrats of the Mainland cities.

For some reason, he didn't like that comparison very much when I told him.

Still: [Fireball]

That's a rare type of magic for monsters to have. Human mages have been known to pursue it, but even among those it would be uncommon to find someone with enough strength to kill a higher-rank monster like a giant bat outright. A creature possessing that sort of magic talent would be an extremely unique find.

Grant is optimistic that it came from much higher in the Dungeon, noting the massive crack that runs along the ceiling. Those run at least thousand feet up, and he's starting to think it might open back up to one of the early Dungeon levels. Maybe even the surface itself.

No way to find out for certain, but it's a seriously compelling thought. If someone found where it opened, now that the floor is cleared as a Sanctuary, Adventurers might one day be able to set up a pulley system. They might even bypass some of the most dangerous levels of the Dungeon. If not the Guilds, then certainly the Empire: the profits of such a venture would out-weigh the risks.

Still, these are the kind of passing thought that would make Grant say *"Talia, quit your day-dreaming."*

He already says that, on a regular basis.

Personally, I think he's the one who's been daydreaming. That bag of crystal on his hip is enough for a small house in countryside. He's probably plotting out the whole thing in his head.

Meanwhile, I've been watching the ceiling and walls a bit more closely since the bat, not just in the sense of daydreams.

Certainly, a Dungeon Sanctuary is supposed to be a safe zone: but those magics only work on the ground. They're limited to the ancient runes- so the air or the walls aren't going to be effected.

Usually, that's not an issue. In fact, the subject is not something I've ever had to take into consideration since I first started Adventuring. On this continent, the upper zones are more-or-less commercialized. There are only so many entrances for people looking to descend any actual distance, so merchants and smithing companies typically have booths set up by Adventure Guild permissions. The Empire takes claim over the Sanctuaries with some form of rolling bounty, crediting whomever it was that originally cleared it, then expanding and paying for further ventures so long conditions look promising. Doesn't happen often, but most of those payments still go towards the larger operating Guilds. Get a foothold like that, a few hundred years later the Empire will still be pushing gold towards an organization.

Even the sanctuaries located deeper have at least some permanent presence of Empire guards, supply lines, and at least one inn-structure that people can use to rest some-what safely.

Not this one though.

We're absolutely the first Adventurers to make it this far.

I can write with confidence: there are no supply chains or mapped paths. There's no smith for equipment, Empire Guards, traders- there's certainly not an inn to stay at.

We're the very first people to make it this far.

This is a feat that trumps almost any other accomplishment (short of coming back with a cart full of ancient weapons and artifacts) so, Grant's absolutely right about what he said. If we can get back to the upper levels alive to prove all this, we're going to be put in the books and handed some fat-sacks of gold.

But that's a big "if."

I wonder how we'll manage that.

It's a long way back to the surface, and a really long way back down after that. Neither Grant nor I have a single clue how to get back up there, and this deep in the Dungeon, there are some serious dangers for a full team of people. With just Grant and myself, it's not going to be a walk in the park.

For now though, I suppose it's back to the simpler concerns: smoked bat-meat with a side of moldy bread.

Beats starving to death.

Journal entry: 54

Another bat landed. Scorched and unmistakably dead on arrival, just like the last time. One is a coincidence, but two is a trend. Grant thinks that the Giant Bats must be having some sort of territory dispute with another monster way above us.

I'm not so sure.

Grant and I roasted it a bit extra with his fire magic., and just to be safe, I decided to cast purify on the meat before we ate it. You can never really know for certain if something is dangerous in a Dungeon. When in doubt, it's safe to assume it might be capable of killing you.

After all we've been through, dysentery would be an embarrassing way to go.

Once we were done eating, Grant and I spent the whole day trying to retrace our steps back out the way we came in.

I've helped him with this, as best I could: marked the walls and floors with runes as we go, but already I think this is going to be next to impossible. Honestly, I don't understand how we managed to get down to this floor alive. Four turns in, and we ran into the largest Tar-Spider I've ever seen. It was easily as tall as Grant, give or take an extra foot.

We had to retreat, and Grant cast more than his fair share of fire on them, so we survived without injury. The problem, though, is now the whole tunnel system is basically a complete disaster.

Smoke, at least two caved-in sections, displaced spiders that are likely going to be starving soon- potentially drawing in other predators.

So, no: we're not dead, but I think we might have just trapped ourselves.

Coming back to the Sanctuary was demoralizing. We smelled like cinders, looked and felt like something the cat dragged in, and our plan was shot. Even after searching the entire Ancient hall that leads to the cleared safe zone, there was only one tunnel system.

One tunnel system, and we set the whole thing on fire.

Grant summoned his magics to pull water reserves from the storage-stone in his bag, refilling our canteens with a grin, but I think this one hit him hard. He's blaming himself for the fire, and we both know we're running dangerously low on supplies. I tried to reassure him that he made the right call. After which, he made some lame joke about us hitching up with a wedding after all this blows over, then he rolled up his cloak and went to sleep early.

With all that happened today, I couldn't sleep. Not at all. I stayed awake, watching the ceiling and the walls as Grant's little mana-bonfire died out over the next few hours.

The Dungeon is a special place. Even in the upper levels, I'd say there's a fierce beauty to the landscape, but the further down you go, the stranger it gets.

Truly though, this Sanctuary is really a marvel of its very own.

Almost like a night sky, the whole ceiling is like a dome: a cracked egg, filled with glowing blue. Deadly but beautiful fungi, maybe even a few growing mana crystals hidden among the mix, all waiting before the gargantuan fissure in the roof leading upwards to the unknown heights.

Laying there, I let my eyes soak in the scene. I stared so long I felt the flow of colors trace when I moved, almost ready to roll over and let sleep take me: but that's when I saw it.

A quiet moving glow of blue, like the mushrooms, but deeper. A more intense color that seemed to blink in and out of existence along the far wall.

The same blue I remember after the giant skeleton was slain.

Watching from the floor, I tried my best not to move. Only my eyes followed it, as it slid out along the walls, just barely rising from some hidden ledge in the stone.

A monster, but not like any I've ever seen.

It's like a basilisk of some kind, but much too small: with scales of crystal instead of black or green. This beautiful shade of blue. It seems to watch me for a time, before sliding out further, striking with an oddly clumsy motion to snatch a mushroom from the wall beside it.

It repeated this several times.

A monster that eats poison deadly enough to kill a whole group of adventurers, I'm not sure whether to be amazed or horrified at what the deep Dungeon has to show me, but it's what came next that really stood out.

A giant bat flew down, terrifying in speed as it soared through the open fissure of the domed ceiling. It seemed to circle as I watched it, and my hand felt for my mace as it came in closer.

Then there was a roaring flash, followed by a heavy burst of flame, and the bat landed on the distant floor, scorched and smoking without so much time as to let out a shriek.

As Grant awoke with a panic, staff fumbling and rolling on the floor as he chased after it, shouting in a confused state of mind, I watched as the crystal serpent stared down at us from the balcony for the briefest of seconds before disappearing back into the stone.

One time... that might be coincidence. Two times, and that might be a trend.

But three?

I think that monster is helping us.

Chapter 44

Snake Report: Day Whatever/Watching Humans Report: Official Day 4

A group of Giant Crabs tried to eat me today. It was terrifying.

You know, I thought I'd get used to monsters trying to devour me by now, but... nope.

Anyways, as a result, I will not be pursuing the Earth-Molding short-cut tactic along the ceiling chasm.

Why?

Three words: *Gargantuan Hungry Crustaceans*.

That's why. Today I made it another forty slithers up, grooving out a pathway along the side of the cliffs. I'd just started for the final stretch of another couple slithers, before a claw shot out of the cliff face and tried to pincer me in half.

Hisssss...

But, after that, I had about half a second warning before ten more of the scuttling bastards made an appearance. Scaling down out of all sorts of divots and breaks along the chasm walls.

They blend in really well: completely ambush predators. Their shells look like rocks, down to the nitty-gritty details, and their legs hide underneath those perfectly.

Best guess, I think they've been surviving eating the fly-through traffic. Something like me popping out of the walls?

They must have thought I was worth a taste.

Either the Tiny Snake God acted with divine intervention, or I was extremely lucky.

Regardless, more magic was burned in the following seconds of that encounter than I'd ever recommend. I'm also comfortable admitting here, that my first instinct is not to fight- but to drill a hole into the wall while hissing in terror.

Which is probably a good thing, because the crabs couldn't follow that.

At best they clawed at the rocks for a bit, with surprising efficiency considering the hardness of the stone- enough to chip away at it, but thankfully nothing more.

From there, though, I had to burrow a straight line down, rest, then burrow another line back out to the lower groove. I used that to get back down to the spiraling peak of camp *Big-foot.*

It took forever.

Honestly, after the crabs did their thing up there, I've started to think using magic is a rare trait for monsters. If they had [Earth Molding] I would have absolutely been snake chowder for their creepy crab mandibles.

They didn't seem to have it though.

All-in-all: I don't believe magic isn't very useful to creatures that have nothing more than a *"eat them before they eat you"* outlook on life. Abstract thought really isn't a naturally selected trait down here. By the time you've thought of something useful, it's a pretty good chance something else has murdered you.

So... yeah. I'm probably a rare-breed.

Due to the lack of spell casting around these parts, I think most monsters probably rock and roll with the [Venom] or the [Massive Perk] or whatever species variation there is for that kind of thing.

I really haven't seen any other snakes, so it's difficult to say.

Well... you know, Mama-snake was huge. Relative to me, that is. I'd bet some money that she took [Massive] but there's no way to know for sure.

Then there was my nameless sibling, devoured by that centipede... not much to go with there, either.

So... guesswork. That's all I'm left with.

If I have brothers and sisters slithering their ways about the Dungeon... well, I doubt they would hesitate to try and eat me, so there's no point in thinking too much about them.

The humans though. On the other hand, they're still down here.

You know... just doing human things.

Like eating the giant bats I shot down. Coming back from the ancient doors visibly smoking. Arguing loudly in a language I don't understand.

They explored the Western passage again too. I saw them go towards it, disappear around the bend, and then I saw them come back running like all hell had broken loose.

It had. I don't know what, but the Wizard shot a bunch of stuff in that general direction before all the commotion settled.

That night, when they set up camp beside the weird magic campfire spell, I think they looked pretty depressed.

I get that.

This is a depressing sort of place.

Everything is dangerous, and most of it is actively trying to eat you. There's no sunlight, only glowing mushrooms and weird moss. Even here, where maybe there's some sort of daylight way up above? That's almost like it's there to taunt, not inspire.

Ssss… it's a rough life.

Before I went to sleep on my stone molded sofa, beside the camp *Big-Foot* snake shrine, I shot down another bat for them. Maybe I should let up on that.

It's tough though. I'm still a human on the inside, even if I'm a some sort of magic-dungeon creature now. This might actually be my element, when you think about it: my naturally intended habitat- but for a human?

This place is downright hostile.

Chapter 45

Snake Report: Day Whatever/Watching Humans Report: Official Day 5

Today- yet again, I came face to face with death.

As always, my day began normally without any signs of approaching doom.

Hisss...

I woke up, curled into the perfect spiral on my stone carved sofa. I ate a few stockpiled mushrooms for breakfast, and then I spiraled up towards my furthermost level of progress, taking it upon myself to grind through into the odd newer-layers of stone.

It was easier than what I've been pressing through up until this point, softer in a way I think. The work wasn't that laborious, and as expected, I soon broke into another section of the Dungeon. Right up and into a tunnel before I could even realize it.

And nothing tried to kill me.

Strange, I know- but the day was still young, and there's a first time for everything.

Still, I maintained perfect form, periscope-snake method.

My practiced technique.

I viewed the tunnel I came out in, saw nothing in particular, and bobbed back down and re-molded the floor.

Safe.

After all the progress, I'd decided that was enough excitement for one day. Honestly, a new layer of the Dungeon, easily a few hundred feet up: That's a good sign in a way. I'm cutting right on through, no freaky magics or creatures have tried to stop operation **[Earth Molding to the Heavens]** so I'm still thinking with a positive outlook about it.

Yeah…

That's the exact line of thinking that made me drop my guard.

When I returned in the presumed evening to watch the humans, only the Wizard was sitting by the weird fire, his back turned towards me and his eyes watching the ancient doorway to the far side of the room. His shoulders were slumped, his staff was laid down in a haphazard sort of way. Even from a distance, it was a look of defeat.

The second human was nowhere to be seen.

And I really do mean nowhere.

The floor below was empty. Where there had been two, no there was only one.

Hisss...

You know, that's a bit of a scary situation, especially with the suddenness of it.

They had both seemed capable, I'd only looked away for a few hours. It's not like I had any real obligation to look out for them, but in my mind, I had it fixed that they weren't going to die down here.

I'd tricked myself a bit, that it would all work out. Like the stories you know? This is obviously a world with magic and adventures, so why not? The great human duo, defeating the odds in this terrible place! Heroes of combat and survival, hurrah!

I guess not.

The Wizard slowly stood, picking up his staff with a heavy sigh as I watched. One hand the staff, the other hand... a Mace. That was definitely the Paladin woman's weapon.

No one in their right might would walk off unarmed down here. That's not how it works. Life… well, life doesn't always work out.

I knew that, but watching the young Gandalf figure in the distance, I felt that was a really sad feeling. I could only imagine, running through a place like this would form strong bonds. You don't just go out risking your life with just anyone.

Which meant that she was really gone.

After that impressive display of power against the skeleton, something else had killed Miss Paladin. Maybe an ambush, or a trap, or poison... it seemed such a waste.

Or so I found myself thinking.

Then, the Wizard suddenly turned. In an instant his posture shifted, his hand released the mace and fell to reinforce his staff as a huge burst of magic lashed out. In my direction.

It was a direct hit. I didn't even have time to let out my typical hiss of terror before I was frozen.

My nerves were a buzz with the feeling of static.

All I could do was stare in horror as two hands, blond hair, and a grim smile pulled themselves up onto my tiny balcony and looked deep into my soul.

Miss Paladin stared at me.

"_____" She said, white teeth revealed with a curling smile.

I couldn't understand a word, the language unfamiliar and strange: but I knew what she meant clear as day.

"Fooled you."

Chapter 46

Journal entry:

Today, with Grant's help, I caught our mysterious helper.

I was right. It's a basilisk: Or, it was a basilisk. I'm not quite sure what it is now.

Terrified, I think.

Grant managed to hit it dead on with some advanced immobilization magic just as I got in position under the ledge. I'd been scaling that wall and waited for a full hour, just there under the snake's field of view. It didn't suspect a thing.

We've put it in a magic barrier at out camp, and rigged it to draw power from a few of the crystals Grant has been keeping in his pouch. There's no way out, and even if there was, I think it knows better than to try.

Soon as that barrier is gone, the snake would fall through and touch the Sanctuary magics on the floor. No doubt in my mind those would torch it with short notice. Thus, "terrified."

Monsters inherently know that sort of thing.

There's a reason most of them stay far away from safe-zones. Some Beast Tamers have told me that their partners can feel it, like a noise or a resonance. It's something they instinctively avoid, so I imagine that's the same for both tamed and wild monsters.

That noted, this is a really strange basilisk.

It's not very big, for starters. Probably less than four feet long, no thicker at any point than my wrist. It has no venom glands, no corrosive breath, obviously not on its way to becoming one of the behemoths that sometimes get spotted along the dark chasms of the Northern depths. Honestly, it looks almost harmless.

But its scales are a deep blue. Close up, I think that they almost look like crystals, if they weren't so small. Grant thinks it's probably because of all of the mushrooms it was eating. He joked that if he got hungry enough, he'd probably find out the hard way.

The tiny snake didn't seem to like when Grant laughed about that very much.

Together though, we did a delve to try and figure out more about the creature. Faith magics can dig deep, and Grant knows more about magic than anyone I've met outside of an Empire-university library, so I think we did a half-way decent job at it. The [Delving] spell did most of the work anyways, Grant just threw in some extra tricks to go along... and then he almost threw up.

Only halfway through the [Delving] and he had to stop to dry-heave.

It was *that* bad.

Apparently, this snake has more toxin in its body than any living creature has a right to have and still be breathing. Grant wouldn't even join back in until he'd gotten a drink of water, and even after he looked a little green in the face. So, it took him by surprise, but crazy at that might seem: that wasn't even a fraction of what really shocked him. It's also most definitely got magic.

Quite a lot of magic.

Very, very strong magic.

Grant made me add another few layers to the barrier after finding this out, sticking a couple more crystal shards to it for good measure. Muttered something about rebounding theories and soul-air element bindings, he worked on the barrier-cage for awhile after that. Needless to say: he doesn't think it's only the fireball spell we need to worry about.

I'll trust his judgement.

All in all, though, I've never season a monster like this. Our team has done more than our fair share of deep dives too, so there's something to be said for that.

Still, they say that the farther down you go, the stranger things get... but a Dungeon creature that eats poison and uses magic? That is just a unique kind of bizarre. To top it all off, though, it's practically docile, which actually might be the weirdest thing of all.

That's unheard of.

Every living creature that comes from the Dungeons will inevitably try to kill people. With the exception of the few monsters taken up to the surface and tamed (and that's topic some might argue doesn't change a thing) the monsters of the underworld try to murder humans. Ten out of ten times, if you run into a creature in the Dungeon: it's going to try to kill you if it thinks it can get away with it.

This basilisk though, hasn't made a single threatening move towards us since it woke up.

No aggressive posturing. No lunges, no teeth, puffs of magic, or violent struggles against its confinement. Instead it just watches us, turning to face whoever is talking as if it's trying to understand.

Really, it's as if some Beast-Tamer died down here and left their partner behind. The snake is acting as if it were a pet, and not a wild creature known to swallow them whole. I've even heard the larger ones can paralyze people with a weird hypnotism skill, and eat them alive.

Yet here we are, and with an utterly tame example of the opposite. A deep-dwelling monster with zero interest in attacking humans.

Whether Grant agrees or not, I've decided: we're taking this thing back to the surface.

Chapter 47

Snake Report Day Whatever/Captured by Humans Report: Official Day 1

Death. It stares at me.

I am imprisoned by a case of magic air and glass, floating over death. Like a super-hero trapped in their evil nemesis's lair, chained suspended above a giant bubbling pit of molten lava-- only in my case it's not lava, it's that scary floor. The same scary floor that turns monsters into roasted meat: and instead of some cackling evil nemesis, there are two Fantasy-set human adventurers staring at me with looks of pure confusion.

It's like they've never seen a snake before, or heard of English for that matter.

I have no idea what they're saying. It's like if you threw me into the rural country-side of East Asia, and then had the natives speak with heavy German accents.

I can't understand at all.

Nothing.

At least not the words, anyways. Human-side logic lets me take some guesses at the rest, though.

They point, they look in my direction, they make gestures. I'm inferring here, and it's a bit of a pseudo-science, to be real, but I'm working out a little bit. There's some knowledge to be gleamed from this, and the fear keeps me nice and attentive.

Sure, for all I know they're talking about adventuring mumbo-jumbo, or their next scouting expedition. I feel like I'm a topic of discussion, but maybe they're just talking about what they'll be having for dinner.

Which better not be me.

On that subject: if they try to eat me, I hope they realize I'm a beautiful flavor of toxic death.

Zesty, with a side of doom.

Actually, if they really do try to eat me, I hope they don't realize it- in fact I hope they choke on me too, while they're at it.

Yeah.

Eating me is like a messed-up version of cannibalism. Whether they realize it or not, that's extra evil.

The Tiny Snake God would curse them, I think.

Maybe the human god too.

I'm rambling. I know it.

I blame the fear.

Whatever. They can shoot down their own bats. I'm really not exactly thrilled with this, but truthfully, as of this moment, I don't think snake-meat is on the menu. Actually, right now I think that the Paladin is actually arguing a case for me. She's really going at it too, the mace is waving around, her fist is shaking. She's sort of scary.

I'm basing some of this off the angry finger pointing in my direction, and the louder tone of voice from Young Gandalf. The Wizard hasn't really been too thrilled with me since he tried some weird magic with Miss Paladin and then almost hurled.

No idea what that was about, but whatever. Serves them right.

Hmm...

They're getting up.

Man, I am tiny.

Really freaking tiny.

Humans are pretty big. Not giant-skeleton big, but I forgot how tall people can be.

Oh.

I guess this magic barrier shoebox of mine can be picked up.

Ah... I don't know how I should feel about this.

I'm... I'm a backpack. The Paladin just wrapped me in a blanket and slung me over her shoulders. Magic can work like this? They can just box me up with barriers and carry me around?

What the hell.

Hisss...

I think I'm being kidnapped.

Chapter 48

"Talia, you know that the chances of us finding our way through the tunnels today are slim right? The snake doesn't have to come with us."

Behind her, the Wizard grumbled nervously as they marched up the hill along the far cavern.

"Last time we ran into a huge mess too. If we need to run from those centipedes again, you're going to have a hard time with a monster on your back."

"I don't care. We're keeping him." Talia replied as she marched on, mace lifted and glowing to light the way.

"Him? It's a him now?" Disbelief grumbled and echoed along the passage way. "How does that work?"

"Call it a woman's intuition, Grant. If we can't make it back to the Sanctuary, I don't want to leave the snake there to die."

"Why not? It's a monster for light's sake!"

"It helped us. It wouldn't be right to leave it boxed up on top of certain death."

Underfoot, Talia noted the scent of charcoal. The stone tunnel seemed to have taken on a scorched earth appearance, as if a fire had swept through at some point in the recent past.

"Watch your step here, it's a bit slick."

"Thank you--"

The reply came off-guard, before launching back into protests.

"And what if it breaks out in the tunnels then? What do we do if it's capable of freeing itself?"

"It won't."

"But what if it does?"

"It won't"

The slow sigh of defeat greeted her defensive rebuttals.

"I think you've lost your mind, Talia. I really do."

"Noted, Grant."

"It better be."

Letting the conversation lapse, Talia continued downhill once more. Just as they had previously explored of this section before being ambushed by a pack of venom centipedes. She knew that, in theory, those should have all been run off by Grant's magics, but they could still be lurking.

Displacing monsters was more an art than a science. They'd rallied up the swarm and then thinned the herd, but there wasn't any guarantee that Dungeon creatures wouldn't try and attack again.

"Holy gods and thunder... It's like the whole cave was set on fire. Look, even the ceiling here is scorched," Talia mumbled. "Did you do this last time Grant?"

"No," the hushed reply came with a level of nervousness.

"I think this level of fire could only have been caused by a very-strong magic..."

He pushed his staff against a stone, watching some of it crumble away, "I couldn't do this if I tried."

Turning back and nodding, Talia continued without saying the obvious.

Extra careful from here on out.

On her back, she felt the captured monster shift, glow of its scales lifting a peaceful light over her shoulder as she marched on. The top of the makeshift bag had slipped, letting the serpent observe as they marched on.

Glancing at the creature, Talia though it seemed curious before Grant rushed to cover it back over with the blanket once more.

"It might give us away," he muttered, purposefully avoiding her disapproving glare.

Irritated, she shook her vibrantly glowing mace at him before shouldering past.

The downhill expanse soon opened into another large and domed room, similar to the Giant's but with a natural formation. Ashen pillars still stood, however burnt and scorched along the ground, and the thick miasma of deep air seemed to permeate with every breath. Every lungful held the taste of mana and chaos, both rich enough to noticeably shift her own levels.

The reason the depths of the ancient Dungeons were so dangerous. Magical fuel spawning all manner of terrible and twisted growths from the natural and mundane. The ruined remains of long forgotten civilizations buried beneath the earth, spawning horrors at every turn.

This... this was the deep Dungeon Talia remembered with a sense of dread.

But, if the Eastern tunnels in which she and Grant had first arrived were now collapsed, there was only one way forward.

Down.

Chapter 49

Snake Report Day Whatever/Captured by Humans Report: Official Day 2

The humans in this world are crazy.

Crazy- as absolutely *insane*. Bonkers, loony, two pancake's short of a Denny's Grand-slam.

They've left the no-monster zone, and now we're going in deeper towards the origin of my birthplace. The zone I accidentally set ablaze and burned rather completely to ashes.

In fact, we've already gone in deeper than that, if my guesstimate of this woman's footsteps have any true bearing on reality. We're in past what I'm familiar with.

Sometimes the cloth falls off my magic barrier-shoebox, and I can take a look out before the Young-Gandalf covers me back up.

I'll reflect on that statement later, I'm sure: The moral of the story is I can't help but recognize anything other than danger everywhere I look.

See ahead? From my tiny vantage point behind Miss Paladin's shoulder I can see bones all over the floor.

Really big looking bones, all gnawed on and such.

And to the left, there's another passage. One that has been quite obviously burrowed out as if by some impossibly strong claws instead of my refined and dignified magic. Even without seeing deeper into that darkness, instinct is basically screaming with a megaphone that I shouldn't go closer.

The craziest thing about the pair of humans, though, is that while all this is going on, they're actually stopping and taking notes. The Wizard has a little book and some pencil-like tool he's been scratching away with.

They've been documenting lefts and rights I think, mapping out a path, all while I've just been trying not to scream.

"_____" Miss Paladin said something with a serious tone. The Wizard has his staff ready now.

"____" Young Gandolf is replying, also sounds serious. The cloth covering is coming a bit loose. I can see a bit more, we're at a fork in the tunnel. A left and a right option- in my opinion both look like terrible choices.

"HISSSSSSSSSSSSSSSSSSSSSssss..."

That wasn't me, if you were wondering.

Oh no: that was the "left" option.

Ms. Paladin is moving right with a sense of urgency. From what I can see of her face, she doesn't seem too thrilled about this.

"HISSSSSSSSSSSSSSSSSSSSSSSSSSSSSSSSSSSssssss..."

Oh shit.

The ground is rumbling.

"HISSSSSSSSSSSSSSSSSSSSSSSSSSSSSSSSSSSSSSSSSSSSSSSSSSSSSSssssss..."

A set of eyes is staring at us, glowing a deep, deep green atop two sets of white fangs.

That's a really, really, really big snake.

It looks hungry.

So much for diligent note-taking. We're apparently just winging it.

Chapter 50

"I can set up a barrier--"

"There's no time! RUN!" Grant's shout echoed off the dark and shadowed walls of the cavern, half-formed spells thrown over shoulder illuminating his panic clearly to any watching eyes. Talia heeded his words without complaint.

A massive basilisk was directly behind them, its stony scales and giant coils filling the tunnel with a terrible grinding sound.

As her legs pumped with wide and high steps, tripping over stones and slick moss, Talia struggled to keep her glowing mace held ahead- providing just barely enough illumination to show ten feet in front of her at any given time.

Down.

Down.

Down.

Down.

They had been trying to find another way up, but all she could do was descend- further and further. Twists and turns, shrieks and startled calls of unseen monsters. Each twist and turn was just another atop the large pile she might never manage to remember.

Finding their way back was already impossible.

CRACK

A huge burst of heat and light knocked her to the ground, feet lifting and body thrown roughly forward with a heavy blast of wind.

"Talia!"

Her vision swam, ears ringing from the show of thunder and pressure, as she sought out the source of the voice. Pushing herself back off the ground, the makeshift bag weighed down her shoulders, glowing blue serpent turning startled in all directions it possibly could.

"I'm sorry this isn't romantic as I planned it," the voice was calm and serious.

Legs shaking, Talia's eyesight pulsed in and out of focus as she fumbled for her weapon. Grant stood with a mass of air magics between his hands, arcs lifting off and strumming like a string under tension as his broken staff sputtered smoke on the ground before him. His robe lifted, catching on the heat and sparks that shattered out along the vibrant air of mana.

From the brilliant glow of the magic crackling between his hands, Talia saw the entire cavern as if in the light of day: Every crack, stone, and detail illuminated as the massive creature towered overtop the Wizard, rearing back for a certain strike. With horror, Talia saw the cliff's edge. The pitch black darkness that had waited not two steps more.

"You need to escape, Talia."

The magic flew through the air, channeled without a tool, by sheer willpower alone. Stone exploded, cinders and sparks flared, and Grant's hands raised up further. With horror, Talia recognized the glitter of color clutched between his fingers. The shades of crystal shards, gripped by the handful in each fist.

"For my sake, for Joan and Rodrick: *Don't give up.*"

Then the Basilisk struck, and the cavern exploded beneath the ungodly force that waited for it. A blast that hit with gale-force strength, pushing and throwing Talia into the air.

Above the chasm, and then down.

Down.

Down.

Down.

Down.

Chapter 51

Snake Report: Day Whatever/Watching Humans Report: Official Day 4 continued

We're in deep.

Really deep.

Figuratively speaking, literally... It's like we've undergone an epic on par with Journey to the Center of the Earth. We just fell at least fifty feet into some underground river, and I don't have a single clue where we ended up after that.

The current took us down further though. That's generally how rivers work. They run downhill. Miss Paladin was somehow able to swim us through, half-dazed and covered in armor- though she lost her mace somewhere in the rapids. She dragged us onshore along a divot in the side of the waterways before collapsing.

I'm scared.

My magical barrier shoebox is fading off. I can see it, visibly flickering out of existence.

From what I managed to see before we fell of a cliff, Young Gandalf's dead.

He has to be.

There's no way a person can survive something like that.

Ssssss…

Brave.

He was really brave.

Braver than Hero-Frog.

Braver than me.

I take back all the bad things I thought about him. He was a good guy, a real good guy. Even though I can't understand the language, I know he said something real proud right before the end.

No fear.

Yeah.

No fear… I don't even understand how he did that, and I'm the guy who already died once. It was terrifying, but him?

He wasn't scared.

Miss Paladin's not taking it well. Not well at all.

Considering everything that's happened, I'm amazed she isn't hysterical. She's still holding composure somehow, but I don't know how.

No idea where we are, way, way down in the darkest depths of this evil place, her friend is dead, and she's go absolutely not shot in hell of making it out alive. Yet, she's still holding it together.

Beside my fading box, she's unconscious now. Sleeping, I think.

Before that she was just crying.

One of those quiet sort of cries, where even though nobody can see it, the act was restrained. Like she's too strong to just break down and let it out. It's not the kind of thing you want to watch.

Watching someone cry is awful. It feels wrong.

Hiss...

Well... there goes the last of my barrier. I'm free, it's completely gone. All that's left are those crystal pieces young Gandalf stuck on the corners, and the cloth Miss Paladin was carrying me around in.

If I wanted to, I could leave and go... I don't even know. There's water. There's this rock... there's more water. Unlike the rest of the caverns I've been in, I don't have any light. There's nothing growing here, no mushrooms, no crystals: just the natural ambiance of my scales.

Black water. surrounding a big rock.

I think we might be stranded.

Hissss...

...

Rock is fine, but water...

> [Water element]
> [Water Manipulation I] - Ability to actively mold and shape water.

Hisssss...

Oh... this might take awhile.

Chapter 52

Talia woke up in darkness, greeted by nothing but the quiet sounds of flowing water. To her eyes, there was only a pitch and terrible black. All around her was darkness, broken only with the scent of earth and mana heavy on her tongue.

The depths. She was in the uncharted depths.

Alone.

Her breath caught as she instinctively reached for her mace, finding nothing, then towards her belt she found... also nothing.

No weapon. No gear. No note book, or dried meats: It was all gone.

Grabbing desperately at what little mental fortitude remained in the growing ocean of dread quickly surrounding her thoughts, Talia began the peaceful and warming chant.

"Oh, Holy guardian of Light. Give me sight in this wicked land of shadow."

Over and over, she repeated it, letting the prayers and magic calm her. Beneath the palm of her hand, the ground began to fill with the glow of faith, slowly falling outward as her mana poured into it. Inch by inch, it grew to intensity, revealing the world around her with the ambiance. As the darkness receded, Talia made sense of her bearings.

She was crouching on a large boulder, no larger than thirty feet wide at its largest. It seemed on solid piece, perhaps a cave formation worn away by eons of weathering, sloping upward to a summit of sorts at its center.

But around this was nothing but water.

Nothing at all.

Even as the magic strengthened further, it was nothing but water. Overhead, she could just distantly make out a cave's ceiling, but around her there was nothing but dark moving water, flowing slowly past towards some unknown destination.

This was some sort of underground lake, or river system, deep beneath the surface.

"Oh no."

The hopelessness of her situation had set in now, nice and deep.

There was nowhere to go, just water, and the island she'd been fortunate enough to randomly stumble upon- by luck or fate of the currents.

"Hisss..."

A monster.

Instinct took over, as Talia raised her guard to a fighting stance, light magics flowing into the shoddy gauntlets at her fists. She could still fight, even without a weapon, she could still put up some resistance.

But no attack lashed out. In place of violence, there was silence.

Light intensifying and eyes peering into the relative darkness ahead, Talia made out the faint glow of a familiar deep blue. The small form watched her from the stone island's peaked slope, perfectly still.

"You want revenge?" she asked quietly.

"Hisss…" In the glow of her magic, the slender body seemed to rise up, lifting a full pace or so off of the ground as it watched her. Even then, it seems pitifully small.

"I really can't blame you." Talia replied. "Bringing you here, I'd be mad too."

"Hisss..." It reared back further, mouth opening to reveal a pitiful set of fangs as Talia steeled herself. It was a magic user, it wouldn't use a physical attack- it would cast something. Something terrible, and that would be the end of her.

All at once, it lit.

In that instant mana sparked. Like oil set to torch, a plume of fire erupted with a fierce surge of heat and movement, streaking past her cheek before she could even blink.

Did it just miss?

A horrible scream sprouted from just behind her shoulder, as Talia ducked and turned- just in time to watch a shadowed shape bubble down beneath the hidden depths of the underground river.

Had it not been aiming at her, in the first place?

"Hisss..."

Turning back, Talia saw the snake lift its tail in a slow wave as its body lowered back to the floor. It watched her calmly as she pushed up the slope to approach, tongue flicking out with a final lazy motion, before turning to the other side of the rock and slithering away.

She couldn't help but interpret the gesture as intentionally rude.

"Well look, you're the weird one here," Talia muttered, carefully making her way to the center of the boulder, looking down at the rest of the space before taking a seat. It was just rock, slightly damp, perhaps from some distant point overhead. It was too dark to clearly see the ceiling, so she had to assume.

Here she was, just sitting in the middle of… nowhere. All around the small island, short waves flowed against the stone. Possibly brought about by the current, sweeping further down into the depths of the earth.

Talia shivered at the thought, before summoning further magic to imbue the stone beneath her. Its **warm** glow of relative safety made her feel a little better about the fact she'd almost just died, again.

She watched as the snake slithered around, pivoting slightly in order to keep it in sight.

"You realize most creatures down here eat people, not mushrooms." She called out.

"Hisss..."

Another sudden burst of fire, and another shriek. Talia leaned in, curious, as the blue serpent continued a slow circle about the boulder's perimeter; slithering a quiet patrol while occasionally spitting out flaming death.

Around and around it went…

There had to be some reason it was acting this way, didn't there? Was it panicking? Pulled away from its natural environment only to be trapped in a much less forgiving place…

Talia stood up with a start. The waves were making an odd sound, as if they were colliding with something.

No, not "as if" they were: because they were. They were impacting a small raise of stone, water splashing overtop ever so slightly.

Had that been there before?

"Hisss…" Talia turned, watching as the basilisk continued its circle.

"You've got to be joking." She watched the stone in front of it shifted slightly. Molding its shape, as if pressed under trained hands.

She squinted, peering closer. It really was changing, not just a trick of the eyes.

"Sssss…" The snake kept moving, earth bulging up as it went.

"Earth Magic too?" she questioned aloud.

It ignored her, as it continued.

On its first pass around the island, Talia had barely noticed what it was doing, but now? Second pass not even fully completed, and half a pace of stone seemed to have risen up: a slight rim, as if a bowl.

She sat back down, pressing more faith into the earth beneath her, and watched as the stone continued shifting. Already, if she were foolish enough to walk back down to the island's edge, it was enough to rise up to about Talia's knee.

By the end of the snake's third time around, it was up to her waist, and with a thickness of her forearm.

"A wall... you're building a wall," Talia stared at the creature as it went about on its fourth trip, significantly slower than before.

"SSSssss."

"You have got to be the strangest monster I've ever seen." The snake continued, raising the wall just a bit higher "Or heard of, for that matter."

"Hiss..." Turning back, the snake slithered along the stone back towards Talia, but never reached her. Before her eyes, the stone underfoot opened way in the form of a small tunnel. Seconds later, the snake was gone, deep into the boulder.

"Light and gods... Nothing makes sense anymore." Talia murmured quietly from her the glowing summit, watching the barely illuminated waters beyond the strange bowl-like walls that raised up around the island's perimeter. "How the hell does something so tiny have enough magic to do *that?*"

No sooner did the words leave her mouth, the stone beneath her buckled as if made of liquid instead of solid rock- and Talia dropped downward with a panicked yelp.

Chapter 53

Snake Report Day Whatever/Captured by Humans Report: Official Day 5

Tiny Snake Camp *Alcatraz*
Current population: 2

1 Human Paladin

1 Tiny Snake

Camp is now at minimum working capacity. Walls have been raised, the summit has been hollowed out, and relative respite has been provided from the creepy eel things lurking in the water.

Super creepy. Nightmare fuel. They're definitely attracted to the light that Miss Paladin keeps making. I'm absolutely certain about that now.

It's dark, I know, but I really wish she would cut that out, for both our sakes. There seem to be quite a lot of them, and spitting fire constantly is exhausting.

Then again, she tripped over the chair I made like three times already, so I guess human eyes aren't very helpful down here without something like that to assist.

Fair enough.

Anyways, it's a lot like a movie I remember watching once. Miss Paladin is currently staring Tom Hanks, from castaway. Only difference is that I'm not a volleyball, and we're stranded in a cave-lake thousands of feet beneath the ground, surrounded by things that want to murder us.

Pretty close though.

Anyways, I've got some other issues of concern to deal with besides the human who keeps talking in a language I don't understand.

[Mana resistance: Rank 21]

See that.

Look real close.

It's gotten so high, the display got sick of using roman numerals.

Yeah.

If you haven't guess already, I might have eaten the fragments of the Mana Crystal that Young Gandalf had fixed to my magic shoebox. My insides right now feel like someone is marinating them with ghost-peppers.

This again.

Again, and by choice no less. Seriously...

The reason? Oh, I just hate myself.

No- that's not it.

That's a joke. I was joking. It takes my mind off the pain and suffering I'm currently going though. All this, after I swore to never again- yet here I go eating poison like it's not going to make my life miserable.

Reasons though. There are reasons.

Thing is, the weird Eel things keep trying to come over the wall. They're creepy looking, and they have way too many teeth.

Mana burn > Creepy Hungry Eels

It's up to me to put a stop to their aggressive encroaching wriggling, because Miss Paladin is not good with Earth magic. At all, it seems.

Actually, I get the feeling she can only use the [Faith] magic I've already seen. Lights, healing, barrier sort of magic: none of which is very helpful right now. It was probably Young Gandalf who could use the rest.

Or maybe he couldn't.

Not quite sure.

I only really saw him shoot fire and lightning, though he did grab me with some weird freezing magic.

Really cold.

And, I guess there was that time he shoot a bonafide Hyper-beam.

Hisss...

Tough to say.

I'm still not 100% sure how magic in this world is intended to work, and the [Voice of Gaia] isn't all that great with abstract questions. "How does magic work?" isn't going to get much of an answer.

"..."

See?

I already tried, that's how I know.

But, honestly, I don't have the magic to waste on that kind of thing right now. Not until the walls are another ten feet up and slanted a bit at the top. No more hungry looking things trying to eat me.

"_____ _____ _____ _____?"

Ah.

Behind me Miss Paladin is saying something again.

She's been talking a lot the last few hours, pointing and gesturing. It's sort of funny, trying to have a conversation with her. I'll hiss, she'll respond, make motions and shapes with her hands and arms. I'll hiss again, she'll do more exaggerated gestures.

The effort is definitely there. She's not wallowing in sorrow like I would be in her position.

Humans of this world are made of tougher stuff than I was.

They're also prettier.

If I wasn't reborn as a snake, I'd earth-mold her a ring ASAP.

Another hand gesture towards the ceiling, then one towards the walls. Blond-hair and blue eyes are looking at me with a serious sort of pondering expression. \

Who am I kidding? Even if I was human, she'd be way out of my league: a strong independent Paladin woman, who don't need no man.

Hiss...

She's pointing towards the ceiling again. Looks a little mad.

No words mentioned have made even a *tiny* bit of sense to me yet, but I think I get what she's trying to say. It's probably something like: *"Can you get us to the ceiling?"*

Hiss... the ceiling though. Not a bad plan, but...

I'm already about 110% sure water magic is not going to help much in this. Beside a small pool of the stuff I left for us to drink, and the other little grated moat I made by the wall's base for... well, *other* things. I'm not about to try and tango with the monsters living in the underground water ways.

They're absolutely terrifying. I'll stick with earth and fire for now.

But the ceiling... If I can get better with Earth magics, in time it might be possible... Eventually. It's way too far for me to manipulate right now, but if I could get closer... Well, it's on the table. In the meantime, it's one "Hiss" for yes, two "Hiss" for no, three "hiss" for maybe.

"Hiss. Hiss. Hiss."

Miss Paladin looks confused. I think the shrug-gesture is universal no matter where you are.

At least we're getting somewhere. I'd call this progress.

Chapter 54

Snake Report: Day Whatever/Watching Humans Report: Official Day 6

Creepy eels taste a lot like chicken.

I know that's a common go-to for what food's taste like, but I'm serious. They taste like roasted chicken. In a world gone to hell and back, that's a big deal.

Adding to that, though: this is also a rather special occasion, on par with a tiny-snake's first fireball, or genocidal sacrifice to the Tiny Snake God. This is the only thing I've eaten that hasn't resulted in tremendous suffering. In fact, it's actually really, *really* good. I never thought I would say this, but I'm glad it somehow jumped over a fifteen foot wall and tried to kill us.

We even cooked it in a stone oven, crisped to perfection. I think I ate a quarter of my body-weight, unhinged my jaw and everything-- the real deal.

I'm snake enough to admit, that wasn't actually my idea. Miss Paladin used more than a fair share of gestures to convey this plan. She's been looking at me funny ever since though.

She pointed at me with an angry expression.

I like to interpret that as "You're one cool snake!"

Yup, that's what I'm going with. Miss Paladin's really keeping morale high, but, as they saying goes: "all good things in moderation."

There are spikes on the wall-top now. Preemptive measures, as Camp *Alcatraz* is really shaping up to form.

I wasn't kidding about Camp *Alcatraz*. I've gone above and beyond even my own expectations in the process of trying to burn off the overflow of excess mana. Below I will list a few of its many features.

> -A massive fifteen-foot perimeter wall (Now covered in sharp spikes)
>
> -A thick stone grated drinking pool (Upcurrent)
>
> -A thick stone grated not-drinking pool (Downcurrent)
>
> -A carved summit interior with a stone oven- complete with external chimney, two bunks, two chairs, and a table.

-A raised watchtower now reaching an estimated height of thirty feet. (Snake use only: Only 70 more feet to go before I reach the ceiling!)

Pretty neat. So far so good.

Chapter 55

Talia: Mental Journal in absence of regular Journal

This basilisk is NOT NORMAL.

Not normal AT ALL.

I knew from the moment it started molding walls that it was weird, but now I'm utterly convinced I've either lost my mind, or I'm sharing an island with some sort of divine-beast of legends.

Oh, and I figured out how it was using more magic than physically possible: It was eating the mana crystals.

Eating.

Mana.

Crystals.

Those pieces of rock that contain solidified magic so powerful that they can violently explode. Those glass-like chunks, where one small shard can be used to create upwards of forty full-strength mana potions. The kind, where each has to be specifically calibrated and measure for the sake of safety, and can only be used when a Magician's mana reserves are low.

Drinking two potions by mistake while at full mana might cripple, or possibly kill a human being. Three would mean almost certain death, four and you're going to die while vomiting blood so magical it's going to burn through the floor.

Five might make a person spontaneously burst into flame.

Yet, this tiny basilisk probably ate upwards of two hundred mana potions worth of crystal shards, and it's not even concerned. I don't know if the crystals just burn slower, or what- but by all rights it should be dead.

Instead it's making walls.

Walls, with sharp pointing spikes at the top.

It's creative.

These wall-top enhancements were added those after a snapper-eel came over, and it fried the light-loving piss out of the poor thing with some sort of flame-breath magic.

Green-fire. Lots of it.

My hair is still frizzy, and I was on the complete opposite side of the island when it happened.

So, the snake has been reacting to things, and obviously working up some preventative measures. Actively adjusting and planning ahead- but it gets ever weirder.

The snake hollowed out the core of the island.

It turned the space into a room, but not just a normal monster lair- the room has bunks. They're made of stone, but they're still very obviously bunks. It also made a table, and chairs.

How?

That's the question that I can't get out of my head. Just how?

There are no chairs in a Dungeon. There are no bunks, or tables. Where did it lean about these things? I mean- It's a light-forsaken basilisk for god's sake! Why is it making chairs? Tables? Bunks?! I don't understand!

Is this just a very intelligent monster? Is this a tamed beast that lost its partner in the Dungeon and went feral for untold years- or is it a human put under some unknown curse?

I'm honestly leaning towards the last one. Ancient and chaos magics aren't unheard of this far down, and at this point nothing else makes sense. Not since it made the oven.

Yes.

An oven, stove, object for the sake of baking.

It made one of each

In the middle of my attempted communication for it to use some fire-magic to cook the eel, it dropped everything it had been doing and slithered off to make an oven out of molded stone.

Then it added a chimney to vent the smoke, bobbing its head up and down as if congratulating itself.

To make matters worse- Light help me: it's beautiful.

Gorgeous

This is the kind of stove a noble might own. The surface is covered with tiny details of a snake and two frogs travelling through scenes of sunsets and clouds. It rivals some of the carving work I've seen in the ancient chapels of the Emperor's City.

And it did all this in under an hour.

I sat down and watched it from the stone table and chairs, chin resting on my hands like some sort of slack-jawed farm-girl.

It defies logic. This thing: a creature like this shouldn't exist. It's beyond improbability. No fluke of nature's own creation could bring this into existence.

I'm entirely convinced the snake has some sort intelligence: so convinced, I've long-since moved to the point where I'm consistently trying to talk to it.

Talking to a snake.

I've used hand gestures, I've try to speak clearly- and it actually pays very close attention. It doesn't seem to understand everything, but it's obviously trying, bobbing along as my hands move, hissing replies.

Responsive?

Maybe I'm insane.

Who can say?

Maybe losing Grant and the others broke me in some irreparable way. Maybe I went under water for too long, and it rattled my mind. I don't know. I'm alone and trapped deeper in the depths of this Dungeon than anyone alive has ever managed to get.

But, if I'm mad? Even if I'm long-since lost to the legendary Dungeon-sickness and now acting without lucid awareness of what's really going on: so be it.

I've been talking to this tiny little blue basilisk. Stories, adventures, history- anything. I'll keep talking to it until it understands.

If there's any chance of getting out of this Dungeon alive, it's this ridiculous snake.

Chapter 56
Snake Report: Day Whatever/Watching Humans Report: Official Day 7

"[Voice of Gaia], show me my abilities."

[Level 42]
[TITLE: DIVINE BEAST, LEVIATHAN]
[BRANCH: Magic essence]

[UNIQUE TRAITS:]
[Toxic] - Toxic Flesh. Dangerous is consumed.
[Crystalline scales] - Increased Defense
[Omnivore] - Capable of eating non-monster food-stuffs.
[Affinity of Flame] - Bonded to the Element.
[Legendary] - A rare being. Not often seen, known only to Legend.

[STATUS:]
[None]

[RESISTANCES]
[Poison resistance: Rank XII]
[Fire resistance: Rank II] - Affinity*
[Mana resistance: Rank 21]

[Skills]
[Healing:]
[Passive Healing 21] - Automatically being to recover from injuries. Mana drained as a result.
[Heal I] - Third rank of healing.
[Flame element] - Affinity*
[Leviathan breath II] - Rare ability. Advanced variation of [Flame Breath]
[Fireball VII] - A ball of flame, capable of long-range.
[Earth element]
[Earth Molding 20] - Second spell rank of [Earth Manipulation]
[Water element]
[Water Manipulation II] - Ability to actively mold and shape water.
[Knowledge element]
[Voice of Gaia VI] - Knowledge embodiment. Spirit of the world.

[Divine element]
[Royal Spirit of Man] - **Acquired**

What the heck is that last one?

I don't know, exactly.

[Voice of Gaia] is being all sorts of taciturn when it comes to that particular subject, and I've run out of mana crystals to eat.

Anyways, that's where I'm at.

Not bad.

To say the least, I've been busy. Earth magic growth has been good, water magic growth has been... well, not so good. I tried splashing some of the drinking water around, but Miss Paladin was watching me so seriously, I felt obligated to stop.

She's following me around now, watching everything I do, everywhere I go (not that hard considering the lack of terrain) but she's been doing this with a super serious expression. She's also been rambling on with a bunch of words I'm not exactly certain of. I get the sense she's trying to make me learn something.

Jokes on her, I was terrible at language in my last life.

Really bad.

Embarrassingly bad.

I doubt this one is any different.

Occasionally she'll go back up to the summit and make the pillar I've been making glow a bit, but then she comes back and follows my every move. Light source, snake, food source, snake, bathroom, snake.

In some ways, it feels sort of nice to be the center of attention.

"____" She'll say, followed by another bout of "___ __ ___ ___" and some conflicted expressions with hand gestures that point at me with a bit of a dramatic flair.

"Hiss" I'll often reply, which is snake for "Yeah, I know I'm the best at this. Thanks Miss Paladin."

I don't know, she's been a little weird recently. Just… strange.

She even grabbed my tail once.

Like, just went for it. Bold move I might welcome if I were a human. Taking the initiative and all that. But I'm not a human, and it scared the ever-living-snake-shit out of me.

I think she apologized afterwards.

Tiny Snake God preaches forgiveness to anything that doesn't try to eat his followers, so it was all good. A good fashion head-bob "hiss" passed that on and along.

We're cool human.

We're cool.

But what's not cool, is the growing number of eel intrusion attempts.

You would think that several of your brethren impaled and bleeding to death atop a wall covered by a large number of sharp and pointy stone daggers might discourage this sort of behavior.

No, it's having an opposite effect.

It's working them up into a feeding frenzy. They're like highly mobile and suicidal sharks. Dead eel on a spike? Better try and eat that, get impaled myself, and repeat the cycle.

It's getting a little scary, actually.

There are some seriously problems with that sort of behavior.

First and foremost: there is currently a very limited quantity of stone for me to play around with.

Those walls are only fifteen feet high for a reason: I'm too nervous to take any more material to grow them, and moving it around is difficult now that I'm running on my own strength alone. No more seemingly infinite mana sources around unless I happen to mine a crystal out of the ground.

Which seems unlikely.

This stone isn't the right kind for that I don't think.

But there is a second issue here. Something I'd like to bring up and communicate to Miss Paladin, if I could talk. Currently I can't manage that though, and she can't climb the tower I'm pushing up towards the ceiling.

I'll say it here though.

Issue number two: it's not just eels out there now.

Hisss...

Those stupid toothy bastards are putting a lot of blood in the surf.

More than just a lot, honestly, gallons upon gallons: it's as if the Boston tea-party had been tomato soup instead of earl-grey.

Yeah.

So, think about that. Eels are annoying and dangerous, but I wouldn't put them at the top of the aquatic food-chain.

Think bigger.

Bigger.

Much bigger.

The reason you don't go swimming with an open wound.

Yeah, you're getting there now.

Remember when you were a kid? When your parents took you to some weird-ass museum filled with bones, and you walked though some giant archway- only to realize that it wasn't an archway at all, but a set of jaws?

Well that's fine if you don't- I do. I totally do.

It's all I can think about now. It haunts my tiny-snake dreams, my waking hours, my everything, because there is a big-ass fin cutting the waves out there. A huge fin cutting through the water with waves, and circling this little island like no tomorrow.

BIG.

Horrifically big.

And it's been getting closer.

Chapter 57

Snake Report: Day Whatever/Watching Humans Report: Official Day 8

Tiny-Snake and Human Camp *Alcatraz* Tower reporting: Forty-five and half slithers tall, and still climbing. For the Forecast this morning, we have nothing but depressing dark waters, overshadow of rock ceilings and cloudy surfaces.

What? What's that? I've been told to inform you that there's a slight chance of Megalodon attack.

A growing chance? Right-o

Now for Miss Paladin with the sports- Miss Paladin?

Ah yes, well said. The blue tinted eels really did beat the orange-ish eels in the latest showdown. Great game, amazing stuff, lots of giant-shark-attracting red in the water. Fought the good fight, that they did.

Hisss...

I really need to get us the hell out of here.

Pronto.

From the tower, I've finally gotten to the height where taking a look at my surroundings is reasonably possible. Spitting a few fireballs long distance helps me get a good picture too. Those things go faaaaaar, pretty fun, though probably a waste of magic.

My findings are about what I already knew.

We're not dead-center, but I'd say that this rock island is about as close as reasonably possible from being relatively-equidistant to every wall of this cavernous underground lake. Hundreds of feet in any direction before "land-fall" and even then, there's no shore to speak of. Some big pillars, but no actual land. You'd be scrambling against slick walls while the eels closed in.

For that reason, swimming is NOT an option, and neither is making a rock-boat.

Those are vetoed.

Yes, I think it's probably possible. An object will float if it weighs less than the amount of water it displaces- Wikipedia taught me that awhile back. I might have to make a pretty big section of rock, but I think it could be done.

That's your Bill Nye moment of the day.

The more you know.

Hisss... no boats, no swimming.

Just looking down, I can see a bunch of dying eels, some weird shit that won't surface but is apparently poking some eyes up just above the surface, and of course: the Megalodon fin.

Circling, circling, circling...

Truthfully speaking: I'm absolutely dumbfounded that Miss Paladin managed to get us here without dying.

Flabbergasted.

Or about as much as a snake can actually be flabbergasted.

I don't know if we were just moving quick with the current, or the explosion scared everyone in the neighborhood, or what. There are a few more islands that I can see in the distance, but getting to one of them and not being dead seems more luck than anything.

Is there a luck stat in this world?

That sounds like it might be a thing: I'm putting that question on the to-ask list.

But Gaia is gonna have to wait.

Up: the direction.

My course is set.

The whole plan since Camp *Big-foot.* Go up, escape, eat human food, live the dream and be the tiny-snake you've always wanted to be.

I've been working hard at it.

At this point, I'm guessing only forty something slithers more from the ceiling.

Far, yes. I agree, it's still far, but I can see it a bit more clearly. Nothing seems to be living up there, but I'll know for sure in a day or two as I get closer.

It's hard though.

Earth molding doesn't make material from thin air, it needs stone to work with. Already, I'm starting to take an unnerving amount of material from the island's core and work it upwards. It's starting to give me the impression of hollowing out the island into a weird looking bowl... or a straw.

Not good.

Sort of a troubling conundrum, considering I have no idea how much of it is safe to take before I break something and the eels come pouring in with the flood.

Years of hitting "random" on Wikipedia can only take someone so far. Here's hoping that can be avoided.

In the meantime, I've made the core room of Camp *Alcatraz* as sturdy as possible in the even of such an occurrence. If everything goes to crap, at least we'll be able to regain our footing from there.

Below though, my fellow islander isn't inclined to staying put in there. As per usual, Miss Paladin is watching my every move. I think she's starting to worry I'm going to abandon her down there or something.

Hisss... Seriously.

I'm a snake, not Satan.

Chapter 58

Talia:

The snake's tower is getting disturbingly tall.

Forty... no, fifty paces high at this point, and somehow the serpent still shows almost no signs of stopping.

On occasion, it will sit at the table, eat a few bits worth of eel before then going to sleep for a short period. I assume that's what the snake is doing, at least. It just curls up into a tight spiral, and lays completely still for a few hours. Then, it's moving again: heading back to work.

This basilisk… it's a productive little thing.

Although some portion of the request has likely been lost in translation, I'm now under the impression that it understood what I was asking for when I pointed to the ceiling a few days ago. The goal is clearly the ceiling, which I expect it's likely going to get to soon.

The real problem though, is that there's absolutely no way I'm going to be able to climb up after. The tower is too thin, and there are no footholds: attempting that would be suicide. If I were to fall, land or water: either way I'd likely be dead.

No way around it.

At the same time, I think this might just be the preliminary structure. Yesterday my foot actually went *through* some of the rock island: the stone crumbled to dust and I slipped in a pace before I hit the bottom. I think it was hollowed out, intentionally.

The earth present there seems to have been relocated.

I don't know much about building, or elemental magics. It's rare a human have even the most basic affinity with earth as it is, but I can tell there's a very complicated operation taking place. To get the rock tower, there has to be material to mold, and the snake has apparently solved that problem by drawing stone out of the ground underneath us.

Quite a lot of it.

Slowly but surely, that tower is taking the only defense we have from the eels that continue to spear themselves on the walls. If this tower fails, we're probably going to be stranded for good. There won't be enough rock left to get us to the ceiling.

Light and gods, that's a tremendous amount of pressure and stress for something I can do nothing about. Faith magic is useless for molding anything but itself, and I can't just pry the stone apart with my hands.

Instead I'm forced to sit on the sidelines, and watch. Take time doing little to nothing, practice my chants, exercise, climb up the walls and pull a lone eel down every now and again.

In essence: I wake, I eat, I wait. There's not much else to do, but watch the snake go about its strange work.

Did I mention the snake made me silverware? Stone-silverware, but still a reasonably useful knife and a thick spoon- both egregiously engraved with a small snake and two frogs looking majestic.

At this point, I'm not even surprised. Why wouldn't it?

Still, I do feel like the snake has been acting a bit strange recently. Stranger than before, I mean. Compared to whatever baseline the tiny basilisk normally has going for it.

The blue scaled critter stopped about halfway up yesterday. For awhile it be surveying, shooting the occasional fireball, but then it just "stopped."

Just sat there, staring at something.

Even now it just sits up there, with the typical happy head-bobbing visibly absent. Just waiting, watching the lake beyond the walls. Slow but sure, I can see it turning, as if following view of something.

At first, I had to assume it spotted bats, or some other flying monster, but I've been watching recently myself, and I can't see anything but dark stone. Not even if I make the stone glow as brightly as possible, I still don't see anything worth watching, but the snake clearly does.

Once it's done building for the day, it just seems to watch. Feelings and emotions are a difficult concept to assume for a monster, but I think it's uneasy. Worried, even.

I'm starting to wonder if there's more motivation to reach the ceiling than the fact I suggested it.

Chapter 59

Snake Report Day Whatever/Captured by Humans Report: Official Day 9

I think that someone is trying to kill me.

By someone, I mean something.

Something with a large set of teeth.

White whale, Holy Grai- No. Stop that.

Not a whale, a shark.

A shark that's the size of a whale, bigger than a whale.

The kind of size that probably would eat whales if put in the same body of water for an extended period of time.

It did a pass by today.

Just a casual circle in, open its mighty and horrific maw, swallow half of the eels gathered, and disappear back under the surface. Just a few dozen monsters, eaten in one bite.

No big deal.

Pfft- that's not even a small deal.

I'm not scared. I'm approaching this subject rationally.

That's why I'm shooting fireballs at the water with complete abandon for aquatic life.

Hisss...

Hisss...

Hisss...

That's not me, that's a portion of the lake boiling.

Lots of steam out there.

I'm mostly out of magic now.

Super calm.

Collected.

All-business and professional snake-persona has been adopted. I'm dealing with the matters at hand. Increased military mana-budgets this quarter, I already built a wall, very much against Cannibalistic Eel immigration. Border protection is of the utmost importance.

Politically I think I'm really holding up my end of the bargain.

If I had hair, I'd probably comb it over.

Hisss...

That one was me. The water around Camp *Alcatraz* is just a bit foggy now. Oh black water, keeps on rolling... all evidence is being swept away by the current.

There's no way to deal with it. One tiny snake can't boil the entire lake, no matter how much he really, *really* wants to.

Oh, if only I could.

I would.

For my efforts though, I leveled up again. It only took thirty or forty eels catching fire, and another thirty or forty taking the bait and following suit. So, eighty eels was about equal to one level.

Long gone are the days of mushroom related advancement.

But eighty eels... That's probably half or less when compared to what the Megalodon gobbled down with a single laid-back pass. It wasn't even trying, that monstrosity just sort of opened its mouth and swallowed everything. Those teeth weren't even necessary.

Right now, an entire level up for me, is probably less than a small snack for them. So, I've gotta wonder: what level is *that* I wonder?

General guess, there's at least one or two gobbles a week, a few hundred eels in each... extend and multiple that back at least a few centuries from the looks of that fin...

Holy shit.

Tiny Snake God: this is not okay.

I thought that falling-back to setting everything on fire might be the go-to plan here, but now there are even more eels.

They're eating each other.

Huge fans of barbecue, every single one of them.

They've let the whole lake know, spread the word
about *Alcatraz* smokehouse Grill.
The critics are raving.

Oh, Tiny Snake God. If you don't send another brave Frog Prophet to show me the way out of this, it might really be the end. I need a sign. Something, anything-

Ah, Miss Paladin is shouting at me.

She's waving a rock-spoon at me, all angry-like

I feel like she always knows just what to say at times like these.

Probably shouting, *"Stop shooting fireballs you majestic and wondrous snake"* or *"Build the tower and show mercy to your pitiful enemies: you're too strong for them!"*

Yup, those both sound like they could fit.

That's definitely what she said.

She's right, I should just keep building the tower. Don't look in the water, don't look down. Just a couple more slithers, and I think I might be able to start molding the ceiling down to meet me.

Hisss...

I think after dinner I'm going to have to try and come up with a way to communicate our situation to her. People have a right to know about giant Megalodons.

That's a basic thing, twenty-eighth amendment. Look it up.

Chapter 60

Talia:

Talia watched between bites of roasted eel, while the tiny blue serpent across the table carefully lifted and set several large pebbles atop the surface. She chewed slowly, careful not to look away from its activities as she made another cut into the monster-steak. Beside her, several more cuts waited on the recently added stone plate, matching to match her stone silverware.

Earth magic was clearly in progress, but Talia wasn't quite sure what kind. Maybe it was making more kitchen utensils? This was abnormal behavior, even for the basilisk. Maybe something had stressed it out?

Swallowing down a particularly tough bit of eel, Talia thought back through the day.

She had yelled at it early... that was true. She might have even said a few rather unpleasant things, but only in an effort to make the strange creature stop shooting globs of streaking fire over the walls.

Perhaps, it was still upset.

The final bite of monster-steak went and followed those before it, as Talia set her stoneware down. In the light of her faith magic overhead, she had purposefully ignore the now-revealed details and finery of the plate's surface. This dish had a three-headed frog wearing a... cap of some sort. The creature was bowed before a another two-headed frog, which was staring majestically over a sunrise and clouds. On the border was a snake wrapping around and eating its tail: face settles with a zen-like expression.

"Ridiculous." She whispered quietly, pushing it aside on the table. From across the way, the basilisk continued its strange work.

If it heard her, it made no motion of recognition as yet another large pebble found its way to the table's surface.

"Hisss..." Out from under blue scales, its tongue flicked out, head lifting to bob slightly as it looked the results of its magic over. Then, it turned to face her, confirming that it had her attention.

"What are you trying to do this time?" Talia asked, eyeing the pebbles. "Is that a game?" She reached towards one of the pebbles, stopping as it hissed again.

The stone shifted.

"Sssss..." Before her fingers could reach it, the pebble molded: shape turning and twisting as if the material was dissolving. By the time her hand reached the stone, it had become a small human figure. Talia paused, staring at the piece. It was like a child's toy, shaped to oddly specific impression.

The blue serpent bobbed its head as if to encourage her.

"Is this... me?" Slowly she picked it up, turning it about. It really was her, her armor, her cloak... even a small but happy looking face. "This is fantastic."

The snake bobbed its head happily, as if agreeing. Another pebble shifted, turning into a snake spiraled up in a coil with its head raised.

"You?" Talia asked, picking up that piece as well to inspect it. "Are you trying to explain what you are?"

Her question fell on deaf ears, as the table surface between them rippled. The stone shifted, churning about into the impression of waves, and in its center, a slow rise brought a distinct impression to form.

Bit by bit, the once flat plane lifted up until it was unmistakable.

"It's the island." Talia realized. "The island and... the lake. It's everything."

What had once been a table, was now a map. Each second that passed, she could see more and more details rising into form. Other distant islands morphed out from the table's surface, and the border edges of what were likely walls came to shape a generally circular outline.

"Sssss…"

Talia watched, as he walls lifted on the edge of the island itself came to fruition. Details of stone and spikes, and eels molded out with frozen thrashing shapes as the familiar tower began to lift up out of the table like a thin spear. Higher and higher, it lifted until soon it seemed an exact replica. As if built to scale: the island they were trapped on was now sitting atop the table.

The snake stopped, and stared at her once again.

"Ssss..." It looked at her hands, eyeing the two pieces as it slithered up onto the table's surface- stopping to direct its tail towards the inside of the islands walls. Then it moved back slightly and did the same thing, pointing to the dramatically detailed figures of the dying eels.

"Alright... I think?" Talia put the two figurines inside the walls beside the tower, leaning in closer to the island to look at the eels. They were frighteningly carved: eyes wild, sets of teeth almost polished enough to glow. "I... I feel as though I understand so far."

"Hiss..." Before her eyes, a single eel moved. Clumsily, it broke off the wall and fell with a "thud" before breaking into pieces. The snake moved closer to it, concentrating as several more eels came out of the table's surface, each one picking up a piece of the first shattered figure.

Talia's eyes narrowed. "I've seen them doing this. It's why they've been so active recently."

"Hissss..." The eel pieces seemed to flatten out, no longer being recognizable portions of scale and flesh, but spreading. Almost as if... a wide puddle?

Talia's eyes narrowed.

"Is that... Blood?" She asked, pointing to the surface.

"Sss..." With a tired hiss, the serpent turned to the far side of the table, contorting it. Slowly, the mold raised up, moving towards the island and the eels, but more specifically: Towards the flattened pool of "blood." Then from the raised lump of stone, a single piece broke free of the mold.

Was that a... fin?

Talia stared at it, as her stomach tied itself in a knot. That's exactly was what it was: no matter how she considered the shape, there wasn't anything else that something like that could reasonably be.

That was a giant fin.

Turning back to the tiny blue snake, head now resting on the table with a quiet hiss. Seemingly tired, the basilisk had flattened out, like a blue cord of rope, but it hadn't stopped just yet. Talia watched as the fin settled back into the table. "Hisssss..." Then the stone around the represented eel blood quivered, and then lifted as a massive head took shape. Jaws of hundreds upon hundreds of teeth lifted up, and over, the carefully shaped and detailed eels.

Thump.

The incomplete scene was left frozen in time, and atop the table behind it, the tiny serpent flopped down still, apparently exhausted. Perhaps it had used its remaining magic on the effort.

Still, as Talia looked it over, there was more than enough to understand the message clearly.

"Oh... Light help us." She murmured, as her hand traced along the half-molded form. One terrible cold eye, scars covering stone skin, with a maw that rivaled the size of the scaled-island beside it.

A giant monster.

Even unfinished as it was within the shaped stone, Talia could tell it looked hungry.

Chapter 61

Snake Report: Day Whatever/Watching Humans Report: Official Day 10

As of midday, the snake and human alliance here at Camp Alcatraz is under siege.

Call it, the *Great War of Deep Waters*: a battle of which bards might one day sing ballads.

I put this on the record, here and now: the enemies we face are stupid as they are numerous.

Yes, it has come to my direct attention that eels are the cannibalistic lemmings of the monster world.

The is no longer a shadow of doubt in my mind.

Over and over again, the never ending storm of toothy idiots has fallen upon the stone-spikes. So many, it has gotten to the point where I'm burning them off with fire magic so they don't legitimately form a barrier of flesh for the hundreds of others looking to make their way over the walls.

The Megalodon has taken serious note of this.

It apparently also likes barbecued eel, just as much as the other monsters do. Several passes already, and it's yet to clear out the growing density of mpsf – Monsters per square foot.

If anything, it's just encouraging more to come and fill in the gaps.

We're now the hotspot for aquatic activity. The prime destination everyone is raving about: Camp *Alcatraz* is a hit.

Worth mentioning, but now that it has decided to make close passes: the shark fin is taller than the stone walls. That means it's at least fifteen feet, probably more.

Also, that means it can be seen from the center of the island.

Yeah.

Miss Paladin refuses to leave the small hilltop for anything now. She's just been staring out, mumbling to herself and watching as it circles us.

She's not happy.

I'm not happy.

The eels are stupidly happy.

The Megalodon doesn't seem to have emotion, only hunger.

Insatiable hunger.

Hissss...

I've been more than properly motivated.

Not by faith in the Tiny Snake God, or love- though Miss Paladin is definitely the type of gal I'd take home to show the family in the circumstance they weren't snakes.

No, I'm afraid Operation [**Upward Mobility: The Snake-erican Dream**] is motivated entirely by Fear.

Fear…

Heights has never been a big thing for me either.

Thought I'd mention that, on account of the fact that I've reached about 70 slithers up. High enough to experience a fatal landing even if I aim for the water. At this height I'm fairly certain it would be like landing on concrete.

Snake pancake.

Still, this is important for *more* than just fostering a healthy source of paranoia-brought-on motivation. As of a few minute ago, I'm just close enough to start coaxing the ceiling to head in my direction.

Just finally there.

Little by little, inch by inch. The closer the rock above gets to me, the easier it becomes to move.

I've been swelling a huge amount of it, just a little at a time. It's like a giant rock-pimple, or an over-sized Hershey's kiss made out of... limestone maybe? I don't have a clue, rocks were never heavily in my sphere of knowledge beyond a few courses I had to take in my last life.

Exams were passed, but knowing myself- I probably slept through the classes.

My ignorance is wide, as the underground lake is deep.

Anyways, it's getting there. Big moment.

Ten feet from first contact:

Slowing our approach, over.

"Roger Roger, this is Mr.Snake to Houston, over."

"Checking Snake-acceleration, descent is coming along nicely. We are a GO for landing, over."

"Eight feet... Check the balance Mr.Snake, rightward leaning- straighten out, over."

"Seven. Looking good from here Mr.Snake, over."

"Six... five...four-three-two-one: *Presto.*"

Houston, we have first contact. I repeat, operation **[Snakerican Dream]** successful. This was one small slither for snake, one giant slither for snake-kind.

Yes: ceiling contact has been acquired.

Now for the hard part.

What I've been dreading.

Getting Miss Paladin up here... alive.

Hiss...

I'll be honest. I wasn't the nicest person before I died.

Not saying I was a terrible human being, but I wasn't particularly charitable or anything. No soup-kitchen shifts, no helping the homeless, no working for the Peace Corps. I'd donate a dollar to the guys who rang bells outside of the supermarket on the holidays... sometimes. I'd let people merge into traffic... when I felt like it. Once and awhile I'd spot a coworker for lunch if they were hitting a rough patch, but it's not as if I was a saint or anything.

I was morally average at best.

Morally average means there is some teetering, back and forth with wiggle room between the two. It also means that the presence of both Good and Evil sit upon my non-existent tiny-snake shoulders to offer advice.

Intrusive thoughts:

"Leave the human, save yourself."

"Don't leave her! She's your ally!"

"Do it! Escape this horrible place!"

"Miss Paladin is your friend! You can't abandon her!"

"Is that friend worth being eaten by a Megalodon?"

"Can you live with the guilt of dooming someone you care about to certain death?"

"She's a human! You're a Snake! The moment you get back above ground, she could turn on you!"

"Miss Paladin wouldn't betray you, that's nonsense!"

"She's the reason you're down here! She and Young Gandalf put you in a Magic Shoebox!"

"... That was a one-time thing."

"Was it? Was it really?"

Geeeeeeez, putting Angel-on-the-shoulder-snake in the corner.

That's some heavy shit.

Real heavy, tiny-snake-devil: You evil little bastard.

Besides, I already told you: I'm a snake, not *Satan.* How the hell could anyone leave a person in this terrible place? You'd have to be some sort of serial killer.
Megalodon or no, I'm with tiny-snake-angel on this one.

No snake or human left behind.

Chapter 62
Talia

It was done.

Before her was a pillar of stone, rounded to a column and widened to three paces. At the top, so far up that she could barely make out the glowing blue scales, was the snake. It was doing... something.

The strange creature was done working on the islands tower, but from reason it wasn't coming back down.

"You better not leave me here!" Talia shouted towards the distance ceiling, voice echoing out into the massive cavern. "You hear me? You'd better not!"

Her yell repeated in the distance, softly dimming as the sound was swallowed by the sounds of water and the splashing of eels beyond the islands walls. The endless cacophony of unorganized noise continued, ignorant of Talia's shouting.

Sitting down beside the tower, illuminated by the peaceful hum of faith-magics imbued there, Talia sighed.

"You'd really better not leave me here." She whispered at last.

The thrashing frenzy of Eels beyond the walls of their strange camp was at a minimum, quiet compared to the noise which would come later. Talia had cleared away the last of the bloody incentives earlier: dead eels removed from the walltop to deter others from following suit.

Still, as they always seemed to, more would return- spurring on their brethren. She'd look away for a moment, and without a doubt, Talia knew another would be there: stuck on the spikes of the wall, wriggling like a worm on a hook. It was only a matter of time.

For the exception of that one Talia had dealt with herself, none of their aquatic neighbors had yet been so daring today. Considering the constant onslaught of the vicious creatures, she was grateful for break. Taking those creatures down could be more than exhausting, and there seemed to be an almost infinite number of them. One would turn to three, and all it took was the blink of an eye. The last batch had grown so uncontrolled, that the basilisk had actually cleared them away with vibrant bouts of green-fire: flames so hot, they had caused clouds of steam to lift off the lake's surface.

Moments like that made Talia very glad that her companion on this rock preferred to eat Eels, rocks, and mushrooms, instead of people.

But what in all the *Light* was it doing up there?

"Creeeeeeeeeeee!" Splashes, followed by a long screech cut through the quiet calm of the cavern air. *"Creeeeeeeeee!"* Talia turned her head to see the first eel of the day, jaws snapping in vain as it tried to pull itself free from the sharp stone spikes.

"I would have expected you to learn by now..." She muttered, leaning back against the pillar of stone behind her. "You're not making it over the wall alive. The basilisk will fry you first."

"Creeeeeeeeee!" Spotting her, the unlucky monster snapped its teeth while spitting blood with wild abandon over the inner wall as it strained to reach towards Talia's direction. *"Creeeeeeeeeeeeeeee!"* Several more were piling up alongside it now, impaling themselves as often as they happened to take bites from one another.

The violence of the splashing beyond her sight increased, shrieks and screams falling atop one another in a dissonance chorus.

"Again, and again, and again," her voice was completely muffled by the following onslaught. "Will you never stop?"

Taking out the small stone knife she'd been given Talia traced along the strange details along the grip, staring at tiny serpent which threaded its way along the handle. Made from stone, she'd expected it to be terribly fragile, but the piece was oddly reliable. If she stared closely at it, Talia could see the stone was worked in a different fashion than the rest of the island, as if placed under tremendous pressure.

Sharper, denser... more than just some small thought had gone into its construction.

"Maybe you were an artist, or a smith," leaning back until her head rested against the stone pillar. Talia stared up towards the ceiling once more, ignoring the screaming eels.

She couldn't bring herself to get up and deal with them, just yet. Up above, the snake still wasn't coming down. It was working the stone, but in the ceiling. So far off, it was difficult to tell.

Talia shook her head.

"Grant liked art too, you know. He used to talk about those things with Joan, just to make Rodrick jealous. Sometimes he would even buy her stone-worked flowers, the really fancy kind- and when she wouldn't accept them, and then he'd give them to me instead." Squinting her eyes didn't help against the darkness of the cave, only serving to make her view more shadowed and blurred. "He always could, because he knew Rodrick would make Joan say no, so it gave him an excuse." Rubbing at her eyes, she leaned forward, curling up over what remained of her worn and ruined armor. "Ah... Why'd you have to do that Grant? Why'd you have to leave me down here alone, you stupid, hopeless, reckless, idiot..."

Screams of death and dying rallied out from beyond the stone wall, further snapping teeth and faces spitting their final breaths as they leapt over one another, but she didn't care. Curling tighter, Talia tried to push it all away as she clutched the knife tightly in her hand, head tucked beneath tired arms.

"Why'd you have to be so cool at the end?"

Alone on an island, deeper than anyone had ever been and come back from alive. Her friends were dead. Her weapon was lost, the rest of her possessions were scattered at the bottom of a dangerous underground lake, and the closest thing she had to a companion in this place was over a hundred paces above her head: a bizarre being of existence that might never be coming back.

"Creeeeeeeeeeeeeeeee!" Talia glanced up, just in time to see an eel fumble its way over the wall to land in a writhing heap. Covered in bites and open wounds, it uncoiled slowly, face searching the environment it had only just arrived. Finally, it settled its stare on her.

"CREEEEEE-"

It had barely finished its call of challenge before another eel slipped from the pile of impaled monsters, jaws closing shut like a steel-trap on the first's neck: abruptly ending its shriek in an instant.

Talia watched the carnage, expressionless.

Was this the kind of world she wanted to live in? Could she do this alone, day after day, after day? What was the point in such an existence? Just surviving... just eating what tried to eat you... just killing for the sake of living another day. She stared as the two eels struggled, one heaving its final bloody gasps, while the other tore into it mercilessly: bite after lashing bite.

She eyed the knife in her hands, slick stone edge almost glistening in the dim light of the pillar's base.

If it came to that, she'd have to choose.

More eels screeched and cried, as another surge of bodies mounted themselves on the wall-tops. The frenzy was truly in full swing now, worse than Talia had ever seen it before.

It wasn't just eels anymore either, Talia realized. The long tendrils of monsters that had long-since been lurking in the depths were now plucking free their meals with barely the slightest hesitation: all as the eels whipped themselves up further into a bloodbath.

Only seconds, and the island was already being overrun. Approaching her, one of the eels began to wriggle forward towards her position.

Talia rose, sucking in a deep breath as she reached beside her.

"Ha!" She bludgeoned the first snapping set of jaws to a pulp with the fanciful stone-plate, which soon shattered. "Be gone!" The second went down beneath the kitchen knife- as did the third and fourth, but by the fifth her knife was dragged away in the corpse of a soon-to-be-swallowed eel, and there was nothing left for her but magics.

How many more now?

"Ha... ha... ha..." Her pulse beat wildly against her chest, behind her eyes and ears. *"Oh, Holy guardian of Light... Grant me strength..."* The mana flowed along her skin, her gauntlets, what bent and broken plates remained of her armor.

Power.

Faith Magics offered little in the way of deadly force, only defense, healing and endurance. Talia knew this well, as an adventuring Paladin, she had been the shield for her companions: a stalling method, of sorts. Her role had always been the one who could drive off the monsters, but rarely have to be the person called on to deal crucial blows.

Talia knew, she was out of her element.

The longer she stood catching her breath, the greater the number of monsters: pouring in with nothing to stop them. Hundreds of them surging and fighting among themselves atop the walls with mindless hunger. Once they made it over the edge completely… she would die down here, even with the walls slowing the tide.

Talia shook her head, clearing away the thought as she wiped the blood that speckled her cheek with her sleeve.

Slowly, she rose from her crouch.

"Who's next?" she shouted, stance ready and watch for the next challenger to break free of their midst and approach as she readied herself back to the pillar.

"Come! Try and take me!" She threw her fist forward, smacking a heavy blow to an approaching set of teeth- impact throwing the dazed creature back to the piles waiting at the base of the walls: dazed creature instantly torn apart by its waiting fellows.

"Creeeee-"

"I am not afraid!" She shouted. "Do you hear me? I'm not afraid!"

Another punch, another caught and redirected bite- teeth barely grazing as Talia ducked it past her shoulder. Without a weapon, it was only a matter of time.

"HA!" Both hands and forearm plates took the next bite, jaw shattering as she parted her arms with a brutal swing. The creature dropped at her feet, and Talia looked up with a proud smile: just in time to see several heads turn towards her.

Dozens of eels, staring at the blood which now covered her armor, and the corpse beside her.

In unison, hundreds of teeth opened wide with a terrible "CREEEEE!"

"Oh, for light's sake-" Talia was cut off rather abruptly by a heavy blue object landing on her head, knocking her backward.

Then, everything was on fire.

Chapter 63

Snake Report:

Daaaaa daaa daa daaaaaaa dududuuuuuuuuuuuuuuuuuuuuuuuh

Hear that?

That's the sound of me being a damn hero.

No devil-snake on my non-existent shoulders. No abandoning comrades in their time of need, no using up almost all my magic on a very dramatic but very necessary fire-storm because I couldn't figure out how to get down here quickly without dying!

Well… actually, about that last part.

We're in a bit of a pickle. I tell you what.

"HISSSsSsSsS!" (That means "Climb faster human." In Snake Language)

"_____ ___ ____!" *(That means "Shut the hell up! Make more hand-holds! I'm going!"* In whatever language Miss Paladin happens to speak)

"HISSSSSSSSSssssSSSsssSSS" (That means "I'm too young and beautiful to die yet." Again, in Snake Language)

"___ ___ ___ __ ____ @!& _____!" (That means… Honestly, I don't have a single clue. The shift-symbols indicate it might have been emphasized more than usual.)

Maybe it's about the cannibalistic ritual sacrifice to the Tiny Snake God taking place below us. Things are getting pretty gruesome down there.

Classic blood for the blood go- No, stop that.

None of that.

Tiny Snake God only.

Ssss… it's bad though.

Here's hoping I have enough magic, and Miss Paladin has enough upper body-strength, to get us to the top of this tower. Only sixty more slithers to go, one earth-shaped hand-hold at a time.

"GRRRRRRRRRRROOOOOOOOOOOOOOOOOOOooooooooOOOOO OO"

Ah... huh.

Rest in pieces Camp *Alcatraz*. Megalodon just made landfall.

"___ ___ ___ __ ____ @!& _____!"

"HISSSsSsSsS! HISSSsSsSsS! HISSSsSsSsS!

Chapter 64
Talia:

"I'm choking you stupid serpent! God-damn you, choking!" Talia coughed the words out, as the snake around her shoulders and neck hissed and spit in a terrible panic.

"HISSSsSsSsS!"

"Still choking!" Talia shouted again, hand reaching for the handhold that quickly sprouted out of the pillar's side.

"HISSSsSsSsS!" The blue coil about her throat loosened as the snake's head leveled with her own, scales flushing to a paler shade she could only interpret as fear. "HISSSsSsSsS!"

"I'm going! Just keep making handholds!" She shouted at it, tired arms reaching for the next ledge. That formed form beneath her fingers, stone sinking in like putty as it molded.

"GRRRRRRRRROoooooooooooooooooOOOOOoooooOOO"

"HISSSsSsSsS!" The basilisk increased its volume. "HISSSsSsSsS!"

"I'm not even going to grace that with a reply." Talia muttered, risking a quick glance to the dizzying distance below. They were past the halfway point by now, but things were slowing down- for both of them.

Her arms were shaking they were so tired, and the serpent was obviously pushing its own magical limits with every tiny casting... but none of these issues compared to the greater threat.

"GRRRRRRRRROoooooooooooooooooOOOOOoooooOOO"

The real danger came from below, where a massive beast had begun ravaging the island.

Stopping to catch her breath, Talia felt another shot of panic take to her veins, as the beached behemoth twisted and shook- vibrations on the island carrying up beneath her hands and feet with every terrible "chomping" bite. Through the glow of her last chanted cast, she could see hundreds of monsters falling in droves to those giant jaws. Contrast to the warm light at the tower's base, the brutality was sickening. Strong or weak, large or small: all went down under teeth and violence the same. Crushed beneath razor teeth and unstoppable force.

As did portions of the island.

In its efforts to take in ever-last living monster below, it was eating the ground, the walls, the stone: everything.

The massive jaws crushed what could not be cut, shattering anything in its path.

"How is it able to eat stone? How in Light's name?" Talia cursed, as she continued her climb. "I've never even heard of a monster that strong!"

"HISSSSSSSSsssssSSSsssSSS" The basilisk let out another bout of panic as more handholds began to sprout from the stone with renewed vigor, pushing ahead of Talia's own pace. Twenty more steps worth, they filled to the ceiling. After those were surpassed, Talia would be at the top of the stone pillar, where she could see some sort of tunnel was present there, reaching out into the ceiling.

"GRRRAAAAAAAAAAAAAAAAAW"

Below, the ground shook again, vibrations running up the stonework so fierce that Talia almost lost her purchase, feet struggling to maintain their stance. Looking down in horror, she saw the monstrous teeth sinking into the tower.

"Why?" Talia couldn't help but let the question out. Why bother with the tower, did it really want them that badly? "Are we truly worth so much trouble?"

"SSSSSS!" The snake turned, head pointing directly down.

"Oh no." Talia whispered. "The light."

Far down below, revealing the scene, was the base of the tower. The glowing base.

She'd left the stone filled with power, and her faith magic was still burning brightly. During the mad-panic of their ascent she'd forgotten to dismiss the spell, and with nothing else left to consume, the beast had taken the unintended bait like a moth to flame.

"No!" Talia reached for the magics, hymn soaring in her mind's eye, but the magic fell short.

They were too far away. To manipulate the magic within the stone from this distance would be impossible- it would carry on until its mana expired.

"GRRRAAAAAAAAAAAAAAAAAW"

The teeth sunk in deeper, terrible shock-waves running up beneath the stone. Rattling measures of force that brought cracks and creaking noises that popped and sprayed dust along the hard-worked rock. It was going to being them down.

"HISSSSSSS!" Wrapped tightly around her neck, the blue serpent fell limp-just in time with the sudden ceasing of motion. As if the creature had used the last portions of its strength with one sudden and desperate gamble, it began to uncoil, caught by Talia's free hand in a split-second of panic. For that instant, handing there by only her feet and one tired arm, dread filled Talia's chest.

The illusion of falling came swinging up over her thoughts: the sudden lack of shaking, of motion, of vibrations threatening to throw her from the tower's ledges.

Then, it was over.

Beneath her feet, the tower had ceased to be. Cut clean and falling away, a perfect slice tumbling down below, breaking into long shards with the earth's embrace approaching. Eyes wide, she watched as they smashed down atop the jaws, crushing the behemoth's mighty skull beneath untold rock and weight. Like spears tossed from a cliff's edge, they rained down with a barrage of destruction.

"GRRRRRRRRRaaaaaa-"

As the beast's scream was buried beneath the stone, Talia pulled the blue serpent like a scale-covered scarf, gaze set to the summit of their climb.

Talia knew then, it was up to her.

Chapter 65

Snake Report: Life as an ascended being, Day 1

[Level Up]

A hole in the ceiling.

[Level Up]

Uncomfortably cramped.

[Level Up]

This is home now.

[Level Up]

Undeniable proof in my eyes that the Tiny Snake God loves his followers.

[Level Up]

I call it Camp *Olympus*.

[Level Up]

It is a happy place.

[Level Up]

Miss Paladin even appreciates it. No complaints from her, she's already asleep- though honestly she's really the one who doesn't have any room.

[Level Up]

I could fit in a shoe box.

[Level Up]

The magic or normal kinds, either way I'm sure I could.

[Level Up]

I'm not in a shoe-box though.

[Level Up]

Still rocking my snake-scarf status.

[Level Up]

No choice in the matter though, I really messed up this time.

[Level Up]

I used way too much magic.

...

...

...?

Ah, good.

It finally stopped.

[Level Up]

Never mind.

[Level Up]

It'll stop eventually, I'm sure.

[Level Up]

[Level Up]

...

...?

Now, maybe? Here's hoping.

It makes this noise that isn't a noise?

Each and every time, no exceptions. Migraine inducing, just thinking about it.

There's a long story there- probably a couple of them. To make it short, the Megalodon died atop the ruins of camp Alcatraz, Miss Paladin has more upper body-strength than I'd imagined possible, and I think I got credit for murdering some ancient evil from the lake of doom.

Heavy pillars of stone, plus gravity. Large chunks of heavy material falling from great heights onto the thing seemed to do the trick somehow. I guess it's really hard to live through a giant rock-guillotine, even as a Behemoth-Monster of the depths.

Well... I mean, I say that, but the Megalodon lived through that part actually. For a few hours it was still making "grrrrrrooooo" noises and such.

Even at a rough count, at least two hours.

Then it died.

Honestly, I think getting stuck under them might have really been what killed it. Far as I can tell the Megalodon just slowly suffocated while a bunch of other hungry seas-monsters went to town on it.

Gruesome, but I'll take it.

I mean, it brings up some interesting questions about damage calculations, experience accumulations, and "last-hit" relevance, but I'll take it.

Loophole victory is still a victory.

Hisss...

But there is a problem. Even with the shark dead, and both of Team Tiny-Snake alive and well atop Camp *Olympus.* I messed up.

Big time, too: a serious error- necessary or not.

Too much magic.

I used too much magic, and then I pushed past my limit right at the end with a huge effort to cut the pillar before we fell and died by impact/eel/Megalodon.

Unfortunately, there have been a few side-effects.

See the above mention: I am now a scarf. Still a scarf. Will likely continue to be a scarf, off into the future until some distant time yet to come.

Atop of looking a bit like some hip-hop artist who might be trying a bit too hard, Miss Paladin hasn't even met my parent's yet. Skin-to scale contact here: we're moving a bit too fast for my liking.

It's embarrassing.

But… yeah, I seriously can't move.

At all.

I'm just a majestic looking scale-scarf. I can breathe a little, and blink. I can make my tongue do the cool "flick" thing, but I can't move.

To make matters even worse, I can barely use magic either.

It's not like it's gone, but it's hard to reach for and use. I still feel the weight of it. I haven't lost mana or anything, in fact I think I have even more than I did before- but [Earth Molding] is working as a trickle compared to what I was managing previously.

Thus the cramped quarters.

It's a left-over from what I managed to complete before the Indiana-Jones Theme started playing before I ended up with snaktile-dysfunction.

There's not a lot of space in this room.

If you look to the right, you'll notice there is a hole in the floor that could lead to certain death, and if you look left there is a wall of bedrock. Just like above- the distance in which that rock continues for is ambiguous.

Anywhere from a few slithers, to half a mile. I'm not exactly clear on how far we fell down in the currents when we went over the cliff. Probably pretty far, but there's no way for me to know with any real certainty.

Meanwhile, beneath us there is only a few steps worth of rock, and then a long fall into a lake filled with hungry eels.

Obviously, Miss Paladin isn't going to be able to chip away at the rock by hand, so I'll have to be the one to do the heavy lifting there. Somehow I'll need to pave the way for us to go up.

But also obviously, I'm having a bit trouble with that at the moment. The only magic that's working properly right now is [Voice of Gaia.]

Which is a shame, because I don't think I can question our way out of this.

...

"[**Voice of Gaia**], tell me my status."

[Level 70]
[TITLE: DIVINE BEAST, LEVIATHAN, GUARDIAN]
[BRANCH: *Divine Being*]

[UNIQUE TRAITS:]
[Toxic] - Toxic Flesh. Dangerous is consumed.
[Crystalline scales] - Increased Defense
[Omnivore] - Capable of eating non-monster food-stuffs.
[Affinity of Flame] - Bonded to the Element.
[Legendary] - A rare being. Not often seen, known only to Legend.

[STATUS: Temporary]
[Paralyzed – Temporary] – Result of Mana-debt
[Weakened - Temporary] – Result of Mana-debt
[Intake - Temporary] – Acclimating to [Divine Element]

[RESISTANCES]
[Poison resistance: Rank XII]
[Fire resistance: Rank II] - Affinity*
[Mana resistance: Rank 21]

[Skills]
[Healing:]
[Passive Healing 22] - Automatically being to recover from injuries.
Mana drained as a result.
[Heal I] - Third rank of healing.
[Flame element] - Affinity*
[Leviathan breath V] - Rare ability. Advanced variation of [Flame Breath]
[Fireball X] - A ball of flame, capable of long-range.
[Earth element]
[Earth Molding 30] – Capped - Second spell rank of [Earth Manipulation]
[Water element]
[Water Manipulation II] - Ability to actively mold and shape water.
[Knowledge element]
[Voice of Gaia VI] - Knowledge embodiment. Spirit of the world.
[Divine element]
[Royal Spirit of Man] – Acquired
[Ancient Spirit of Depth] – Acquired

Phew, that level though.

That seems high.

I think I would feel very proud of this if I wasn't wrapped around someone's neck like an old-country fox-pelt.

"**[Voice of Gaia]** What is the [Divine element] - [Royal Spirit of Man]?"

...?

Nothing. No answers.

That's okay- This is fine. I expected this from the last attempt.

Annoying, but fine.

"**[Voice of Gaia]** What is [Divine element] [Ancient Spirit of Depth]?"

...

...

...

Nothing.

…

…?

Yeah-no, that's absolutely nothing.

Seriously, I hate this magic sometimes. Takes my mana, and doesn't answer. It's like a vending machine that eats your hard-earned quarters.

What is this even- ah! Hey, you know what? I just remembered something.

"**[Voice of Gaia]** How many skill points do I have?"

"[Assessing...] - [10,000 Skill points to allocate]"

Hmm, I take back what I said about this magic.

That seems high...

"**[Voice of Gaia]** Is that a lot of points?"

"[Assessing...] – [Tally rounded to nearest fitting rank. Number is equivalent to Advancement]"

Uh… uh.

Yeah, that still seems like a lot. No doubt, this is a lot more than I was ever anticipating.

"**[Voice of Gaia]** Are there any [Divine magics] I can buy with those?"

"No. [Divine Magics] cannot be purchased, only earned. Once used, their effects become permanent."

Hisss...

Answers.

Many answers, in fact, more answers than I was expecting.

Rare for [Voice of Gaia]

Suspiciously rare, even...

Hisss...

If I still had facial hair, I'd probably stroke it with an expression of deep thought and reflection. While I'm at it, maybe I could have some old-style pipe too, to puff away with in solemn and troubled silence.

And a rocking chair.

On a wooden porch, overlooking some distant valley, and a beautiful sunset.

Yes... Yes, I can see it clearly now.

Indeed.

I'm both terrified and intrigued by these answers.

I'm also out of magic.

The life of a scarf has become more interesting.

Chapter 66

Snake Report: Life as an ascended being, Day 2

It is morning here in Camp *Olympus*.

Miss Paladin is awake, but I'm still too weak to be anything but a scarf. Thankfully, she doesn't seem to mind much, although she keeps staring at the hole in the floor.

Long way down.

Looooong, long way down.

That's probably the first thing on my to-do list: Seal up that space so neither of us fall to our deaths by accident.

Tougher than it sounds.

Despite a full night's rest, I'm still almost useless.

I can feel a bit of my [Earth Molding] has come back, but it's pretty weak. I'll be running on low-power snake-settings.

It'll be enough for now.

First thing is a barrier for that dropping point. An ornate stone lattice...

Now, if you've done earth magic with me before, you know this is the fun part of this whole technique. It's important that we focus our chi, relax our scales, and really focus on our mana. There it is, you've got it now: shake loose any non-magic related thoughts- just beat the devil out of them. This is where you can take out all your hostilities and frustrations. It's a lot of fun.

Okay, now we can let the magic out, wash away the old stone and make it new stone. That's the fun part of all this, shake it off, cover everything in the snake-studio just like so...

I'm sure you've had enough of the Bob Ross impression, but that's sort of what this feels like when running on low-power.

If I was some sort of industrial stone melter and carver before, I'm more of a hobbyist right now. I figure if three sets of hands were working soft clay, that's about my molding capacity at the moment.

It doesn't take too much thought though.

Even with limited power, and I've got progress. Widening out the room a bit, adding some barricades to keep us from falling through the floor, raising the ceiling a tiny bit.

I think I might try and go with a rough staircase this time. Human-sized, built right.

Hmm... might take a while.

Still, Miss Paladin isn't exactly capable of fitting in a tiny-snake-tunnel. I'm going to need to think of something.

She's looking at the lattice I just made, pointing out my detailed inscriptions of the Tiny Snake God and his holy Frog Prophets.

I can tell she's a big fan, probably going to convert from human religion and join me in my worship.

All hail!

I can hear it now.

Sort of.

I really wish I could understand her. These conversations are tricky without any context. Good ol' communication... I guess I never realized how important it can be. Language is like some sort of super-power really, like telekinetic mind-sharing powers: it's basically magic from the outside view.

Magic…

Oh.

I'm such an idiot.

"[Voice of Gaia] Are there any language-related spells?"

"Beneath [Knowledge element] there are Language Magics that can be unlocked and purchased by [Level] and [Skill Points]"

Oh, you have got to be kidding me. I feel so stupid right now.

"＿＿＿ ＿＿ ＿ ＿"

Yes, Miss Paladin, you're right. I'm definitely missing that ever-crucial intelligence stat.

"[Voice of Gaia] List them."

Chapter 67

Snake Report: Life as an ascended being, Day 3

Wow! So soon? Where was the rest of day two oh Great Snakey One?

I can hear those questions being asked, even without ears.

Even without someone asking them- oh, I can hear, and I can tell you.

Yes, I'll tell you where it went.

Down.

Down the insatiable appetite known as the [Voice of Gaia]

It's a greedy, greedy bastard.

As a result of my unavoidable ignorance, the rest of the day went together with no small fortune of points and mana.

I'm honestly starting to think this spell is toying with me, telling me just enough, timing the market and prices...

Rigged.

It's a rigged game.

[Human Language - Northern Continent Dialect: Comprehension] - 2,000 points

Purchased. Still didn't understand what Miss Paladin was saying.

Oh. That's right. Even in my last life, there were HUNDREDS of human languages. At least, and those were just the ones that were around in present day.

Hiss...

[Human Language - Southern Continent Dialect : Comprehension] - 2,000 points

Next on the list, and mind you: it's a long list.

Purchased.

All was well.

...

This time it worked.

I'll admit it.

But *tricks*.

How was that sorted, I wonder? Most current speakers? Top rated?

I don't know, it doesn't say.

Like making deals with a genie. [Voice of Gaia] is a lot like that. I feel like I should have been given this sort of thing from the start, and instead I'm forced through an awkward process- like I'm trying to buy a car at a dealership, and they keep tacking on more fees.

Oh, right: As if that wasn't bad enough, each purchase costs points.

… and mana.

… and time.

Time?

Yes, that concept of which I'm beginning to think we're running out of, considering neither of us have eaten anything in a few days. There were some tiny bits of dried eel-steak Miss Paladin had in the pouch on her belt, but that's it.

What was I saying, though?

Oh, well… yeah. Downside is that each language purchase knocks me the hell out.

Just… Poof.

D-U-N: done.

I wake up some time later with a terrible migraine.

But, it's not just that- notice the fine print: *Comprehension*.

Give it a minute… sink in yet?

That's right: I'm still a snake.

Snakes can't talk.

"*Hiss*." That's what I sound like. Even after buying these outrageously expensive things, I still sound like "*Hiss*."

Fine print.

Tricks.

Yes. It's a total rip-off.

The type that forces me down a desired path, leading me now on the concept of a sunk-cost to my last intended purchase. Scrolling through skills and spells left and right until…

[Knowledge Element]
[Spirit Attendant] - Bonded Spirit of the Earth, a tool for its master. Known to accompany Divine Beasts of Legend.
[8,000 Points]

Hisssssssssssssssssssssssssssssss.

That means: *"This game is rigged"* in Snake Language.

Somehow- SOMEHOW, I don't have enough points.

Starting at 10,000, I never would have considered this possible.

Rigged.

Hisss...

I'm complaining.

Too much, I think it's all I seem to do recently.

Gotta cut that out.

Honestly, I don't have a right to complain.

I died a mediocre person at best, and I came back to life as a snake. Instead of disappearing from existence forever, or going to hell, or being reborn as a sea-barnacle, I came back with my mind still present.

This isn't so bad.

Sure, this is a messed up reality filled with danger and death, and I'm not even possessing arms and legs- but everything here is gravy.

Round two.

I really shouldn't be here at all.

Perspective: it's important to remember.

I have no right to complain... But*

But, I'll say this. Here and now, on the record: I almost wish I couldn't understand Miss Paladin.

I really almost wish I could turn back the clock, and give back this rigged comprehension.

Yeah.

Snakes can do okay without food and water.

People can't.

Trouble.

We're in trouble.

Chapter 68
Talia

Thirst.

It was all she could think about. It crept into her mind, down past any rational defense: terrible and unrelenting thirst.

Hunger could be stalled, pushed away, ignored for a time. Talia had the foresight of drying out some pieces of the eel meat, and though it hadn't tasted well, she could chant and channel magic well enough to heal through most-any illness that might have carried with it.

But she had no water, only stone.

Beneath her was a thick layer of dark and cold rock, beside her was an elegant lattice of much the same, and above her was nothing but the blackened bedrock of the deep Dungeon. Layers of rock so deeply soaked with mana, that it might as well be poison.

Talia couldn't drink stone, mana, or poison- though she might be tempted to try. It had been almost two days since her last sip of water. Before she had climbed straight into the air to come and rest in this small space over an ancient lake. Even laying down with little movement, breathing controlled and focused, she was slipping into madness.

Thirst was everything.

"Water..." Her voice rasped, like sand and glass were pulled taunt on strings of metal in her throat. "Please... Water." As always, Talia spoke to the quiet glowing shape of blue which hovered along her shoulders. More a specter than a reality, it moved almost as little as she herself now did.

"Hisss..." It replied softly, as if to try and put a stop to her words. As if to say that it heard her desperate pleas, and understood them.

"Water..." Even to her own ears, the voice that begged for such a thing was unfamiliar. "Please, god... please."

Why had she ever come to this horrible place?

The thought floated above her conscience mind with all the others, questions and unfinished bits of logic and understanding disjointedly spinning about before the abyss of forgotten. Why had she come down with Joan, with Rodrick, with Grant... What was it they had wished to achieve?

Greatness... Riches... Knowledge... Adventure... Power?

All were possible, for a price. They had been a great team, known even to the larger Guilds on the continent, and yet: they had been so foolish.

The risk was always there.

For an Adventurer, be it in ancient tools or weapons found far beneath the earth, in monsters and their wild magics, or the bountiful wealth one might obtain with the scavenging of mana-crystals and precious metals: a life's dream could be obtained in the depths. Even for those held and tested by the upper layers of the Dungeon networks, those first tunnels long since picked clean of anything but the manifestations of dangerous creatures and malignant tides of tainted-earth magics, Greatness and riches were still within one's reach should they be willing to work for it.

So… why did they ever choose to go further?

That was the reason for all of this, wasn't it? That they left the safety of familiar ground, and went out looking for… what, adventure? To see that which none might have ever seen before. To discover, to trail-blaze a path those others might follow after?

Or was it for power? To grow, in experience, in skills: To acclimate to an environment that will only accept the strong, and make them stronger. To turn those with promise, into legends, to be one of those figures immortalized in history...

Talia didn't know any longer. She couldn't know, not through the fever pitch of haunting dreams. Unable to see beyond the black of the hollowed cavern, the glow of mysterious blue scales, the scream of Grant's voice, of Rodrick's final shouts, of Joan running terrified into the darkness- never to escape those which chased after. They left her, one by one. Friends and companions of years and seasons.

Rodrick had a dream of Legends. To be the man in the stories, to be remembered, to be known, to have fame. He pushed ever onward to the next challenge they could overcome.

Joan had love, and she sprinted after. A desire for something she could never have completely, but could never quite let go. A one-sided affection that pulled her deeper than most might dare.

Grant had pride and will to achieve, and a curiosity for those ancient mysteries long forgotten by the noble races. He had the desire to learn, to understand the forgotten and make it his own.

But herself... What was it that brought her here?

Desire for fame, riches and status? Love of another? Pride? Unanswered questions? The simple wish for adventure?

She didn't know.

"Water," she begged the glowing blue spectre once again, watching through the haze as its strange eyes lifted to stare back at her. Deep and strange, a poison blue of ocean depths and a setting-sun sky. "Water..."

It wasn't until the cool damp of rain touched her lips, that she let rest take her once again.

Chapter 69

Snake Report

Something from nothing.

There is the single greatest trick with any magic: a certain condition, maybe better classified as a law.

Earth can be reshaped and molded. Elements can be moved, and the force to do this can come from my own body- somehow. Fire, while not controllable, act under the same principle: devouring my mana with a hunger as it bursts into existence, but the fact stands: I can't make something, from nothing.

Magic is not all powerful.

Earth needs to exist to use earth-magic. There can be no stone tower from the sky, without stone to build it. Earth requires earth. That cup of stone can't be molded without stone, and neither, can it be filled up.

Water magic is no different than the other elements. Without a source, it can't be done. It's forever out of reach.

This… I think this is where I think many might find their end. Trapped in this cavern, settled above certain death, where there is nothing but air and stone.

Air, stone, snake, and human.

It's frustrating. I can do nothing with air, no matter how much I pry through the lists of spells: there's nothing.

I have no air magic, though I strongly suspect such a thing exists.

With the human, I can heal, but I can only heal *wounds*. Bruises, cuts, burns and injuries: but that's it. None of those are going to help now. After several attempts, I feel at this point I might only be making things worse.

I can't heal someone who is dying of dehydration.

That's not how it works.

By that same logic, I can do still things with stone, but what good is stone right now? An empty cup? A device to mock the poor person slowly succumbing to their body's most necessary and essential need?

To anyone's eyes, snake or human: there is nothing but air and stone in this room.

This is where the line should stop.

Should.

The trick is, I can see something else.

No, not with eyes, but with my mind: the mind of a person from another world. Useless as it might often be in this godforsaken Dungeon, the knowledge held in this head knows things that it shouldn't know.

Logic... science... chemistry... these are all subjects I forced myself through as a human.

I know them. Not to the level of a doctor, or a researcher- but they're not alien to me. Where some might look at this room and see nothing to work with, I look and see a solution.

In air, there is oxygen. There is what we need to breathe, but that's not the only thing.

Nitrogen...

Oxygen...

Carbon dioxide...

Some others as well, even mana. In this world, there are likely others, and I know there are many elements I don't remember well. Not even enough to repeat the names: material I simply can't ever interact with.

But, of all those: if I reach out, I can feel something else waiting there.

Something I can even touch with magic, and slowly, it reacts... piece by piece, they react...

In this air, there is a single thing I can touch. An "element" in which I do have power over, however weak.

Drop by drop, it collects:

Water.

There is water in the air.

Barely a fraction, but it's present, waiting for someone like me to reach out and... take it.

As if from nothing.

I am creating something, from nothing.

Hisss...

That's basically magic, while using magic.

[Water Manipulation III]

Science rules.

Bill! Bill! Bill- no.

Stop that.

This is serious.

My magic is still weakened. Physically I'm almost useless.

I'm learning to multi-task on a serious scale here. Pulling water out of the air, aiming it, pouring a cup by method [Earth Molding] alone because my body won't move. Carving out stone and shifting things to make more space. Making a new altar for the Tiny Snake God.

Lots of things here.

Serious things.

Even a normal human would have some serious trouble with this stuff.

The stair-archway has been started. I plan to wind it in a spiral similar to the way I originally intended at camp *Big-Foot.* There was a table made, and two chairs, as well as a bunk. I had the ceiling pushed out a bit... I'm just trying to come up with more things to do because [Earth Molding]'s effective range isn't so efficient if I can't move.

I managed to lift my head a bit earlier though.

That's progress, but... it's slow progress.

There is nothing left to do but wait. Let her drink a tiny sip, then wait...

[Water Manipulation IV]

Water magic is different from working with earth. It's fluid... I suppose that's obvious, but with earth, things mostly stay where I put them. With water, it seems that nothing ever stays put longer than I'm holding onto it. The second- no, the instant I let go the magic releases: the structure is gone, the work is left to run its course.

So, I have to go one drop at a time...

Collect the water like condensation, as if it were dripping from the ceiling.

Cool it down, slow it down... catch it, then pour... carefully.

Fill... then pour...

Tiny sip...

It's all I can do.

Hiss...

Miss Paladin, I'm very sorry all this happened to you.

I wasn't certain I would get along with a person that captured me, but I think I've gotten past the trauma of being kidnapped. To be fair: I was a suspicious monster creeping about beside your hard-won sanctuary, and you were rightfully concerned.

I honestly think I might have tried to do the same thing in your circumstances.

Still, you shouldn't have been there in the first place.

This is no place for a human to be.

Trust me when I say that. No one else would know better.

This terrible place is for monsters, not people. Emotions, hopes, dreams: they aren't meant to go this far down in the depths.

No, things like that: they rise up, like heat.

It's why people build cities, and artwork, and sculptures and crazy inventions.

To go higher.

To keep themselves out of the pits. Away from places like this.

I'm rambling.

It's a bad habit, that comes out when I'm under a lot of stress.

I talk.

Well, I *hiss*, nowadays anyhow, but it makes me feel a bit better when I can't do anything about the world around me.

You know?

I don't really have a choice.

Things die down here.

Lots of things, ever since I was born in this world: all around me, all the time. Even if I'm not the one to cause it. Even if I try to stop it, to avoid it all entirely.

Things die.

It's what happens in a place like this, all too frequently.

It gets... tiresome. Heavy, I guess. Like weights. Bit by bit, those add up.

I don't know.

Sometimes, I can make up as much as I want to hide away from it. Build things of my own.

Sculptures.

Tunnels.

Pillars.

Camps.

I can make crazy and wonderful things. The stuff of dreams in my last life, more than dreams even. I can do more than I ever would have thought possible.

But then, sometimes I can't.

Even now, I can't do everything.

I'm sorry.

I guess after all the horrible stuff, I just really don't want you to die.

Chapter 70

Snake Report: Life as an ascended being, Day 3.5

After a few hours, Miss Paladin woke up.

No... That's not the right description.

After a few hours, Miss Paladin began to talk.

It was quiet, really quiet at first. So much of a whisper, it sounded more like breathing than speaking, but then I started to make out the words. Really strange and unfamiliar things, suddenly shifting to a language I understood completely.

Between every tiny sip of water, she let out a few more syllables. Just a few more words, sneaking along on the harshest and ragged heaves.

As the hours passed, I realized she was telling a story of some kind: a fable, maybe.

Not to me, not even to herself... No, this was a fever dream being spoken aloud. A legend, from long, long ago, stretched out into verses. Prayers, but fit together like a song that isn't meant to be music, of a story hidden within.

Whispers in the dark.

As time stretched on, my magic steady with the tiny drops of liquid falling from the air: I could do nothing but wait.

So, I listened, as she whispered the words.

As it is known, as it is sung, there was once a King who could not die.

Long ago, he ruled.
Before the oceans came to rest.
Before the sky came to form.
Before the world was as it was.
The First King, of the First Men, of the First Era of the world.

Lord of the weak, of the lessers, and the destitute.

For the Forests held their own kind, of beasts and power.
Those mighty Mountains held another, of stability and knowledge.
And Oceans cared for nature, alone.
But for men, there were only the space between- of pieces and fragments

unwanted.
Yet, the King ruled them, all the same.

While the Forests withered.
While the Mountains crumbled.
While the Oceans filled with storms.
The First City of Men rose up.

They were weak, no longer.

Upon the horizon,
Where buildings cut the sky, and forges twisted the earth,
A place stood where men working the soil until the world held no power.
Where those who were once weak and unwanted, could become strong.

But it was not the City, which called to the hearts of men.
Nor the towers, nor the walls, the riches, or wealth.
They came for the truth behind the legend.
The chosen soul, gifted by the gods, and destined to guide them.
Wise, kind, strong- they came seeking something more.

All came, to bow before the one who ruled it.

Humbled by the years, the King stood above them all.
Wise in ways only age can gather, yet so skilled: none could rival him.
He would take what knowledge they could share, and pass it on through the ages.
Gifted and blessed, unlike other men.

Forever outside of death's reach.

No sword, nor arrow, nor poison could end him.
No passage of time could age him further, or disease that might hope to ruin him.
Whatever danger threatened him fell away like rain on glass.
For some, this was a blessing in true form.
The sign that the King was destined to lead them.

But what for some, might be a gift: for others is a curse.

Strong as the First King of the First men could be, untold years weighed down upon him.

Heavier and heavier, its burden grew until it filled him with sorrow.

Though he found meaning and purpose in his role as rule, in the love for his people as a whole, he was forever in mourning.

Surrounded by thousands, beloved by the people of his great city, the price for love has always been the same.

Loss.

His blood had mingled among them.
By lovers, sons, and daughters: all who came after them.
Worse by every year, it ate away, wearing down like waves upon the sand.
Just like all the others before them, all he cared for would one day leave his side.

Like fleeting moments, each came and went until his own descendants were indistinguishable.

In the passing of countless lifetimes, that weight piled like the bricks of his great city.
There inside of him, rose a structure building atop itself.
Building, and sinking, deeper and deeper into despair.

Too heavy for one soul, this knowledge gripped the King so horribly that he often wished for an end.

He prayed for the great solitude of death- even begged.

But the gods did not answer his prayers.

He could not end.

Violence could not stop him.
Poison, or the elements themselves could not break him.
No weapon could bring that which he crave.
Instead, the King could only try to erase- to push away those who cared for him.
Those who served and lived beneath his rule,

As the years pressed onward, the King grew cold even for his purpose.
To rule, to protect, to guide: these were duties for another to fill.
While the city grew larger, when nations formed about it, the King faltered

in his rule.
No longer did he walk among his people.
Never did he travel further to witness their achievements, as they met the great oceans of storm, and crossed the jagged mountains.

To every corner of the world: soon he was known to all, and yet to no one.

In time the people began to think of him not only as a ruler, but as a God.
As men spread across the world, with them came his legends.
To the people of the Forest, he was divine.
To the souls of the Mountains, he was like the stone beneath their feet.
Yet, to man: he was all.

Some even believed the King a deity meant to guide them onward towards greatness beyond all else.

But the King claimed to be none of those things.

He had said the gods did not speak to him, nor answer his prayers.
He swore to never have met the creators, and he knew nothing of the heavens.
He knew only that which he had lived.

But that did not stop the people from their faith.

They strayed from the old ways, their desires grew with each generation.
No matter what they learned, built or achieved: their King was the Light in the sky.
Those privileged to speak with him interpreted his suggestions.
No longer as experience and mortal toil, but as divine proclamation.

The King's words were Commandments!
To be heeded, to be followed, to be taught as law.
To be enforced.
To be enforced cruelly.

Lost in sorrow, the King did little to stop them.

Even with his protests, the cries only grew.
Tainted by a fervor of faith, he watched from his throne as men changed.
Those passing familiar faces, descendants of his friends and families over the ages: all twisted and wrong.

His blood was among them, but they were no longer his kind.

His final purpose was lost, and the King found then, that he could bear life no longer.

Yet still, the King could not find his end.

He secluded himself: deep and away, travelling down the stone staircases of his castle, far below the city atop it.

Deeper and deeper down into the most sunken and ancient ruins, farther down than any other might ever reach.

Farther, and farther, and down into the Earth where the first blocks of his first city still rested beneath the others.

Until there was nothing but stone.

Nothing but soil.

Below the footsteps of man, the King found himself surrounded only by graves.
The place of ages long past, of lives long forgotten and replaced.
Left alone with his thoughts.

There, through the great knowledge of all his years upon the earth, he pursued the greatest question upon his tired mind.

How could he die?

And so it was, that time passed.

Onward...

And onward...

As it does, and as it will continue to do, time marched towards the endless horizon, and the people of the King began to forget.

Some even began to forget him, not just his teachings: but his presence.

Had there ever been such a man?

Was it a King that once ruled them- or a god?

*Who can say, for the people lived short lives and held even shorter
memories.*
The living need proof, and the dead cannot speak.
Their descendants, passed him on towards legend.
His blood forgot their own source.

Generations came and went.
Greed and ambition began to sprout.
The people changed further.
Shrinking in on what they were in both form and mind.

*Some wished to rule in his stead: to fill the position and throne left
abandoned, and in time, some did.*
Inventions of tremendous power clashed, oiled by the blood of its makers.
The sparks fell upon the fuel, and they began to burn.
Mankind fell to war.

For ideals.
For gain.
For the sake of glory.
Empowered by the knowledge of their heritage, but too foolish to control it.

*Across the land, a Triumph of Death was proclaimed for all to hear and
know.*
It crumbled the greatness of man to splinters and fragments.
All while the broken pieces stabbed at one another.
Shattering again and again.

And yet, still: time passed.

And still, the King worked.

Deep in the long-forgotten tunnels of his ancient castle.
*Covered and hidden by the ruin of the ages, surrounded by layers of
bedrock.*
Where strange things lurked, and gods might roam.

He worked.

There was a secret hidden, grasped within the clutches of his tired skull.
It pressed with the long-held years and secrets of his mind.

Of thoughts tying thoughts, and knowledge melding together endlessly.
Forming on an art that had never been tamed.

Thousands of years, of lives, of experience and insight.
They bent to his will as he carved the grooves.
The voices howls, as they sunk beneath the stone.

But he did not stop.

Deeper than any had ever dared.
Farther than any among the living should pass.
In search of answers, in search of secrets: it was there he discovered the answer.

Not only for what he had hoped, but greater.

By blood spilled, by the privilege granted: the First King of Man opened the Gates of Magic, and the world was forever changed...

Miss Paladin kept talking for a long time.

Eyes closed, face sweaty. I think she was losing more water than I was giving her at first.

For every sip, she probably lost at least as much before the next.

But the hours passed.

With time, I got a little better, a little more controlled.

Every so often, some improvement came as the skill pinged its rank. Some more came as practice, but I could see the difference.

One drop found itself turning into two drops.

Then into three.

Then four, then five…

So on, and so forth: it was working.

Miss Paladin stopped looking so close to death, and her fever seemed to fade off a bit. Still looked as though she had been surviving in a Dungeon. But it was an improvement.

Her weird words rolled out, with her voice a little less dry, a little more lucid.

I listened, and I poured. Listened, and poured. Musical, her voice fit with the acoustics of our small space but then, finally, she stopped.

I was so set in my routine, it took me a few minutes to realize her voice was absent in the room. Nothing but the sound of water dripping out of the air into a stone cup.

Nothing.

Silence.

Then panic.

Was she dead? After all that?

I cast heal a more than a few times before I realized she was just asleep. Finally, truly asleep, resting peacefully. No more words, but there was a slow and quiet breathing. A lazy lift and fall of her ribs, rocking me on my perch like some strange boat.

So, I began to fill the cup again.

She would need more water when she woke up, I reasoned. Setting it on the floor, I made it into a large vase with a wide and weight base. Then I mesmerized myself into a quiet trance, watching the flow of water, feeling the vapor condense and fall with a quiet pitter-patter of artificial rain.

Miss Paladin left me with a lot to think about.

Chapter 71

The history of the world, or possibly just a story... a very long and detailed story, that sounded a lot like she'd heard and told it before hundreds of times.

I suppose maybe that was just a mad-ramble of some half-dead person, but I'm not quite convinced. To me it was much more like a single person in a church choir than delusional muttering.

Hisss...

An Immortal... a long but painful life.

The wise and ancient King... *The Gates of Magic...*

With a story like that, I can't help but miss books.

There are no books in the Dungeon, which is a crying shame. There's nothing to do but sit and think in a place like this, unless I'm running away from something or getting eaten alive.

I'd rather sit and think, compared to the alternative options.

There is quite a lot to think about if I have the time, after all. Existential crisis and confusion, magics, stone working plans, and fever-ramblings of an almost-dying person...

Humans, for one.

Those were the center of Miss Paladin's story, aside from the King, of course.

The King...

The Immortal King.

I guess he must have gotten what he hoped for at the end of that. After searching for an answer in quiet solitude, forgotten deep beneath the ground...

Make me wonder.

Death?

An exaggerated way of saying the Immortal finally died?

Sounds about right.

The Immortal King died then... It seemed like that might have been implied. But more than death, he got more than death... Or maybe he got something better than death?

I feel like there are a lot of better options than being dead, but perhaps that's just a biased perspective having reincarnated.

The Gates of Magic though... did those mean actual gates, or some sort of metaphor?

Sort of vague…

"[Voice of Gaia] What are the gates of Magic?"

"[Forbidden]"

Hisss...

It answered.

That was a non-answer, but it still did it… which is weird.

Not sure what that means, but it's obviously something.

Stuff to think about, for sure.

That's all quite a lot to throw at a half-paralyzed snake trying to concentrate on water magic and earth magic at the same time.

Chapter 72

Snake Report: Life as an ascended being, Day 4

Gooooooooood morning rocks!

Gooooooooood morning fancy lattice covered hole to certain death!

Gooooooooood morning shrine to the Tiny Snake God!

Gooooooooood morning empty water-holding vase!

And gooooooooood morning Miss Paladin! It warms my little serpent heart to see you well, and as miserable you might be, you don't look dead. That's progress!

Hisss...

I've learned a few human swear words.

Hisss... rough language for a woman of faith.

What a wonderful day this is. I can move, freely, slithery and the like, I'm back to 100% operations here in Camp *Olympus*

Well, maybe 85%

It doesn't matter. I'm moving around, I'm using magic, I'm feeling good. Today is going to be a thing of progress, I can feel it.

[Water Manipulation VI]

No more multi-tasking. Aquatic necessities have been taken care of for the time being. Focus on the air, focus on the beautiful Snake God vase: finish the work and move on.

That's the routine now, no more "tiny one drop a minute" sort of pace. Instead, my focus is once again on the familiar.

Rocks, stone, dirt, walls, ceilings, floors... the staircase I'm carving looks absolutely beautiful. I'm telling you right now, it's great, it's gonna be great. I make the best staircases. Just like I make the best walls.

Believe me.

First a wall, then a tower, now a staircase.

This staircase, believe me- It's gonna be great. I have a plan, I'm going to make it pay for itself.

Yes, I really mean that, and no, it's not going to be fun.

But Operation **[This Time For Sure]** is now a go.

Chapter 73

Talia

Talia watched as the odd little basilisk melted the wall as if it were putty, or glass under high-heat. From a height that would reach over her own head to the floor, the stone just "compressed" and fell away, edges spinning out beneath the patterns of shifting stone.

It was impressive progress.

Grant had always told her earth was the most stubborn of the elements, all but unwilling to bend before a Mage's power. Yet, for the snake, that didn't seem to be the case. If anything, the earth was more than happy to move along as the small creature continued its advance. The pressed and molded rock reformed with strange and spiraled motions, encapsulated before they were fixed in place.

The power at work made this all seem almost too easy.

After watching it raise the tower up, right out of the island, Talia had known the snake was strong. There were probably only a few Mages alive that would have performed a similar feat, and none of them would have been able to have created the walls and interior of the island in a single day. Especially not while fending off monsters at the same time.

She'd assumed that it was the raw mana crystals at work, there. The irrationally solid resistance to mana-burn had helped it channel far more magic than any living creature had a right to. Not without the assistance of a group channeling their powers together, or a large quantity of very carefully crafted potions.

Now though, the strength she was witnessing seemed befitting to the category of pure… power. Sheer strength, perhaps coupled with a small spark of genius.

From her stone seat in the small room, Talia watched the visible flair of artistic talent that seemed to fix itself with every new-formed step. There was efficiency in place, and as the magic continued, she could see it finding a stride. Any mage with power over earth might replicate the motions and the purpose of creating a passageway up through stone, but in the swirling echoes of rock and mana, Talia could see the signs of a master.

Here was sculptor of stone and trade might make a carving, perhaps even a staircase similar to this in function and purpose: but only a master could make it timeless.

"Clunk."

The foreign sound brought her attention to the final step created so far, earth still swirling apart as the blue scales illuminated their twisting patterns with a strange magnificence. As she peered closer though, Talia soon realized there was something else glowing, present atop the newly formed steps.

There, waiting quietly, a perfect glowing crystal had just been pried from the bedrock of the worked stone. Barely a few paces away, sitting in plain sight was the kind of stone that went to the market for bidding no more than a few times every decade. The type some nobles might use to power airships, or massive machines. An object that could lift up an ordinary adventurer into the class of a rich and wealthy noble: what equaled an entire vault's worth of gold, right in front of her.

She stared at it.

The snake stared at it.

It was massive, easily larger than her hand. Not blue, but a perfect shade of emerald green, not even the slightest hint of a flaw or crack in its perfect spherical shape. No impurities at all.

Truth be told, in her current state of mind Talia would trade it for a loaf of bread and a warm bowl of soup, but staring at it in a light-headed wonder from her seat, the green glow seemed to memorize her. Her gear was missing, her armor was in pieces, her weapon was lost, but sitting there on a freshly made step of stone was a gem that could buy a mansion in the peaceful countryside twice over. It was such a foreign beauty she couldn't even fathom.

So much wealth, just waiting for someone to find it, and take it away. On careful steps, Talia approached it, hand outstretched- before gasping in horror.

It disappeared.

Slowly.

Painfully.

Talia watched speechless as it was swallowed up by the lesser blue luminescence of a tiny basilisk, who then let out a small burp before turning towards her with a single flick of its tongue. She saw an expression there, to which she could only interpret as the reptile's way of saying: *"I may have just made a terrible mistake."*

Chapter 74

Snake Report:

"Spit it out you idiot! Spit it out!"

The shout is loud and clear as the beating of my heart.

I hear it.

I respect it.

But I'm afraid it's too late for that, Miss Paladin.

I've prepared for this.

It's the only way we're getting out of this mess before we die of old age, or starvation.

Operation [This time for sure.]

This time, we're making it out of this terrible place.

We're going all the way to the top.

All the way up to the surface world. No more Dungeons, no more spiders, eels, no more Megalodons.

This is the only way.

The only way.

Oh, it's there now. I can feel it.

No going back, the magic is rising, earth magic is continuing... should level out soon...

Soon…

Soon…

Any second now.

Alright.

Alright.

Uh... huh...

It's not leveling out.

Nope.

Not even a little bit.

Oh god, this is way worse than I remember.

Holy smokes.

Phewwwwwwwwww

Shake it out, shake it out.

My body isn't just on fire, it's undergoing nuclear-fission. Not just spicy peppers here, this is something else.

"I HAVE THE POOOOOOOOOOOOOOOOOOOWER"

Like that. If I could say anything other than Hisses, I'd be yelling that at the top of my lungs.

Woooooo... Oh boy. Forgot how awful this was, this is the worst.

Ah, Miss Paladin looks very worried. She's trying to get up out of the chair.

Don't be concerned Miss Paladin.

I'm a professional.

I swear.

[Mana resistance: Rank 22]

See? No problems, what doesn't kill me makes me stronger. I'm cool like that.

[Mana resistance: Rank 23]

Wow, that was fast.

[Mana resistance: Rank 24]

Hmm...

[Mana resistance: Rank 25]

Do I smell smoke? Is something burning?

[Mana resistance: Rank 26]

[Passive Healing 23]

Oh.

[Mana resistance: Rank 27]

[Passive Healing 24]

It's me.

[Mana resistance: Rank 28]

[Passive Healing 25]

I'm on fire.

[Mana resistance: Rank 29]

[Passive Healing 26]

Shoot.

[Mana resistance: Rank 29]

[Passive Healing 27]

[Heal]

[Mana resistance: Rank 30]

[Passive Healing 28]

[Heal]

[Heal]

[Mana resistance: Rank 31]

[Passive Healing 29]

[HEAL!]
[HEAL!]
[HEAL!]
[HEAL!]
[HEAL!]
[HEAL!]
[HEAL!]
[HEAL!]
[HEAL!]

Chapter 75

Snake Report: Life as an ascended being, Day 5

Today, a lot of things happened. I can go chronological, good to bad, or bad to good. Or, I can just ramble like I usually do.

Hiss... Let's just get the bad part out of the way.

Today, I became an enemy of mankind.

It was terrifying.

It all came down to [Earth Molding.]

See, I've gotten really, really, *reeeeeeally* good at using this magic. So good, that it now calls itself [Earth Sculpting.]

Ranked up in a big way.

I used it to build an ornate and winding staircase up through the Dungeon bedrock, with Miss Paladin following me all the way at a slow walking pace. That's how fast things were going: the more I used it, the easier it got. Eventually, it was getting so easy to do that the magic wasn't enough to keep me from suffering serious mana burns.

I mean, it was getting to easy. Literally, too easy, I was too efficient- so, I had to use it even more.

And more.

And more… you can see where this is going.

How the dangerous cycle began.

I'd make a stair, start another stair, begin to inlay detail and tiny scripts, then start a third stair, then a fourth, inlaying all the way up that chain of steps. The tiny detail work normally took more magic than it was worth, but I felt like I had to use more- MORE, or I was going to experience combustion into fireworks and blue scale fragments.

So, I found more.

More to do, more to spend magic on. Anything I could think of started to happen. I carved hand rails, and then I domed the ceiling on a gothic sort of style. I made sculptures along those surfaces. But it was easy! Too easy!

All these happening at the same time *still* weren't enough, so I made fake windows and molded Tiny Snake God shrines as I went to match them- and

I made the stair case even wider. Expanding by several slithers in every direction and adjusting the slope, so it was more like one of those giant mansion stair-cases you see in the movies.

More, more, more, more: I was multi-tasking to extremes. Magic makes this a lot easier than I would have expected, but I couldn't even count how many patterns I had rolling at once. The motivation of bursting into flames and dying a terrible death also provides some serious incentive to work at it. I seriously felt like a bucket of gasoline being put towards an open flame.

And that's about where I think I pretty much lost it.

Eventually, my memory starts to skip. Right around this point, I'd call it a haze: a mana-induced haze.

I lost track of direction.

My vision went funny.

So far as I can remember, I think this went on for half a day or so.

At least.

Distantly, I recall Miss Paladin giving up her encouragement about the time my tail caught on fire, perhaps switching her to a more serious mode: actively following me around casting heal with long and extended chants.

She stopped when she realized I was casting it too, and then complained with something along the lines of:

"Monsters can't use heal like that. It makes no sense."

And I was like: "Well, duh" / "Hiss."

None of this makes any sense Miss Paladin, get with the program already. I'm not a monster, I'm a disciple of the Tiny Snake God. Even the [Voice of Gaia] agrees, I'm a "Divine Being" or some-such-something.

Yeah.

So... Hazy.

The influx of mana was frying my brain a bit at that point. I was either turning into gibberish, or channeling some sort of holy-snake-spirit.

Hiss, hiss, hiss.

You know how cats will purr sometimes when you put them by a nice warm fire?

Well, apparently monster-snakes will "Hiss" a lot like that if you set them on fire from this inside out. I don't even know what kind of things I was saying, just basically rambling my way up towards the far-off surface world of my dreams.

I let it all out, I think. Told Miss Paladin my deepest darkest secrets.

About who I was, now- and way before all this.

About person I'd grown up wanting to be, and the person I'd actually turned into.

About how I'd wasted my shot at existence, and how my existence had wasted me with a shot (a bit too literally for my liking) and how I'd died.

How I was the absolute worst pick to be woken up as a serpent in this terrible place, and whatever had plucked me out of my last existence to drop me here could have done a much better job.

On, and on, and on...

There was so much magic swirling around I wasn't even sure I was spiraling upward after a certain point. For all I could tell, I was spinning us in a lazy circle, around and around and around again, wider and wider but going nowhere fast.

So...

Really, it's my fault.

Looking back, Miss Paladin was trying to warn me of something. She repeatedly said things like "The stone looks different here" or "I feel like we're near something."

Well.

She was right of course, let me tell you.

Humans don't like it when a powerful monster with almost unlimited magical power burrows up out of an inhabited sanctuary floor.

They don't like it one bit.

Chapter 76

The floor was lava.

Not real lava, but monster lava.

There were those runic scripts all over the surface around where I'd breached via operation **[This Time For Sure]** and I was under the clear suspicion that touching those would result in a similar occurrence to what might happen if I stopped using magic.

There was also a large quantity of splintered wood, several broken wheels, a few large portions of timber: all smashed to bits. Whatever had been in place before I'd shown up, had been quite effectively ruined.

I noticed this, only after finishing the railings and carving them out to look like serpents being lofted upon the raised webbed hands of frogs. At that point, there was nothing reasonably left for me to sculpt, and the magical buzz in my brain was finally starting to subside.

Like someone who had been running on a treadmill and suddenly found themselves back on solid ground, I felt somewhat confused.

I mean, I'd been living in the depths of… well, basically hell. I'd been in hell since I woke up in this world, so suddenly looking up and seeing a bunch of human buildings everywhere threw me for a loop.

My mind went and skipped for a minute, facts processing like they were floating in tar.

We were still in the Dungeon, this was still a cave, but there were buildings. Cabins, more formal structures- maybe something that might have been a tavern? Everywhere around, I could see them, windows glowing with light.

But, there was also that scripting. The type that I knew from experience would burn me if I touched it was all over the ground.

But at the same time there were even animals in the distance, spooked and making noises- but clearly penned up together.

So… this was obviously still a cavern: a huge cavern. If I looked up, there was stone, not sky…

Putting two and two together took my brain an embarrassingly long amount of time.

I was still in the Dungeon. This was like before, when I momentarily popped up in a new tunnel, only... different, somehow.

It's funny, in retrospect. How I thought of all that, and skipped over the more obvious.

I guess my state of mind was a bit frazzled. It didn't help, of course, that I realized "not using magic" was exactly what I'd just started to do. Having nothing left to [Earth Sculpt] which was of course, leading back to the feeling of bursting into flames

That urgency forced me back towards my panic option of [Plan B:] Throwing mana down the insatiable and greedy gullet of Gaia before I exploded under the build-up of heat and energy beneath my scales.

"[Voice of Gaia] What's the deal with the floor?"

Ah... I remember that feeling even now: The feeling of switching from a fire set as "Open Flame Roast" dropping to "Slow Toast"

Huge relief.

Mana burn is no joke.

"Scripts of Magic created by the First Men. Created as a defense during the Era of Tragedy."

An interesting reply: Not a non-answer. For someone barely half-conscience of anything outside of fire and pain, I was intrigued.

"[Voice of Gaia] Why does the floor fry monsters?"

This momentary peace. I think it might stay with me until the day I die. The inner flames of overflowing mana drawn back to feel almost normal for a few seconds.

"[Scripts of the First Men] ... [Status: Broken] ... This floor no longer has the capacity to repel corrupted-beings due to scripting damage."

...Hiss...

Awareness.

Even in a mana-induced haze, that was a statement to bring me back to lucidity. Just enough time to contemplate and process a bit. It's that sort of *Instant-blank-thought* where a mind can realize something very important was just said, but can't quite wrap its thoughts around exactly "what."

"Wait, [Voice of Gaia] repeat that last-"

Before I could finish that, Miss Paladin stepped up past me. Step by step, tired to the point of her legs trembling, and body frail, she fell to her hands and knees. They she held herself, just barely off the floor, heaving with deep gasps, before turning to me at eye level.

"You've done it," she said, smile on her face wider than I think I had ever seen before. "You saved me," her tough facade of unbreakable grit fell away to a single grateful sob, smile quivering as her tears sprouting to the air faster than any water magic.

"Thank you."

Chapter 77

Those words hit me.

They hit me hard.

Like the fist of a god, those... they were beyond me.

Words that I think I'll probably carry on with me for some time yet to come.

In that moment, thoughts swirling and hazed to limits I can neither recreate or accurately describe: what she said to me then solidified into something.

Something real.

From survival, stress, panic- all coming off of the bitter tailspin of a previous life. One filled with selfish, worthless, morally ambiguous decisions.

Then, suddenly: "Thank you."

I had been given a chance to do something good in this life just like my last, but this time I hadn't wasted it. Those descriptions of myself, those quiet little titles I'd adopted as a matter of reality: somehow, against all plausible odds, I'd **beaten** them.

Even if it was only a tiny victory.

Even if it was only temporary.

Staring at Miss Paladin's smiling face, hearing those words- that proved beyond any doubts in my mind that I had finally done something worthwhile. At the start of this, I remembered setting out for some undefined goal in my new life, and this was the closest I think I'd come to reaching it.

For once, I'd done something right.

I felt pride.

Then, the moment was over.

Reality came crashing back down, with a bitter vengeance:

"ATTACK! WE'RE UNDER ATTACK! THE SANCTUARY HAS BEEN BREACHED!"

"A BEAST HAS BROKEN THE SANCTUARY! TO ARMS! TO ARMS!"

There are only a couple certainties that I can clearly remember in the chaos that unfolded in those following moments.

"KILL THE MONSTER!"

People with swords, with spears, with bows, with staffs: They rushed out of the buildings with screams and shouts as lights and torches blustered and exploded to life, and animals kicked and screeched in panic.

"KILL THE MONSTER!"

Fear grabbed me in that pandemonium, panic rising quicker than thought as the sounds of magic casting through the air matched the whistle of shafts and fletching.

"Flee!" Miss Paladin shouted at me with harsh tone. Her grateful smile was long gone, replaced again by that fierce warrior disposition. "Escape! Quickly, before they kill you!"

Too much was happening at once, it was all I could do just to stare at her in confusion. I guess that left it to her own initiative.

Without warning, she picked me up and gave me a hard throw before I could even think of resisting.

It put me airborne, soaring overtop heads and armor, weapons at torches. My landing was painful, but not nearly so painful as the shots of arrows, fire and unidentifiable mana whizzing past my panicked slithering.

"THE SERPENT! THERE IS A BASILISK IN THE SANCTUARY!"

I was hit by magic, at least once.

Arrows glanced off of my scales, several thrown axes and at least one sword cut at me.

I scrambled, fast as I could: I slithered until my body ached and shook from exhaustion.

I spewed magics to cover my wounds, and more to blast away the ruthless attacks. [Heal] and [Leviathan Breath] and [Heal] again, mana spent without the slightest reserve, my head ducking, dodging, weaving, hissing in a blind panic as more and more attacks flew my way.

Before I even knew it, I was out of the human-territory and back into a Dungeon tunnel. The shouts and hollers were still hot in pursuit as I dived down, safety abandoned as I went about picking the first turns I could to [Earth Sculpt] into the bedrock and escape.

Chapter 78

Snake Report: Life as a Wanted Criminal, Day 1

"[Voice of Gaia] Tell me my status."

[Level 70]
[TITLE: DIVINE BEAST, LEVIATHAN, GUARDIAN, ENEMY OF MANKIND]
[BRANCH: *Divine Being*]

[UNIQUE TRAITS:]
[Toxic] - Toxic Flesh. Dangerous is consumed.
[Crystalline scales] - Increased Defense
[Omnivore] - Capable of eating non-monster food-stuffs.
[Affinity of Flame] - Bonded to the Element.
[Legendary] - A rare being. Not often seen, known only to Legend.

[STATUS: Temporary]
[Mana burn – Temporary] – Result of Mana-debt
[WANTED] – Bounty issued for capture, or proof of execution

[RESISTANCES]
[Poison resistance: Rank XII]
[Fire resistance: Rank V] - Affinity*
[Mana resistance: Rank 40]
[Steel/Iron resistance: Rank I]

[Skills]
[Healing:]
[Passive Healing 38] - Automatically being to recover from injuries. Mana drained as a result.
[Heal V] - Third rank of healing.
[Flame element] - Affinity*
[Leviathan breath VI] - Rare ability. Advanced variation of [Flame Breath]
[Fireball X] - A ball of flame, capable of long-range.
[Earth element]
[Earth Sculpting III] – Third spell rank of [Earth Manipulation]
[Water element]
[Water Manipulation VII] - Ability to actively mold and shape water.

[Knowledge element]
[Voice of Gaia IX] - Knowledge embodiment. Spirit of the world.
[Divine element]
[Royal Spirit of Man] – Acquired
[Ancient Spirit of Depth] – Acquired

I am a criminal.

A wanted snake.

There is apparently a bounty issued. Dead or alive, it matters little.

For my head in a sack, there is a reward.

From my hollowed-out hole in the tunnel walls, the echoes I've listened to have informed me of what [Voice of Gaia] did not.

I am known as the *Blue Death*: a fearsome monster that wishes to destroy mankind's only footholds within the Labyrinth of the Northern Continent's Dungeons.

What's worse is that I'm a "*Sanctuary Destroyer.*"

The most terrible beast of legend: the type of creature only rumored to exist in the dusty tomes of ancient books. I have taken away the most valuable of resource for humans in this terrible place.

They think I'm evil.

To make matters worse, according to the passerby of this area, the Sanctuary I ruined was extremely important to the newer adventurers. The ones not quite capable yet of venturing farther into the Deep Dungeon safely. It seems that this Sanctuary was the last "Upper-level" area before the terrain dropped into much more dangerous places.

There is a reasonable chance my actions will lead to people dying, trade routes faltering, businesses failing...

Guilt.

I feel a lot of guilt.

My own people, or at least my own mentally-identified species, consider me their enemy.

After all this time, hoping beyond hope that maybe I could go to the surface and find a way to live outside of this horrible place, my dreams have been crushed.

The surface is for humans.

Humans hate me.

Sitting here in my new Camp *Solitude,* I know this because I am listening. Burning out the last of this insane amount of mana, feeling both sick to both my stomach and my heart, and letting the sounds of their voices roll in along acoustics of my lair.

Listening for adventurers.

There are many of those in this region.

I feel as though there have to be hundreds of them. Groups and parties of them walk about, weapons and equipment clanking with heavy steps, all scouting around the ruined Sanctuary. Many have armor that's almost as loud as their voices.

A few days ago, I might have found curiosity enough to go and check: to go look at all their weapons, and gear.

Not now though.

Hearing their conversations are enough.

It's not good.

Almost all the talk in the tunnels that reaches me, is about what I did.

There are only a few other topics, and most of those are indirectly related. Issues like *"Reconnecting with the cut-off Sanctuaries"* or *"Passing on word to the newer adventurers and returning safely."*

Rescue missions and the like. It seems like I've thrown the network here into total chaos.

The worst are the people returning, who don't know.

Desperate.

Lot of them sound desperate.

Many of what I presume to be the veterans are patrolling in groups, rounding up inexperienced people and sending them back up towards the surface. There's a serious sense of comradery now palpable in these passageways.

Humans against the "Wanted Beast of Destruction."

Humans against the "Blue Death."

The big bad monster: who isn't really very big, didn't really intend to be bad, and mentally isn't a monster at all.

If I could talk, I think many things might be clarified. Maybe I could argue my case, my situation.

I still can't talk, though.

Not yet.

Missing a crucial number of points.

[Knowledge Element]
  [Spirit Attendant] - Bonded Spirit of the Earth, a tool for its
  master. Known to accompany Divine Beasts of Legend.
  [8,000 Points]

I have 6,005...

So... "5" from a level up, the rest from the Megalodon?

Still seems like I'm a little short.

Never going to be able to grind those points from leveling, it would take centuries. Even if I got as big as the megalodon and became the top of the food chain, there's just no way.

It's troublesome to acknowledge that getting the rest of my needed tallies here won't be coming from leveling. That still only gives me five, apparently. Not exactly a reliable plan.

But then, there were some other things that gave me points. Killing that giant skeleton gave me a few, and then that Megalodon...

Those sort of things... well, at least the Megalodon for certain, gave me skill points.

Super powerful monsters have them, normal monsters don't.

So, to get those next 1,995 points...

Hisss... I'm drawing unfortunate conclusions here.

Yes.

I have to earn them. If I ever want to clear my name, grinding the little guys isn't going to cut it.

I'm going to have to go monster hunting.

Chapter 79

Snake Report: Life as a Wanted Criminal, Day 3

Day three as a [Wanted] Snake: my head is still attached to my neck... or body... or maybe my body is my neck.

I've been burrowing in and out alongside a Dungeon tunnel, trying my best to follow after a relatively capable group of adventurers that aren't evacuating the area. From eavesdropping on them, I've learned that they're on a mission to locate and escort a group of "Rank D" adventurers that belong to the same guild.

So, as far as I can tell, that means they're looking to rescue some less experienced folk.

I started trailing them mostly by chance. There were only so many tunnels in the walls I could make to listen for things without being drawing attention, and their conversation sounded promising.

"Large packs of Goblins." That's what this group expects to run into.

It seems there is a very well-explored, well-mapped area that's off and on its own from the rest of the so-called "Deeper Dungeon" and it comes with a few untracked upper tunnels that supposedly lead to the surface.

The zone is referred to as the "Subterranean Forest."

Which, sounds "great" to me.

Forest? I personally think that sounds preferable to a lot of other terrible choices out in the labyrinth of this terrible place.

I don't really want to go monster hunting. I have to do it, but I don't want to do it.

Monsters are scary.

They do scary things, like eating other monsters.

Honestly, I'd rather avoid them, but a place like the one these adventurers have described?

Dangerous, but not too dangerous: The* Goldilocks-Dungeon-Danger-zone.*

I don't want to go looking for the most dangerous creatures this world has to offer, but I feel like even in a "easy" zone there have to be a few monsters there I can get some points out of.

Right?

At least a couple.

I think I can handle that.

Probably.

But at the moment I have bigger priorities than exactly what's ahead on the trail. Keeping up with this group without getting spotted is really, REALLY difficult.

Like, Tiny Snake God-damn.

They're hauling ass these last few hours, and if the speed of their travel wasn't bad enough: there are four of them, and they're always watching for danger.

I think they don't even have to see it, to know.

It's like they can sense it.

I've seen them cut down monsters on the way, they don't even stop.

Anyways: three are warrior-like folk, and there's one bowman. Far as I can tell, there is no Gandalf in this group, and no Paladin either.

High damage… I think they're the types to play aggressive.

After watching them completely slaughter a group of oversized spiders, I'm also thinking they're probably a high-level.

If humans have levels.

Which I suspect they do, although I have no way of confirming this. [Voice of Gaia] won't answer those sort of questions- instead providing a very stern sort of "..." response.

Just "..."

Like it's mad.

Oh, another thing of noteworthy value: the leader of the group has an almost "Buster" sort of sword. It's gigantic. One-edged, curved a bit like an over-sized falchion. I think just dropping it at the right angle would be enough to kill most smaller monsters.

Pretty terrifying, honestly.

Humans like this one are probably on par with some of the monsters deeper down. The sword-wielding, grizzled, bearded type of guy, who's covered in scars: that's their Group Leader I think.

Instinct doesn't like the look of him.

The others are strong too. Besides the bowman, one of them uses and axe and another uses a spear, but none of them compare to that sword guy.

So far as I can tell, they call giant sword man Master Zane.

Sword Master Zane, and his fellows: Daxton, Knox, and Ryker.

Knox is the bowman. For some reason I find that a lot funnier than I probably should. Daxton and Ryker and spear and axe respectively. The only other trivia I've picked up is that they all know the group they're heading to retrieve pretty well. I think they're mentors of sorts, they talk about the others like a teacher might speak of his prized students.

All except for Zane, who barely talks at all. The strong, silent type. Unless I count the violent yells when he slaughters some unfortunate pack of monsters.

Yeah.

I'm beginning to think Humans are pretty overpowered.

Monsters are scary, but humans can do some really crazy things in this world. Super-human things, at least when compared to the last world I lived in. No one back there was picking up sharp bits of metal with the equivalent weight of a small Honda, and chopping up animals in the wild with it.

I don't think, anyways.

I didn't get out much before, all I did was work.

The typical Birth, School, Work, extremely early Death routine.

Took a shortcut at the end there, but "boring."

I'm trying to say I was boring.

Still, I think this kind of behavior breaks the old-rules of reality, which I was still kind of taking for granted.

Hiss... a little concerning.

Normal physical limits are clearly not to be trusted. Going to have to try and wrap my head around that concept, but: O-P as some humans might be in this place, I have to believe there are conditions in place. Even this Swordsman would have had a seriously difficult time dealing with that Megalodon.

No matter how good someone is with a blade, a giant shark can still eat them, or squish them. The only reason I won, was because I cheated.

Heck, I'd imagine it would be much the same with all those eels too.

I had a safe match up, using fire magic. That's a great catch all for swarms, but I bet a person with a sword might eventually have some trouble. One mistake, and then it's probably over pretty quickly. You can chop up a ton of monsters, but in a place like this there might just be another group waiting around the bend: humans need a team to survive down here.

Like I've said before, it's a scary place.

Only the impossibly strong seem to survive for any serious length of time. Giant serpents, giant sharks, giant skeletons- swarms of giant bats and spiders... the strong live off the weak, and they monopolize their position. At the first sign of competition, and they're up in arms to attack.

Other monsters, humans- anything. Dungeon life is kept in a very ruthless environment, and there only a few ways for the only other way for weaker creatures to survive.

With numbers: just swarm the enemy with chaotic abandon and take them down one way or another. With some sort of lethal danger, like venom or toxicity, so nothing would want to both... or, I suppose they can just hide.

Hiding works well, in my experience.

But I'm barely hiding at all now.

The way this group is moving, you would think they were being chased. Their voices seem worried... nervous, concerned. O-P swordsmen and his gritty looking warriors shouldn't be any of those things, but they sound it.

This is shaping up to be more of an adventure than I had originally anticipated.

Chapter 80

Swordmaster Zane:

Zane's pace picked up, as they rounded the next tunnel. His sword flashed, cutting down whatever foe had been lurking to intercept him.

There was no time to waste.

Originally, yhe Wayside Guild had assigned Salazar to retrieve the younglings, but Salazar was on a charting expedition when the Sanctuary was broken. Several noted groups had gone with him on that trip, as well, heading farther down in the deeper zones. That meant a large majority of the Guild's own man power was occupied, along with a large list of problems when they finally did get back. More importantly though, it meant that someone else would need to go in Salazar's stead.

So far as ventures went, deep below, there were Mages and Paladins drafted up from the mercenary banded lists. Cartographers, scribes, and a small escort of Empire forced: this was an expedition put together for an impressive amount of gold in the expectations of securing a reliable pay-out for the intended production of deepest known regional maps.

So it was, that Three of the most precious of Guild resources were deep within dangerous territory. What had begun as a time-honored routine of sending the newest members to retrieve a single Goblin Shaman's Staff, had turned into a terribly dangerous mission.

Youth that were intended to one day inherit the traditions and the teachings of their veteran members. The Secrets, the knowledge, the traditions of the Wayside Guild itself. They might complete their task, only to return and find themselves trapped out of their depth. With no food, no supplies, and nowhere safe to rest.

No one could have predicted the zone's fall, but had Zane not been at the 23rd Sanctuary during the Blue Death's breach, this oversight might cost the Guild its newest members. He'd gathered the group from those who were willing, and left immediately.

Already, the 23rd was under siege from the local monsters. They'd come, trickling in at first, but growing more aggressive by the way. Small engagements for now, but these had begun forcing many of the non-combatants to evacuate. The likes of the traders, the merchants, the inn and build staff: convoys were being formed by the hour to retreat from the area. Once they were gone, all that would be left behind, were ruins.

It was the worst possible situation.

The trio of younglings ahead of them five leagues farther from the next closest sanctuary- and if they retraced their route with intent to return, it would probably be over ten leagues depending on what route they took. The 23rd Sanctuary was the last human refuge in the Northern Continent Labyrinth before the truly difficult zones began. Both back up towards the 22nd Sanctuary, and down towards the parallel zones of the 24th and 25th respectively, would be a terribly dangerous distance for new-Adventurers to attempt alone. Especially ones already exhausted by a previous mission: even with more than a bit of luck on their side, the odds were not kind.

Zane knew this well. It was why he volunteered to retrieve them.

As the many years piled atop him, it would not be all that long before the final seasons of his prime were burnt away. Truthfully, most his age might have already settled into a retirement from the Dungeon expeditions. Many of his fellows were already taking their places above ground as a Guild caravan escort, or a low-risk desk worker for the Guild halls: but Zane felt strongly he could not leave the danger of this work just yet.

It even wasn't about the money. For a few it might be, but not him. With someone of his strength: Zane knew, there would need to be another to take his position before he could move on, and despite his hopes: a fitting candidate (even by his most generous standards) hadn't yet appeared. Even with three other veterans of over three-decades of combined experience present, and Zane would still be hard-pressed to deem any of them suitable replacement.

They hadn't fought the battles he'd fought.

They hadn't risked themselves to the brink of death time and time again- they hadn't slain beasts that could decimate a full party.

But Zane had.

He dove deeper than any of them, and it showed. He had [Skills] most could only dream of, knowledge that took a lifetime to gather. Should he step away from the Wayside's Dungeon Guild too early, there could be disastrous consequences. As the strongest sword within the Wayside Guild, he had a duty to protect the future of the organization.

Perhaps some of this was his own ego.

Zane was not so arrogant as to ignore that he had one. As with all men of talent and skill, he felt more than just some small measure of pride for his capacity, but there was serious truth in the matter beyond his own personal feelings. When there was no one else the Guild could rely on, Zane was the final call.

The end of the line.

Be it dealing with a threat, or rescuing a comrade. He was the final safety net for the men and women who served the Guild: the sword in his hands often held between success and total disaster. To take that away would mean the deaths of his companions, unless there was someone to take his place.

"Knox, any signs yet?" Zane continued his pace, pulling off left at the next division of the tunnel-ways, incline now sloping up in elevation towards the alienated region.

They were close. The goblin inhabited area would begin once the caverns opened up in the massive expanse beneath the Great Forest. Root systems beneath those trees had been twisted and corrupted by the mana of the Dungeon long-ago, since becoming as much of a ceiling as the stone they had once burrowed through. The signs were there around them now, cracks along the walls and earth.

"We're near the terrain, but I haven't seen any sign of recent camps. I don't think that they've come back this way yet." The archer replied from the back of the group. "Only a few markings, goblins, and maybe some tar-spiders."

"That's good, right?" Ryker cut in, heavy pace thumping on the stones beneath his boots echoing over Zane's shoulders. "Means we didn't miss them."

"Or it means they're still deep in the Gob-zone. We'll probably have to comb the damn place to find them." Daxton grumbled, short spears clacking softly in the leather on his back, steel lance leveled and ready beside him. "Not even our great leader can cut down all the Gobs in the world."

Zane didn't reply to that, instead keeping his pace as the incline grew steeper, feet digging into the loose deposits of soil atop the tunnel floor. Now was not the time for conversation.

Already, Zane could see the evidence of what lay above them. The roots and soil, small tendrils of gnarled wood breaking through the walls of the wide tunnel and creeping further in. Along the floor many of these were more prevalent, forcing more careful steps as their paces slowed, eyes alert and watching for other signs of life. They were very close to their intended destination, and likely quite near the surface- not that any sane human would want to surface here.

Being beneath the Great Forest was preferable to emerging up within it. Even to his own vast knowledge, there were few places above ground that could be more dangerous.

"Keep moving." Zane growled.

In a quarter league Zane knew their group would be at the next rally point. They would make camp there if the younglings weren't nearby, and the search would begin from there. Out into the massive nether-forest of roots and glowing fauna of mana bloat plants and poison in all shapes and forms.

Not something most would look forward to.

It had been years since Zane had been there, and for good reason. Even if the monsters of the area tended to be weaker: the terrain was difficult, isolated, and unforgiving. The area would be true test of an adventurer's skills: a perfect confirmation of someone's readiness for the deeper Dungeons.

But, in equal measure: not the ideal setting for a search party.

Zane had a feeling this mission might grow complicated.

Chapter 81

Snake Report: Life as a Wanted Criminal, Day 4

We're in a forest.

Well, under a forest.

In a forest, but underneath a bigger forest?

I'm about mostly certain of it: the ceiling is covered with giant interlocking roots. It's so far away it almost feels like I'm outside, taller than the area of the underground lake where Snake-camp Alcatraz was. Lots of rocky pillars, lots of crazy roots winding all the way down from the ceiling along them, lots of glowing- probably poisonous plants and mushrooms.

It's pretty, it a scary way. My inner late-night British-Nature-Documentary voice might call it a "Primal Beauty" as I overlook the vast and bizarre landscape. Instinct is just yelling "DANGER: KEEP OUT"

These are all important observations we should hold with respect, although "We" is probably a relative thing.

I'm still following the group, and I'm currently hiding in a big rock I found. The people I've been trailing are circled around a small campfire eating some sort of dried meat. I think it's "morning" in the cavern right now, and they're preparing to for the day ahead.

Very serious looks are being passed about, but the conversation it much too distant. At a best guess, they're going to start searching this cavern.

It's there, I won't lie: the temptation.

I'm tempted to follow them, but that's more curiosity than anything else. When I was with Miss Paladin, I think I got a unique impression of the people in this world. I felt like I was on a team, and it was a good feeling.

These guys though: I'm their enemy. Not the same team, they would try to kill me if they saw me.

I have to squash those thoughts.

So, the mission here is not to watch humans do human things. The mission here is a simple one: to kill the biggest-baddest monster in the area and earn some points. I get the feeling small-fry aren't going to cut it. I need another Megalodon-esc beast, and I need it to die by my hand... tail... fangs?

To Die by my Fangs!

Well... "Fangs" certainly sounds the best, but my bite is useless for anything but mushrooms. Absolutely useless. A gardener-snake sized bite is laughable compared to the rest of the dangers down here. I don't even have venom, honestly: they would have to bite me to get poisoned.

Hisss....

I pity the fool that tries to eat me.

But, the struggle is real.

Time passes slowly like this, sitting in a rock, but things are happening.

The group has made their moves and gone deeper into the area. They've also left some gear, a bag or two, a spare weapon and such nonsense. I think that means they'll be returning at some point, so I'm going to make a tiny-snake camp nearby to match this.

This is a large bit of solid stone, so it will do for now.

It's probably at on-point cosmetically too, having been a portion of the ceiling that fell or something. Outside it's covered by the weird-roots reaching off from the walls and ceiling that dome this place.

About thirty feet tall, twenty feet wide: this is now Snake-Camp [Lighthouse] and has all the typical amenities.

Took little to no time at all, honestly. Working stone is a very natural feeling now, it's barely an effort ever since the [Earth Sculpting] designation.

Water is still troublesome, but I'm getting there.

Wood though? I don't even know what to do with wood.

Set it on fire, I suppose?

That's the closest I can get to manipulating it. There doesn't appear to be a [Wood Molding] magic option for me, and I wasted a bit of mana to check.

Seems I'm still stuck with those first few avenues for magical abilities. No signs of that changing anytime soon.

That's fine.

Troublesome in a way, but I'll make do without it somehow.

The ground is still mostly "earth" after all, even if that's now basically were it stops. If everything is giant roots and weird plants from here on in, my normal method of diving into a wall and sealing it up behind me might need to be rethought, but I'll find a work-around somehow. Maybe I'll just burn the plants to ashes and then dive into the wall.

Are ashes dirt?

Is that a cheat-code, burn things down to their base elements and then [Earth Sculpt] them?

Hisss...

Something to think about later, I hadn't even considered this.

For now, I am beginning my own adventure, out into the great unknown of the massive Gob-zone of the nether-forest. This weird subterranean landscape, complete with pillars and roots and what seem like winding paths made by either people or just monsters walking down the same trails a few hundred times.

As always, I'm proceeding with utmost caution. The humans went towards the Arbitrary West, so I'm going Arbitrary East.

There is no rhyme or reason to this, I feel like monster hunts are best played fast and loose. It's not like a grand-plan would work or for me anyways.

I've got pretty bad luck when it comes to this sort of thing.

But this cavern really is amazing- not like the rest of the Dungeon at all. It reminds me of a book I read a long time ago: Journey to the Center of the Earth.

This place is obviously massive, to the point in which, honestly, if I couldn't look up and see the ceiling I might feel like I was on the surface. It even seems to have a hazy fog that glows a bit with the pale light coming off the ceiling and the odd pseudo-forests along the ground.

Surveying from a high-ground, it looks like a large crater depression, with a deep plateau that goes on for miles within it. Beyond the occasional pillar or giant root that comes down to the level I'm now on, connecting the ceiling and the floor past the far-off cavern walls, it's all fairly uniform. Almost a forest beneath a forest, there are massive mushrooms and other strange plant-like things covering the fairly level floor. I'm also pretty sure there's a river somewhere, or a stream.

It makes the class "sssss" noise, and it's not me, and Instinct isn't screaming in horror, so it's not my Auntie or Uncle Snakes either.

Weird place. Geologists would be shitting their pants at the sight of it, I'm certain.

"How the hell does something like this come to be?"

No clue.

That weird root and rock mix over there?

Some sort of weathering maybe?

Honestly, no clue. My lifetime of Wikipedia related knowledge holds no power here. Besides, I'm a snake, not a scientist.

Probably magic or some such nonsense.

Pretty sure I remember Miss Paladin said a bit about that at one point or another: "Magic influencing the world" or some such.

I'll just settle on magic.

It easily fills the gap so I don't start to question absolutely everything and go completely insane.

"Magic! That's how!"

Cue the laugh track and the infomercial with some bald guy and a few stained towels.

But...

Well, slithering down this path, I have to think magic didn't really cause something like this to form. I feel like something living would have had some sort of influence on it.

It's a carved slope, any rocks seem to have been worked or carved, or maybe molded away intentionally to give a route you can travel freely.

This would have taken a lot of work.

It has a spooky effect, though. Not sure if that was intentional, but the ominous glowing plants overshadowing each aside of the trail, giant wooden roots twisting up in dark-foreboding shapes, fitting for a winding and disorienting path that doesn't seem to stay straight for longer than a couple slithers.

Creepy stuff.

Creepier still when I'm pretty sure there's something watching me.

Much creepier when I'm pretty sure I'm staring back at them.

A bunch of them.

Oh.

That's not my imagination after all.

Hisssssssssssssshit.

Chapter 82

Snake Report: Life as a Wanted Criminal, Day 5/ Life as a False God, Day 1

When I was a kid, I remember people telling me I could grow up to be anything I wanted.

Maybe a maintenance guy, or a janitor.

A garbage pickup person, or a state-worker.

Maybe, if I worked really hard and persevered, I might even become a:

[Project Manager]

Hisss…

Well, I suppose they didn't set my dreams to far out, but hey: they never saif I could be a tiny snake. So, I guess I surpassed some expectations.

Then again, some of them did say "anything" without clarifying, so I suppose it was somewhere in the mix.

Hisss...

If only they could see me now.

Not just a tiny snake, but a deity.

Yes, a god.

I have become a worshiped god of brutal carnage.

Respected, beloved, and feared equally by my followers. Praise be to me.

As always with these circumstances in my life, it was terrifying. I wish never to repeat it, and I truly thought I was going to die.

A theme?

Yes, that's the theme. I've been flirting with death so much recently, you'd think we would just seal the deal already: get hitched and pop-out a couple of kids. Maybe build a nice white-picket, gothic fence, and adopt a dog named cerberus…

And yet, I think perhaps it's time death and I started seeing other people.

The spark is just lost, you know? It's not them, it's me.

Me, being worshiped like a god.

Hiss...

Where do I even start with this one?

I'm not sure exactly how to explain in a linear sort of way. Quite a lot has happened, snowballing rather quickly onto itself.

Going off towards the relative and arbitrary East on that Forest Trail, winding in along confusing paths for a few miles...

Losing track of direction, becoming hopelessly lost, eating some mushrooms- almost getting eaten by something that "looked" like it was mushrooms but wasn't...

Getting more lost, giving up hope on ever finding my way out of this god-forsaken subterranean nightmare of glowing plants and weird roots as the growing sensation of someone watching me seemed to grow at an exponential rate...

All that happened, and probably some extra bits I've overlooked, but I'll just skip ahead to the feeling I was being watched.

It was like a chill down my spine, only it wouldn't go away.

It was enough to send instinct into [Statue] mode.

Everywhere I had the guts to slowly turn my head, I thought I could make out creepy eyes. Wide and feral, they were staring at me, lurking within the forest beneath the forest.

They never blinked, and that made it so much worse.

Hunted: I was being hunted.

Not a good feeling even when you recognize it- but by the time I realized this,: no matter where I looked- something was looking back at me.

Yeah.

Goblins.

A metric-butt-load of goblins.

Goblins, goblins, goblins: everywhere.

I really don't know what I was expecting.

In retrospect, this was probably the extra reason that the humans went West and not East. Apparently, they knew something I didn't, and they clearly recognized this way was a bad plan.

This area is called this place the "Gob-Zone" for a reason.

If even that OP-sword-wielding Zane thought it was a good idea to go the long-way round... even half-listening from a distance to the human conversation, I should have put two and two together and guessed that there were going to be full-on hordes of them.

But I guess I'm just a bit off my game recently.

Yeah.

Off my game and surrounded by hundreds upon hundreds of goblins. That strange breed of monster that's apparently smarter than your average Dungeon creature.

Capable of pack-hunting, rudimentary tool use, and also staring for a really-*really* long time without blinking.

It didn't help that they're also great at creeping around.

I went and slithered right on into enemy territory.

Just minding my own business, wandering straight into a trap.

One second it's a happy sort of wilderness hike, and the next it's like that scene from the hills-have-eyes. Everything is still, and then it's complete and utter madness.

Being abruptly surrounded by goblins waiting-in-ambush is a bit frightening, but having no clear escape path is even more so.

The ground- well it wasn't ground. I was on top of a root or something by them time I realized, so no immediate downward escape could be performed (Not that I could focus on much of that after a crude looking arrow "twacked" right in front of my head) so human-side really just fell apart.

Hands off the control, Instinct-override went straight into [**Terror mode**] and from there, things might have gone a bit haywire.

I might have taken a walk on the wild-side, in all the worst ways.

[Terror Mode] is not a joke.

Arrows and stuff coming down at me, human-mind shut-down right into the pitiful state of "NONONONONONONO-" sort of panic where you just do whatever it is you can do without much of a plan.

I imagine we've all seen it.

An emergency- people just flail around.

Running back the wrong way, ignore the posted exit signs, or just do something uselessly stupid.

But, I'm not really a human anymore.

Not even close.

Terror Mode, in my case, was no longer curling into a ball and screaming while I waited to die.

Half of me maybe, but the other half?

I'm a monster: an animal, and I was backed into a corner.

You don't back an animal into a corner.

Not ever.

Hiss...

Yeah: it was like a full-on conversion of every bit of mana I had, turned into [Leviathan Breath] to be thrown about every plausible direction.

Like one of those light up spinning toys you see in amusement parks.

Just twirling around in a panicked circle.

You can imagine it, I'm sure. Around and around, like someone going full-tilt voms off the hurl-a-wurl at the county fair.

Like when the silly orange-fish uses flail, only it's super-effective: that was me.

And in the fire... well that was all the Gobs.

... yeah.

Up front, no real points were earned here. I'll start with that.

I got maybe... 10 points... pretty lousy for killing a few dozen unfortunate goblins, and maybe their chief.

I leveled up once, so really I think I only got five points.

Which is sort of a bad-trade, when risking death.

I don't know.

I mean, I should have figured getting points wasn't going to be easy, but I'm actually wondering if those 5 might just be some form of pity "style" points, and not really something I can count on reproducing.

Maybe it was the Goblin Chief.

I'm leaning towards one of those "bonus-points" options like when you hear the announcer shout "double kill" or something and the game gives you a little medal as if to say, "*Great job, have a sticker!*"

Ugh.

Probably the Chief. Worth a tiny bit, but nothing more.

Really though, I never want to experience that again.

The [Leviathan Breath] twirl-a-whirl is horrible. Besides the constant urge to vomit, it comes standard with flaming mushrooms, flaming roots, and flaming Goblins.

All-around nightmare fuel, even without the screams.

Oh, the screams... straight to the vault with those.

100% repressed.

I don't mind killing monsters if I have to survive. Monsters are evil things that only think about eating me and murdering stuff, but goblins?

Goblins talk: they have real voices, with words and stuff.

I'm not about that.

Not at all.

Anyways, for some obvious reasons: there weren't too many survivors who came out of that mess, and as the smoke cleared away it all settled down quickly enough.

It was a bit embarrassing.

Outside of the blast-radius, there were still dozens more gobs- even after that crazy-spinning. I could see them, weird eyes all staring and looking scary.

I can't keep up [Leviathan Breath] magic for a super long time. It has a cool-down of sorts depending on how much I use, and I'm not a big snake. My lung capacity is lacking a bit, and [Leviathan Breath] seems to put an emphasis on the "breath" part.

End of the day, even with magic I'm just a snake.

Small, no venom to speak of, with fangs that fail to puncture mushrooms 9/10 times I try and practice my [Super Deadly Bite] attack.

So, there I am, looking for any swath of ground not covered in plant matter. My mind's set completely on escaping my inevitable doom, still wriggling and spinning around to try and face all my enemies at once in an effort to look dangerous.

I was ready to spit fire balls in vain as I pissed myself to the early grave... and I basically missed the fact that none of the goblins were even making a single effort to try and attack me again.

It took me a full minute of doing the [Special Worm Roll] and waiting for the next round of arrows, or swords, (or axes and sick-looking spears) before I noticed that instead of another assault, they had all thrown down their weapons and bowed.

Bowing, towards me.

Not just ordinary prostrating: they were legitimately heads-on-the-ground-style groveling.

Their ambush had failed so badly, that they were actually begging me for forgiveness.

Hisss...

So, I thought maybe I'd gotten a bit stronger after the Megalodon.

But it's more than a bit, I think.

I've also been travelling up. In every game I've ever-played, "up" in a Dungeon typically means weaker enemies.

I don't think a magical serpent from the depths of hell was something they expected.

Hiss...

Well, anyways: that's more or less how I became worshiped.

As of this moment, I am the Tiny-Snake God's Mortal instrument. May all tremble at the force of reckoning beneath his name.

I'm a bona fide Divine Being.

Praise the Snake.

Chapter 83

The Pugly Tribe is a great and ancient group of Subterranean goblins.

Apparently formed long ago by the ancestors of the castaways who lived in the grounds overhead. Since then, these goblins have adapted to the environment, using their wits and ingenuity to carve out a living in the underground of the Dungeon. Together, they have survived in a zone beneath the Great Forest, rallying together to defeat the beasts and creatures which once threatened them. It seems that the solution for maintaining a Dungeon-zone's difficulty is adding goblins, and waiting a few generations.

Of course, after a few hundred generations, you're bound to have a feud or two. One goblin taking another goblin's favorite rock, or eating the last fried snake-sandwich. There's likely going to be a bit of bad blood.

So, occasional tribal wars.

This sort of thing leads to fractures, which leads to tribes splitting, which in turn leads to Goblins worrying about their own kind, as well as the usual monsters.

Still, through constant vigilance, the Pugly Tribe has apparently defended its odd borders and homeland, since growing in population, fractured off, and growing again. Eight times, if I'm supposed to believe what I'm hearing.

They've even got some cave-doodles.

Interesting stuff. Looks like they used to not look so goblin-ee, but I guess the Dungeon will probably have that sort of effect over a couple thousand years.

Anyways: seems likely that all goblins found in the great Dungeon Networks of the Labyrinthian region, or even the "Deep-Dungeon" (if goblins live that deep) have originated from this very place.

Ah, yes: how do I know all of this?

Well...

[Goblin Language - Comprehension]*
     1,000 Points.
Ha...

Ah, well. It wasn't actually called *[Goblin Language – Comprehension]* but that's a lot easier to pronounce. It was *[Lukra-blah-blah-something-something]* but that wasn't hard to figure out when they kept repeating it over and over while pointing to themselves. I'm wise to [Voice of Gaia's] tricks by now.

You're shaking your head. I know you are.

Listen, just because I talk to myself all day in an effort to maintain sanity doesn't mean I can't tell.

Oh, I can tell.

Before you judge me, by all means, please: let me know the last time an entire species started praising you as god.

Anyone?

Anyone at all?

Yeah? Nobody?

That's what I thought.

Hiss...

Well, if you're wondering: it's awesome.

I'm living the dream here.

Sure, I spent a bit of my hard-earned points, I've still got a ton more. I'm positive I can find a way to get about 3,000 or so.

Can't be that hard.

I'll use the Goblins to help me find bigger monsters, and then I'll get to work. So, no problem. Spending those points was totally worth it.

No regrets.

Hiss....

A little regret.

See, the Goblins in the Pugly Tribe are probably smarter than the average Goblin, they can talk and use some sentences and such- though that's not really saying much in the grand-scheme of things.

They're like Tarzan when he tries to speak with Jane, but midway through the movie- where it's basic sentences at best.

So yes, you got me. Just a tiny-little-itty-bitty portion of regret for spending those points.

But it's still convenient.

And it was a lot cheaper than the [Human languages]

I mean, it was totally half-off. Like [Voice of Gaia] wanted me to buy it.

Of course I would.

Of course.

Anyways, most of the knowledge I've gathered so far came from a mix of talking to [Voice of Gaia] and looking at the cool cave-drawings that the Elders of the Pugly Tribe were very proud of. There is a detailed history there, if a little bit confusing and scatter-brained, I can put the pieces together with a bit of help.

The Elders, they're like wizards almost: but more adorable and a little harder to take seriously. They have cute little staffs, they smile- but they're missing a lot of teeth.

They laugh a lot, cackling sort of like you might expect.

Adorable.

I think they're harmless.

No way something so cute could be dangerous, right?

Right?

I'm completely right, I know- but that's not really the best part! You might right now be asking: why Pugly? Has he finally lost it?

No- maybe? Doesn't matter.

You're right to ask both those things, no judgement.

I mean, the Goblin tribe's formal tribe title is *Lukra'Dotreka'Mahabitu*, which means Tribe of the Shadows: Lessers to the Great Ones Above the Root and Stone…

Or whatever.

They're totally goblins, exactly how one might imagine them to look...

Only with pug-like faces.

Pugs.

Like the dog, pug. Scrunched in, wrinkled, sort of adorable disproportionate eyes and nose. They sniff everything, and if they run around, they do a funny "panting" thing after it.

Just "Woof" y'Know?

Thus "Pugly." Pugly Goblins.

I remember when I was a human: pugs were great! Of the little canine variations, they were far superior to their competitors, such as- but not limited to that evil little chihuahua I used to have to dog-watch all the damn time.

It's not like I can talk anyways, so I'll think about them however I want.

Pugly, woofly: they're adorable little guys, every last one of them. I never owned a Pug when I was alive as a human, but I always thought they were funny dogs. Friendly too, when they weren't adamantly barking at some perceived threat:

Mail-men, joggers, cars, unlucky guys taking their mother's pet-Chihuahua for a walk at night before then abruptly getting robbed and murdered.

Hissss...

Bad memories there. Push those down, way to the back- wayyy back there.

No, the Goblins of the Pugly Tribe don't bark, they talk a lot like grunts and guttural sort of noises that form up into almost-like sentences. Even the smartest of the elders seem to speak that way, but if I could find a way to specifically demand it- I'm sure they would try to bark.

The closest I've heard is the sound/word for "danger." That comes out a lot like "Worf" or "Wort" depending on if it's a bad, or really bad.

Wort Wort Wort.

But yeah... goblins.

Goblins, goblins, goblins.

I'm sitting on a throne in a half-dome auditorium sort of cavern where they set me up. There's an attendant feeding me as many glowing mushrooms as I can eat, and there are a couple "Guard" gobs with clubs and bows looking at me with great respect, and there are about three hundred others just cheering for me.

It's gotten pretty loud, and all their words are overlapping, but I think they're saying things like "Divine Beast!" and "Benevolent Savior" and "Champion of our people!" Fists in the air, jumping about, excited adorable little faces.

The Elders are even making cool magic swirls and such with their weird root-staffs and crystal pieces. I feel like they're showing off a bit.

Meh, whatever.

It's nothing to worry about. I'm a gosh-darn deity. I've never felt better about things.: This is the kind of reincarnated life I would have been hoping for.

It's nice.

Seriously, what could go wrong with this?

Snake Report - Blatant Foreshadowing: **"Everything."**

Chapter 84

Snake Report: Life as a False God, Day 5

Being the all-powerful ruler of a Goblin Tribe is something everyone should have a chance to do.

Being in charge is great.

Very fulfilling work.

Goblins have been coming to me with problems, usually with sober looking and adorable faces close to tears- and I solve them.

Example:

> *"Great God of Tiny Snake. Homes Ruined, monsters destroy."*- Hunched back old-man Goblin

Ah ha! An interesting problem indeed, but have no fear my faithful follower!

Using my advanced and (currently) unparalleled intellect, I understand the Tarzan-like request to mean: *"A horde of giant horned lizards came and destroyed one of the small Pugly Tribe villages nearby."*

It seems only the main camp of the Tribe is here, and there are smaller settlements tucked away around its perimeters.

So anyways, to continue: with a prideful hiss, I can slither off to investigate such claims with a healthy escort of tough looking Goblin warriors.

As it turns out, giant lizards are scary, but [Leviathan Breath] is much, much more terrifying.

Couple "Hoooos" and "Haaaas" followed by some [Earth Sculpting] and reconstruction efforts: presto.

Brand new village, nicer stone houses instead of shoddy root-carved messes, and more roasted lizard than a tiny snake and a band of goblin warriors know what to do with.

Or so I thought.

Goblins can eat a lot. Seriously, like a LOT. It's a wonder they don't all look like the blueberry girl from Willy-Wonka's factory.

I only partook at few nibbles.

All in all, not quite up to par with barbecued eel, but pretty close.

Additional information: giant lizards each net a whopping 0 points.

So... yeah.

I guess I'm going to have to look a bit harder for those than I thought, but that's okay.

Anyways, it's this sort of thing. My daily grind as supreme ruler.

I've been on-call saving the tribe from outside threats, or rebuilding things with Earth Magics, or just slithering around and getting a feel for how the Pugly tribe lives on a daily basis.

All I can say for certain is that life as a goblin is tough.

Hisssss... Very tough.

I've only been supreme goblin diety and ruler for a few days, but I think in a strange way I might have been lucky to have been born a snake instead. Not that being born a snake is starting off any easier, but Goblins have... well, conditions attached to their prolonged survival.

There are no solo goblins in the Pugly tribe. Instead, they all live in family units, usually of one strong looking male and a few females with their litters of goblin-children.

The stronger the Goblin, the more females, it's that sort of logic from what I can see.

But there are reasons for this.

Survival for a Goblin is almost as rigged as being born as a helpless snake in the deep Dungeon. One on one, a goblin really can't defeat anything but the weakest monsters. Even the ones who are good with a weapon.

In short, even the strongest Goblin is still pretty weak. The toughest Goblins I've seen are Mike and Ike, and I think they're no more than the equivalent of giant bat or a couple Spiders in basic strength. Probably a bit weaker.

But goblins are a lot like people in some ways.

People that went backwards and sort of... devolved or something.

They use tools, and bows. They have weapons, either salvaged from unfortunate humans or made from the natural resources around them. Stone axes, chipped iron swords, primitive short-bows. More important though, goblins work together against threats.

Like when I was ambushed and roasted a bunch of them, or like when that other goblin tribe came and messed with my goblins- and I roasted the ground in front of them and sent them all packing, or like when that other tribe came and I...

You get the idea: they were working together to take on a threat.

Their tactic is numbers, but alone, they're almost nothing.

At best, I'd call them the upper bottom of the Dungeon barrel.

The dregs.

The weakest of the weak, with no obvious chances of getting significantly stronger over time.

So far as I can tell from the Pugly tribe, they really don't grow much stronger. They don't seem to unlock skills or abilities that are very good for anything but eating poisonous things or going long periods without eating anything at all. I've seen nothing usual or exceptional from the ordinary Pugly goblin.

Really, to my eyes it looks like they hit a long-plateau of slow progress on their development at some point after adolescence, and they're more or less trapped there forever.

For but one single exception, this is true.

99.9% of the goblins seem to follow this exact track record.

They're weak, they can't survive on their own, and they don't seem to improve.

But that other 0.1% is a different story.

Hissss...

Those guys.

The goblin shamans.

Remember those Elders I mentioned? The cute and harmless ones with the cute staffs?

Well... yeah.

Them.

Let me be honest, I might have misjudged their character.

I got a bit distracted with how adorable they all were, and maybe took that to mean they weren't really all that scary.

Looks are misleading.

I should know by now, it's better to just assume everything is danger.

It's a reasonable rule to follow in the Dungeon.

But yes... those shamans. They're horrifying.

Wool over my eyes, fool me once- shame on me.

I need to boost my intelligence stat or something, because these sort of situations are really unpleasant.

Currently I'm surrounded by about five of them.

Hissss...

Shit.

> "Small Snake God, You bless us."

The first Shaman is speaking with a gravely sort of Grandpa-Goblin voice, face so wrinkled and scrunched it might as well be a crumbled bag with eyes peering out. He's raising his staff, gnarly old wood sort of oddly fixed with a rather large mana crystal, and he's pointed to the history drawn on the cave walls of the open room beside my throne.

> "You slay Chief. Terrible Chief, ruthless Chief. You slay enemies, and their chiefs bow. You build home. Many new to tribe. We grow much with your powerful magic. "

Funny thing to say. Really funny actually. They might have bodies as fragile as the family heirloom dishes you only take out on holidays, but if anyone has powerful magic here, it would probably be them.

Hiss...

I'd like to think that was meant as a joke, but there isn't a drop of humor in those words.

Very serious tone.

Violent, almost.

> "Yes."

The others are nodding in agreement from equally aged stoops and hunched backs.

> "Yes. Worst Chief... Terrible Chief dead. You grow tribe. Better, much."

Maybe they're trying to convince me.

Or, maybe they're just agreeing with themselves.

> "But more mouths... More feed. Too many, then not enough."

"Yes."

"Yes, not enough."

"Trouble..."

"Keee- trouble!"

I'm beginning to suspect becoming a Goblin Shaman takes a very long time.

If I had to compare this situation to anything, I feel like I'm in an elderly home, but all the old-folk have loaded P-90s instead of walkers. Those staffs are just radiating power.

"We know. Serpent... sacred. Touched by... gods."

The eldest figure is continuing, staff raising to glow with an intimidating swirl of mana to form patterns in the air.

"We see.... We know: you are Divine Beast. Still young..."

More murmurs of agreement in response to that. As much as I like being flattered, I'm starting to get a bit nervous from all the magic swirling in the air. Without even looking I know each one of them has more mana than I do, and that's seriously saying something. Frail looking bodies, old and hunched over, but absolutely overflowing with magic.

"But we have lived... Long."

"KeeeKeeee- Long! Long!"

Shouts are joining in, hisses through teeth-less gums, and awful grins. Their laughs are falling upon one another, and those eyes... Their eyes watch me now: Eyes holding to a far greater intellect than I anticipated. Dark beads hidden beneath terrible folds of aged skin and scars.

"We know."

Holy crud.

Horror movie line right there. All of them looking and turning their heads at the same time.

Crap.

With great effort here, I'm swallowing the urge to try and dig into my throne and escape. Instinct is just screaming to freeze: **"Don't move!"** is what it's telling me.

Over and over, just like that first encounter with the centipede.

I am greatly outmatched. To make matters worse, I've never fought anything that used magic.

I think that's why this is all so scary. Barely any monsters have magic, so far as I can tell. Unless you count the humans... who put me in a box, the Stone Crabs that almost killed me are the only thing I've seen, really.

"You seek power."

The eldest whispered.

"You lack attendant."

Another cackled, hoarse throat like dust and crumbled stone.

"You lack voice."

The maddening laughter was lifting up.

"We can give you, all."

The staff fell to point towards me, swirls of magic and energy spinning about as if an invisible hurricane.

The praising me and worshiping my actions definitely brought my guard down. They seemed so harmless my first few days. Magic nothing more than fancy lights and swirls.

They'd been hiding it.

"A trade... for Tribe, we will give."

"Yes!" The others shouted. "Yes, a trade!"

Oh, I don't know if I like where this is going.

"Slay creature, that guard surface."

The eldest Shaman leaned in, toothless smile widening into a disgusting grimace as the others broke into another bout of terrible laughter.

"Then we give, what you seek."

Snake Report:*Kill Quest Received*
Difficulty:★★★★★★★★★★

Chapter 85

Snake Report: Life as a False God, Day 8

There were more basic requests the next few days. I fried a few more lizards, built some more stone-houses, I sat on my throne: but once all was said and done I set out without an escort.

This was mostly due to a growing sense of anxiety.

Still, I was familiar enough with the area to feel reasonably confident I'd end up in the correct place, and the directions from the creepy goblin shamans were pretty clear.

Up the "Great" root tower, and defeat the beast which lurks at the exit to the Forest above.

Their brooding hints and creepy laughter was also strong hints this wasn't exactly a *"Request."*

More of a polite: *"You're doing this, or else"*

Both instinct and human perspective settled together in agreement with the gut-feeling they were probably going to try and put an end to me if I didn't ramble on out of their roost.

They wanted me gone.

Adorable little pugly faces are great until they start laughing like wild-jackels and letting out uncomfortable amounts of magic from their staffs. The harmless old-folk 180 degree switch to dark and powerful warlock thing wasn't exactly a source of comfort.

But then: neither was the late-night glowing light illusion of a snake getting its head chopped off while green-dancing figures jumped around wacking the corpse with wooden poles.

Hints.

Lots of strong hints.

Maybe just open statement, but I made my expected bow-out to go off and deal with this [Kill-Quest] of sorts.

That's what Heroes do in a fantasy world setting right?

I might not be the greatest hero, but I suppose that's not the worst goal to strive for. It's important to have those.

Goals, I mean.

Get to the surface, eat real food, avoid death: These are all pretty reasonable goals I'm working towards. I guess I could tack on something heroic, to the end there.

But to be honest their offer was fairly appealing, implications aside.

If I interpreted it all correctly, somehow they were going to give me points- or maybe something similar to points? Maybe the points came when I killed the monster?

That was probably it, it's not like I want to go back down there and ask them.

I mean, they knew I was divine beast, which only [Voice of Gaia] had been able to note previously. They probably knew a few other things too.

More importantly though, they had obviously just given me a clear target. Somewhere ahead was a strong monster, and that was what I wanted... wasn't it?

Strong monster = Points.

Reward = More points?

Hard to go wrong here, long as I can keep myself from dying.

But, I'll admit: as I slithered off from the main goblin camp, I did feel a bit guilty. Leaving behind the many slumbering figures in the large cave, I had a feeling I could probably have been happy there.

It was a home, of sorts.

Goblins weren't bad company, and I was doing a lot of good for them. In the week or so among them, I'd improved their lives dramatically.

Better homes, safer villages, less danger from the local monsters that roamed around their borders. Even that main camp had been shaped and carved: the likes of which was now reinforced and carved away with rooms, and gates, shrines and large walls all fitting with traditional Tiny Snake God themes.

But it wasn't meant to be.

Slipping quietly past, unnoticed by the two watching pairs of eyes I had come to know as the goblins Mike and Ike, I pressed on along the upward trail without looking back.

Upward in a long spiral above the main camp, along a roughly carved staircase on the edges of a giant root towards my intended destiny.

It hadn't been that long since I'd come to this place, but for Monsters, Goblins really weren't so bad. They were a lot like people, and I guess that's something I've really been missing.

Human interaction: you don't get a lot of that down here.

Makes me wonder what happened to Miss Paladin.

After all that chaos at the Human Sanctuary, I never did find out what happened to her. All the talk in the halls was about what a nightmare the safe-zone magic being ruined was, or how horrible the "Dreaded Blue Death" had been.

Not a single peep about a Paladin who miraculously appeared that night.

Hiss...

In all the confusion, she probably went back to the surface with the first chance she got.

I certainly wouldn't blame her, if that were the case.

Probably just got out while she could, before someone tried to pin the blame on her too.

But thoughts like this... well, there's a time and a place. Right now, I'd say I'm probably in both the wrong place, and the wrong time.

I mean, looking down... I'm pretty high off the Dungeon-ground now. It's giving me flashbacks to a certain tower above a Tiny Snake Camp Alcatraz. If I peer over this wooden stair edge, I might see...

Hiss- no.

Bad plan.

Makes me queasy. Way too high up.

Phew.

But, while I'm looking, up ahead is something pretty neat. Snake-Periscope can be utilized both horizontally and vertically, after all.

It seems that the root here meets up with a bunch of others. They interlock all over the ceiling, and if I'm not mistaken I think a bunch of them are carved out. Like a weird set of roads in the sky.

Or the ground?

Well, they're all up there, and a ton of them too.

According to the Shamans of the Pugly Tribe, I just need to go up, but I feel like having a bunch of hallways carved out up here is probably convenient for getting around.

Huh...

I wonder... why don't the goblins don't use them?

A surprisingly insightful question coming from me, but now that I'm looking up here... I never saw anyone come up this path. Honestly, it looks like these things could act as highways from one side of this region to the other, no problems.

This is a serious convenience being ignored.

...

Or avoided.

...

Hisss...

You know for some reason, all of a sudden I have a terrible feeling about all this.

Chapter 86

Snake Report: Life as a False God, Day 8

Today I was bamboozled into being eaten alive.

It was... you already know.

To brush off a classic analogy: it was like walking a really long and spiraling plank while some old goblin-jerks threw back goblin wine and cackled over their stupid goblin faces.

Alright, the concept I was aiming for got thrown-off there a bit, but I'm still a little flustered. Mostly on account of being gobbled right on up like a stray piece of blue-scaly-spaghetti.

Being eaten alive will shake someone up.

Yeah, listen here: I don't care who they are: until they're drowning in stomach acid, they have no damn clue. It's really scary, watching yourself be dissolved, watching your healing be outpaced and the burning sensation start to... Hisss...

I'll stop there, and just say the following: it's dead.

It's dead Jim.

This is really the only thing that matters, in the end. The tiny snake struggle is real nowadays.

Death on all sides.

If I think I'm safe, I'm probably wrong.

Still... there's another object of concern I think should be considered now.

I really have no idea where I am.

Absolutely no idea.

See, when this all started- I did know (relatively) where I happened to be. I'd made my way to the top of the giant root pillar like I was supposed to.

All the way up, to where it carves out as a passageway, and. I slithered on by past hundreds of crazy Goblin-carvings and ritualistic looking symbols, as I made my way with my tongue tasting cool and sweet air.

To the surface.

Honest: I was so close.

Closer than I had ever been.

It was in plain sight.

My body just sort of locked up when I realized this. That breeze of fresh air was something else- like a once in a lifetime moment. After living my entire snake-life in a dark and gloomy Dungeon of ancient mysterious and terrible monsters, fresh air is like a magic, in and of itself.

It's like a drug, ittakes a hold and doesn't let go.

I wanted to stay wrapped up in the feeling forever.

I was totally and completely dumbstruck.

So, maybe you can imagine: when I came to the final expanse of the root, I might have let my guard down a tiny bit. Right where Dungeon gave way to roots and soil, to a final open portion before the outside world.

There on the precipice of a rough gathering of earth, branches, and feathers: I sat like a statue.

Total ignorance.

I was wrapped up in the beautiful light of an early morning- not a presumed morning where I just took a guess and judged the glowing fungi and crystals to mark some rhythm of time passing, but a *real* morning.

The sun rising through distant leaves and branches, with the warm embrace of wind and heat that made me think it might be summer somewhere beyond the massive expanse of tree trunks the size of sky-scrapers.

They billowed out in all directions I could see, colors of green and brown and faintly above: blue.

The sky.

Hissss... How long had it been?

For a few precious seconds, I was thinking of nothing else.

I'd achieved Snake-zen.

No Quest. No scary Goblin Shamans. No Monsters to kill. No humans calling me a calamity on mankind, and no need for Points. None of these things mattered.

Beneath the crazy green glow of an impossible forest, I was a total peace. The leaves shifted in the distance beyond the root-cavern's opening, the songs of birds and air sweeping through rustled and chirped with the echoes of my memories from a previous life.

And so, in this state of mind, I just sort of sat there defenseless. In awe of everything, soaking in the first true light I had really ever seen in this life, as the Giant Owl whose nest I just rudely intruded on turned its head and then swallowed me whole.

Yeah.

I messed up.

Hisss...

I messed up pretty bad.

Seriously bad- I mean, I was eaten alive. I didn't even have time to complain before I ended up down a gullet and into a bunch of stomach acid. My second life flashed before my very eyes, followed shortly by my first one, and maybe the faintest glimmer of one before that?

All up in the air at this point. Or it was, really.

I was, more specifically.

I was in the air.

See, the Owl... Well, it made a big mistake.

After swallowing a tiny snake, if decided to spread its wings, get a bit of movement in after breakfast. No matter how big and impossibly strong a giant Bird-Monster might be though, you know what it really shouldn't do?

Eat something **[Toxic]**

Chapter 87

Snake Report: Life as a False God, Day 9/Lost in the Surface World, Day 1

[TOXIC]
Toxic Flesh. Dangerous if consumed.

[Unique Traits] are things I haven't ever really considered much until after the fact.

I mean, sure- I read them, but I guess I never really thought them through.

Never in my mind did I consider getting eaten whole a serious method for achieving victory.

As they saying goes: A win's a win.

The bird wretched me up at an altitude of a few thousand feet. I was showered like a 747 dumping on a fly-over state, surrounded by odds and ends- bits of bones and droplets of Bird-stomach-related things.

It's raining snakes, hallelujah

I guess owl-monsters in this world can cough up more than just pellets, not that it really mattered. Apparently, by my actions of surviving on a diet of almost nothing but poisonous Mushrooms and mana-crystals, I've gone and made myself a really unpleasant meal for would be predators. So unpleasant that after coughing me back up, the Giant Owl went and died.

How do I know for sure?

[Northern Forest Guardian - Legendary Owl Slain: 1,000 Points]

Hisss... A very encouraging message to receive, if not for the other circumstances requiring my attention.

[EXTREMELY TOXIC: UNLOCKED!]
Extremely Toxic Flesh. Fatal if consumed.

Ah, there's another one.

Off in the yonder distance of the horizon, I watched its body plunge lifeless through a canopy of giant trees with a shower of feathers and tree branches before disappearing from my sight. I might have taken a bit of satisfaction in this, if I didn't promptly follow-suit by doing much of the same.

"SMACK"

A shower of leaves and a shower of pain.

"CRACK!" That was a branch, "CRASH" Another branch.

"SMACK."

"THUD."

It's important to stick the landing with at least a portion of your body unbroken, but if I could see my health bar, I think there's a very high probability it might be in the red. If I could even lift my head to check, I imagine I might seem more like the letter "Z" than any living snake has a right to.

Hisss...

Active, passive, magical Healing or not: this might be time to take a breather.

Chapter 88

Unlike many other portions of the known Dungeons, even when considering those with regions of arguably higher difficulty and danger: The Nether-Forest has long since been considered unique. More so, it holds a rare title as an "Open Network."

In essence, this is the description of a Dungeon zone as an "Open Network" is typically reserved for regions that present more a massive-expanse than a series of tunnels and passageways. Though there are certainly other examples known and explored, there are none that quite match the Nether-Forest's sheer scale.

Quite the contrary to most zones (where caverns rarely open up to even a tenth of the region's great size) no matter how thick the foliage of the plant-life can gather along the bedrock, a group can never be directly separated from any other region within the expanse. Beyond those few and rare side-tunnels which have been noted to lead out towards deeper depths and zones beneath the earth, the entire area is a massive and open cave.

Known and infamous for its position beneath the core of the Great Forest (one of the few portions of the Northern continent not established and occupied by mankind) the Nether-Forest was long sought as a potential trade route to the far northern-most regions of the continent's Dungeon. Tracing back along known history, Entire Merchant alliances have tried and failed to establish some level of profitable lines within the region, none quite managing to do anymore than waste their coin. The terrain, while lacking high-class monsters, is still rugged, and occasionally frequented by mana-swells during the Northern Storm season.

Still, up until the destruction of the local sanctuary, it was favored as one of the more unique and accessible areas possessing an attribute of "leveled" terrain, both in context of danger by local monster inhabitants and geographic manifestations. While not quite as useful to merchants and investors, it has been known as an ideal location for Adventurers (Either Guild sponsored or of private means) to learn their craft with a lower rate of fatalities than what might ordinarily be expected.

In one final not of reference: the Subterranean Nether Forest is also one of the few known Dungeons to possess direct influence and contact from the surface (however dangerously inaccessible this might be) due to its unique physical interruptions.

Those famous and alluring structures, twisted and gnarled along strange routes. Some of petrified and ancient stone, but most of living root. These

Pillars, their forms diving deep into the earth from the mighty expanse of the Great Forest above ground with intertwining and enormous size, are the means that most Adventurers seek to travel this area. Either by route in which to safely enter known hunting grounds and harvest the Dungeon monsters which prowl the region, or for the naturally occurring plants or crystals which form in the mana-rich environment.

For Zane, climbing up to the root-network was never a simple task.

Even for trained and professional adventurers, the effort was always pushing the limits of excessive both in planning and execution: first was the challenge of plotting their route.

In his younger days, still eager to prove himself to the Guild, Zane had often roamed solo or as an escort for hire. Those first years especially, he had seen numerous expeditions to the region of the Labyrinthian region known as the nether-forest (more infamously known as the Goblin-zone, or as some might call it: the "Gob-zone") and he had in turn witnessed a wide variety of successes and failures. Many of those last, had come from ignorance.

Zane had made certain to learn from them.

Pulling on the line, a thick tethering of rope consisting of both twine and Iron-Bison hair, Zane dragged the last of his companions upon the small ledge of the overlooking pillar with a heavy puff of exertion. Each and everyone of them was drenched in sweat from the effort, but it had finally paid off.

They had taken to the last portion of the stone, reaching the rally-point often referred to by the Guild as *Citadel.* After climbing several hundred feet to reach this ledge, the reasons for this title were perhaps more obvious than most. Looking down might make any but madman dizzy, below the expanse of the cavern stretched out in the distance.

"Knox, keep look-out here. I'm going to scout ahead up the tunnel." Zane issued his command as he dropped the rope into waiting hands, turning back towards the material waiting behind them, feet carefully pressing on along the thin space of stone no more than a full pace wide. "Daxton, Ryker- follow when you're ready."

"Yes sir!" A voice replied somewhere over Zane's shoulder, as he pressed around the bend of rock and thick root, hands feeling the smooth surface of the root for thin but present handholds. carved out painstakingly for this specific purpose. The Citadel rally point was perhaps one of the safest places in the Subterranean Forest, with the sole exception of falling hazards. Not all of it was out in the open though.

Feet carefully places in a slow scooting motion, Zane finally felt the root give way beneath his left hand, finding air where wood and fiber had been before. Pulling the rest of his body along to find it, he stepped inside the passageway: into the true *Citadel*. His eyes adjusted slowly, darkness of the space barely illuminated by a single over-sized glowing mushroom. Stepping in closer Zane kneeled to the floor, fingers tracing along the wooden surface. The evidence was there, though not the source.

Closer, but not quite there.

"Younglings?" A voice called out behind him, as the Spearman Daxton stepped through the crevice of the root into the hollowed room. "Younglings, are you here?"

"They're not. Best you keep quiet." Zane replied, rising from the floor..

"Anything?" Another voice joined them, funneling into the hollowed space of the root beside them. "Knox says he can remain a lookout, but he's not seeing much of anything out there. [Keen-eye] or not."

"They were here." Zan replied. "Recently, if I were to guess. My bet is they came here after their first scouting efforts, so we're not far from the trail."

"That's good! They're still focused on the mission then?"

"So far as we know." Zane replied, considering. "Tell Knox he'll stay here. You too, Ryker."

"Me too? Why?" the man questioned. stepping in from the crevice-way with irritation clearly in his tone. "I can help Zane."

"No." Zane spoke with finality as he moved deeper into the room, looking up at the carved latter of handholds ascending a vertical tunnel far above their heads. "No, we'll need two of people if they come back injured. Climbing down from here isn't a simple matter."

"But-"

"I said no, Ryker. Leave the red-seal as proof if they show, and get them out. We'll catch up."

"What if they don't come back?" Ryker asked quietly, hushed tone in the sheltered space barely a whisper. "Do we just sit here and wait? Should we follow?"

"Yes, you should wait." Zane replied with a gruff voice. "Stay put until we come back, understood?" Zane waited, before turning back to the brooding face.

"Understood, Ryker?"

"Yes sir." The reply came, if forced.

"Good." Zane turned back to wall, motioning to the other man present. "Daxton, lets get a move on. If they're still on mission, we'll know where to find them."

"Yes sir." The Spearman replied, beginning to climb with a renewed vigor.

"And Ryker?" Zane set his hands onto the carved sections of root, beginning his own ascent with quick and efficient motions.

"Sir?"

"Don't worry." Zane said. "We'll find them."

Chapter 89

Snake Report: Life as a False God, Day 9/Lost in the Surface World, Day 2

This forest is 100% horrifying.

If all of the surface is like this, I might be better off in a cave beneath the ground, because this is nutter-butters.

Extra-stuffed nutter-butters.

That "*Legendary Owl*" I killed?

Yeah, well that's not the only dangerous than that up in here, let me tell you something: there are god-damn Dinosaurs.

Dine-Oh-Sores. Like, chase your jeep wrangler through a fucking jungle- "Think they'll have that on the tour?" Really big and hungry things, with way-WAY too many teeth.

Some of them seem to hunt in packs.

Yeah.

As per usual, it's me against the world.

Take no prisoners: Snake Camp [*Isla Nublar*] is in full effect.

It's a one snake team. We've hired no Newmans, we've left no chance for error. There are no electric fences or computer programs to go awry.

I've pulled out ever single trick in the book.

Kill or be killed.

Dog eat dog.

I stick to what I know.

My human life might as well have been a long and convoluted method to train someone on how to fight these terrible things- because unlike the other monsters I've had to go up against so far, these had their place in Hollywood.

Childhood movies my family used to both terrify and fascinate me.

We had safety locks on all out door-knobs from age 7-12 just so I could sleep at night without fear of velociraptor attack. I veto'd a manual transmission car after driver's ed, simply because I thought if a T-rex were chasing me I'd most-definitively stall the clutch and die.

What I'm trying to say in a convoluted and rambling manner, can be summed up like so: unlike everything else in this world, I was mentally and theoretically prepared for these exact kinds of scenarios.

My human life had actually readied me for something.

Know thy enemy.

Instinct has no place here. This is purely based on a human's most powerful motivating force.

Yes... no it's not intellect.

It's obviously fear.

Lots and lots of **fear**.

See, I know very, very well: there is only one thing you can do when faced with dinosaurs.

I've seen the movies, and there is only one thing that has proven successful for those not possessing the beautiful and beloved Plot-Armor.

That's right.

You follow the tried and proven plan of [*NOPENOPENOPE*] and turtle up your defenses like a Terran on their last mining base with a full 200/200 of nothing but Siege tanks and Mules against a Zerg with every base on the map.

Lock the doors, bar the windows, pull the blinds: stall- but not bathroom stalls, because those will get you killed.

Tiny-Snake Camp *Isla Nublar* was created with that exact plan in mind.

Operation [**No Thank you**] was drafted and put into action.

To the best of my potential, this was in full effect by the time I got attacked. Hisss...

Prepared or not: as always, it was terrifying.

Chapter 90

Snake Report: Life as a False God, Day 9/Lost in the Surface World, Night 2

Night has arrived, and I am still alive.

The Forest is quiet, but in the distant trees I can hear the faint sounds of movement, of calls and shrieks.

I know: they're out there.

Beneath the unreasonably thick canopies of the giant trees, it's almost as dark as the Dungeon tunnels. Pitch black, and lacking the once taken-for-granted bioluminescence of the blue mushrooms. So, in some ways, it might actually be worse.

Even me, a being who has lived an entire life beneath the ground: as the sun has now set, it's very difficult to see much farther than ten feet in any direction.

Not that it matters, currently.

I don't really want to see what's out there. Far as I know, there is nothing in this forest I want to be friends with.

There are the only hunters, and the hunted.

Unable to safely leave camp *Isla Nublar,* I'm hesitant to say anything further. If there are other species of forest-dwellers not intent on devouring all and every, I'd love to meet them, but I'm confident natural selection weeded out the friendly folk a long time ago.

Even if that isn't the case, I'm still not going to leave the shelter. These are deeply troubling times.

Behind the scrambled wall of rock, small peep holes let in the night air and what little moonlight seems to find its way down to the forest floor.

It's like camping, only I have a vault instead of a tent.

Hiss...

The small shrine I've made to my lord and savior, the Tiny Snake God, brings me little comfort.

Beyond the obvious threat of powerful predators, there is a much more obvious set of problems presented.

The human-logic that picked Magic at the start of all this has most definitely paid for itself in full. I'd be dead a hundred times over if the applications weren't so versatile, and I have a feeling survival in this world would been close to impossible with those other options.

[Venom] or [Consumption] or [Massive] probably wouldn't have cut it.

No matter how strong I could have been using those, there's no way in hell I would willingly tango with the creatures prowling around outside my make-shift barricade.

But magic has some limits.

For example, [Earth Sculpting] only works on earth.

If a Forest floor is made up almost entirely of inter-woven roots, with just a tiny little bit of actual dirt and stone in-between them... well, that doesn't seem to be very helpful, now does it? There's stone underneath, but it's having a difficult time getting up to where I can use it.

I ran into this scenario before. You might remember.

Now, you would think I might have thought of some sort of alternative plan for this type of situation after the goblins scared me so bad I might have peed a little. I couldn't burrow into the ground and escape, so human-side froze up and left everything on [Instinct] to handle.

It appears that when being unable to use choice number two with "Fight or Flight," Instinct's immediately implemented default-setting is to try to and everything on fire in a blind panic.

Not always the best plan, despite what some might tell you.

I guess it doesn't matter if it's goblins or dinosaurs, this plan works about the same way, and that's good.

Lots of magic fire = Lots of possibly assailants being on fire = Tiny snake not being dead.

But, you know what this is not good for?

Maintaining a low profile.

Burning down a more or less perfect circle of forest is a very good way to attract attention. Hisss...

Quite a lot of attention...

Fire, smoke, trees and foliage aflame with a brilliant blaze of heat and natural light. It's eye catching at first, especially with the magical elements of it mixed in. swirls of green and mana turning over the whipping grasps of ember as they simmer out to coal.

If I could have hidden my presence before, the possibility is more or less gone in its entirety. This tiny dome of earth is like an obvious and ugly pimple on the scorched forest floor. You couldn't overlock this if you tried. I quite literally, stick out.

I would stick out more, if possible- but there's not even enough actual earth for me to do it. The ground might as well be entirely choked over by roots, and as much as I've listened to [Voice of Gaia] tell me I have an affinity for flame, I'm not really sure that flame has an affinity for me.

Sitting in the shoddy and magical molded version of a primitive slow-cooker, my efforts to set anything else on fire are pending. I'd rather not be baked alive.

But...

"Grrrraaaaaa... Creeeee! Cra! Cra!"

The sounds that leak in through the makeshift earth-pimple I'm calling a Snake Camp are deeply troubling.

I'm quite soundly trapped here, unless I want to slowly try to burn my way through a few dozen layers of roots and possibly melt into a snake-puddle.

"Graaa?"

I can't speak dinosaur, but instinct is telling me that's probably *"What's this weird rock?"*

"Creee?"

That's probably a *"Can we eat it?"* sort of question.

"CRACRA?"

Translation: *"Yes, I think so!"*

Hmm... Something is most definitely chewing on my little rock-camp.

I can't see much of anything, but they're moving around out there now. I can tell from the saliva that smells like certain death, dripping through my peep-holes.

"CRA! CRA! CRA!"

Yep.

"CRA! CREEEEEEEE!"

Wow, they've pulled my camp out of the root, they're really going at it now. This little rock-bubble is making uncomfortable crumbling sounds.

"GRRRRRAAAAA! GRAAAAAAAA!"

Yep. This is fine.

A whole pack is out there, unless the sounds are deceiving me.

This make-shift rock bubble is absolutely not going to survive the night. I can hear the walls cracking.

I think I've got maybe five minutes left before they're on me.

But this is fine.

Totally fine.

It's times like this, I'm reminded of a famous quote from my human life.

> "When life gives you lemons, you need to make lemonade."

To hell with it all.

I came here to get some points.

Hisss...

Let's get some points.

Chapter 91

Swordmaster Zane:

Along the ceiling vine-networks overlooking the subterranean forests, Zane lead at a fierce pace. Step after upward step, his muscles had long since fallen into the regular and established rhythm he'd often trained for, strength pushing him on along the twists and turns of the wooden and twisting halls.

Glowstone in hand, the glass illuminated those strange walls with a peaceful light, odd shadows muffled and catching the hand-scratched carvings of instructions and guides throughout the ages. Some were almost polished away, etchings barely slivers in the fiber, while others looked fresh: almost brand new. Zan stared with intensity as he passed these by, but in the end it was Daxton who called out for his attention with true findings.

"They posted a seal! Far-left tunnel!" Daxton shouted from down the ways, echoing stomps of heavy boots plodding along back to the agreed intersection. "It looks like they were trying for one of the larger-tribes in the center-region." His spear dropped with a loud thump against the floor as he raised up the wax coated parchment for Zane to read himself.

"*Lukra* then... It's got to be." Zane hissed with displeasure, mind racing ahead. "They're not confident enough yet to head directly there, so we've got a good chance at catching them before they reach a downward route. If we're lucky, they'll still be making their way towards the center." Zane took the paper and scanned it over once more before reaching into the small pouch on his belt and pulling out a portion of chalk to mark a quick symbol alongside it and handing it back. "Post it back up, we'll move out from there. Double pace."

"Yes sir." Daxton replied, voice determined.

As they began again, Zane took lead down the twists and turns- more than living up to his command. Double-pace, glow stone lofted barely enough to properly illuminate more than twenty paces in either direction: Twice he stumbled direction into a monster's den along the passage-way, and twice his sword struck down any foes that happened to make effort to slow their pace.

Still, as the hours stretched on, and Daxton's heavy breath made echoes through the confined tunnels and winding-nature of the root-passages, Zane found himself forced to slow. They couldn't afford injury, and without

Daxton, Zane's options for rescuing multiple injured would be greatly reduced.

Three younglings, especially injured, would be a severe test to his capacity alone.

"We'll make camp along the next open passageway. I'll take first watch." Zane spoke quietly, slowing his jog to a brisk walk as they turned the next bend. Glow-stone raised up to confirm, the markings carved matched those of his memory: Not a safe zone, but a relative refuge.

They could rest here, if only for the night.

"Yes sir." Daxton replied, grateful as he sat down with a loud clunk of armor and weight. Leaning his spear against the wood behind him, he sat back, breathing still not quite settled from the exertion of the day's travelling.

In the moments that followed, as Zane scouted to final edge of the hall, he was soundly asleep.

There was skill Zane considered no less desirable than mastery of any martial weapon: to be capable of slumber at a moment's notice.

In a Dungeon, even in the weaker zones, it was truly a blessing only given to the rarest few. Even now, having been an Adventurer for most of his adult life, having acquired skills some might only dream of: Zane still needed time to find himself at rest outside a sanctuary. Even then, it would not be true sleep. Not like the peaceful snores of his companion in the distance, anyways.

Setting himself to meditative stance, Zane watched and waited, focusing on the air and sounds within the root-carved tunnels. Reaching out, he sensed for motion, awaiting its presence in any of the usual forms.

Though monsters were far less common in this area, there were still some beasts which roamed the ceiling highways- especially off the beaten trails and among the smaller routes Zane and Daxton now rested. Though not a threat to someone of Zane's own caliber, an ambush could wound or maim even the strongest of warrior.

So he focused, and listened.

To the far off echoes of distant things too far to understand or identify.

To the brush of faint wind, whipping in from the open air passages off in the far-off routes they had no need to take.

To the strange rumblings overhead. The many... strange rumblings. As if distant explosions were crashing atop and among the Great trees of that dreaded forest, Zane could feel them shaking through and rippling along the ceiling and the roots. Even their path, carved from within the excessive size of a great-root seemed to trembled at the onslaught.

A battle of behemoths was undoubtedly occurring. Forces of true power, than few could ever hope to rival. Beast that might make even Zane falter with fear. There were many reasons that men remained apart from the Great Forest. Such was the realm of Elves or beasts, where human-kind had even less of a place than the Dungeons beneath that cursed soil.

Another thunderous boom rippled on through the ceiling and wood, shaking beneath and around them enough to rock Daxton's spear from its resting place along the wall- perhaps waking him with a loud clatter if not for Zane's intervention- trained hand catching it and setting it quietly on the floor instead.

There were things more powerful than any man.

On nights such as this, Zane found he needed little to remind him.

Chapter 92

Snake Report: Life as a False God, Day 9/Lost in the Surface World, Day 3

Well... good news everyone.

I have those precious points.

Apparently.

Although most of the small monsters didn't seem to give anything (and I use the word "Small" loosely) the monsters that did must have added up.

It also probably helped that there were some rather large monstrosities involved in some of the recent events. Jeep-wrangler in 5th gear, sort of monsters.

It's a relative scale, that sort of thing.

Think one of those diagrams where a person is standing next to an image of a blue-whale. When you come at the world from my perspective: that's pretty much everything in this forest- but, even when put next to me, there have been some examples where the [Kaiju Emergency Alert System] might've started ringing.

Still, I've managed to obtain what I came here for. All of it and a little extra. I've got the stupid points. I've conquered my enemies and fashioned a throne from their bones.

Or something close.

Not that close.

I'm laying in a bush, covered in vomit actually.

No throne to speak of, not even one made of porcelain.

Was it worth it?

Hiss...

No.

No, it was not worth it.

The lowest point in my existence has been reached. In line with that, actually I've got a new title.

"[**Voice of Gaia**], tell me my titles."

[Level 86]
[TITLE: DIVINE BEAST, LEVIATHAN, GUARDIAN, ENEMY OF
MANKIND, *CALAMITY*]

Hiss...

Yeah. Calamity: *an event causing great and often sudden damage or
distress; a disaster.*

I'm a disaster.

Grew up hearing that often enough, but now it's official.

[Voice of Gaia] is like George Washington. It can't tell a lie.

At least I don't think it can.

Sometimes it just chooses not to talk, but it doesn't lie.

Hiss...

Well, it all started off well enough. Battle and violence and all that.

Combat to the death is something everyone should probably experience at
least once in their lives. I mean, maybe- in a controlled sort of environment,
where you're not actually going to die... wait, no. That would totally defeat
the point.

Maybe if you get tricked into thinking you're going to die, but it's actually
all safe?

Yeah, like that.

Everyone should experience it. I seriously think that the crazy fight-to-the-
bitter end is sort of like an existential journey of adrenaline.

It's a rush to say the least.

When my tiny-snake camp got broken by a pack of hungry monsters, and
there was no longer anything between my thin little scales and a bunch of
sharp teeth: I went and just embraced the chaos.

Kill or be killed, my instincts were all over the board.

Attack! React! Dodge! Move, move, move!

Human mind might as well have been completely blank. I was definitely in
some sort of nirvana-like "This is how it ends" peaceful mode. A weird
synchronized mix of complete calm, and absolute panic. While Instinct was
blasting magic and green-fire in massive swathes of dino-killing
destruction, Human mind was directional at best.

The quick "Hey, maybe shoot left, then right, then up" sort of communication.

It mixed well.

Extremely well.

Hundreds of dead, trees on fire, roots and bushes all burned to ashes and smoldering piles of dust. By the time I ran out of magic and got swallowed whole by a T-rex looking sort of fellow, I think I'd probably obliterated a solid mile of forest territory.

I fought the good fight, y'know?

Really did.

Still, can't win them all.

Not fair and square, anyways. Sometimes there's just no other way around it.

Combat ended with me laying immobile on the ground, much like some sort of scaly. A few loud "Stomps" and a bunch of teeth later, I was down someone's gullet with a clean gulp and swallow. Right down that giant lizard's throat before I could even realize it, on through into a sack of stomach acid.

Landed in there with an uncomfortable "splash" and realized that I couldn't breathe, could see, couldn't feel much of anything but a very nice burning sensation that started up pretty quick-like.

I think this is typically how most stories end.

Getting eaten is generally a death sentence after-all. Only known comeback from that was Jonas and the Whale.Really, that's the only way I've managed to live so long.

So that big lumbering idiot of a dinosaur didn't even have a full three minutes before it puked me back up and died.

[TOXIC] Strikes again.

But not just [Toxic] anymore…

[EXTREMELY TOXIC]

Took its sweet time, even with a title like that. Enough time that I was starting to think I might have been goner after all, but it finally worked its magic.

Victory with half my tail in the grave, I was coughed out onto the forest floor just in time to watch the creature that tried to eat me stumble off and give one last dramatic roar before collapsing with a heavy thump.

Dead on impact.

Impressive stuff.

That decision to eat almost nothing but poison might have been some stroke of idiot-savant type genius. First the Owl, now the dinosaur. The bright blue "don't eat me" scale coloration apparently isn't enough of a warning, but I guess I should just be thankful that none of the monsters I've run into so far seem to bother chewing their food.

Still, what I didn't realize at the time, was how effective it would be.

Let me ask you an honest question: What's more appetizing? A giant dead dinosaur, or a puked-up snake laying with half-digested contents of some other unfortunate creatures that were eaten for the previous meal?

Obviously, the dinosaur, right?

Right.

No tricks this time, that's exactly how it goes. "Big dead pile of food in plain sight? Better chow down! To hell with that weird squiggly blue thing in the pile of vomit over there healing all of its half-digest scales back together, we've got some good ol' fashion Dinosaur BBQ and Grill! Woohoo!"

That's how all these monsters seem to think.

It's just a big circle of fucked-up life out here: eat or be eaten. Nothing seems to go to waste as the scavenger types crawled out of the woodwork to do the dirty work. Teeth and fangs and claws... pretty gruesome. I wiggled away from that madness to tuck in under a tree root.

I closed my eyes to sleep, mind already fading off into the wonderous oblivion where Dinosaurs weren't real, and I was sitting at home on a nice sofa without any concern of something trying to eat me-

[Level Up]

... Hiss...?

[Level Up]

Hiss?

[Level Up]

HISS? I was just laying here, half dead. No action, all the other monsters I had fought with died awhile back, and it's not like the leveling system works on a time delay.

[Level Up]

So… what the heck?

[Level Up]

I don't get it...

[Level Up]
[Level Up]
[Level Up]
[Level Up]
[TITLE: CALAMITY]

What-

Oh.

See, then I heard it. Scattered out among the trees and singed forest floor, the sound was unmistakable.

Like the aftermath of a massive Jurassic Frat-party gone horribly wrong: Hundreds of puking and dying dinosaurs.

Chapter 93

Snake Report: Lost in the Surface World, Day 3

Ever heard of the terms *Biodegradable, Biomagnification,* or *Bioaccumulation*?

No points on the Snake-Report test if you haven't. That's probably normal.

I'd guess that most haven't heard of these, much less learned enough about them to pitch-in for team-trivia.

They're all slightly different, after all, but they're all equally important to consider sometimes. Ecological impacts can be had when considering each of them as a separate attribute to a substance or specific mixture of chemicals.

See, back when I was a human, I think there were probably millions up millions of dollars spent on trying to determine if substances or chemicals had any of those qualities about them. Companies, Governments, 3rd party Agencies: people had a pretty big interest in knowing the details on these thing, and the basic premise behind why they were so important is fairly straightforward.

A chemical that isn't easily biodegradable, that can bioaccumulate, and also naturally biomagnifies through the food-chain?

Well, that chemical has the potential to wreck just about absolutely everything.

I present you with an example:

Imagine you're a mushroom, with a very-very-very-*very* concentrated level of certain-death poison in your body. That "chemical" is apparently not very biodegradable, and can be bio-accumulated by any creature it doesn't happen to kill.

So... if say, a tiny snake eats a mushroom with this poison in it- and doesn't die... then eats more and more mushrooms with that same poison... well, obviously the snake is going to become much more dangerous than the mushrooms ever were-- right?

It's going to have a higher concentration of this bad "chemical."

That right there is both Bioaccumulation, and a very lesser degree of biomagnification. From the mushroom to the snake, that poison just got worse.

You picking up what I'm putting down here Tiny Snake class? That's science.

Boring human stuff, that fantasy monsters don't normally care about.

But see now, if you're a snake that eats poison, you probably just do it because you're hungry and you don't want to starve. You're probably not thinking "*Wow- I'm a slithering death-package for the next thing that tries to eat me*" you're just thinking "*Mushrooms don't try to kill me in a horrible manner now that I've gotten used to the delicious poisonous flavor, so they're safe to eat.*"

But,

Now imagine that a really large predator eats you.

Logically, that large predator is probably going to die, right?

"Duh," says the class.

Right, right, I hear you. Hold the boredom for a second.

So that giant predator obviously dies from poison... eventually. Maybe it takes some time, but after digesting a significant amount of healing flesh it dies at a slight delay.

In a perfect world, the poison in what it digested might dissipate with time, but we already confirmed it doesn't really- considering our tiny snake has been accumulating it. So, it sticks around- and though logically some other creatures besides the snake or predator might be able to break down that poison at a different/quicker rate, but what if they can't?

What if any predator that eats something this poisonous, dies before that can make a difference?

Well, there's the start of our problem.

If that poison sticks around and doesn't disperse naturally... well, then the next logical question is: what if a bunch of other predators come and eat that big dead one?

Well... they're going to find that the big dead predator was full of that very same poison, and if that poison was so concentrated?

Well, then it's probably going to kill them too.

So, Tiny Snake Class, what comes next? Let's follow the Monster-world circle of life. Things, die, and other things eat them (generally speaking) so now what?

Right.

What if even more predators come and see all these tasty looking and conveniently dead/dying creatures succumbing to poison- and then they eat them?

Hiss...

Connect the dots yet Tiny-Snake Class?

Yes: they're all equally screwed.

Equally screwed until the poison is diluted enough for the next in line to take a bite is able to NOT die from it, or whatever magical attribute the **[EXTREMELY TOXIC]** passive has in-play wears off.

Apparently eating highly toxic mushrooms and mana crystals for a living has turned me into the equivalent of a chemical disaster. I've magnified so much terrible stuff into my scales and flesh, I'm basically death turned adorable.

This ain't just PCBs and bird-eggshell integrity here: this is a bona fide **[Calamity]**

Hiss...

Carrying capacity for most predatory species is going to be significantly out of projections for the next few years. I can only imagine the long-term devastation that's going to follow as this sorts itself out.

In the meantime though, I willingly dedicate this unholy and merciless slaughter of the Forest's natural ecosystem to the Tiny Snake God.

As their faithful and devoted follower, it is my hope that at the very least this sacrifice pleases them.

Chapter 94

Snake Report: Lost in the Surface World, Day 4

Waking up, I can say I feel deep unease.

This is only made worse by the pure and uninterrupted silence outside of the root I had managed to drag myself into. The sound of nothing but a slight breeze, calmly overtaking the pleasant smell of stomach-acid-covered snake skin with a faint loft of wind.

Quiet... too quiet. Unnervingly quiet. My senses still seem to improve with every "level up" but I really can't hear anything.

Nothing at all.

From this safe and tucked away location, I can't hear anything stomping around, or screeching, or fighting. I can't even hear birds cawing. Instead, it's just... the wind? That's it... really, there's nothing else.

Not much like what I remember.

I'm not sure if this is a good thing or a bad thing, but the longer I wait down here, the more it's starting to freak me out.

Best to just get it over with.

Hiss... activating the periscope.

Ah.

Yes.

Nature.

Nothing but nature.

The only things in motion are the rustling branches of trees and the shifting light of the rising sun beyond them. It's as if the world has been emptied of its inhabitants, and the scenery replaced by a world free of everything but nature itself.

Beautiful.

Instagram-worthy.

This is, of course, if we ignore the hundreds of half-eaten dinosaur corpses covering the forest floor.

Like one of those ancient portrayals of a battlefield, bodies scattered along on top of bodies in complete and utter disarray. The carnage brought down upon this place is far past what I would recommend any young and aspiring natural disaster.

For once, I firmly believe that my oddly-bestowed title was rightfully earned.

Calamity... calamity indeed.

I truly feel like I might be the last living creature for miles.

Even the bugs are dead.

There are tiny piles of flies and beetles, just sort-of back down, legs up.

No one was spared.

Hiss...

I don't know how I feel about this, really.

The implications are... troublesome.

I didn't- and still don't like dinosaurs (and I've never been a huge fan of insects) but there is most certainly a sense of loss here. I've ruined a functional ecosystem just about as effectively as the Black Death ruined Europe. My presence alone has absolutely destroyed everything but the scenery. It's just me and the trees out here now.

I really am the *Blue Death*.

Eating or fighting other monsters fair and square is one thing, but I think this has a sense of "wrongness" about it. Strange as it sounds, slithering along the ground past the numerous examples of evidence present, I feel like I've committed some sort of grave taboo.

It also brings up the moral dilemma of using the tiny snake restroom. I think I'm permanently on the hook for burning my compost.

Hisss... avenues of thought I could never have expected.

Leaving the scene of the crime seems like the best course of action.

That's typically what I think most mass-murders or eco-terrorists would recommend.

So, I guess the only real choice is which direction to go... if I remember right: arbitrary North hasn't turned out badly yet.

Arbitrary North it is.

Going North...

Over the dinosaurs, and through the woods...

Ugh... slithering is not the best for long-distance travel.

When I had legs, I didn't appreciate the convenience. Going over stuff, taking longer strides-- it's easy-mode. I mean, if I hadn't been slightly out of shape, I could probably have jogged or run- sprinted even.

Slithering is more of a leisurely pace.

Variable speed, but nothing all that quick.

Maybe like... a couple slithers of panic mode, that's close to quick, but then I'm tired out.

I should figure out how to side-wind, like one of those desert snakes on the national-geographic specials. That would be faster.

If I move like... this- and this... and...

No... I suck at it.

This is slower than normal slithering.

I really thought I was onto something for a second there.

Hisss...

On the bright-side, dead dinosaur concentrations are finally fading off a bit.

Only after a full hour's worth of slithering, but they're not so prevalent among the landscape. Just a couple here, a couple there.

More or less seems to have run itself out.

Maybe [Extremely Toxic] degrades over time?

Not sure.

Still, nothing much is moving yet. Maybe a bird or two, way up there. No more giant owls, but at least a couple far-off signs of life.

I guess I didn't ruin everything. At least I've got that going for me.

Honestly, was starting to wonder if I'd unintentionally brought about the end of the world for a few minutes there.

I figure [Voice of Gaia] doesn't just hand out titles for no good reason.

But I guess I'm in the clear.

That's good.

Really though, I just wish I knew the full size of the forest.

From my unfortunate flight before being ejected from Owl-Airlines, I remember it being pretty damn big, but logically if I go straight in any direction long enough I might be able to come out on the other side.

It might take me awhile, but I think I can manage that.

Still... so far, I can't be sure I've made much progress, and it's very strange to be in a forest like this and have everything be so... empty.

Looking around, I can see the trees. Of course, they're everywhere: giant and towering things, like the big-brother of those famed Redwoods- only on steroids. I can see the smaller underbrush in patches where the light somehow makes it through, but it's mostly just flat forest floor of leaves and gnarly roots, and giant trunks.

Slither, slither, slither, a quiet stroll as the morning is slipping towards afternoon.

Hiss...

I have no idea where I am.

More or less I'm just following the beaten path, some sort of game trail. Avoiding the tall bushes and the more ominous shadowed areas, keeping the sunlight breaking through somewhere to my right side, but the further along I go- the more I'm starting to notice.

There are other things present here. If I look closely, I think in some places among those roots I can see ruins sticking up. Carvings and stone blocks scattered around- halfway to the grave via weathering. The trail I've been following seems more or less the same.

There is the occasional block or gravelly chipped portion, as if maybe it had been an ancient highway or something.

I'm getting a tomb-raider kind of vibe the further I go.

If the human side of me knew more about the world, I'm sure this might all be very fascinating. This was probably a city, or something like that. Ruins overgrown and covered by trees over ages and ages until barely anything is remaining visible on the surface. An ancient civilization lost to the passage of time.

Weird stuff... it's giving me the heebie-jeebies. Some weird ruins in the middle of Giant-Monster woods, everything is too quiet, there are creepy looking carvings on scattered stone blocks and open tunnels under roots seem to go down pretty deep. Probably connecting back down to the Dungeon root-forest beneath all this stuff.

Actually, that would make perfect sense.

The Publy tribe's root and stone pathway to the surface couldn't possibly be the only one. There were a ton of other roots that seemed to do more or less the same kind of thing, and there were a bunch more that winded along the ceiling down there.

Hmm...

Weird as it sounds, I almost think that maybe I should try to find a way back down. The Goblin Shaman-folk said they would give me a reward, after all. I mean, I did kill the owl- sort of. Just because I have a surplus of points now doesn't mean that the rigged nature of the whole thing isn't going to find a way-

"HAHA! TASTE MY SPEAR!"

Instinct: "Hardstop. You're a statue now."

"TAKE THIS YOU VILE BEAST!"

Is that a human voice? Here? I thought this was monster-country?

"EMBRACE YOUR DEATH!"

Ah... no, wait. Wrong language I think. Still getting used to that.

Not a human.

"FOR THE SPEARS!"

I mean, it sounded a lot like a human, and it sort of looks like a human too, but humans don't have pointed ears. No... neither do they have perfectly tanned skin or flowing dark hair, or features that rival any abercrombie and fitch model.

Actually, they sort of look like wonder woman from that one movie, what was it called?

Wonder woman?

Only not.

It's not like humans in this world are really setting the bar super high anyways. Miss Paladin was a beautiful lady, but some of those other adventurers I've seen looked like they were a few purchases short of free-shipping, if you know what I mean.

We can't all be Gal Gadot.

Hisss... but seriously: Not a human.

No, I'm actually about 99% sure that's an Elf.

"DIEEEEEE"

"YIYIYIYIYIYIYIYI"

Several Elves, actually.

That's a full hunting party of them, running around jumping off trees, ducking and weaving- cursing?

It's like a barbaric, foul-mouthed, woodland-band of Legolas-style supermodels over here. They're just absolutely wrecking a particularly evil looking dinosaur.

Really running the show here.

"Woosh" goes a spear. **"Thwap"** goes a bow and arrow. **"DIE MONSTER!"** Goes a rather attractive looking lady with a stone sort of knife in her hands.

One flip, a duck beneath a quick-swung tail, a jump- a spin! **"HA!"**

"CRraaaaaaaaawwwwwwww" Goes the monster, as it topples down with a stake through its skull.

Color me impressed. That was bonkers.

"I DEDICATE THIS KILL TO THE GOD OF THE FOREST!" Miss Elf over there is shouting from on top the dead dino. She's waiting for something, I think.

From here in the bush, I'm pretty sure there's a... oh... yeah, that's a knife of some sort alright. Oh...

Ug... She's really going to town on that poor bastard.

"FOREST GOD! I DEDICATE THIS BEAST'S HEART TO YOU! MAY YOUR BLESSINGS BE UPON US!"

Listen, I'd appreciate if you just used your imagination for this one. Honestly, I'm about to puke. There's killing something and eating it, and then there's going full Aztec Temple on them.

Phewwwww... I'll just close my eyes for a bit, and wait for all this to blow over.

"FOREST GOD! PLEASE! WE HAVE NEED OF YOU! SHOW US YOUR MAJESTIC FORM! COME DOWN FROM THE SKY!"

Hiss...

Yeah, they all look super serious. Fantasy-world bucket list aside, attractive as Elves are, when they're all covered in blood and looking grim-like I personally like to think there are better folks to meet.

I'll just slither away now before whatever or whoever they're waiting for shows up.

Slowly.

Quietly.

Pretending I didn't see or hear any of this-

"FOREST GOD! I OFFER YOU YET ANOTHER TRIBUTE!"

Instinct: "HOLY-SNAKE-SHIT SHE'S FAST"

Human: "HOLY-SNAKE-SHIT SHE'S FAST"

What I actually managed to say: "Hissisisisisisisisissisisisisisisisisisissssss."

In snake language, that means: "Hello, nice to meet you Miss Elf. My what strong hands you have, please don't kill me and rip out my heart as tribute."

Chapter 95
Snake Report: Time out

Listen, I'm calling a quick time out.

You can throw a hand down on the record to make a cool-skip noise as we pause here.

Hell, if you want I wouldn't even mind rolling the pre-made audio clip of: *"Hey! You're probably wondering how I ended up in this situation-"*

Hiss...

Honestly, I don't even know how to follow that up.

I mean, I know where to start- it's just... well look, I'll admit up front here: I'm not particularly proud of my actions.

To push that one further, I really didn't mean it to turn out like this.

Really, I just sort of panicked, and did the only thing Human-mind could think of.

I spent the points.

[Spirit Attendant] - Bonded Spirit of the Earth, a tool for its master. Known to accompany Divine Beasts of Legend.
[8,000 Points] - Purchased!

[Spirit Attendant] – Activated

"YOU DARE PLACE YOUR HANDS UPON THIS DIVINE FLESH, ELF? BOW TO THE GOD OF THIS FOREST!"

Hiss...

If you're wondering, that was me. Well me, as in my *[Spirit Attendant]*

Y'know.

Just digging my very own tiny snake grave.

Chapter 96

Imra, Daughter of the Lukra'Dotreka'Suma

It had taken them an entire day to find a suitable tribute.

Hours upon hours of searching the forest- far longer than Imra had ever anticipated, just to find a sizable beast, but finally the hunt was finished. They had slain it: a beast of the wilds, untamed and ferocious as any warrior could hope to face, brought back to the earth by her own hand and the ritual knife of black-glass.

Imra felt the rush: the quickening of her chest and lungs, her skin.

It was an accomplishment few could rival, and she felt the gifts of the world swirling at the edge of her vision. For the briefest instant, she almost fooled herself into thinking she could cling to that power. That her hands could sink in and take the lurking strength for her own.

But then it faded: replaced by the warmth of the sacrifice's blood. Trails of ruby and life, as its heart was offered to the sky. If the gifts of the world had given her anything, it was but a fraction.

No matter.

Just as the Elders had instructed, just as she had trained, almost all her life: this was the moment of her purpose.

Her entirety.

To the wind she had shouted her intentions with confidence. She'd waited for those mighty wings to come crashing down, without trace of fear: but now terror gripped Imra so tightly than even the strength of divine talons might not rival it.

Not only had she offended the God, her unworthy hands had touched its noble flesh without permission.

She had committed the greatest of taboos.

"DO AS I COMMAND!"

As the glowing spirit lifted up, wisp of tiny flame rising from the strange blue scales of the small serpent in her hands, Imra felt the panic well like the rapids of the Northern River within her chest.

"BOW!"

The voice boomed again, small orb of white flame circling towards her face with sudden command.

"BOW BEFORE YOUR GOD!"

The words rippling through the air took weight in both wind and noise, sending distant birds to flight in the canopy far above.

Stunned to silence, Imra's hands released the scaled beast, expression of total horror slipping atop shock as the Basilisk which stared back at her less out a slow Hiss. How had she not seen the divine nature of this creature? Such pale blue scales could be nothing more than a sign from the heavens, and those eyes: they undoubtedly possessed intelligence beyond the mortal capacity of such a small frame.

"Forest God!" Imra bowed low, hands planting flat upon the forest floor as she prostrated herself before the great voice. "I beg for your forgiveness! I did not know! I did not realize!"

"DID NOT KNOW?"

The Orb of wisping flame spun about the blue scaled diety, sparks of mana and fire lofting out into the air.

"YOU DID NOT RECOGNIZE YOUR MASTER? THE GOD OF THIS VERY FOREST?"

"I beg for your mercy!" Imra shouted, joined in by the many others of her hunting party behind her- the other elves among the hunting party bowing low, dropping their weapons to set their heads to the ground. "When I last saw you as a young girl, you were in the form of a Great Owl! I did not realize you had come to find yourself another body!"

"Hiss..."

Imra looked up from her bow and watched as the Forest God bobbed its head slowly, eyes seeking along in a slow assessment.

"Hisss..."

Again, its tongue tasted the air, almost thoughtful as the glowing spirit of flame settled beside it once more, bobbing in rhythm beside it. Even to Imra's eyes, unfamiliar with the scene, it almost seemed to be consulting something- considering.

Finally, the bobbing stopped, and the divine spirit spoke once more with a pulsing flare of light.

"Be thankful, young Elf. Your God has accepted such a pitiful excuse."

Wisping upward, flame rose above all those present, circling in a slow orbit.

"Against my counsel, the God has decided to spare your lives."

"Thank you, oh Forest God! Thank you for your divine mercy!" Imra bowed once more. "Please, let us continue with the ritual!"

"Continue... the Ritual?"

"Yes! Please, oh Great and noble Forest God! I will bear responsibly for my wrongs, but please let us take you to the village, let us offer you the tribute we have prepared in honor of your expected arrival!"

"Hiss..." The god once again seemed to consult with the divine spirit, "Hisssssss." Imra watched, fearful. If it was known that she both dishonored their god, and offended it so greatly that it did not complete the ancient ritual of tradition, she would certainly be exiled.

Or worse.

"Count this as yet another undeserved blessing, young Elf! The God agrees."

The flame soared high once again, looming over the many bowing figures with a scattering of sparks and cinder.

"Your God demands escort to this village of yours, and hopes that your tribute is not lacking!"

"Thank you, oh Forest God!" Imra shouted, as the cheers of her fellow hunters were raised to the wind. It seemed not all was lost just yet.

Chapter 97

Snake Report:

I'm in deep.

Hooooooo-boy.

Deep cover here.

When it was just the goblins, I was okay with it. I mean, I sort of convinced them I was a deity fair and square. We had a mutually beneficial relationship based upon the [Right of Might] which is a tried and proven methodology.

They were worshipping me, sure- that was pretty nice, but it was more in a "He's the toughest Snake around" sort of way.

No deception involved, my conscience was clear.

With the Elves though... with these guys, it's a totally different story.

My conscience is <u>not</u> clear.

Remember what I said about how the Goblin Shamans were creepy? I mean, much as I like to think I came up to the surface here on my own volition, but the reality is I just didn't want my insides turned outside, so I took their quest and left.

Then BAM: Lo and behold, I was eaten by a giant Owl.

Coincidence?

I think not.

In all seriousness though, I don't think the Elders wanted me hanging around for the long term. My presence I was messing with the typical order of things, and those guys... they were starting to give off a certain sort of "murder-ee" vibe.

Capacity for magic, or not, I'm physically not exactly a fearsome example of monster-kind.

I'm smaller than your average tabby-cat, and I've probably got a rounded down "0" for attack and defense stats. All it would take... I'd guess one well-placed attack and I might be dead- and that's from an ordinary Goblin.

Conservative as they were with their weird magic, if the Elders happened to take me seriously, there was a probably good chance that they could have killed me.

The Gob's had me pretty-well convinced of that.

They were just waiting for some decent odds to take a gamble. Subtle as it was, they had the vibe.

"Dangerous."

Hisss...

The feeling of a predator, watching something it wanted to eat... by now, I believe I've gotten fairly good at picking up on that sort of feeling. Each level I've gained has added to it in some way, and though it's not quite to the level of a [Skill] as [Voice of Gaia] would indicate, I'm willing to lump it beneath the natural radius of my unrecognized talent of **[Paranoia]**

I think it's safe to say, in sharp contrast to pugly Goblins: every single Elf in the Forest Village has that same vibe of: *"Dangerous."*

Every.

Single.

One.

I should have guessed it might turn out this way. The big hint was probably in the millisecond of reaction time I'd had before Miss Elf-warrior put hands around my neck.

With a grip tight enough so that I might as well have met up with death herself and flirted over coffee.

I guess we're seeing each other again.

Ug.

Yeah.

They're fast, they're strong, they're undeniably lethal, and unlike dinosaurs: none of them seem the type who go about swallowing monsters whole. From what I can gather, they're much more inclined to chop/stab/brutally bludgeon them to death.

There goes my get out of jail free card.

The ancient wisdom and peaceful mannerisms? That "being one with nature" cliche? Those are either totally off the mark, or just grossly misinterpreted. Fairy-tales and fantasy books about Elves had it all backwards.

For folks live in a terrifically dangerous and violent place filled with horrible violent and dangerous monsters- of course they're "one" with nature! Elves fit right in as terrifying monsters of their very own!

So of course, I've had no other choice but to ramp it up a bit myself.

"BOW TO YOUR GOD! BOW AND GAZE UPON HIS SCALES!"

[Spirit attendant] has been cranked to 11 at this point.

"BEHOLD! THE MASTER OF THIS FOREST GRACES YOU WITH THEIR PRESENCE!"

I can tell it what to say, but it basically has things down pat. Mystic mumbo jumbo, talk about how great and powerful I am, how everyone should grovel at my feet- tail? Well, the important thing is that just that they know that they should be grovelling: and that they're doing it. Hundreds of elves are bowing, kneeling, prostrating- they're really laying down some serious respect.

"BEHOLD YOUR GOD'S WONDER! STARE IN AWE AT HIS MAGNIFICENCE!"

Yup.

My master plan **[Just fool them until I can run away]** seems to be working pretty well.

The whole village is definitely buying it.

They're carrying me around this place like some old-age emperor, four elves walking around a platform they whipped up for me, flowers and offerings strewn about it.

Elves are looking out of carved tree-trunk houses, waving and shouting.

Beautiful women are throwing pedals from windows. Some are dancing around and placing baskets of fruit onto my odd little procession's platform. The warriors are chanting and jumping about, spinning spears and shouting out the glories of my presence.

It's all very exciting.

The goblins might have worshiped me, but it wasn't anything like this. Goblins were much more of a struggling sort- and they're not exactly super-model types. Elves though: these guys are thriving. They've got the food, the looks, the strength, the devotion!

The Heck with proving my innocent to humans, what was I thinking? This is fantastic!

"OH great Forest God! The Chief and Elders of our humble tribe wish to speak to you!" Miss Warrior Elf is calling out to me, bowing as my Elf-carried altar is lowered: all those carrying it taking knee. "Will you honor them with your presence?"

Hmm... a meeting with the Elders...

You know, the last time this happened, it turned out they were really sort of terrifying and probably wanted me de-

"THE FOREST GOD SHALL ATTEND THIS MEETING!"

Wait-what? I will?

"THE FOREST GOD IS PLEASED BY YOUR OFFERINGS!"

Oh, damn it all.

The [Spirit Attendant] really does just roll with things, doesn't it? That glowing floaty bastard.

Time to pull that back from 11 to a setting that's a bit more manageable. Gotta' rein it in a bit here, avoid repeating any mistakes.

Would have helped if it came with an instruction manual or something.

"Your God demands that he be taken to a suitable place of rest, and the Elders brought to him."

That's a bit better, you weird ethereal orb.

Let them come to me. I'm in charge, that's how it works. The gears are turning here. If they're anything like the Goblin Elders were, I should be on my guard. Safety first.

"It shall be done, oh Great Forest God!" Miss Elf seems pleased with this.

Alright, perfect. This is fine.

Everything is going exactly as it should be.

Yup.

Nothing could possibly go wrong.

Absolutely nothing.

Chapter 98

Imra, Daughter of the Lukra'Dotreka'Suma

In the Sacred worship tree of the Lukra'Dotreka'Suma, a glowing orb of spirit and magic flew above the Forest God's divine body, bathing the ground below with light as it continued a slow, methodical pace.

As Imra knelt before it, awaiting the inevitable command of the power before her, she believed her skin could feel the pressure of its gaze as it passed her by. Like a heavy wind, or the weight of an invisible rain within her mind. How could it be, that so much strength had ever been gathered into such a minute physical form?

Imra truly found no answer, beyond that of a god's own will.

Still, seated here not ten paces from its majestic scales of crystal, her thoughts raced. Moving quickly in sprints that would not end, unable to settled themselves into a manner of reliable action. Before this creature, she could not find her peace.

Was the god pleased?

It seemed content for now, but she'd wronged it in perhaps the greatest of ways. Had it truly forgiven her transgression- or was it simply still testing her? Waiting patiently for her to prove unworthy of its blessings?

Imra couldn't know.

"Hisss..." A quiet sound, like thunder on the horizon beyond the trees. It ushered out, filling the Sacred tree with echoes upon echoes as the Forest God coiled itself, rising with blue scales catching in the lit torches as it raised neck and head to stare about the room. Atop the great Shrine's highest altar, the God's servant of flame responded in turn, motions changing to a slow halt as it levitated with wisps of white to cast strange shadows.

"Young Elf," the spectre of fire spoke in a careful tone. **"Your Chief and Elders... Why are they not here? Did you fail to summon them? Or... do they intend to disrespect?"**

"No!" Imra panicked, bowing her head towards the wooden floor. "No,

Great one. The Elders and the Chief have promised their arrival. They will be here soon! Please believe me, we mean no disrespect."

"Good... Good." The orb bobbed slightly, as if nodding. **"The Forest God is understanding, but he does not wish to be kept waiting much longer."**

"I understand, oh great one."

"Good..." With that reply, it was as if Imra had been released: invisible pressure lifting and floating off as the wisp of flame glided with it, illuminating another portion of the shrine.

As the shadows took her within once more, Imra let out a careful sigh, silently counting her blessings.

The God and its servant seemed appeased for the moment. Content to hold back their anger and wrath for a greater reason. Truth be told though, Imra had to agree with the spirit of flame: The Elders, the Chief- they should have been here long ago.

Waiting here, alone with the Forest God, Imra felt far from her place among the tribe. This was no place for someone of her status.

As the hair on her neck began to prickle, looking up, Imra realized with horror that the serpent's eyes were staring at her once more. From the edge of her vision, she could sense the deep blue as it rested on her shoulders. Eyes like gems, holding within their depths the faintest hint of green and murky black; each that spiraled about the longer it held her.

The eyes of a Divine Beast.

The gaze of a legend.

What had those eyes witnessed? What ancient secrets did they hold within?

All her life she had been taught of the power held by the great creatures- by any of the forest's legends, certainly: but above all she had been taught of the Forest's Guardian.

The last true God of their people.

The Forest's Guardian. The great keeper between the world below and the sky above: a being of violence and death- but also great power. Unlike the cursed blood of her people's enemies, its gifts were not stolen- but earned.

Earned on those ancient battlefields of legend, laying waste to all who opposed its rage.

For Imra to grow and learn of such things was a natural part of her life within the tribe. For decades, Imra had been conditioned. Her body had been trained, her mind had been honed like the edge of a glass blade, and her spirit conditioned for the role of *First offering*, but to witness such a creature first hand was something else entirely.

The radiance of its power, the pressure of its gaze, the beauty of its form. Imra found herself wholly unprepared, and yet somehow a small portion of her mind found excuse. A tiny voice that defended with the thought that perhaps, a small part of this was not such much her own fault- but simply that the god had chosen a new form.

Truth be told, never in her heart of hearts had Imra ever imagined such a body as "this."

No longer was the Forest's deity in the form of a bird of night, with wings that shattered wind, and feathers that no arrow or blow could pierce. No longer was it a massive beast that stood rival to the great trees of the forest. For the first time in her tribe's history, since the breaking of the clans and the lost legends of long ago: The God had come to take on a different body.

It had taken the form of a Basilisk. A hidden beast of the depths: vibrant with strength- yet appearing so fragile it might be made of glass.

"You have bold eyes, Young Elf."

With a start, Imra realized her gaze had shifted. Not only shifted- but also held far too long, as the spirit of flame settled beside her once more. Still try as she might to pull away from the serpent's sight, it seemed only to draw her in- further and further.

Down into a well of power beyond her wildest dreams.

Only as the sound of footsteps and voices came about, and the Forest God turned its own gaze elsewhere, did Imra finally break free to return to her bow with a grateful gasp of air. She had been holding her breath, and not even known.

"Oh Great Forest God! I beg that you forgive us for our late arrival! I beseech you for mercy!"

The voice shouted out as the first to enter the shrine rushed forward with a bowing flourish, landing in a deep and graceful kneel directly before the altar.

Imra lifted her sight, just in time to see Chief Vulre take his place before her- casually bowing low before the raised altar. His hands came up, raising to the ceiling followed by half a dozen others in the dark robes of the Eldest how stopped short to kneel as an audience behind him.

"I beg forgiveness for our warrior Imra as well! I have only just heard of her unforgivably transgression!" Vulre shouted, pulling free the black glass of his dagger to the light, as Imra bringing her eyes down in both terror and shame.

To her back, she could feel the pressure as those many Elders behind him shifted faces to stare in her direction- each undoubtedly with wise smiles, brought of cruel years.

"Shall you only utter the word, I will have her offered to you as tribute! I shall plunge the knife and perform the deed myself!" He turned on her so quickly, Imra had only time to gasp as the hand wrapped about her throat, and the blade rested on her chest. "By your honor, it shall be done!"

Imra had fought in many battles as a Tribe warrior, but in that moment her fear was all too real. To die in combat was how any would wish, but ended at the hands of her own kin? The shame! Her memory would be stained for generations to come, and none would take up her name again.

"HOLD YOUR TONGUE ELVEN CHIEF!"

The spirit of the Forest god did not shout, so much as it boomed, voice and words echoing throughout the hollow trunk of the shrine room. So powerful, it seemed to shake Imra's bones.

"IT IS NOT YOUR PLACE TO SAY WHAT CAN BE FORGIVEN."

Imra's breath caught again, eyes unable to keep from the dark tint of the blade waiting in Vulre's hand.

"ONLY GOD HAS SUCH A RIGHT, AND YOU WOULD BE WISE

TO ACKNOWLEDGE THIS!"

"Great one, I-" Vulre tried to speak, only to have his words snuffed out beneath the pressure of the serpent's gaze.

"The Forest God has found it in his heart to hold forgiveness for such a loyal subject, if only just. This warrior has already been pardoned for her crime."

As Imra let out the air in her lungs as Vulre's hand release her, allowing her body to settle back to the floor with a crash. But, even as she sucked in air- Imra could make out several others doing much the same: Elders gasping with surprise.

She could not blame them. It was nothing short of a miracle, the likes of which that Imra would never be worthy.

As bringer of the *First offering*, her blood was planned to grease the wheels of the Ritual surely as the other sacrifices the tribe would prepare. That she returned from the coveted beginning of the Ritual alive was already unusual enough- but to be spared for such an offense as touching a God?

Imra's life was forfeit.

"Bow your head, foolish Chief."

Eyes wide with surprise, Vulre dropped the knife to the floor and knelt: further to the wooden floor of the shrine than Imra had ever seen. He placed his forehead to the wood itself.

"Oh great one, I do as you command."

The gasps from those elders behind her turned to hisses. Whispers among their own went with looks exchanged, and words were traded beyond even Imra's trained ear. The quiet noise of those who had lived far too long, and knew far too much.

Finally one rose above the rest to speak.

"Oh great God of the Forest!" Spreading apart their arms, Imra saw the pure white hair of the elder from beneath the shadow of their hooded cloak break free to the barest glimpse of light. A sign of great age, long since passing from the pure black of youth. Compared to Imra herself, over even the chief- whose own head was mingled with silver, the elder's own was like the moon: Ancient beyond measure.

"Let us honor your kindness! Let us bring you forth a feast! Our finest wine! Our most precious fruits! Let the coming night be spent in celebration!"

"Ah..." The spirit seemed to lift, careful and gliding, as it flew up above the scene, resting over the blue serpent body of the God: a rising sun. "The God welcomes this. Let it be so."

Though Imra could not be entirely certain from where she knelt, she was all but sure of a cruel smile as the hooded elder bowed.

Chapter 99

Snake Report: Life as a False God - Round 2.0, Night 1:

I'm in.

Seriously, like- skin of my teeth, thread the needle, almost panicked and botched it three or four times, but I think that they've really bought my performance now: in.

All these Elves think I'm a god. I am worshiped. Anything I say seems to go.

More food? Consider it done. *More wine?* Need not even ask. *Mealtime entertainment?* Now there's a bunch of Dancing Elven women.

This is the life.

More than a chief, or a king: more than a ruler- I'm just a straight up deity.

They're bowing to me, their elders are deferring to my commands- the leader obeys my every word. They're both reverent of me, and terrified.

Honestly, this is the best combination of circumstances I could have hoped for.

What the heck was I thinking, trying to find my way back into human society? That's just disaster waiting to happen, I mean, I'm a monster now! Miss Paladin is probably the only one in the world who *wouldn't* try to kill me on sight.

Yet Elves, on the other hand...

Listen, I know originally the plan was to bail out as I had a chance.

I know.

That would be the smart thing to do, but... I'm just not really sure I want to ride off into the sunset.

Not yet, I mean.

This is all a tiny snake could really ask for in life. I have everything a person could ever dream of, ignoring the lack of post-industrial technology. Respect, power, food that isn't trying to murder me: what more could someone want?

"So, Great one, what was it that made you decide to give up your previous form?"

Ah.

Suddenly, I *can* think of something I might want.

Escape from these annoying questions.

"Yes, we are all greatly interested in your decision, oh Great one."

Here we go again... another round of questions from the Elf Chief and Elf Elder #1. The uppity bastards who were about to literally cut out Miss Elf's heart in a sloppy attempt to appease me.

With festival-company like this, it really makes a Snake wonder what the world is coming to.

"The Forest God wished to view the world of his domain from a new perspective."

Ah, good work my [Spirit attendant.] Unlike most things, I'm really starting to think you were well worth the points.

"But truly, a small serpent? Compared to your previous form, of all the creatures which you could have taken shape, it amazes me that you would choose such as this. It is almost as if-"

The Chief is being very persistent, but that's okay. The best part about being in charge of a conversation, is that I can freely interrupt whenever I want.

"The God can now see the close, where there was once only the far. From the sky, the Forest was small and insignificant, but now it is large and intricate."

Well said, [Spirit Attendant.] Very Zen-like, good timing, fortune-cookie perfect right there, couldn't have managed anything better. From the look on the Chief's face, I think that might have shut him down for a minute or two. He's obviously thinking about it, starting to... there's the nod: Good work, he definitely bought it.

Hiss... Tiring stuff though. The guard is up, weird questions and things I don't understand- I've been faking it like a pro, or avoiding those questions entirely. As a God, I think the fact I even bother to answer them at all is probably enough for most, but the Chief and Elders have been a bit relentless since the wine started flowing.

It's good wine, by the way.

Really good.

Sitting here in the shrine, Elves all around, wild and crazy tribal forest party in full swing, buzz of alcohol on my tiny-snake brain, I'll admit it all evens out.

Weird or annoying questions aside, they're a fair trade- though I can truthfully admit that the only person in my company I'm not 110% fed up with already is Miss Elf Warrior. I think that's probably because she's the only one who isn't questioning me and looking for divine insight.

In fact, she's just sort of sitting there not doing much of anything. Not drinking, not eating, just staring at me and probably hoping I don't notice.

Hisss... that's alright.

It's the questions and conversation that are making me a bit nervous though. Now, I say they're looking for divine insight, but really I'm getting the impression they're testing me a bit: poking around the edges and seeing if I react.

It's annoying, but I feel a bit obligated to put up with it for now. Every rose has its thorn, so I guess being a "god" sometimes means dealing with the questions of those who worship you.

I can dig it, roll and slither with it- but it's just... Well, I'm getting the growing suspicion that maybe the Chief and these Elders don't quite trust me.

Like, *maaaaaaybe* they have a tiny bit of doubt.

Now hold on! I know, I know- that's totally crazy talk. I mean, seriously: the whole village here has completely and utterly bought in to the fact that I'm a mystic deity born in the flesh- I'm sure.

My acting and [Spirit Attendant]'s lines and delivery have been spot on, my actions quite godly.

But... y'know... I'm startingto get the feeling that *maybe,* just maybe these last couple guys aren't 110% on board with everything just yet.

Maybe they're only like 99.9% on board.

Like they're leaning back and forth all wibble-wobble on that last bit, in determining how godly I really am, and you know what?

I totally get that.

Yeah! I do, really- I do. I mean, I don't *appreciate* it, but I'll go the extra mile for a bit here. It's the least I can do, y'know, considering I *am* a Monster snake from the underworld who is sort of pretending to be their one and only Precious Forest God.

A Forest God I'm now beginning to strongly suspect might have been the Giant Owl that ate me, vomited me, and died.

Hisss... So, here's a Hypothetical question:

If you kill a Forest God, and then impersonate that very same God in front of the people that worshiped it, what's the worst that can happen?

DING!

[POISON RESISTANCE: Rank up!]
[POISON RESISTANCE: RANK XIII]

Here's a Hypothetical Answer:

They might try to murder you.

Chapter 100

Imra, Daughter of the Lukra'Dotreka'Suma

As the festivities began, Imra found herself alone.

Even as the first night of the ritual was raised with cups of wine to the heavens, and the mood fell into one of success, none approached her. No one dare, of those who she had once called friend, enemy: not even family came closer than a passing glance. She had cut her ties in the weeks and months before her role, as had they. That she was still among them, changed little.

Truth be told, throughout the entire evening, it was only Chief Vulre who stepped within ten paces of her. His lips curled back, with a look of sheer disgust.

"What a god gives, is the gods' to take back." Vulre had loudly claimed, so that anyone might here. "Even now, you are tribute. Your place among our people has ended."

With that, the Chief had walked back among the celebration, taking his place at the head of the table beside the altar. Expression once more settled among the laughter and merriment.

So it was, that Imra had remained in solitude. Just close enough to watch and listen, but far enough away to do just as instructed. Beside the altar, beneath the spinning light of the spirit that glided in a strange orbit: Imra waited for the Forest God's will to call upon her.

Waited, and waited... and waited.

It was almost as if the God had forgotten her as well. Surrounded by the tribe, its spirit of fire bellowed and jested while the wine was poured.

The early night passed into the late, and still it had not addressed her since, while the Elders and Chief brought forth questions for its divine mind to grace them with answers- one of the hooded figures instead came to her. With a strange scent of herbs and spice, the white hair was all Imra could make out from beneath the hood, as they spoke aloud.

"You have failed as tribute," came the whisper. *"Exiled, now and forever."*

"Please, Elder-" In that moment Imra tried to speak, but found she could not.

The swirl of magic held her throat like a vice, and she saw the trail there upon their fingers. Single drops of gemstone red: the old ways.

"The Chief has told you already, has he not? Do not leave the God's side. Your purpose is at an end."

With that command, the invisible grip about her throat released, and the Elder stepped away, cloak merging into the shadows of the shrine until they entirely disappeared.

As the hours passed, like smoke to the wind, Imra watched as the others did much the same.

The festival of the tribe was in full-swing, dancers and warriors performing showmanship and skill before the shrine, but Imra stayed put and watched until only Chief Vulre and herself remained of the original entourage. She watched as Vulre poured the sacred wine, bowing as the Forest God accepted the holy offering, and drank from the wooden bowl.

The Rite of Servant and Master.

This was a long-held tradition, passed down for thousands of years, but the longer she watched the stranger it seemed.

Like all meant to offer tribute, Imra had been trained from a young age to know the spiritual ways of the Tribe. She knew all the traditional forms, the routines necessary, and yet it took her full moments before she realized what had been amiss.

Chief Vulre did not drink from the bowl himself.

As the night stretched, Imra remained, even as the Great Forest Serpent curled upon itself, and the glowing orb of its Attendant seemed to dim. When the Chief stepped away, Imra watched as he bowed in perfect form facing the shrine- an immaculate motion of utmost respect. It wasn't until he passed her by with a harsh stare, that Imra realized the knife he had dropped before was once again at his belt.

"So we part, *First offering*." She heard him say, hand resting on the grip of the black-glass blade with a dangerous stance. "Enjoy this privilege while it lasts."

Chapter 101

Snake Report: Snake Report: Life as a False God - Round 2.0, Day 2:

"[Voice of Gaia] Tell me my status."

[Level 87]
[TITLE: DIVINE BEAST, LEVIATHAN, GUARDIAN, ENEMY OF
MANKIND, CALAMITY]
[BRANCH: *Divine Being*]

[UNIQUE TRAITS:]
[Extremely Toxic] - Toxic Flesh. Dangerous is consumed.
[Crystalline scales] - Increased Defense
[Omnivore] - Capable of eating non-monster food-stuffs.
[Affinity of Flame] - Bonded to the Element.
[Legendary] - A rare being. Not often seen, known only to Legend.

[STATUS: Poisoned]
[Poisoned – Temporary] – Brought about by consumption of a toxic
substance
[WANTED] – Bounty issued for capture, or proof of execution

[RESISTANCES]
[Poison resistance: Rank XII]
[Fire resistance: Rank V] - Affinity*
[Mana resistance: Rank 40]
[Steel/Iron resistance: Rank I]
[Acid resistance: Rank XI]

[Skills]
[Healing:]
[Advance Passive Healing I] – Advance healing, mana drained as a
result.
[Heal V] - Third rank of healing.
[Flame element] - Affinity*
[Leviathan breath X] - Rare ability. Advanced variation of [Flame
Breath]
[Fireball X] - A ball of flame, capable of long-range.
[Earth element]
[Earth Sculpting V] – Third spell rank of [Earth Manipulation]
[Water element]
[Water Manipulation VII] - Ability to actively mold and shape water.
[Knowledge element]

[Voice of Gaia IX] - Knowledge embodiment. Spirit of the world.
[Language Comprehension]
[Human Language – Northern Dialect: Comprehension]
[Human Language – South Dialect: Comprehension]
[Luthra'Dotre'Ka Language - Great Forest: Comprehension]
[Spirit Attendant – Rank III] Bonded spirt of the Earth, known to accompany Divine Beasts.
[Divine element]
[Royal Spirit of Man] – Acquired
[Ancient Spirit of Depth] – Acquired

You know how to tell if it was a bad night?

If you're sprawled out like a wet-noodle on top of a giant tree altar for some barbaric and ancient "Forest God."

Sure, that's probably right up there with waking up to find a tiger in the hotel bathroom. Some might actually argue that could also point towards the potential that it was a really *good* night, so maybe alone it's not much of an indicator.

But context is everything.

Want to know how I can really tell if it was a bad night?

When I wake up on a level higher than the day before, and find *[Passive healing]* and *[Poison resistance]* have scaled right up along for the ride.

Significantly scaled.

As in, much more than should ever be possible under ordinary circumstances.

Hungover as I might be, I'm pretty confident that wasn't due to alcohol poisoning. I think that someone tried to deal me out like Socrates.

Hisss...

The question, is who?

Strewn about the shrine, there are numerous suspects. It seems I'm not the only one who can't hold my drink, and it looks like Elves everywhere just sort of dropped where ever they happened to feel like it. Some of them are piled up, others are showing a bit too much skin.

You know, it's a bit weird that they still look like super-models, even passed out on the floor. That hardly seems fair.

During my human life's University years, I never remember looked like a Greek-statue when laying face down in my own stupor.

There were pictures, you know?

Geez.

You know, reincarnation being possible, I think there was probably a small possibility that maybe I could have been reborn somewhere as an Elf.

It's really making this whole ordeal seem a bit like a rip-off. I just had to random-roll "Snake-Monster" didn't I?

Right up there with the points. Rigged, rigged, rigged...

Ah- sorry.

No offense is intended by this, oh wise and Tiny Snake God.

I know you've been looking out for me, and I know I shouldn't question your ways. You really haven't let me down yet, I'm still alive and well after-all, but I'm just saying.

I mean- look at these guys. That couple over there is laying in a pool of their own vomit, and they still look perfect. Meanwhile, I'm over here, still trying to squeeze off this extra skin like a fat-kid in blue-jeans.

I probably look like a flaky blue pool noodle.

Hisss...

No, you're right tiny Snake God. It's what's on the inside that counts, that's important to remember.

On the inside, I'm... a horrible calamity.

Hisss

Damn it all.

From my raised altar, I've got a pretty good view of the scene here. Dancers over there-abouts, warriors over there... No elders though. Maybe they went to bed early? Maybe not...

It might seem a bit odd, but you know I just noticed the Chief is missing too. There's no masculine looking figure surrounded by Elven beauties laying down there- or at least not that specific example.

Chief gone, Elders gone... weird. The whole celebration thing was their idea, I wonder where they've run off...

Oh. Of course.

Of coursssssse... Rule number one to establishing yourself as a local deity: Never trust the Elders.

They poisoned me and ran away like pointy-eared turd-nuggets.

I bet they might even think it worked, those sneaky little bastards.

They probably left the scene of the crime, set themselves up with some sort of reasonable alibi- and OH: would you look there. How strange! Only little Miss Elf Warrior seems to have stayed the night, sitting over on the mat just where I remember- she's even still in that perfect bowing form.

That's so *weird,* considering how the Chief wanted to cut out her heart and have me eat it or something- I really would have thought she would have run off the moment I pardoned her. It's almost like someone higher in the hierarchy around here told her to stay put.

Hissss... the plot thickens.

I'm not the brightest crayola in the box, but I'm not a complete idiot.

I'll bet she was their planned fall-guy. They leave, she stays- they're cleared, she's blamed. It all makes sense! I can see it clearly! This is some house-of-cards level shenanigans.

Somehow, they realized I was fake, but they were too scared to take me head on, so they tried to take me out all sneaky-sneaky.

What a bunch of jerks.

Also, still bowing? After a whole night? Dear Tiny-Snake-God, Miss Elf, that has to be wicked uncomfortable. Also sort of counter-productive. Looking at the floor isn't helpful.

"Hisssss"

No... still looking at the floor.

Hey, [Spirit Attendant] get her attention for me.

"YOUNG ELF! THE FOREST GOD DEMANDS YOUR ATTENTION!"

Woah-woah-woah, too much! Too much! Simmer down there champ, you're waking up the sleeping beauties.

Look at that, seriously.

And while you're at it, look at Miss Elf. She seems like she might be in the process of a heart attack.

Yeah, dial it back a bit [Spirit Attendant] and just ask her to take use outside.

"THE FOREST GOD WISHES TO BE CARRIED OUT OF THIS SHRINE! MAKE IT SO, YOUNG ELF!"

Hisss... I literally smell terror.

It's not a good smell.

Trust me, every time I level up, I've noticed I get better at recognizing this sort of thing.

0/10.

As much as I know I should really feel a smug bit of satisfaction for the crazy warrior who was about to offer up my still-beating tiny snake heart as tribute to a giant owl... geez.

Miss Elf looks like she's about to scream in fear or cry, and it's making me feel a little guilty.

"With what shall I carry you, oh great one?" She's desperate right now, looking for anything not covered in puke. "What would suffice?"

There's groveling, and then there's straight-up fear. As something of a professional at the second option, I'm pretty good at recognizing that when I see it

"IT MATTERS NOT, DECIDE QUICKLY."

Geeeez, quiet already. I know I'm a bit hung-over, but I'm pretty sure I turned the volume down twice in the last minute alone.

Really, I'm starting to think that [Spirit Attendant] has a bit of an ego. It went and woke the whole place up, the other Elves are all scrambling now.

I feel like that uncool dad busting into the party-house a day too early.

"Will this do, great one?"

"YES YOUNG ELF. LET US GO."

Hiss...

So much for an unnoticed bit of fresh air. It's not every day you get paraded through a village sitting in an empty wine-bowl.

Majesssssssssstic.

[Spirit Attendant] make some small talk.

"WHAT DO YOU FIND MOST IMPRESSIVE ABOUT THE FOREST GOD?"

[Spirit Attendant] you suck at this.

"The Forest God?" At least Miss Elf seems to understand the concept of "small" talk. See how she's not shouting at the top of her lungs?

"YES, THE FOREST GOD. YOU FOOLISH ELF."

[Spirit Attendant] you really suck at this.

"I apologize, oh great one. I am not accustomed to speaking with such divinity."

"IT MATTERS LITTLE. TELL US YOUR ANSWER."

"Well, oh great spirit of fire, if I am to answer- then I must say his strength, of course."

"WHAT OF HIS STRENGTH?"

"It protects us, all of us in the Forest."

"WHAT ELSE?"

"Well... His gifts are earned, given fairly and not stolen like our enemies. He is a true Guardian of the world, chosen by the world."

Hiss... I have no idea what she's talking about, but it sounds sincere.

Up ahead though, small talk is coming to a close.

"YOUR WORDS PLEASE THE GOD, YOUNG ELF. NOW SILENCE."

Miss Elf and I made it about fifty slithers. Fairly decent distance, for an Elf wearing a wine dish with a snake in it, but it seems we've found the Chief Elf and his old-folk cronies.

Earlier than expected.

I don't know how they're so calm about this, really. None of them are running away yet, but I think I would be- in their situation.

I've never tried to kill a god before, but I imagine that could end rather badly.

Still, here they are: walking back to check up on their handy-work no doubt. Calm faces and lack of running away in terror noted, I think they looked anything but pleased to see my beautiful figure peering over the edge of the wine-bowl.

"Greetings, oh Great one." The Chief is already taking a knee.

Here we go...

The bows, the pleasantries, the questions on whether I was happy with things so far: I'm not that stupid. That chief and a couple elders looked like they were one good "hiss" away from shitting their britches, and those formalities were all just stalling and smokescreen as one of the farthest Elders tried to duck off and made their best efforts to disappear.

Listen, I see what's going on here. I've been through this before.

Ah, look- another Elder went and did that weird "fade off" thing they seem to do... and another one. Soon as they think I'm not looking, they're like rats jumping from a sinking boat.

Off to some secret meeting, no doubt.

Look, I'm admittedly not the brightest crayon in the box- but I'm also not a total idiot. I have eyes, way to many levels elevating my senses, and a glowing ball of ghost-fire floating over their heads.

They must think I'm some animal that stumbled onto intellect or something.

This is called misdirection.

Oh: they're all smiles and excuses now, but it's so obvious it's painful.

Like, what do they take me for?

I mean seriously- they've broken out the dancing maidens again. Look at that- there's wine flowing, there's even confetti in the air!

They have to know I'm onto them. I mean, I've been onto them since the moment Miss Elf was instructed to walk me up to the top of this Giant-Stump-stage and those warrior guys started juggling fire.

How the hell Elves can manage this hung-over is beyond me.

I mean, how the heck can elvish woman move around like that after drinking their own body-weight in wine just a few hours ago?

Hisssss...

It is good wine though...

Really good wine.

Anyways, just because the misdirection is working doesn't mean I don't know what they're doing.

All I'm trying to say.

"THE FOREST GOD DEMANDS MORE FRUIT!"

"Yes, right away Great one!"

"THE FOREST GOD DEMANDS A SHOW, MORE DANCERS!"

"Yes, certainly! Anything for you, oh Great Lord of the Forest!"

Okay, I'll admit, I kinda-sorta like this.

I know I shouldn't, but you know what? It's okay.

I'm cool with it.

Being appreciated is nice, even if the source of motivation behind it is a bit sinister. If those Elders are too scared to try anything other than poison, I'm not really even all that worried.

Besides: they really call that a poison? Pleeeeease: they should try eating nothing but Dungeon-shrooms for a few months. I could probably drink that stuff by the bucket every night and only come out stronger for it.

This is all good.

All part of my master plan: see, I can use this as a chance to find out a bit more, learn a few things. I can figure out what the deal is with this crazy place I've landed. For example, Miss Warrior Elf. It's about time to get her talking a bit, and she's been way more formal than necessary- obviously taking this God thing a bit too seriously.

See, she's bowing again.

Soon as she set down my fancy wine-bowl, right back to bowing.

We're basically alone atop a giant Tree-stump for god's sake, that really can't be comfortable. Slivers and such, but I'm sure I can get her talking soon. I'll get this talking-through-a-medium thing down eventually.

Ah, that brings me to my most recent break-through.

"MORE WINE! THE FOREST GOD DEMANDS MORE WINE!"

"Stop groveling Young Elf, the Forest God wishes to speak with you."

Eeeeh?

Hear that?

That's the sound of [Spirit Attendant #1] and [Spirit Attendant #2] respectively.

Oh yeah, I'm making [Progress]

Took a bit of magical poking and prodding, and I might have tinkered with a few forces beyond my comprehension, but it's looking like I can split the ability now that it went and ranked a few times.

It's a lot like my [Earth Sculpting]... sort of.

Not really.

Close enough.

As long as I leave about half of it on auto-pilot in the background, I can speak quietly with the second half. Two floating wisp-wisps instead of just one.

Pretty neat.

"The Great one? Speak with me? It's..." Miss Elf is pulling a deer in head-light sort of face. I'd say this is pretty comical for a warrior who cut out a dinosaurs heart with a knife, but then again- she cut out a dinosaur's heart with a knife. "It's not proper. Only the Chief and the elders should speak to The Forest God."

"Who decides what is proper, little Elf? The Chief, or The Forest God?"

"The Forest God, of course."

"Then there is no problem."

Oh wow. [Spirit Attendant #2] has some spunk. Anymore of that and Miss Elf is going to start bowing again. Relax a bit there lil' fella. Leave the crazy stuff to numero uno.

"AND HE DEMANDS GREATER TRIBUTE! MORE! MORE! MORE!"

See? [Spirit Attendant #1] has that sort of thing under control. Let's just ask her a few questions, keeping the threats to a minimum. A little bit of tact goes a long way, you know?

"Young Elf: Why did your Chief poison the Great Forest God?"

Ah... sheesh. That was blunt [Spirit Attendant #2] and great- see? Look what you just did, now she's terrified! Might as well have frozen her solid you little floating jerk-ball.

[Spirit Attendant #1] get back in here and fix this.

"WHAT DO YOU FIND SECOND-MOST IMPRESSIVE ABOUT THE FOREST GOD?"

Tiny-snake-god-damn: you guys suck at this.

Chapter 102

Vulre , Chief of the Lukra'Dotreka'Suma

As the village rallied about the Great Stump, Vulre watched with tense posture beside the balcony. Below him was a view rivaled by few other places within the borders of the tribe's territory: carved out from within one of the oldest trees by the wisdom of those who had lived before the great wars of the past.

Everything, from the room behind him, the floor beneath his feet, or the balcony in which he rested his hands, was heritage.

"I believe our immediate need for concern has passed." Behind Vulre, a confident tone spoke. "Our transgressions seem to have gone unnoticed. This... *creature* is content, for the time being."

"So it appears." Vulre replied, letting his fingers drum along the wood, silently appreciating the sturdy replies the motion granted. Perfect and powerful, the fibers of the great tree were as strong as they were malleable. An example to follow, if there had ever been one. "The beast may not have noticed, or it may simply be testing us."

Eyes narrowing, Vulre peered down at the festivities below: listening as the booming voice of the God's servant reached out through the surrounding air.

The words were lost at such a distance, but the power of them... it reached even this place. Sitting atop the Great Stump, Vulre could clearly see two spirits of flame orbiting the divine beast. An almost insignificant of blue, thin and fragile as blown glass. Weak... harmless, pitiful, and yet it was deception: a lie so great, that it might drive even a warrior such as Vulre to know fear.

Waiting down below, was a God-slayer.

"You've summoned me here, and now you speak in riddles among yourselves." Another voice spoke, and Vulre recognized it as Yules. One of the Tribe's oldest.

The elder continued with a withering tone from the council table. "Did I not know your father, Vulre- were it not for that, you'd be short at least one member in this council." Several murmurs rose in agreement.

"I understand, Yules. You have my utmost thanks for your attendance." Turning to the room, Vulre nodded in the elder's direction. It was honest, respectful: but only because it had to be.

The faces that watched him, some curious, others without a visible expression: these were the being of true power within the tribe. While Vulre himself was indeed the acting chief, he was not a king. Without their blessings, absolute authority and power were not his to wield.

"Are we truly certain that the Forest's Guardian has perished?" another Elder, one beside Yules, questioned. Their face was a bitter scowl.

"Are we're absolutely certain this Serpent is not the Great Owl reborn? I too find it difficult to believe the Guardian of the Forest- the strongest being of these lands might fall so easily that we not already know of it." Another prompted.

"Having witnessed the creature below myself, I am yet to be convinced they are not simply one and the same." Yet another voice joined the mix. "What else could command such power? What other beast could call forth such worldly strength?"

If he left this to continue, the shouting was only moments away. Vulre cleared his thoat, loudly.

"Elders, council, for hundreds of years it has been your blood, your kin that have guided our people," Turning about the table and those seated about it, Vulre let his eyes rest upon the many faces. "From the reckonings of the ancient war, to the calamities which followed. From the edges of a final defeat: it is this blood that protects our people by cost, and bargain, the sacrifices of our ancestors are a mantle we must carry," carefully, he reached his hands to the wrapped cloth hanging snug upon his belt, lifting it free, "so it is not without great consideration that I say: our God is dead."

Some were with him, some were not. The room was still split, with many undecided. Still, he only needed a few.

Someone rose.

"Then you must give us proof, Chief Vulre." Ancient Yules lifted from his sear, before slamming a fist to the table's surface with a deafening crack that silenced the room. "Proof! Before you brand us all heretics, or worse!" Haggard and furious, the elder glared at him. "Did I not know your father! Had I not watched you grow from a boy, I would never-"

The elder's shout found itself abruptly silenced as Vulre raised his hand, and all eyes fell on what it held.

Wrapped cloth, carefully folded to the length of one's forearm.

Vulre stared back at them, expression grim.

"I understand the need for proof, my council. I understand your concerns all too well, for I too found myself uncertain: torn between two paths I might travel." Stepping forward to his place at the table, he laid the cloth in his hands down for all to see.

"That was, until my most trusted scouts returned from the ruined-region last night to deliver this," his hands settled once more on the fabric, nimble fingers beginning to unwind the knot of cord that fastened it together. "It is worse than we feared."

"Worse, you say? From what is known, half of the southern lands are stricken with plague! The feral beasts which guard the borders of our lands are dead, or dying! It will take decades to recover even half their numbers- how can it be worse?"

Many at the table rose, fingers pointing as angry shouts lifted, but again they were silenced.

Silenced as Vulre began to peel back the fabric, his hands reaching down with reverence to lift the contents of the cloth for all to see. One by one, the words of protest died on their lips.

There upon the table, lay single feather.

Pale, almost white were it not for the strange tinted glow that still hummed from it, in anything but size it appeared almost plain. Yet, it was not ordinary. Longer than a warrior's forearm, it seemed disproportionate to any common avian species, and those markings... for those who knew: those who had travelled down the roads of learning and secrets, ritual and sacrifice, it was clear as day. There within the feather, lay the pale tint of ancient magic. The steady glow radiated out upon the cloaked and hooded faces, revealing their horror.

They knew: this was no ordinary feather.

Judging their reactions, in silence Vulre waited. Watching, observing as all those who'd shouted against him not a moment before seemed to wilt, like vines beneath the sun. Soon, all their eyes had returned, meeting his own.

"The God himself lays upon the soil, and our ancestor's efforts with him," Vulre stated solemnly. "Our Guardian, has fallen."

"Gaia have mercy," Ancient Yules coughed out the words as his hood fell back. "What horror has happened for such to occur within the Far-Forest? How did your scouts come to find *this*?""

"We must know, we must!" Others joined in, shouts and clamor atop one another reaching a fevered pitched before Vulre raised his hands to quell them. Their attention was all-but reverent now. None so much as whispered, while they waited for him to speak once more.

Vulre basked in it.

This... this was how a Chief was meant to lead: not by following the demands of politics, but by taking the reins himself.

"My scouts witnessed the Great Forest God lift wing and soar above the lands, as it always has in the past rituals. They followed as best they could from the canopy, with the close proximity to our planned offerings and tribute- and yet! It was then that they saw tragedy: a long and terrible fall."

"It fell? You mean to say that the Great Forest God was defeated in the sky? Such a thing is not possible! It has defended these lands for centuries! None can rival it-"

"SILENCE!" Vulre shouted above their interruptions, watching the fear grip them. Without delay, he continued. "The God was struck by a force invisible to my scout's eyes! As we all know, there is not a single beast that could have dared approach the Guardian- not among the wind and sky."

"Invisible?" A question rose among the fearful faces. "What could it have been?"

"The cursed ones?"

"No, they would never dare-"

"In flight as it was, the Scouts were too far to see clearly!" Vulre spoke above them, lifting the feather from the table in his clenched fist, "But they could see something had struck it, for its wings faltered, and its movement seized!" He opened his hand, letting the glow of ancient magics settle towards the wood below, twirling down through the air. "As it was, they were soon forced to search for its body to confirm- but before they found it..." He let his tone simmer, anger replaced by fear. "Elders, ancients, I must ask for your advice. The feather alone, the god alone- I fear it is still worse."

"Worse? Worse you say? While we bow and grovel for some *impostor*, you claim this can be worse!" One of the Elders rose with a shaking fist. "We should draw back our bows and raise spears this instant! We should strike it down by our final dying breath!" The others in the room gave nods and shouts, many murmuring agreement.

"Yes, Elders: I fear there is a calamity upon our lands. Like none other I have ever known." Vulre let out a heavy sigh, sorrow gripping his words. "As you know, to the Far forest beyond our village, beasts have died- but I come to you now with grimmer facts."

"It is worse…"

"Oh yes, Ancient Yules. It is much worse. No longer does a single beast still draw breath. All lie dead or dying before the coming hours. The village scouts suspect that even their very flesh to be tainted- twisted and corrupted by some terrible plague, and at its center..." He trailed off, relishing the looks of yearning: their faces desperate for his every word. Ever so slightly, Vulre smiled. "At its center, the forest floor was burned."

"Burned! Then the creature below-"

"Has undoubtedly brought disaster! Not only to our God, but to the Forest itself!" Vulre slammed his palms to the table, harsh shout startling those closest. "It slays without mercy. It takes and does not give! This Serpent is DEATH!"

It was in that moment, that instant, Vulre knew he had what he'd long sought.

At first it was but a few, then another- then another still. One by one he saw their expressions change, twisting from the calm and unreadable, to the look of rage. Of anger- but more importantly: of loyalty.

At last, he had them.

The great families: not simply one, or two- but all of them.

"I will not stand for it!" An ancient spoke firmly from the far side of the table. "My sons will gladly fight, and my daughters as well!"

"Our family has long been faithful to the Lukra'Dotreka'Suma." Another rose. "If the Forest God has been slain, then we must drive this terror from our village! We must slay it before it can spread its horrors! We are with you, Chief Vulre!"

"Yes! We must!" Others rose in agreement, their voices joining "It must be defeated, here and now!"

"NO!" Vulre shouted above them all: jumping upon the table with a resounding stomp to look down at the shocked faces among him. "NO, we cannot! For as a rare few of you might know: that has already been attempted."

The elders voices silenced immediately, looks of concern and astonishment showing clearly as an uneasy hush befell the many figures gathered about the table. Scanning their faces, Vulre continued with tension in his voice.

"You have not misheard me. Late last evening, upon word and witness of the proof, I made my greatest effort to such a cause. Twenty drops of the refined and bitter Gnarn Root were counted, placed in flask, and mixed upon the creature's wine by my own hand." Gasps came at this, many pulling back hoods in shock.

"Twenty drops?"

"Is such even possible?" The murmurs began anew. "By the ghosts of blood..."

Of the many astonished faces though, only the Ancient Yules nodded in understanding. Cane in hand, the elder slowly rose from his seat with a grimace of pain, before turning towards Vulre once more.

"You used a poison more dangerous than any other known to us. So terrible that it might be used to kill every man, woman, and child in this village- yet somehow the beast still lives." He stated, withered hand gesturing towards the balcony below. The others turned to look down and the unknowing sounds and sights of celebration. "Unharmed, no less... such a creature is truly powerful. It would rival to any force we might hope to gather, perhaps even win."

"You mean to let this, this thing take the place of our beloved God!" Another Elder raised a hand slamming the wooden table loudly in objection. "I will not stand by it! My sons are true warriors- my daughters are trained in the magics of our tribe! We will fight it!"

"Settle your nerves, foolish boy!" Yules cracked the cane against the floor with anger. "Inciting panic and bloodlust is the worst thing we could do! From what Chief Vulre has told us, I fear it may be much too powerful for us to take on directly. Not only a god, but the creatures of this forest have fallen. Were it strong before, now I can only imagine! We cannot be so eager to rush towards shallow graves."

"Such a creature should not exist." Vulre stepped down from the table with the perfect grace of a warrior in his prime, to stand beside the Ancient elder, pointing back towards the balcony behind them. "Look there, all of you. See the creature we face, and witness its weakness! It has made no complaints of suspicion, only arrogant demands." Gesturing the the scene below, the sounds of celebration filtered up over the open-edge of the room. Voices of merriment singing out into the early afternoon. "We must be cautious, plan carefully. Only then can we strike."

"But how?" Another rose, shouting, "With what plan? If it cannot be poisoned, it must be slain by the spear! By the bow! By the knife!" The protests began to rise once more, before the "clack" of a wooden cane settled them.

Ancient Yules turned, with a grim expression.

"We know little of our enemy, but what knowledge we do possess is clear: the creature is strong. More powerful, perhaps, than even the God who once protected us." Yules spoke with a bitter- yet stern tone, hand pointing towards the celebrations soon clenched to a fist. "Raising the banners of war will only bring death to our people. We cannot, and shall not, act rashly."

"Then what can we do? What choice remains?" The question settled all into dismal silence, none certain enough to propose another solution.

Finally, Ancient Yule spoke again.

"Vulre, as Chief and warrior you have learned the great wisdom from those who came before you, and on this you have already acted bravely once- failure or no. In the teachings of your father who was Chief before you, and perhaps his fathers before him, forgive me. I must ask a difficult task of you." The many Elders stared in silence, all eyes falling upon Vulre as he looked to Yules, letting himself sit down upon the stool of wood. "I ask you, who has already acted once on our behalf, yet I must ask again: do you have a plan for which we might find victory over this evil?" Yules and the others watched and waited as Vulre's hands slowly and reverently covering the glowing feather once more with the thin cloth.

He took his time, smile hidden away beneath a stoic facade. He let them watch, as the feather and cloth found itself tucked upon his belt once more, and his hand traced the wood on which it had laid.

Finally, after that long moment of consideration, Vulre gave his reply.

"My father spoke to me often of the forest's wisdom. How even the weakest creatures might have their strengths." He said softly. "My father... he once told me that a spider of the vines does not fight its enemies with strength, but instead with careful planning. Preparation of a trap, and then a single decisive blow from the shadows." Vulre watched as many of the elders nodded, and he turned towards the attentive and experienced eyes of Ancient Yules.

"If we are to defeat this creature, I believe we must build a web of our very own."

Chapter 103

Snake Report: Snake Report: Life as a False God - Round 2.0, Early-Night 2:

I've had some time to think, recently.

Time to reflect.

There have been questions and answers, though they weren't necessarily in that order.

Still, a lot of thoughts have been spinning, up in that ol' tiny snake noggin of mine, just waiting for a day to unwind.

The gears have been turning: finally setting themselves to puzzling out the real existential confusion that's been riding passenger's-side for this whole ordeal. Past the where, the what, and the how: I'm moving onto "why?"

Reviewing and considering how it is I've ended up here, on this very stump. From birth, survival... everything.

It took a while.

I suppose this wasn't exactly a linear "A" to "B" sort of travel, that lead me to this place, but I've mulled it over from start to finish. Reflected on the ordeals, trials and tribulations of my tiny snake life. From life, to death, to birth and life again... I finally think I understand what's happening to me.

An answer, as to why I'm sitting on this giant stump, while hundreds of people bow to me. It's so simple, all this time- was so simple.

I've gone insane.

Legitimately, actually, really-truly gone crazy.

Flown the coop, off the deep end- so far out I've missed the pool.

Long-term logical thought has been losing more than just a few battles: it's gone and lost the entire war.

And the weirdest part of all this?

It makes perfect sense.

From the moment my tiny little eyes poked out into the world: every living creature and its mother was trying to kill me. Decisions I made were spun up and thrown strictly on a survival state-of-mind.

Can I eat that?

Will that eat me?

How do I make sure that *doesn't* eat me?

Human-mind has been running for cover and losing pieces along the way, and even when Snake-instict isn't shouting at me, it's whispering. Poking and prodding me in the directions it thinks will keep me alive, fat, and happy.

But I'm not a snake.

That's just the crux of the matter. Up until now it's been such a go-go-go panicked worldview that I hadn't really stopped to think.

At the start of this, maybe I really was something of a helpless creature with unusual circumstances, but now?

What the hell am I?

I'm not just a tiny little defenseless reptile, and I'm not just a human either. Unofficial [Glass-cannon] I very-well might be, but I think I've become something else.

Still becoming, I think.

I feel it at work, just like instinct has been at work.

With every level-up, it's trying to mold me into... something. Leading me down the natural path towards some unseen goal.

I'm not really sure to where, but whatever that is: enough is enough.

That's what I'm getting at right now.

I've finally had time: a lot of time.

To rest.

To think.

To just sit and acknowledge that for the first time since I was born in this messed-up world: I'm not in immediate danger.

I'm... safe.

Rational thought has emerged from the wilds, beard so thick it has bird-nests tucked in it- but still, it has emerged.

I am alive.

I am well.

And, for the first time in who-even-knows, I can think without the pressure of certain death weighing me down.

There are so many things I need to do.

So, so many thing, that I logically should have been doing all along. Questions I should have been asking, magic I should have been practicing, skills I should have been buying.

Above all- there's a decision I need to make first: one I've placed a great degree of thought into.

Do I go back out into the lunacy of this world-gone-mad, to try my luck surviving alone? Or... do I stay here, and take my chances with the Elves to become a Forest God?

I've finally escaped the Dungeon, after all. That had been the goal which kept me stable, kept me moving. I don't even know how far up I had to travel to get here, from that hole in the cave floor, waiting for a centipede to eat me, to this place... it easily could have been miles, but I can't really be sure. All I know for certain is I'd much rather not go back down.

Deciding where I go from here: this is a bridge I hadn't actually imagined I'd live long enough to cross.

But now... now I can make a choice.

So where do I go?

Travel on the surface, perhaps?

I've asked Miss loyal Elf, Imra, a few questions. Just general things, nothing too descript, but it seems that she's never been beyond the borders of the forest.

It's large, apparently. To the North eventually there's an ocean she knows about, and that ocean that extends to the East and West.

To the South, there's apparently enemies.

"Cursed Bloods" she calls them.

So... I could South, but that's probably not my cup of tea- yet, I'm not about to try and swim across an ocean. My water magic is way too pitiful for something that intense.

But... I could practice.

What better time then now? While I'm safe, while my needs are provided and there's nothing to stop me: maybe in a few years, I could a boat out of ice and stone, and sail across the world...

But to do that, it's not so simple.

Looking around, all these Elves, dancing... bowing... singing... I'm their God. I don't think I'm allowed to just "leave" scot-free. That was half the reason I didn't try and run away in the first place.

For now, I think any one of them could snap me in half.

Heck, the "Loyal" Miss Elf Warrior over here almost did that by picking me up. If I'm going to leave, I'm going to have to check off all the boxes.

Improve my magic, learn their secrets, earn their trust. I'm going to have to be smart about this. There's more going on in this world that I need to know.

So... I guess I'll just lay this out in simple terms and say it plain. Just put it down, and commit:

> I think I'm going to try being a god for the long-term.

Hiss...

I'll let that sink in for a minute or two.

"..."

Any complaints?

"..."

No? Well, I guess I don't really expect any. Nobody in my head but me, right? Right?

"..."

Right?

Maybe?

Hissssss...

Well, whatever. I'll imagine a few complaints. That'll make this more interesting for me. I'm sure I can come up with a few pressing ones.

First and foremost: "But what if the Elves find out you killed their God?! What if they try to get revenge?!"

And to that I say, "they won't."

Seriously, they just won't.

Sitting on this stump, drinking wine, watching Elves all bow and grovel at my scaliness: I've come to realize the truth.

This whole village is legitimately worshiping me.

This isn't fake.

They are 100% on-board with how great Tiny-Snakes can be, and they're super thrilled about me being here. Wine, dancing, merriment all around: I even saw some of their craftsmen carving sculptures of me a few minutes ago. They're not perfect, but they're totally getting close enough for me to think there's some potential to work with. To hell with all the Owl looking sculptures, they're moving out the old and bringing in the new.

Ah, I hear it- the other complaints now. The rising tempest of brackish waters: "But what about the Elders? The Chief? Didn't they try to MURDER YOU?"

Woah, woah wooooah. Simmer down, relax a bit. Everything is under control.

Now, you're right about that. It's true: they might have tried to test my greatness a little.

Maybe just a tiny, itty-bitty, little bit of poison in the wine- you're not wrong. But hey, I've thought about that.

I've reflected a bit, and decided it's not that big a deal.

It's really not. Not to me, anyways. Besides, I've got a fool-proof plan in mind if they try anything else- which I'm actually pretty sure they won't.

Why?

Because Imra told me straight-up that no Elf would ever dare challenge a Forest God. She's so convinced about this, she thinks the poison was a mistake, and when I pressed her she said she would take responsibility for it and cut out her heart with a knife.

Obviously, I had to pump the brakes there.

Bit much, really.

But, well... it does kind of clarify a few things.

The hierarchy is not something up for negotiations here. The order is: Forest God first, and Elves second.

Divine Forest Guardian keeps the peace, protects the village, and the Elves worship them for it.

Very straight-forward.

So that poisoned wine was probably just a test. I'm thinking that must have been a confirmation for them, to see if I was really as powerful a creature as I've been saying I am.

Just a quick check, to confirm.

That's all.

I mean, any normal monster would have died, right? Their Owl was suddenly a snake, they weren't super sure about it- and eh, what's a little mortal poison to a god?

No big deal.

I'm just going to write this off as a bit of basic suspicion. Besides: the hangover was way worse than whatever was in the drink anyways.

As a benevolent God, I'm willing to let it slide, it's all good.

It's not right to make a good thing awkward, and as long as I keep everyone convinced that I'm *"Holier than thou"* I don't think anyone is going to get up and complain. Imra the Elf Warrior said it's complete taboo to go against the God's word. Their whole culture is based around worshiping the Great Deity who defends their lands from other dangerous things that might try to threaten them.

That last part might suck a bit, but if I've got an army of Elves to back me up, I think I'll manage.

I might not be the biggest, or the baddest: but I can *totally* do that.

Dinosaurs weren't that big a problem until they went all pack-animal on me, and I think I can get some rocks and dirt organized and available if I try hard enough. Time's on my side, after all. I'll get some nice walls, make a few Tiny Snake God Statues, set a couple monsters on fire. Deal with whatever those "curse bloods" are. Vampires or what-have you... probably.

I did most of this for the Goblins anyways, and they were terrible helpers- so I think I can handle the same for the Elves.

So, it's settled.

My resume has the work experience, I'm qualified for this position. I've obviously already nailed the interview. I'll build a Forest Empire here, starting today, here and now: sitting on top of a giant tree trump and drinking wine before five o'clock.

It's five o'clock somewhere.

Probably.

If clocks exist.

Actually... come to think of it, I'm not certain if this world even follows the 24 hour routine. Not even a crude sundial lying around, I'm thinking maybe people don't.

Elf people at least.

Speaking of which...

"Oh, Great one."

Ah, my loyal subject number one: Miss Warrior Elf Imra. I'll leave this to you [Spirit Attendant #2]

"The Great and Legendary Forest God requests you simply call him God, young Elf."

Excellent, you're getting the hang of this. Good work magic minion.

"Ah... God, my humblest apologies. I just wished to inform you that the people of the village wish to see a display."

Bowing too low again, gotta work on that.

Display though... hmm. I'm not exactly sure what that means. Open-ended sort of request if I've ever heard one.

Wing it [Spirit Attendant #2] but be all royal and regally about it. Think arrogant Roman Emperor from that one movie with Russell Crowe. But like, just a bit humble. Hug the line there.

"A display, young Elf? Is the God's presence in this place alone not enough? You desire more?"

Nice, nailed it.

"No! Oh Great Forest- I mean, God! No, Not at all! It is just that such a thing is custom upon the second day." Miss Elf Imra is looking a bit nervous. "A simple display of your power, a simple show will do- surely." Nervousness is starting to turn into full-blown panic here, she doesn't know where to look: The weird floating orb of magic fire, or me. Honestly, it's a good question. "It's tradition, for the ritual!"

Ah... it's not right to toy with my loyal subjects. I feel a bit bad.

Alright, customs huh? Don't know any of em' but I probably shouldn't overlook something like that. I don't mind a bit of showing off: I mean I am a God now, after all. That's exactly what all the gods do, right?

That was like rule number one: Do crazy stuff and gain mortal affection.

Alright, I'm game.

"The God has chosen to accept this request: Behold the power of your lord and master!"

Ohh, nice line [Spirit Attendant #2] Fantastic work.

Time for a lil' bit of razzle-dazzle: [Leviathan Breath]

Relax the jaw, shake it out- limber- limber... now aim... up, yeah- let's go with aiming up. And a one, and a two, and a

BRRRRRRRAAAAAWWWWWRWRRRMRMRMMRMRMMMMM

-urp.

Oh wow, some of that wine got stuck in the pipe there. I guess shooting a torrent of green fire can do that to a Tiny Snake.

Eighty slithers up... Twenty slithers wide... That was an alright shot I think. I could have done better, but I guess it's just not the same when vicious dinosaurs aren't trying to devour you. The motivation just isn't quite the real-deal.

Never been much of a performer anyways, and I think I might be a bit drunk already.

Hiss...

You know, everyone is dead quiet now.

Miss Elf Warrior looks... Terrified? Awe-inspired? Bit of both?

Those Elves beneath the stump seem pretty much the same. Yeah... yep, that's fear alright. Ah, couple of them look like they want to run.

I mean, it wasn't that scary was it? Just a bit of fire, straight up too- I didn't even hit anything with it. It couldn't have been that bad, could it? I didn't torch anyone. I don't think anyways.

Maybe a bird or two.

Hiss... [Spirit Attendant #2] ask how that was. Let's get an opinion, poll the crowd here.

"Young Elf, The Forest God wishes to know if such a display was acceptable."

"Y-y-y-yes. Yes, it was."

Oh great, and we're back to the groveling. Bowing, the whole lot of them now. Lot of Elves bowing. I know I'm great and all, but seriously. Enough with the Grovelling.

I read somewhere that it's better to be feared than loved, but this is a bit much.

"BEHOLD THE POWER OF YOUR MASTER! BOW TO THE FOREST GOD'S ALMIGHTY POWER! BOW!"

Oh for fudge-cracker's sake, [Spirit Attendant #1] chill the heck out, they're going to pee themselves if we lay this on any thicker. Just a Tiny Snake playing the role of a Forest Guardian, not some Invincible Evil Demon Lord from the Dark beyond.

[Spirit Attendant #2] do some damage control.

"Are there any further requests, young Elf? The God worries perhaps that was insufficient."

"N-no. Oh God, no."

"Good, now tell someone to get the Great Forest God more drink. The lord's throat is parched."

Hiss...

Being a God is tough work.

Chapter 104

Snake Report: Life as a False God - Round 2.0, Late-Night 2:

Luck and intelligence are probably my lowest stats.

[Voice of Gaia] continues to refuse any form of confirming (or denying) the existence of such convenient categories, but I know it's true.

They're a thing, I'm convinced.

As a human, I'd be willing to go out on a limb and say my ranking in "smarts" had to be average at best. Good, but only for useless trivia and things that weren't on the exam. Mine was a coddled existence, spoiled by the new-age of modern technology.

There's a deep sense of irony, having once been self-classified as a "hands on" learner: but that brings me right to luck.

Luck.

See, I *know* I didn't have a lot of that.

If I played a scratch off, I lost every time.

When the clubs in college did a raffle, my number was never called. Winning at ro-sham-bo was similar to lightning, striking twice. I was the kind of person who only played the office-lotto out of fear that the one time I didn't: they actually might win.

Unlike my on-and-off relationship with death, Lady Luck never really had a thing for me. After all, I somehow managed to die while walking taking my mother's Chihuahua around the block.

In the suburbs, no less.

But, you can get by with about what I had.

Average intelligence, terrible luck- but I countered that out with being able to do at least a couple pull-ups, half-way decent work ethic, and being really good at putting up with bullshit. High tolerance to inconvenience, that was the key.

Obviously though, I've never been the maxed-out sort of character.

That was never in the card, but I'd figured myself to be at-least average. Maybe I wasn't the kind of person to hit homeruns or draw aces, but I didn't wander into terrible mistakes very often either, and I had a half-way okay job for a few years. So, up until now... I guess I was thinking that I couldn't really be that far off the mark.

As a human, average in luck and intellect can get you by in life. Society sort of... removes a lot of the difficulty.

[Easy Mode] is selected.

But, as a reincarnated monster-snake?

Hisss...

And, well... now I'm starting to reconsider.

This might be a new low.

See, afternoon turned to evening, turned to night, turned into a blur of wine bowl, after wine bowl... after more wine bowls.

I'm stupid drunk right now.

Human-side is feeling it about half as bad as Snake-side due to some sort of ethereal buffer zone, but the world around me is a bit muddled-up.

Spinning.

Blurred on the edges.

Pretty easy to lose focus.

Those things alone aren't really a big deal (in fact- that was the intended effect) but there's some weird stuff happening out front of the giant stump and I've got no real idea what to make of it all.

There are torches.

There are chants.

There are Elves wearing masks, dancing with those crazy black-glass knives they all seem to have.

This is not what I really want to see right now.

Bad-mojo.

Loud and clear: Bad Mojo.

If this hits a boss cutscene, I wouldn't even be surprised.

[Heal]

...

[Heal?]

...

Alright, well... not a bad attempt.

Good idea, poor execution.

That would've been mighty helpful, but I guess healing magic only seems to work on the hangover aspect of sobriety, and not my actual snake-blood to alcohol content.

Hisss...

Man, you'd really think poison resistance would be functioning here... maybe it's a context thing?

Some sort of fine-print that rules out beverages meant for consumption?

I can almost see the super small font scrolling down the page really quick at the end of the imaginary info-mercial.

Crap.

I'm not going to claim to understand how magic works behind the scenes, but [Heal] isn't helping. I need some sort of detox spell- which is not *actually* impossible.
Hang on a second, I know I've got some points lying around-

-*Urp.*

Oh geez.

Hey, [Voice of Gaia] show me the-*Urp*

Wooo, deep breathes, deep breaths of fresh air...

Come' on.

No... no, still spinning.

Ugh. Alright, that's not happening. The vertigo is a bit too much.

I'm way too drunk to pull up the [Voice of Gaia] skill menu at the moment, and short of leveling up, I've never been able to get it to cooperate in the least.

Bad to worse, I think.

No, I'm not going to try again.

Motion-sickness is hitting me just thinking about it. No way I can read like this anyways. I'd throw up everywhere, and that wouldn't be very god-like.

I've got an image to keep. There are a whole heck of a lot of Elves watching, and I can't have them not thinking I'm something that I'm not.

Right?

Probably right.

Reasonably correct.

Best not to arouse any suspicion if I can help it. They all seem serious this evening. I should have thought through the fourth bowl of wine a bit more... or the fifth?

Can't be sure, but a little bit of level-headedness is coming back now.

Human side is still sober enough to make some moves: [Spirit Attendant #2] Pry some details from Loyal Elf #1, my snake-sense is tingling. No matter how I spin this, the night is taking on a [Bandai Namco] sort of theme pretty quickly.

"Young Elf, The Forest God demands your attention. He wishes to know the meaning of these displays."

Got her attention with the blunt and condescending route. Overbearing, with a touch of disinterested curiosity. Very godly [Spirit Attendant #2] you're working your way up in the world here. Promotions in your future, surely.

"My God, I..." She's trailing off, looks nervous. "This is the dance of reckoning."

"The Dance of Reckoning?"

"Yes, but as you've surely noticed, it is a day too soon. Perhaps the Elders and Chief thought it necessary, but I don't... I don't know the reason."

"Hiss... Alright, I might have misheard that. Loyal Elf Subject Imra the Warrior just said she doesn't know something about the weird stuff happening around us.

Shoot. Shoot, shoot, shoot: alarm-bells might as well be ringing out Morse-code for "T-R-A-P."

[Spirit Attendant #2] do a follow up here, I'm going to start spamming [Heal] in the meantime and find out if it does anything.

"You mean to tell The Forest God that you do not understand the significance of these rituals?"

"Oh great one, I know the ritual as a whole: They are offerings that have kept us safe since the world was shattered. An exchange for your divine power, a contract of blood to shelter our village from the forces outside our borders."

"Very good young Elf, but you claim to know nothing of why this Dance has begun tonight?"

"No, I am truly sorry. I was only told that a great and rare offering has been prepared for you-"

Oh.

The music stopped.

That's ominous.

[Heal] doesn't really seem to be doing anything, capped itself out. I'm as healthy as I can be.

This isn't good.

I'd say Human-side is running on 80% operations, bit of fear is sobering me up somewhat, but snake-side is... woo, even instinct is royally toasted. It might as well be out of commission entirely, so I'm on my own for this one.

Shit.

Alright, spin up the noggin' and let's go: [Paranoia] activate "Tactical assessment."

Still on the giant stump, no stone or earth.

There's a bit of dirt in the clearing, but I feel like it's most organic. Not as useful as the packed stone bedrock, if I remember correctly. It's not completely uniform, so that's going to take some work.

There's at least one drunkenly manifested stone statue down there, so that's something.

Mana?

Oh, we've got ourselves a decent amount of mana... Fire maybe? Can I even aim like this?

Elves are fast... I have some options here, they're just not that great-

"OH GREAT FOREST GOD! THANK YOU FOR HONORING US WITH YOUR PRESENCE!"

Hissshit! Shoot, where is that voice coming from? I can't be that drunk, can I? Was that some sort of acoustic effect?

Hiss...

The crowd is parting.

Alright, there's the Chief. Plain sight, he's got some of his cronies with him. They're bowing respectfully... good start, the Chief is getting back up.

"WE PRAISE YOU, GREAT ONE!"

"WE PRAISE YOU FOR THE SHELTER YOU HAVE PROVIDED ALL THIS TIME! FOR OUR ANCESTORS! FOR US! FOR OUR FUTURE INTO THE COMING DAY!"

"SINCE THE TIME WHICH THE CURSED-BLOOD SHATTERED THE WORLD AND LEFT OUR PEOPLE IN RUINS, YOU HAVE PROTECTED US!"

Praise is nice but... I have no idea what he's talking about.

"IN HONOR OF YOUR POWER! IN HONOR OF YOUR STRENGTH! WE BRING FORTH THE BOWL OF SACRIFICE!"

Uh... okay... I don't really want anymore wine though.

"THIS BOWL IS TRIBUTE TO YOU, OH LORD OF THIS LAND!"

Wow, that's a big bowl. I mean, I guess that's cool. I don't think I'm really that thirsty anymore, but-

"ON THIS NIGHT, WE BRING FORTH THE FIRST TRIBUTE!"

Ah, there's a dinosaur tied to a bit of wood. It looks decisively unhappy about the circumstances.

"WITH THIS KNIFE OF MY FATHER! I OFFER THIS TO YOU!"

Oh.

OH.

I guess that bowl's not for wine.

Nope... that's a whole lot of blood. Rest in peace dino.

"WE BRING FORTH THE SECOND TRIBUTE!"

It's bad-form if a god throws up, but I think I might.

Another dinosaur: This one is absolutely not thrilled to be tied to a log. It's thrashing about.

"WITH THIS KNIFE OF MY FATHER! I OFFER THIS TO YOU!"

And... now it's not thrashing about. The Chief already looks like he took a blood-shower.
That bowl isn't even half full.

"WE BRING FORTH THE THIRD TRIBUTE!"

Okay, so I see where this is going now.

Make delicious Monster offerings to the Forest God, use them to buy the God's favor. It probably made a lot more sense when the forest God was a

Giant Owl that liked to eat just about anything that crossed its path, but as a Tiny Snake I'm not so sure this is my thing.

"WITH THIS KNIFE OF MY FATHER! I OFFER THIS TO YOU!"

But... at the same time, I'm not so sure I want to try and put a stop to it either.

"WE BRING FORTH THE FOURTH TRIBUTE!"

Oh no.

Oh god. Oh, Tiny Snake God, I'm reading you, loud and clear. There's no way they'd just happen upon a giant frog for no reason. This is a sign.

Oh, I'm so sorry.

I can see the look, in its eyes. Not of hatred, not of struggle: acceptance.

I can see it all so clear. Sitting upon a giant lily-pad, it heard the voice of a higher-power that said *"Go forth, my son. Go forth, and do what must be done."*

From there, it hopped. Hopped like no giant frog has hopped before: towards its destiny.

"For you, faithful disciple of the Tiny Snake God: for you, I pledge my life."

Oh- I'm so sorry Mr. Frog.

Your sacrifice won't be in vain. I swear it. I'll find a way to live through this.

I will.

"WE BRING FORTH THE FINAL TRIBUTES!"

Ah, this time it's not frogs or dinosaurs. They're wheeling out a wooden cage or something, covered in cloth.

"IN YOUR HONOR, WE HAVE BRAVED THE WARRENS AND DEPTHS THAT ONCE FRAGMENTED OUR PEOPLE!"

"IN YOUR HONOR WE HAVE RETURNED VICTORIOUS! BEHOLD THE FINAL SACRIFICE TO YOU THIS NIGHT!"

"YOUNG SOULS- INHERITORS OF THOSE WHO SHATTERED THE WORLD!"

What the heck is he talking about? Whole lot of dramatic flair involved here, obviously intended to impress me, but I'm willing to bet there's just going to be some weird monster or something in the cage and- Oh god.

Oh no.

No no no.

Nononononononononono.

Those are humans.

"WITH THIS KNIFE OF MY FATHER! I OFFER THESE TO YOU!"

Fuck.

Snake Report: Calling another Time out.

Time out. Freeze frame, record skip, step back and view the screen.

There are three humans.

Teenagers from the looks of it. One girl, two boys, each decked to the nine in standard looking adventurer clothing.

Matching badge crests on their shoulders, shredded ropes on the floor of their cage- so an escape attempt. Badge seems familiar, but that could just be the wine. I'm an intoxicated deity, I'm probably making connections I shouldn't.

They're like the... monster-hunting Eagle Scouts or something. I don't know.

One of the boys is is visibly terrified and the other one looks hopeless, meanwhile the Girl has pried off a chunk of the cage and is holding it like sword. Defiant, tough... setting the bar pretty high.

Calm, collected: Just another example how some Adventurers in this world as just cut from a different cloth.

Like Young Gandalf, she's staring death in the eye where I'd be hissing about being *"too young to die"* or some other standard line.

I probably have a lot more in common with the crying boy- although that one also seems to have a lot more composure than I'd personally expect of myself.

I'd have peed already.

"Release us!"

Ah, time-out's over. The girl is shouting in the Southern Human language. "Release us!" Now the Northern one. "_____ ___" Now an *I have no idea* one.

Talented, gotta respect that. I think I knew one language as a human in my previous life. English, with just a tiny hint of Spanish: *"Working Proficiency"* is what I believe I had falsely listed on my LinkedIn profile.

Without magic, I'd be hopeless.

"We're from the Wayside Guild!" The girl is shouting in Southern Language again. "We're sanctioned by the Empire! Harm on us is an act of war!" That bit of wood she pried off the cage somehow is leveling towards the front now, pointing towards the Elf Chief. "Do you understand? You can still fix this! Release us!"

I wonder what sort of training these kids have had to go through to be this capable.

Attempted escape, an improvised weapon, and now negotiating tactics? Adventurers are tough. I'd be too busy peeing myself to talk to a blood-covered Elf Chief holding some Aztec-looking knife.

"Oh great Forest God!" the Chief is shouting now, shaking his fists and visibly dripping blood with every gesture.

"These Children carry the blood of those who shattered the world! They defile your holy realm by their very presence!"

A nice spiel there, but I'm not exactly certain I want-

"Drag them out!"

Ah, there's the signal. The Elf Warriors are coming forward now, spears are poking through the cage. No way to fight that, the girl's disarmed. The Boys are both looking rather grim now, girl is still surprisingly calm- but all of them have been dragged over to the bowl.

The blood bowl.

Hisss... Just looking at that thing makes me want to throw up, additional context notwithstanding.

This is the type of thing I should probably put a hard-stop to before it goes any farther. Maybe I'm just sentimental, but as a former human I'm not a big fan of sacrifices that fit this particular variety.

"OH FOREST GOD!

WITH THIS KNIFE OF MY FATHER, I OFFER THESE TO YOU!

Alright, I might be drunk but this party is getting a bit too wild.

Hey, I know *[Spirit Attendant #2]* has been stealing your limelight *[Spirit Attendant #1]*, but this is your chance to shine. Go get'em champ, do what you gotta do.

"YOU DARE INSULT THE GREAT GOD OF YOUR FOREST? RELEASE THOSE HUMANS AT ONCE!"

Nice.

Ah... well, okay.

The Chief stopped, and that's *good*, but...

Hiss...

You know, I won't claim to have much predicted or planned out *that* far into the future, but I really didn't expect the Chief to be smiling.

I'm pretty sure that's *not* good.

Chapter 105

Vulre , Chief of the Lukra'Dotreka'Suma

"RELEASE THOSE HUMANS AT ONCE!"

Hush had fell upon the clearing the moment that shout emerged, crushing whatever noise had once been beneath a great and rumbling tone and pressure. The sudden silence came quickly, but stretched on far longer.

Not even the wind seemed to dare intrude.

Thought his heart was beating like a tanned-drum and waves of fear were rushing through his veins, Chief Vulre couldn't help but smile: a wide grin, that pulled back glowing teeth.

Never in a thousand years, had he thought this would be so easy.

Vulre turned to those around him. Dozens of faces in the torch-lit night, and none of them against him. Of all the reasons he'd brought these defilers here, he'd never anticipated such a reaction: there would be no better opportunity than this. To all those that had supported it: the imitator had finally revealed its true nature.

"Release them, you say?" The question fell like glass knife to strike, quiet and fatal as it ushered from Vulre's throat, all eyes in the tribe turned to stare as the once revered God. Letting the disbelief rise in his voice, Vulre asked again. "You ask me to release- to spare these *humans*?"

"I do not ask, Chief of Elves: A God does not need permission."

The reply came harsh, glowing orb of fire flickering with each booming word.

"Release those children and send them back to where they came. They will bring this village only suffering."

Vulre felt the unease around him building, swelling like a storm on the distant seas. The Tribe had many sects and many families, and many levels of faith: but this was far beyond any of those.

"You... You demand this? That I break the most sacred of vows that we of the Lukra'Dotreka'Suma have sworn?" Vulre cursed the name with a violent hiss, "You ask me to spare this filth! Beings whose very blood did shatter the world?"

"Do you dare to disobey me, foolish Chieftain?"

Vulre turned raising his hands to show the ceremonial knife high above, smile widening further as the black glass glistening in the torchlight: painted deep crimson with blood. "My people! Hear me! Witness my shouts, for I stake my honor and name, my lineage and family: I claim this God to be *false*!"

Letting go of their bindings, Vulre roughly shoved the final would-be sacrifices forward, ignoring their yelps of pain as the humans crashed against the bowl of sacrifice. On their impact, the stone slipped from its wooden perch, heavy carved-rock leaning forward to pour its contents out upon the ground of winding roots with a flood of crimson.

There it spread forward, a rolling tide flowing past what had once been massive cables of fibrous growth, carved and polished down by meticulous detail. Careful architecture that began to drink the swell with a desperate dry-thirst. Grooves and pathways filling along all-but invisible channels, slowly the patterns began to emerge as the blood rolled onward. Even in the dim light of the torches, Vulre watched their passage reveal the lost language of a different era, ancient and terrible rites of necessity.

It had begun.

"A false god!" From the far back of the astonished crowd, a sudden shrieking shout broke free. Vulre recognizing it instantly as a youth- ears catching the voice, recognizing to which it belonged.

"A demon!" The shout was continued by another, this time recognized as the second son of Ancient Yules.

Finally, they came to his aid.

"It has come to lead us astray! To turn us from tradition!" Another voice broke through, old and gravelly, an Elder this time- again from the far back of the gathering. "It is a poison! A plague upon our Sacred Land!"

"It is a serpent of Evil!" Yet one more shout joined in, more and more suddenly picking up as the sparks of the mob were lit. "A creature of deception! A false God!"

The original plan may have already been in tatters, but Vulre's smile only grew wider as further voices joined the fray. Shouts and denunciations that turned the crowd, and began gaining momentum.

The being atop that stump might be a terrible danger to any sect alone, but united the Village could have few rivals in strength. As the shouts of astonishment and disbelief turned to anger, glares and hatred directing towards the glowing blue scales that waited in the distance, he raised his weapon higher.

All were right on time.

From the deathly silence that waited in the space around him, Vulre could see faces turning: towards the God atop the ritual stump, back to Vulre, then back to the stump again.

Nervous expressions, mouths working as if they wished to say something-anything, but were too afraid. Fear, terror, surprise- little blame could be placed on them: for how could they not be? Drenched in the blood of ritual, Vulre's hands were stained, and much more deeply than the simple red on his skin.

This was a moment of eternity! Ancient magics now swirled about the air, laced into a thick fog of aura and mystic while more blood still soaked along the grooves of the ancient carvings that guided them. In this, he was bound to something long-since forbidden.

Vulre acted not a power of the world, but a bargain of the soul. No longer was the ritual acting as a restoration to the seals that bound their Forest's Guardian to its service: this was the ritual of its very creation.

"Hear me, my brothers! My sisters! Long ago, when the world was broken: our fathers gave their blood as an offering to the flames of madness!" Vulre shouted to his tribe, willing their sights to rest on him and him alone. "And long ago, when our enemies came, our fathers took the world's beasts of hatred for their own!"

Shouting above the loudest of the outrage, Vulre stepped forward to plant his heel heavily into the back of the closest human. Their gasp of pain a sputtered against the blood still pooling around them.

"My people! This False-God has not only taken the place of our Guardian through deceptions and lies, but it has done worse! Our scouts have returned from the far forest, and for all the horrors they have witnessed: they have returned with this!" From the pouch on his waist, Vulre pulled free the sacred feather, raising it high with a blood-soaked hand, for all to see. "This beast has not only deceived us! It has slain our beloved god!"

Vulre watched the people of his tribe as their anger boiled to a barely contained hiss- ears twitching and fists shaking as weapons began to emerge within white-knuckled grips. Already he could see knives cutting against fingers and palms, trailing smoke of bargains offered to join that which had already been spilled.

He smiled at that: it seemed they would not need the wretched power of the cursed-ones, after all.

"SILENCE!"

The booming sound of words crushed into Vulre's chest, into his bones, into his mind with an impact so terrible it seemed to shake the ground on which he stood. From atop the Great Stump, it seemed that patience was finally at an end.

"You DARE to make such accusations? To threaten? To disgrace a GOD?"

Two flickering spirits, once small and insignificant, now floated beside the basilisk with a rage of color brighter than any torches. Both to grow, larger, and larger still, as a burst of burning green light erupted towards the sky with a sickening wave of power and sound.

BRRRRRRRAAAAAWWWWWRWRRRMRMRMMRMRMMMMM-

The magic ripped through the air.

"YOU SHOULD BE THANKFUL THAT YOU'VE NOT ALREADY BURNED TO CINDERS!"

Reeling from the noise of those spirits, the ground began to shift beneath his feet. Piles of gravel, boulders and blocks were now sliding out about the base of the massive trunk, formed together. Shifting and slithering with disturbingly life-like movements to amass beneath the sculpture.

"THE GOD DOES PRACTICE MERCY ELF. YOU DO NOT KNOW WHAT HORRORS HE COULD BRING UPON YOU, SHOULD HE ONLY COMMAND THEM!"

There, a coiled serpent of rock turned towards him, body raising higher, and higher still: carried by the lifeless eyes of a massive stone frog. From its sides, further heads sprouted, each more hate-filled than the last as the monstrosity advanced upon Vulre and the humans at his feet. The many carved faces stared at him, expressions twisting with rage, while behind them the voices of fire shouted.

"RELEASE THE HUMANS, ELF! SEND THEM BACK FROM WHERE THE CAME, AND THIS CAN STILL BE FORGIVEN!"

"Y-you-" The fear had taken Vulre, wrapping him up within its chill as the stone moved closer, and the heat of the green flames lifted into the darkness with the hair on his neck.

How powerful did a creature need to be, to command such worldly strength? What terrors had it survived, in order to amass so many of the world's gifts? Somewhere within Vulre's terror though, was resolve. Buried within the embers of anger and hate still smoldering- but more importantly fanned by ambition.

What did it matter if this demon was powerful?

That was all the better, when Vulre took it for his own. He found his voice with this, once more.

"You see! My people, witness this heresy! Our so-called god threatens me! In defense of our enemies, the Forest's Guardian threatens the very beings which it has sworn to protect!"

"YOU FLIRT WITH FOLLY, FOOLISH ELF!"

The flames boomed again as the statue moved forward to strike, but Vulre continued- fervor in his voice only rising by the second.

"The god I know of would not have hesitated to slaughter these humans! Yet instead this beast raises effort to save them!"

"RELEASE THEM! BEFORE YOU ENDANGER US ALL"

The Flames shouted so loudly that the ground seemed to tremble, but Vulre turned without hesitation.

"I WILL NOT!"Vulre shouted as he let the knife fly, glass edge cutting deeply across his own palm to join the blood below: swirling within the torrents of magic, life, essence and ritual. He could already feel it, the heat within his hand. Not of pain, of not flesh or bone: but soul. He was bound to it now.

"As the ancient rites demanded! Let it be done!" Vulre shouted, foot lashing out with a brutal kick to topple the last contents of the bowl forward, final splash of red pouring forward like a river set free of its dam- soaking the statues, the stones, the earth: running along the ancient grooves carved along the trunk's base. "The price has been met!"

"What have you-"

As Vulre watched, the growing spirits flickered, pushed back as if against a thick layer of polished glass atop the stump that muffled their shouts. Even with their ghostly forms, the weight pulled them down, pressing them in. The statue of stone, mere paces from where Vulre stood, slowed, then froze: immobile.

"You fools! Those humans are-"

The voice was cut away, silenced at once behind the fog of barriers now forming. Centuries since it had last been called upon, and yet he could see: *it was working.*

Vulre's grin turned to a wicked smile as the Magics soaked in along the ancient pathways, mana upon the air sealing tighter and tighter on the stump.

Beside the false god, Vulre saw the warrior Imra struggle in vain fists pounding on the barrier as it began to slide in closer. Her shouts were muffled to the point of mute, and Vulre could see the truth plainly as she most certainly did: *there was no escape.* But such had long since been the way of the First Offering.

This was little different.

BRRRRRRRAAAAAWWWWWRWRRRMRMRMMRMRMMMMM

Vulre reeled back with the show, hair rising with the feel of intensity along the air as he covered his eyes to avert the horrible crash of light and power which smashed against the forming barriers. A brutal green glowing like a tainted sun, as hundreds of cracks seemed to coalesce on the shrinking orb of mana.

Heat, power, intensity: It forced the ritual to bend, crushing it beneath its mighty strength...

And then it failed.

The cracks of the barrier lasted only for an instant, before molding together once more: reforming stronger than they were previously. Where fear and astonishment were first held, Vulre now felt laughter rise in his chest as he watched another blow strike, and fail as the serpent struggled, twisting in vain as it unleashed its desperate fury. Such efforts could only make the end come quicker.

BRRRRRRRAAAAAWWWWWRWRRRMRMRMMRMRMMMMM

Futile.

The blood had been spilled, in order and rites. There was nothing the beast could do now. This was the old way: the bargain had been struck, and soon the creature would helpless. Unable to defend itself, unable to resist the blood-ritual's true purpose.

"You see! My people, this is not a god at all! It is but a demon with its power contained! An imitator and embodiment of falsehood! A beast who wished to trick us!" He shouted, turning to the crowd pointing his knife at the humans. "Our god would never spare these children of the First Men! Our god would never forgive them for the deeds they brought down upon the world-"

"IEEEEEEEEEEEEE!"

A spray of blood erupted, seemingly from nowhere, covering Vulre's chest and face with a violent burst. With loud thump beside his feet, Vulre turned towards the source, his eyes widening with horror.

The terrified face of Elder Yules stared back from the ground, face still half aware, eyes still blinking in disbelief.

"Who dares!" Vulre barely brought the question before another cut of the wind swept past him, his feet just barely pushing body aside as one of his warrior rushed towards the source- only to be toppled to the ground in two pieces. "Who betrays us? Who spills this blood now? Speak and I shall strike you down!" Uncertainty rising, his free hand grabbed at the the humans, pulling the unwilling participants like shield towards the sounds of struggle beyond the torchlight. "Speak! Damn you!"

"AHG-"

Another warrior fell, arm still clutching at their weapon landing not three paces beside where Vulre stood, and the orange flames of torches soon follow: falling to the ground with a rough scattering of sparks and light. They hissed and crashed, lights extinguishing

"Huaaaarrr-"

Another body fell, their weapons flying- glass blade landing in the dirt: covered in gore.

The panic quickly began rising anew as the warrior's instinct within him forced his body to turn and raise his knife towards the coming danger, a century of training, learning, perfecting- all to move just so.

Sparks and pain were his only reward.

A horrible shattering that travelled down his own weapon, and up along his arm as Vulre intercepted an attack by the thinnest of margins. With a terrible shattering, the blade of his fathers burst to ten-thousand pieces in the night air, shards flinging themselves off into the darkness of the clearing.

It would defend him no more.

"Who dares?" Vulre screamed as the darkness beyond the ritual's torches seemed to fit upon a silence of deathly still. His people had fled, his warriors had fallen. In his moment of triumph, someone had come to steal it all away.

Desperately reaching with his unwounded arm, Vulre stepped back as he dragged up an unwilling human shield, ignoring their struggles as he turned- trying to face his opponent.

Where were the rest of his warriors? Where were the shouts? The rising crest of the ritual and violence sure to follow? He had made the Elders each rouse their entire bloodline! There should be full generations of Kin, ready and awaiting their signals to strike the final blow upon the beast, but instead there was nothing.

"WHO DARES!" Vulre shouted once more, pivoting towards the sound of footsteps, warned only soft crunch that walked on without a single care for the bodies and blood upon the ground.

Then, Vulre heard the voice.

<You God-damn Elves and your filthy pagan magics.>

A foreign tongue cut through the sudden silence, words slipping in between the muffled cracks and glow of the False-god's futile attempts to escape the ritual's seal.

<Who in the bloody hells do you think you are?>

A flash of silver steel whipped through the air at impossible speeds- not the slightest hesitation held for the living shields still positioned between its arc and Vulre's own flesh.

Eyes widening, the Elf Chief only had a bare instant of pain and awareness before a second flash of agony burned at his throat, throwing his vision in a horrible spiral which offered but a single glimpse of the being who struck him. A tiny flash of recognition, before the world went dark at the feet of a human swordsman.

Before death took him, with his blood running rampant along the grooves and routes of sacrifice, Vulre heard the cruel and hate-filled words of a language he did not know.

<Those younglings belong to the Wayside Guild.>

Chapter 106

Snake Report: Life as a False God - Round 2.0, Late-Night 2: Electric Boogaloo.

What was that?

No questions for now, too much is happening.

I'm trapped, [Spirit Attendant 1] is trapped, [Spirit Attendant 2] is trapped-we're all trapped and it almost seems like a good thing: because being outside sounds like a terrible plan.

I remembered where I saw those badges.

Badges? We don't need no stinkin- No, stop that.

Damn it all, maybe I am crazy, but I remembered where I'd seen those before. Instinct might be useless at the moment, but Human-side's strong suit is recalling trivial information. An affinity for mental games of "connect the dots."

Those badges are **Guild Crests**.

Yes, I knew that.

So, in my own acknowledgement of that recognition, I found myself lead along right onto the next obvious question. "What human guilds do I actually know?"

Immediate answer: none.

But that's a good hint. Opens up another question:

"What *humans* do I know?"

Answers: Young Gandolf: presumed *KIA*. Talia: presumed *MIA*. Those people I had been following, and their leader Swordmaster Za-

Oh.

Connect the dots complete, but instead of crayons we've got blood. Buckets of blood, and whatever's left of this metaphor is covered in it.

Tied up humans = Missing adventurers, and the person looking for them? Well, he's outside killing the people that tied them up.

It's a problem.

One of many problems.

It's like a finely blended smoothie of concerns and potential danger, but I'll summarize the three main issues.

Problem One: I used a lot of magic in the last couple minutes.

Earth magic was pushed to the limits, Several [Leviathan Breath] attacks were mounted, I literally shoved mana into [Spirit attendant 1] and [2] which (though it seemed to work better than expected) did absolutely nothing to prevent this situation from spinning out of control. Icing on the cake is that I've wasted more than just a couple [Heal]s trying to grapple my way back into sobriety.

So... we're running at 35-45% capacity here. The back of tricks is only halfway full, rounded up.

Problem Two: The Elves have weird magic.

Apparently, this stuff is blood-based, or some sort of ancient bargaining system. I'm not 100% clear on the details, but I saw some of this before with those elders, or I smelled it. Whenever they did a spooky vanishing act, it smelled like blood.

Still, I hadn't expected anything to this sort of magnitude, and I hadn't expected them to blitz me.

We're trapped in a shrinking and unstable magic-bubble of pressing death. There's a building sense of both dread and air pressure; neither of which are probably good for us. Static bursts of mana like a tesla coil going wild, smoke, wind, fire... It's bad news, and it's only getting worse now that everything outside has devolved into a bloody melee.

Ah, what's with that plural there? We? [Spirit Attendants] are people now?

Well, I'm not quite sure about the [Spirit Attendants] but yes: we.

Miss Elf warrior Imra is along for the ride I guess. They didn't hesitate to throw her right along and under the bus. Tough gig, being a Fake-God's Servant.

We're a duo for the ages here.

Just a little, itty-bit my fault I think.

Then again, I'm pretty convinced that her original job was to get eaten by an owl- so it's probably a fair deal.

I took one for the team there, checked that box off for her, so it probably balances out.

Hiss...

Not something which I have the luxury of time to consider. My conscience will have wait for the dodgy excuses I'd surely have come up with, because right now the walls are closing in... they're actually closing in.

It's like a shrinking bubble of invisible steel, or some wacked-out blood-ritual compression chamber. Shimmering air, glassy sort of texture, pretty much 100% impossible to break.

Not good.

Which leads me on to number three.

Problem III: Roman-numeral worthy.

None of my efforts to bust us out of here have resulted in any sort of progress.

Earth magic is useless. All the rock and soil are outside, so that's no good, but what's worse is my statue seems… tangled. It's still trying to move.

Water Magic is even MORE useless, on account of the significant lack of the stuff and it being... well, mostly useless anyways.

[Leviathan breath] hasn't done much more than make it extremely uncomfortably warm, and my helper here isn't really doing anything. Miss Elf seems to have more-or-less given up hitting the barrier and slumped over in the first stages of severe heatstroke.

No heat [resistance] I guess. Or maybe no [Affinity] for fire?

Either way, not good.

Maybe it's just the wine sloshing around in my system, but I think my Spirit attendants are actually giving me a "that's rough buddy" impression. They're squished up against the bubble, but I almost feel as though I can make out some actual details there.

I'm starting to question their intelligence.

Then again, they're stuck too... so they can't be that smart.

Hiss...

I'm also starting to question my own intelligence.

It's sort of surprised how badly I messed this whole "Ruler of the Forest" thing up.

But maybe I just lack that... edge. They say historically, people at the top of society are psychopaths. Cut-throat sort of people that don't blink at doing nasty shit to keep power.

"Burn the fields and put their heads atop stakes" kind of people.

I guess I'm just not really made for this sort of environment.

Still, I think I was doing a pretty good job to start out. Honest, it all seemed to be going to swimmingly up until they filled a giant bowl with blood and dragged out some human prisoners.

That was the obvious catalyst for all this.

BUT, apparently trying to warn people this is a bad-plan makes me the asshole.

Helter Skelter out there, and I'm the asshole! You don't see me killing people right now! I'm all about live and let live! That's the kind of God you want to have: The Tiny Snake God forgives!

Damn it all.

I tried to be a good person here. Just because the Elf chief was a bit of a bastard didn't mean I was about to roast him- chaotic evil just doesn't suit me.

But I tried peaceful diplomacy, and look what it got me.

"Don't mess with those kids!" I said. "They've got some sword-wielding maniac looking for them!" I tried to say, before freaky cult-magics cut me off- but noooooooooo: big-chief on campus had to try and ursurp the living proxy of the Tiny Snake God.

Well, it serves you right: you headless chiefy bastard.

Hisss...

Oh, we're so screwed.

If I die after this, well... I really don't want to find out what a double [New Game Minus] is going to be like. I'll probably end up a freakin sea-banarcle or something.

Ah... that's going to suck.

This is going to suck.

Outside this evil blood-magic bubble of doom, it's basically just a gale-force of smoke and lighting. I can follow the mana around a little bit, smell it, taste it... this was all organized before (in its own creepy way) but now?

Absolutely not the way it's supposed to be working.

Definitely not.

I might not know a whole lot about ancient magic or blood-rituals, but I can tell you there's way too much energy in this system. All those weird grooves in the ground have overflowed, and every poor-sucker who's been dropped headless out there is just fuel on the fire.

I mean, this was a blood ritual wasn't it? An ancient Lovecraftian sort of thing, based on living sacrifices? In a situation like this, what's all that extra supply going to do?

Any sort of spell-organization here has flown the coop: this all looks like it's about two pints from disaster.

Yeah.

Nothing left to do but pray at this point. Reflect a bit, make peace with it all. Hope for a third shot at life.

Pray it's not as a barnacle

I know, I shouldn't be greedy about it, but I've always heard that the third time's the charm. I could make it work. Honestly, I really think I'll be trying to avoid these kind of situations if I ever get out of this mess.

I've learned from my mistakes, I well and truly swear.

This is all coming loud a clear, it's definitely a sign. I should give up trying to be a ruler: obviously I didn't fully comprehend what I needed to do in order to make this type of thing work out. Praying to the Tiny Snake in the sky is fine, but I should seek alternative forms of employment and lifestyle. Maybe a roaming priest, or a part-timer. Maybe I could start a magic bakery, or a coffee shop, or something.

In the name of the Tiny Snake God and your faithful prophets, I swear: I'll use my magic to build you a giant shrine, I'll spread tales of your benevolent tail far and wide.

In the name of the Tiny snake God, I swear, if you save me I'll-

Sword-Master Zane

Through hell he had travelled, but one by one: he cut them down.

Their warriors, their leader: Zane cleaved through them as a scythe cleaves wheat. First in silence, then in open combat. The ancient pagans of the Northern Forest, the legends themselves: it mattered little to his sword.

It was steel, after all.

From both sides, spears had flew towards him- yet Zane spun. His blade shifted in his hand, twisting with the afterglow of [Counter] before it flew along the form [Diving Hawk] to run a third opponent through.

"_____ ___!" a voice shouted, language unfamiliar. "____ ____!"

Zane ignored those shouts, as he continued to cut down another striking form, letting the two halves of the body crash to the ground: one still screaming amid the swirls of chaos in the air.

He would show them no mercy. They had brought this upon themselves.

More came at him, and more fell. Stone and wood, glass and fiber: his steel separated them just as simply as the flesh behind them. He felt the rush, flowing through his skull, through his veins- deep within his chest. His sword moved, quicker- fast, stronger with every blow exchanged, until the battle found itself ending.

"_____ ___!" the shout had turned to a scream, and though Zane did not understand the words, he knew the sound of terror all too well. "___ ___!" His final opponent retreated, back stepping into the blood that soaked the ground. Filthy hand now grappling with a struggling hostage.

As he charged, sword swinging- Zane found his attack deflected: a glass knife lashing out at his side as it blocked, cutting shallow as Zane let his own follow through. [Razor's Edge] swung clean, resonating with a deep exhale from his lungs as his side burned as the blood trailed won down both steel and cloth.

It was done.

One of their arms swung useless at their side, weapon broken or discarded, while step by step, Zane moved forward. The pain in his side was throbbing worse with every push and pull of muscles and tendons, but his sword... his arms: they were still ready.

[Ethereal Blade]

Zane swung with a skill that surpassed all the rest he had ever achieved. The greatest achievement of his lifetime, he felt it reach past his palm, his finders, his sword itself, as he gave no pause and the blade passed through his target in a horizontal sweep, two sets of eyes watching in equal horror before the deed was done.

A single head fell to the blood-soaked ground.

"Those younglings belong to the Wayside Guild." Zane heard his own words, as his knees gave way, and he found himself leaning heavily on his sword while unknown magics swam in the air around him, twisting and turning with the crazed laughter of some far-off plane.

Upon the massive carved stump in the center of the clearing, a creature waited. The center of the wretched ritual itself, a body of blue and crystal that seemed to stare down at him. Not with anger, not with rage: should Zane not know better, he would have thought it almost seemed to watch him with pity.

Pity, as the magics in the air grew to a tempest, grew to a storm to rival any Zane had seen in his life, lifting up and higher to the treetops, the clouds and sky: pressure building as horrible screams seemed to rise from very air itself. From the carved wood, from the stone sculpture, from the wind and the blood now climbing along with it.

"Shame," Zane muttered, as he fell forward towards the waiting lake of crimson, vision fixed on the strange cerulean glow in the eye of the storm. "I could have done more."

Then, the screams of the wind and blood were silenced, and there was only fire.

Epilogue
End of Act I

Urgent Report: *Elite Dungeoneering team missing, presumed no survivors. Further details enclosed.*

Urgent Report: *War threatened from the Old Country borders. Dwarven armies rallying along Far Eastern Front of Empire Controlled Territories. Further details enclosed.*

Urgent Report: *Strange Monster patterns detected in all known Dungeons. Alert level raised for all active Guilds. Further details enclosed.*

Urgent Report: *Volcanic eruptions spotting off Southern Continent Coasts. Elevated Monster activity reported. Further details enclosed.*

Urgent Report: *Dungeon Sanctuary destroyed. Hundreds stranded and awaiting Imperial rescue. Further details enclosed. Witness testimony included.*

Urgent Report: *Dozens killed or wounded in Dungeon Depths! Trade Routes in disarray! Empire Forces drafted! Details enclosed.*

Urgent Report: *Unknown Sculptures and Unidentifiable runes traced in Dungeon Network. Sanctuary impossible to recover. Unholy origins. Details enclosed. Artist Sketches and Witness Reports included.*

Urgent Report: *Unsanctioned religious activity recorded. Inquisitors sanctioned and dispersed to known locations.*

"When in all the gods names will this end!" Yelled Royal adviser Eduard as he leaned back in his chair, hands rubbing violently at his temples. If only such motions could fight off the painful headache approaching for the umpteenth time this evening, he might find some measure of solace. "Truly these are dark times, but why is it that I must suffer personally? What have I ever done to deserve this?" He grumbled, giving in to the exhaustion of the late hour, letting his shoulders slouch in temporary defeat. Within the room of secrecy runes carved atop every brick and board, he knew it would be a rare occasion indeed if someone were to answer his questions anyways.

With a long sigh he stared at the overflowing documents atop his wide wooden desk. Headlines of ink and ledger waiting ever so patiently for his return to their seemingly endless swarms, most yet to be so much as glanced at. He was months behind at this point, and every day further he fell was another step towards the executioner's chopping block. Three straight weeks now: late nights and little sleep- but yet the reports only seemed to increase.

What has begun as a post envied by most any scribe, was presently a sickening nightmare. The *Dignified Leader to the Investigation Post of the Second Privileged*, Eduard found the easy life had begun nothing but a distant memory, replaced entirely by stress and horrors unbound like the books opened for reference about the floor and little remaining available surface area. It was almost every other day now that the Seers were pulling him in for further council, prying at questions for answers he simply didn't have.

Their demands worsened by the week.

Two years of apprenticeship, working his hands raw to scribble out runes and etchings with endless repetition. Three years as Ledger assistant, proving himself first among equals for those desperate few seen to hold some measure of promise among the droves of poor-yet-educated among the striving lesser houses. From there his career was soon advanced by two more as a Noble's Scribe, signed in oath to a house of kin-ship to the Imperial blood, and then another as Seal keeper for the same province.

Loyal, ambitious, dedicated: these attributes were the foundation which lead Eduard Rosel of the Lesser House of Ertra to be selected from the masses for higher privileged. Of course, when telling this story himself, perhaps he might admit to leaving out a few details among the many. Certainly, he'd rarely burden someone listening with the messy promotions that came after his early years, maybe all but totally passing by the topic of yet another failed coup gone awry, or how the Empire and its noble lines might have suddenly come about to an immediate (and impressively large) demand for educated servants completely simultaneous with the Palace's choice color of decoration shifting from white to red.

No, instead if asked, Eduard might simply pass such trivial explanations by with a brief statement such as "There had been open positions to be filled" or "His services were in utmost demand." For he was a man ever of the mindset that his accomplishments were more of personal association than just a few random strokes of luck.

Perseverance, back-breaking work-ethic, and unwavering loyalty to the Empire: these were the reasons Eduard had found himself seated in the most coveted position known to scribes. Hard work was what had earned him his place in the world, and he'd be damned if anyone was going to tell him otherwise.

Still, even he had to admit: if it was hard work that brought him here, it was the same which might see him removed as well.

"Blasted Seers, all they care about are their stupid prophesies." He grumbled at the thought of them, leaning over the stack of papers awaiting his review. "A few accidents in the Dungeon, an earthquake or two... As if the world will come to an end in our lifetimes. It's ridiculous, preposterous, utterly insane what they're having me do." Eduard continued, Heresy muttered freely from his lips, as if daring the shut door by the hall to open and spring forth with court inquisitors foaming at the mouth to damn his sorry lot to the Dungeons beneath the Palace not five miles East. "I doubt the Emperor himself would bear the burden of this god- forsaken duty."

Perhaps that was just the manner by which he tempted fate, but as he sat their, fuming with anger and staring with his best impression of rage at an innocent ink jar, the ground rumbled beneath him.

A heavy rumble that sent his arms flailing backwards, shook papers, dropped books, and wavered candles running low with liquid wax sloshing to and fro before settling with Eduard's own aching backside heavy on the floor- astonished and fearful.

"What in all the world was that?" He uttered, clawing at the side of his desk until he might find enough purchase to drag himself back into his chair. His eyes scanned the room, darting from shadow to shadow, finally resting on the thick door, still shut and locked tight against any who might enter. "Just an earthquake?" He wondered aloud, secrecy rune and wards acknowledged as the breath he'd held back for more than a tense moment finally freed itself from his chest.

He winced at his own foolishness.

"Of course it was... of course it was." He answered his own question. Still, it was a painfully long-while until Eduard's heart-rate settled back to a normal rhythm, and he was thankful that the few who had held witness to his moment of stupidity were limited to the many stacks of papers, books, and half-emptied glass bottles of ink. "Coincidence." He muttered finally. "Absolutely just coincidence."

However little logical basis a soul should feel for fear when speaking heresy of the Empire at the farthest of the witching hours, Eduard knew that many unlucky men had likely been struck down for less, and in far more terrible ways than an earthquake. Still, perhaps he should keep himself in greater check.

Though the very thought of what madness drove those old and crusted magicians of the court to torture him with endless assignments and an impossible disregard for his well-being, they still held the favor of the Emperor himself. They might literally chew grass and shit patty like a bison in pasture, but just the Emperor's favor alone would have him picking up after them until his service had reached its final term, and it wasn't his place to say otherwise.

Not unless he fancied himself dying young.

Well… perhaps middle-aged.

"So what if the Earth shakes a bit? There are beasts aplenty to stir, have been for ages." Eduard's growling tone returned, hands reaching about the papers to reshuffle and align the shaken pages of documents. "Always have been, always will be. Monsters and wicked things below, men and heavens above; perfectly natural." Eduard truly believed those words.

The *Dignified Leader to the Investigation Post of the Second Privileged* was meant to be a cushy job: a career founded on maybe one, perhaps two passing investigations in a lifetime- often without the need for travel.

If a particularly strange happening occurred within the empire, or the Seers had some odd mystic prediction, Eduard's task was to investigate. A simple enough thing to demand from a man, especially someone with half a drop's blood away from being a commoner. Eduard didn't mind holding down such a commitment one bit, but that wasn't what this was turning out to be at all. "Ever since the blasted astronomers opened their bloody mouths. Had to report that hogwash on the celestial bodies, didn't they? Just had to make a fuss, get them all riled up, spouting nonsense about that blasted ancient prophesy!"

Just like that, his dreams of a simple and rewarding career had been ended. Abruptly shattered to ten-thousand sheets of parchment, and dropped on his desk for review. The whole sum of the Seers' divinations were ridiculous. and though Eduard lacked even the status to whisper that aloud without inviting his doom, their madness was ruining him almost as surely. One missed night of sleep at a time, it was breaking him down like a stone left to weather and crumble. Another month of this stress and he might be claiming the world's own reckoning himself, shouting visions of the coming catastrophe at specters like a daft lunatic roaming the streets and sleeping in alleyways.

For honest thought, Eduard had to admit that might be preferable to this. Truly, he often felt as though the mere act of continuing on his entrusted duties was encouraging the high-seated fools. The past several months especially, what with the Royal astronomers passing along warnings and shouts from their mage-assisted looking glasses. It pained him, really, handing such diligently collected information off to be grossly misinterpreted by mad-men chosen by the great Emperor.

"All because they learned the Ancient Language, all because of that." Eduard tisked again, picking up his quill and dipping it carefully in preparation, "Dabbled in chaos and then went too much too far behind the curtains if you ask me. Not something I'd wish ever for. Believing a few stone scribbles from our grandfather's father's, father's, father's great grandfather's presumed King. Utter foolishness. Stupid, crazy, no-good nonsense." He was pushing his luck today, lips all but singing him to the noose, the ax, or worse. Muttering against the very fabric of the Empire, especially while being employed by that very same thing, was a terrible idea. "Foolish, foolish, foolish." He muttered continually, whispering the words as his quill scribbled notes along in no particular rhythm.

Heresy uttered or not, Eduard was wise enough for a man his age, and every fiber of his being sided in the camp of logic. Logic that said the secrets of the First men weren't for the likes of those living in the current day. Blood like that was cut from a different cloth than the men who resided in the land of mortals now, and as far as Eduard was concerned: prophesies about the world ending were hogwash. One misinterpreted statement from a few thousand years back, misconstrued and used by some war-lusting maniac to take over half the known world and crown himself emperor. If Eduard knew anything about life, it was certainly that a common man need not concern himself with such things. To meet one's purpose and contentment, a man only needed a faithful woman waiting at home and a warm meal twice or thrice a day. Everything else was simply misdirection.

Though maybe some mugs of ale wouldn't hurt anything much.

On the holidays, of course. Those of faith and service had conditions to adhere to, after all. The thought of a nice mug, or even a chilled glass of wine though...

"Aggggg..." Yet here he was. Not a home, not with a woman, and most certainly not enjoying a hot meal with ale! All because of these blasted reports! All because some Crazed magicians thought they were witnessing the world's end! "Has it ever been this bad?" Eduard let his tongue click against stained teeth as he picked up the last report atop the pile, the likes of which had arrived only just hours passed by a tired looking messenger. It bore a blaring red wax- recently stamped with the magic-crested seal of glowing ambiance. Highest of the orders it seemed. Impenetrable to seeking hands and scouring eyes, likely rigged with all manners of clever traps-Eduard had little doubt.

Sighing in heavy resign to his duty, he lifted his hands, the barest sweep of his post's ring lighting the spark that burst the wax aside like a priest might banish a ghoul- material falling off to the shadows beneath the desk. His tired eyes watched as the paper unfolded and the ink ran from a jumble of unreadable patterns into something more legible. A practiced swirl of elegant and practiced penmanship conveying information of apart utmost importance.

Urgent Report:
> Strange lights seen in the Great Forest.
> The Wayside Guild...

Eduard paused, squinting at the words, uncertain.

"...Younglings missing..." He stared at it. "Sword Master missing, multiple casualties... Monster extinction event..." The headache began to creep back in, growing worse by the passing second. "*Goblin tribes committing ritual suicide? Evidence of suspected Elven Blood Rituals?*" He looked back over the words again. "What in all the gods is this? Is this even the correct report?" He muttered aloud, eyes squinting for some deeper insight and finding none.

If skimming only turning his mind about in confusion, he had to reason trying with a heavier level of attention might make the difference as he tried for a third pass at the weighty pile of words. Not just a summary, but actual collected testimonies- a significant rarity that caused his eyes to narrow, gaze slow turning to disbelief until his hands shook careless drops of ink from the quill he'd prepared. "Lords above, Kings below, this is madness itself." The ink scrolled further, and further, and further. The more Eduard read, the more it pressed words onto the paper- seemingly endless as it carried on with witness testimonies, artistic sketches, government and local reports, trade and ledger information. On and on it pressed into his tired mind, building up like the pressure between his eyes. It got worse.

And worse.

And *worse.*

Worse, worse, worse!

Everyday it was worse!

He couldn't hand this to them! He just couldn't! Everyday he handed those blasted Seers more wood for their flaming bout of insanity! They would have another mountain of work for him after this! By the First King of men himself- Eduard was absolutely certain of it, they might even send him to investigate personally! Knowing the position, he might have to bend knee and mount a bloody expedition; it was common knowledge that men on expeditions rarely got three warm meals or faithful women.

Reading it again, Eduard came to recognize the absolute nightmare held in his shaking hands. Hands trembling once in fear, now gone white with rage all but uncontained.

"Damn it all!" Eduard set down his quill with anger, seething at the unfairness of it all. He should be home, tucked in bed by a warm hearth and his wife. If ever got to the bottom of who or what was behind this, be it a Demon- a god, or the first King of men in the flesh himself: he swore by his father's own name and honor and pick up the sword to deal with the bastard himself. "I'll deal with you myself! You hear me? Myself!"

"Deal with who, yourself?" A cold voice answered, striking an immediate chill to the fires of anger that burned to fiercely in Eduard's chest not the barest of instants before. Gasping in horror, Eduard turned to see the black cloaked and hooded figure of a Seer's informant waiting silently beside the doorway, noiseless presence almost impossibly molded with the shadows of the candlelight within the room.

"How... how long have you been there?" Eduard asked, shock and fear composing themselves as quickly as he found possible, hands rushing to straighten out his robes as he rose from his seat. "I didn't hear you come in."

"Ah, they never do." The shadowed figure replied, voice arriving and ceasing with unnatural suddenness. As if the words snuffed out to silence the second they arrived, not resonating further beyond the passing of their purpose. "And not long ago... I have only just received my commands."

"Well? What is it then?" Eduard replied, taking the gruffest tone he dared to muster with the eerie figure. "I've got more than enough to deal with at the moment, and no time to waste."

"That you do, Dignified Leader to the Investigation Post of the Second Privileged." The coldness of the reply cut Eduard like a knife. "Much to do... So very much, I wonder if you'll manage?"

"Out with it. Why are you here, and at this hour no less."

"Ah... to bring you this." The parchment emerged, old-fashion roll fitting and prim with seals and decorations of the Royal house unmistakably clear upon the material's borders. The faint outline of a sickly white hand emerged with it, as the roll of paper was set carefully down atop a towering stack of papers waiting beside the door. Though Eduard wasn't able to see the man's face clearly, his detected a smile along with those eerie words and form, as the man stepped back into the blackness of the hall, shutting the door once more behind him. "I wish you luck, dealing with it *yourself*, Dignified Leader. Best of luck, in fact."

The moment stretched. One, then two, then three, before Eduard finally had the courage to approach the seal, hand setting carefully upon the fine and delicate casings to pull it open and heed its message. As it turned out though, there was little for him to read.

For the glorified eyes of the Privileged alone:

The Great Forests of the Northern continent have been lost in their entirety beneath the flames of Chaos. By confirmation of the Royal seers and the Emperor himself, it is known:

The Prophecy has begun.

End of Book I

The Snake Report continues over at thesnekreport.com!

About the author:

Wercwercwerc, otherwise known as Jakethesnakebakecake, otherwise known as the Jake, is known to the literary world primarily though his writings online. As of the release of this publication, his ongoing web serial The Snake Report has accrued close to two million views, and worldwide readership. Shared through social media and going so far as to be translated into other languages, his writing prompt response "Scars" has been met with global success.

When not writing The Snake Report or working his day-job, Jake enjoys camping, archery, guitar, and spending time with his partner-in-crime and their two dogs.

All Hail the Tiny Snake God!

As always, thank you for reading.

Made in the USA
Middletown, DE
01 July 2019